Praise for

Perilous Bliss

Book Three of *The Star-Seer's Prophecy*

"After eagerly waiting for the third book of *The Star-Seer's Prophecy*, I found myself enthralled as I dove into this final volume on the world of Kyr and the land of Khailaz, now recovering from the hell of the Soul-Drinker's long reign.

"Book Three builds upon the substantial foundation of Books One and Two, and culminates in a well-crafted, page-turning and unpredicted climax that is deeply satisfying and authentic to the characters and the story. The author has woven everything together beautifully.

"In psychological terms, this is a story of the depth of human suffering and the laborious and miraculous ways in which human beings can find healing. Rahima Warren's description of Kyr's recovery is inspirational and instructive. It is a testament to her knowledge of the process and principles of psychotherapy and the development of a mature human being, as well as the healing power available to those who have the courage to tread the 'hard path.' I highly recommend *The Star-Seer's Prophecy* to healers, therapists, and those in need of healing—in other words, all of us. (Note: I do not recommend this book for children.)" — Merideth Bowen Shamszad, MFT; Author, *The Story of Little Feather*

"Longtime psychotherapist Rahima Warren brings her daring, passionate, and compassionate trilogy to a most satisfying close in *Perilous Bliss*. Brave and reflective readers may find more in these books than excellent fantasy set in a masterfully built and richly detailed world. If you're ready to encounter your wounded side, to understand and release its pain, and to walk with it to a more serene future, then let yourself experience the fiercely potent, healing magic of *The Star-Seer's Prophecy*, because it was written for you." — Jodie Forrest, Author, *The Rhymer and the Ravens* and *The Ascendant*

Praise for

Fierce Blessings

Book Two of *The Star-Seer's Prophecy*

"*Fierce Blessings* is a wonderfully compelling read. A page-turner of the highest order. But more than that, it is a powerful spiritual teaching. A step-by-step guide on how to keep our hearts open in the face of unimaginable suffering, how to forgive the unforgivable, and what it means to allow the sweet mercy and compassion of the Divine Feminine to be an ongoing healing presence in our lives." — Chris Zydel, Author, *Conversations with the Brush; Love Letters from the Creative Heart*

"*Fierce Blessings* brilliantly explores archetypal themes of life, which have coalesced in the heart and soul of the heroic yet tormented protagonist, Kyr. His awakening and struggle to become the hallowed vessel of the Goddess are poignant and heart-wrenching, yet readers of his story will be well-rewarded as his transcendent and redemptive spiritual path unfolds. This is a profound and inspiring work that grapples with the universal themes of brutality and forgiveness, trauma and recovery, and the liberating power of compassion." — Merideth Bowen Shamszad, Psychotherapist; Author, *The Story of Little Feather*

"While exploring the depths of darkness, an essential stream of healing flows through *Fierce Blessings*. This is a profound and extraordinary book that will reverberate in your bones long after the story is over." — Robin Winn, Psychotherapist and Teacher

[Note: The following are Five-Star Reviews on Amazon.com]

"Gritty and uplifting! The author uncovers the depth of human suffering in order to create the vision of healing and growth. Sharing the character's journey supported me in accepting my own journey from suffering to growth. A richly rewarding story for those with the courage to seek the fullness of being alive." — Richard Schieffer

"The content is graphic, however this story is worth telling on so many levels. Kyr has suffered and been abused, and he has also been the abuser and learns a new way of being. It makes you stop and think: if he could forgive and go on, maybe there is hope also to forgive things you thought not possible before. I like the fact that you find yourself rooting for Kyr throughout the story. I am looking forward to reading Book 3 to see how Kyr navigates the third Hell." — Rena Scarberry

"A multi-faceted book. Beautiful work! In *Fierce Blessings*, the author continues the saga of Kyr, a young man who has survived unspeakable horrors, and his healing path. Like the first book in the series, *Dark Innocence*, I couldn't put this book down. The book is a little challenging to read, in that the author describes rather vividly what Kyr undergoes at the hands of his sadistic captors. But the way that he is supported in healing from these abuses is beautiful and poignant, and the reader heals from the shock of reading about his experiences along the way. There are a number of underlying messages in the book, such as the connection between our spiritual wellbeing and the health of our planet, and hope for healing severe trauma. I found this particularly lovely. I think you will greatly enjoy this book, and personally I hope Book 3 comes out soon!" — Abena

"Have you ever thought that you could never forgive someone? Kyr, the main character in the book, has had the unspeakable done to him and he has done the unspeakable to others. Yet he learns what true forgiveness is, …grows spiritually, and learns about love. This book is fascinating and I could not put it down! If you are looking for a book to get lost in, this is it! Be sure to read the first book of the trilogy, *Dark Innocence*, before you read this one. It's another I-can't-put-it-down book." — Caren Myers

"*Fierce Blessings* is an aptly named journey into discovering what practicing compassion and forgiveness truly means. The story itself is so skillfully written that it carries the challenging themes of violence and betrayal, rather than forcing the reader to bear their full weight. It is a timeless story of healing and profound growth. One well worth the hours spent reading, in my opinion." — T. Nichols

Praise for

Dark Innocence

Book One of *The Star-Seer's Prophecy*

"This novel can take its place amongst Tolkien and the best of science fiction writers such as Ursula LeGuin. It is a well-sustained, exciting and suspenseful narrative written in a lucid and powerful style." — Harris Smart, Author, *Passion Play; Tom Bass: Totem Maker*, and *Sixteen Steps and Other Journeys in SUBUD*

"*Dark Innocence* is a can't-put-it-down, page-turning adventure story, deliciously abducting you into an enchanted world that is brimming with powerfully complex characters, and both dark and light magic. But the true genius of this book is that the hero, Kyr, is not the only one embarking on a healing pilgrimage through the treacherous and liberating underworld of the psyche. I can't imagine how any reader can take this soulful, spiritual and creative literary journey and not come away deeply and personally transformed." — Chris Zydel, Author, *Conversations with the Brush*, and *Love Letters from the Creative Heart*

"I had the pleasure of reading *Dark Innocence* several years ago as a manuscript. At the time I was reading many manuscripts, writing book reviews, and working as an editor. *Dark Innocence* stood out almost at once. The story is compelling, gripping, even. The journey is intense, rich and rewarding. I highly recommend *Dark Innocence*. This is a book that is at once action-packed and deeply provocative. It will resonate with you for years to come." — Stephanie Rose Bird, Author, *No Barren Life* (A Young Adult fantasy), and five non-fiction books

"Rahima Warren has written a daring, taboo-breaking, visceral, intensely felt and moving novel. It's impossible not to get wrapped up in the characters and their passions, only to be surprised again and again…. You won't be able to let go of this book, any more than it will let go of you. Highly recommended!" — Jodie Forrest, Author, *The Ascendant*, and *The Rhymer and the Ravens* (An historical fantasy trilogy)

"*Dark Innocence* is a beautifully written and richly woven tale of the archetypal themes of wounding and redemption. The author looks fearlessly into the darkest aspects of human experiences and explores the true nature of healing. Her wisdom as a psychotherapist permeates the story, but this is no dry textbook...it is a gripping and inspiring page-turner! The story has stayed with me and continues to amaze. Highly recommended. (For adults only!)" — Merideth Bowen Shamszad, Author, *The Story of Little Feather*

"Potent, magical, and unforgettable. Rahima jolts us into a stark, horrific world of humanity gone awry. Then, with lucid ease, she skillfully guides us through the complex and often tumultuous terrain to reclaim the lost treasure of compassion and embodied being. This riveting story is a call to awaken, to face the unfaceable and to find the heart of being human. This story will grab hold of your bones and live with you long after you've put the book down." — Robin Winn, MFT, Diamond Logos teacher

"A must-read for everyone...I could not stop reading this book. Not only was the story fantastic, but you could see each little step of self-healing, discovery, acceptance.... It's beautiful and sad and hopeful and inspiring." — Tiffany H., from her Five-Star review on Goodreads and her blog, "A TiffyFit's Reading Corner"

"In the beginning, the author, Rahima Warren...makes it clear that there is more to *Dark Innocence* than just a fantasy fiction tale, and that her purpose is to provide a deep, meaningful, healing and spiritual fantasy story. 'Wow, fascinating concept,' I thought, 'a therapeutic story written in Tolkien style' — MUST READ." — Tetje Ann Barbee, from a letter to the author

Perilous Bliss

ALSO BY RAHIMA WARREN

Dark Innocence
Book One of *The Star-Seer's Prophecy*
Rose Press, 2012

Fierce Blessings
Book Two of *The Star-Seer's Prophecy*
Rose Press, 2015

All three volumes of this trilogy are available from:
www.starseersprophecy.com and www.rosepress.com

ALSO PUBLISHED BY ROSE PRESS

**Healing Civilization: Bringing Personal Transformation
into the Societal Realm**
Claudio Naranjo, M.D.

**Starting Your Book: A Guide to Navigating the Blank Page
by Attending to What's Inside You**
Naomi Rose

MotherWealth: The Feminine Path to Money
Naomi Rose

**The Portable Blessings Ledger:
A Way to Keep Track of Your Finances and Bring Meaning
and Heart into Your Dealings with Money**
Naomi Rose

A New Life: Poems
Ralph Dranow

All are available from www.rosepress.com

The Star-Seer's Prophecy

Book Three:
Perilous Bliss

Rahima Warren

Rose Press
Oakland, CA

The Star-Seer's Prophecy, Book Three: *Perilous Bliss.*

Book Developer & Editor: Naomi Rose
www.writingfromthedeeperself.com

Proofreader: Gabriel Steinfeld
gstein@sonic.net

Cover Illustration & Design: Brenda Duke Murphy
www.bdmillustration.com

Typesetting: Margaret Copeland, Terragrafix
www.terragrafix.com

Original Interior Book Design: Joe Tantillo
www.tantillobookdesign.com

Publisher: Rose Press
www.rosepressbooks.com
rosepressbooks@yahoo.com

The Star-Seer's Prophecy, Book Three: *Perilous Bliss* / Rahima Warren
First edition. Published 2018
Printed in the United States of America.

ISBN #: 978-0-9983928-0-6

Dedication

*The Star-Seer's Prophecy Trilogy is
dedicated to all those who suffer
and inflict suffering
in the dark innocence
of the world.*

Rahima Warren's
Mission Statement

The Mission of my metaphysical fantasy trilogy, *The Star-Seer's Prophecy*, as well as my own inner work and my career as a psychotherapist, is to end the personal and societal culture of hatred, revenge, and punishment, and evoke an inner and outer culture of compassion, forgiveness, and healing.

The Star-Seer's Prophecy Trilogy

An epic metaphysical fantasy of sacrifice and redemption on the healing journey toward love and awakening

Please enjoy the trilogy in sequence, as these books take the reader on one continuous journey from evil and suffering . . . through healing and transformation . . . to love and awakening. Book 1 sets the shocking, poignant stage for Kyr's healing journey. Don't miss the continuation of the story in Book 2, or the completion and fulfillment in Book 3.

> *"[Perilous Bliss] builds upon the substantial foundation of Books 1 and 2 and culminates in a well-crafted, page-turning and unpredicted climax that is deeply satisfying and authentic to the characters and the story."*
> —Merideth Bowen Shamzad, MFT,
> Author, *The Story of Little Feather*

Dark Innocence: Book One

Kyr struggles with suffering and evil, and moves toward healing and forgiveness

Fierce Blessings: Book Two

Kyr fights with fierce compassion to protect his soul against familiar seductive evil

Perilous Bliss: Book Three

Kyr faces betrayal and despair on his path toward love and awakening

―◦◦◦―

The Star-Seer's Prophecy confronts the evil and cruelty that we humans suffer and inflict in our dark innocence, and holds forth a vision of healing, compassion, and forgiveness that is so needed in our world. Not for the faint-hearted or straight-laced, these books are recommended for adults who want to be challenged, touched, and inspired.

For more about the Trilogy, visit https://starseersprophecy.com/trilogy/
For reviews of the Trilogy, visit https://starseersprophecy.com/reviews/

The Star-Seer's Prophecy

When the Wanderers
form the Dire Cross
under the Firebird's wings,
sorcery and murder
must give him life.
He must be abandoned.
May we be forgiven!

Star-cursed, twin-souled,
knowing only evil, pain, and ice,
the dark innocent
is our salvation.
He must be forsaken.
May we be forgiven!

Through three hells,
through blissful heaven
and its loss,
he surrenders all
yet never yields.
He must be betrayed.
May we be forgiven!

Hollowed by suffering and evil,
Hallowed by expiation and submission,
the Vessel of the Goddess is created.
We must ensure his Fate.
May we be forgiven!

Author's Note

The Three Hells of *The Star-Seer's Prophecy*

Dear Reader,

If you've stuck with Kyr through the first two hells he's been through, you are very brave! I thank you and hope that Kyr's journey on the hard path thus far has been helpful and inspiring to you. [If you have not read the first two books of this trilogy, I suggest that you do so before reading *Perilous Bliss* (Book Three), as it is one continuous story and will have far more meaning for you that way. Visit **www.starseersprophecy.com/books** for more information and links to online bookstores.]

In *Dark Innocence* (Book One), Kyr ends the generations-long reign of horror by the evil sorcerer-king called the Soul-Drinker, and is rescued from the only life he has known — a life of suffering and inflicting suffering as a Slave of that malevolent sorcerer. Discovering strange but wonderful aspects of this new life — kindness, friendship, and love — reveals to him his own crimes, and his own pain and suffering. This sends him into the first of the three hells foretold by the Star-Seer: a hell of anguish and remorse, guilt and anger. With the aid of many people — Rajani and Tenaiya at the Safe Houses; Svahar at the Great Tree; and Naran and the Kailithana Jolanya at the Sanctuary; as well as the divine forgiveness of the Goddess Zhovanya — he begins to recover and become a kind, courageous, and loving person.

In *Fierce Blessings* (Book Two), Kyr undergoes the second hell: a return to the kind of torment he knew as a Slave, at the hands of his worst enemy, Gauday. Kyr must fight to keep from succumbing to all-too-familiar depravity, and to protect his soul against Gauday's insidious cruelty and malign sorcery. Yet his only weapons are the compassion and forgiveness he learned at the Sanctuary. With his inner guide Dekani's help and Zhovanya's fierce blessings, he manages to survive with his mind and soul intact, though still tainted by the remnants of the Soul-Drinker's evil sorcery.

Now, in *Perilous Bliss* (Book Three), an unthinkable betrayal destroys Kyr's faith in his friends, himself, and even his beloved Goddess. Utterly devastated, he flees into this third and final hell alone to confront the truth of his life beyond all lies and illusions. In the face of this harrowing ordeal, will he give in to despair, and abandon the hard path of healing and forgiveness? Or will he find the courage and willingness to fulfill the Star-Seer's Prophecy after all?

Perilous Bliss deals with vengeance, forgiveness, and love . . . despair, hope, and enlightenment . . . intense emotions and equanimity . . . and above all, sublime mysteries. It is dedicated to those who — even if coming from difficult origins — follow the hard path of reflection, healing, and forgiveness toward the fulfillment of the soul's potential for love and illumination.

I hope you enjoy the dark revelations, soul-deep healing, and astonishing transformations of the conclusion of *The Star-Seer's Prophecy*.

Rahima Warren

March, 2017

A reminder: Although this is a fantasy, it is not for children, the faint-of-heart, or those seeking light entertainment.

The Story So Far

Book One:
Dark Innocence

In an ancient world of blood sorcery and healing magic, the Soul-Drinker, a vicious necromancer-king, is draining the life from the souls of the people and of the earth itself. Worse yet, he has banished the land's rightful Goddess and disrupted the Sacred Balance, sending the mortal and divine realms whirling toward destruction.

The only hope for salvation is a youth named Kyr, born and raised as one of the Soul-Drinker's blindly obedient slaves. Kyr knows only the pain, evil, and cruelty of the Soul-Drinker's hell — and nothing of the Star-Seer's Prophecy that declares him to be the long-sought Liberator.

Rescued by strangers, Kyr embarks on a bewildering journey into a bizarre new life, where kindness and love are real. If he is to fulfill his destiny, he must battle his inner demons and fight to find his buried capacities for compassion and courage. Will he be able to surrender the inner ice that has been his soul's only protection in time to save the world from disaster?

Book Two:
Fierce Blessings

No longer the dark innocent, Kyr has survived the first hell of the Star-Seer's Prophecy and become a man of compassion, courage, and integrity during his year at the Goddess's Sanctuary. To atone for the terrible crimes he committed as the unwitting slave of the Soul-Drinker, he plans to help his slave-brothers find the blessings he received from the Goddess Who saved his soul: healing, forgiveness, and love.

But, torn from the safety of the Sanctuary by his worst enemy, Kyr now faces the second hell foretold by the prophecy. Left chained outdoors like a dog for months, he is subjected to beatings and derision by his captors. When the rains come, he is taken inside as servant and whore by their leader, who subjects him to sorcerous torture, aiming to turn him into his will-less, mind-bonded slave. Far from any help, Kyr struggles to protect his soul from the seductive pull of all-too-familiar depravity.

Will Kyr keep faith with the Goddess? Or will he return to the foul slavery he has known for most of his life? The fate of the land and the Goddess Herself depends on his choice.

Book Three:

Perilous Bliss

"We must become so alone, so utterly alone,
that we withdraw into our innermost self.
It is a way of bitter suffering.
But then our solitude is overcome, we are no longer alone,
for we find that our innermost self is the spirit,
that it is God, the indivisible.
And suddenly we find ourselves in the midst of the world,
yet undisturbed by its multiplicity,
for in our innermost soul we know ourselves
to be one with all being."

— Herman Hesse

Table of Contents

Prologue ~ Jolanya's Dreams

Jolanya's empty stomach twisted with apprehension as she trudged through the priestesses' complex of caves and tunnels beneath Zhovanya's Temple at the Sanctuary. Her own shadow loomed and shrank as she moved through the light and shadow cast by oil lamps hanging from the stone ceilings. Full Moon Mother had summoned her, and she feared she knew why.

White-haired Dyrni awaited her inside her simple meeting chamber, standing erect in her formal white robes in front of the silver Moon disk on the wall. Usually Dyrni was serene and kindly, but this time her voice was stern.

"It's been nearly a year since Kyr was taken from us," she admonished. "We know you are saddened by this, and have been unable to carry out your duties as the Kailithana. Luckily, there has been no potential kailithos for you to help — until now."

Jolanya felt a chill take over her bones, and remained silent. Her throat ached with repressed sobs; as she remembered the dreadful calamity that had overtaken her beloved Kyr shortly after he completed a year of deep healing work with Naran and herself right here at the Sanctuary. This very morning, she had awakened from the nightmare that still haunted her sleep.

No, no, no! she wails silently, watching Gauday and his band taking Kyr away from the Sanctuary, beaten and bloody, dragging him back into the kind of hell he had endured most of his life, from which he had so recently recovered his soul. "Zhovanya, Jeyal, how can You let this happen?" she demands of the Goddess and God. "He is the Liberator, the one who freed all of Khailaz from the Soul-Drinker's evil. "Help him!" she begs, "please help him!" But neither the Goddess nor the God respond to her pleas, and her heart aches with unending grief.

The Full Moon Mother's voice broke the silence. "Are you ready to fulfill your duties as Kailithana?"

Jolanya jumped, and came back to face her present dilemma. "I'm sorry. I can't." She winced at Dyrni's frown. "I don't want to break my vows as Kailithana, but in my heart, I have already. I love Kyr, and haven't been able to let go of him. The thought of sharing the kind of intimacy the Kailithara demands with another man is…unbearable."

"I understand." The elder woman's gray eyes softened. "There is always one."

Surprised, Jolanya asked, "Oh, you fell in love too? What did *you* do?"

"I sought a Moon Dream from Jeyal for guidance, and He cooled my heart."

Jolanya frowned and met Dyrni's searching gaze head-on. "I suppose I must do this, too. But if Jeyal tells me to let go of Kyr, I fear I cannot."

Dyrni gathered her full authority, and the Full Moon sigil on her forehead glowed bright silver. "You must. You are the Kailithana."

Defiance flared in Jolanya's eyes, but she merely said, "I will seek a Moon Dream tonight." She bowed, and stalked out of the Full Moon Mother's chamber.

She spent the rest of the day in tears, prayer, and attempts at meditation. That evening, Jolanya plodded through the tunnels to the Dream Cave, dressed in her sleeping robe and carrying a pouch containing the Dreaming herb. Stopping before a round door set two steps up in the stone wall of the tunnel, she commanded, "Kaa'atay!" and the door slid up. As she climbed into the dark warmth of the cave, which was just big enough for her to sit or lie on the comfortable bedding on the floor, she heard the door slide back down behind her, leaving her in utter darkness.

One candle, only, was allotted to Dreamers. "Shai," she murmured, and a golden flame sprang to life on its wick. Then, sitting cross-legged, she chanted softly, "Jeyal, sumarali. Volara donoruli. Jeyal, sumarali. Volara donoruli." But soon she choked to a stop, her throat aching. Tears came, and kept coming. She sobbed into her hands, wiping her face on the hem of her sleeping robe, until after a while her tears ebbed. "Jeyal," she whispered, "I love him. How can my vows as Kailithana keep us apart? He *must* be the one You promised, or why would my heart keep insisting that we belong together? Please, please grant me a Dream of clear guidance."

She lifted the pouch tied to her waist and took out a substantial pinch of the Dreaming herb and a small moonstone flask. Chewing the bitter herb made her start to gag, but she washed it down with the flask's sweet contents. She placed her hands together before her heart, bowed her head, and prayed, "Jeyal, please show me the path You wish me to take." A few moments later, she sagged down onto the bedding, closed her eyes, and soon began to dream.

She kneels before the sacred silver-blue flame of Jeyal in the Council Cave, watching as the flame shapes itself into a man of lunar fire, with a crescent moon glowing upon His brow.

She raises her hands from her heart up toward the shining god. "Jeyal, I offer you my heart." Tears streaming down her face, she begs, "Please guide me. Am I to remain Kailithana here, even though my heart so longs for Kyr that I cannot in all conscience continue with my work? Or am I to carry out the secret mission of the Kailithana?"

"THE TIME IS COMING WHEN YOU WILL BE CALLED UPON TO FULFILL THE MISSION."

His Light flares up, bright as the Full Moon, and begins to diminish.

"Wait!" she cries. "When? How?"

But His Light swiftly wanes to Half Moon, Quarter Moon, Dark Moon.

In the darkness, Jolanya awoke, and wept again. For joy, this time.

"Kailithana?" Golden lamplight filtered into the Dream Cave from the open door. "Kailithana, it's time to get ready. The Council of Sisters will meet with you at Moonrise."

It was Tovali, one of her closest friends among the priestesses. "Thank, you, Tovali. I'll be there."

Jolanya left Zhovanya's Temple and walked down the mountain to return to her cottage. In the valley below, the Sanctuary complex spread out, gilded with late-afternoon sunlight. Seeing with the eyes of the soon-to-depart, she noticed anew the white-washed buildings with their peaked slate roofs; the large dining hall with its wide, wooden porch separating the rows of small rooms lining both sides of the tidy brick courtyard; the large fountain in the courtyard splashing peacefully. She treasured the Sanctuary's order and peacefulness, as well as the community of her sister priestesses. *I'll have to give this all up to go be with Kyr*, she sighed. But her heart glowed at this thought, and she took a little skip of joy.

In her cottage, as she washed, dressed in her indigo robes, and ate a bowl of oatmeal, she considered how to tell the Council about her Dream and her decision. She knew many would object, and she wondered how to convince everyone of the rightness of her decision. The thought of days of debate made her head ache.

Just before Moonrise, she returned to the priestesses' complex below the Temple. She marched through the familiar tunnels toward the Council Cave, but, halfway there, she stopped in mid-stride. "Oh, Jeyal!" she whispered. "Let

3

that not be necessary!" The oatmeal in her stomach suddenly felt like a ball of mud, but she shook herself and strode onward.

The Council Cave held a small pool of still water with a round, white boulder in its center. From a cavity in the boulder arose the sacred Flame of Jeyal, burning a luminous silver-blue. The Council of Sisters sat around the pool on pillows of four colors — gold in the East; green in the South; red in the West; and black in the North, each woman in the Direction she felt most attuned to at this moment.

Dyrni and two elder Sisters were a solemn presence in the East, the Direction of Learning and Discernment. In the South, the Direction of Wounding and Healing, sat three younger Sister-Healers. Jolanya sank onto a pillow in the West, the Direction of Obstacles and Transformation, beside her friends, Tovali and Lanya. She glanced nervously toward the North, the Direction of Completion and Death, but it seemed empty. Staring into the darkness, she thought she saw a flicker of movement, a quick flash of silver, but she couldn't be sure. She frowned, her apprehension growing. What if her gamble didn't succeed?

As soon as Jolanya had settled herself, Dyrni led the Sisters in the invocation: "Jeyal sumaralai. Volara donorulai. Jeyal, we call You. We offer You our hearts." When the silvery-blue flame flared high, the women fell silent, leaving it up to Jolanya to begin when she was ready.

Shaking with excitement, Jolanya tried to keep her tone neutral, not wanting to reveal her joy to her Sisters. "Jeyal gave me clear guidance." She took a breath, and plunged onward. "He told me the time is coming for me to fulfill the Kailithana's ultimate destiny, a secret mission that has been handed down from Kailithana to Kailithana. This means that I will be leaving sometime soon. I don't know when, but Jeyal said I will be called upon."

"You can't leave," Lanya protested. "You're the Kailithana!" Most of the Sisters voiced their forceful agreement.

"What secret mission?" demanded Tovali.

"Hush!" commanded Dyrni. "We are in Council. We *will* be calm and contemplate this development *quietly*."

With some sighs and rustling, the Sisters settled down. The silent, silver-blue flame burned steadily. Not a ripple disturbed the water of the pool. Jolanya tried to meditate, but her heart beat too fast. In contrast, the time passed so slowly that she felt sure the Sun and Moon had frozen in Their paths. Just when she thought she would have to jump up and *demand* that they start the discussion, Dyrni opened her eyes and said, "We begin in the South."

The younger Sisters spoke to each other quietly, at first. Then Marnya spoke for the South. "Perhaps Jolanya's grief for Kyr has distorted the Dream she received. We suggest she spend time in fasting and prayer, then Dream again."

Jolanya wanted to protest, but it was not her turn to speak.

"Who speaks for the West?" asked Dyrni.

Tovali and Lanya conferred in soft voices, and then Tovali said, "We know how difficult the loss of Kyr to that evil madman, Gauday, has been for Jolanya. But we too question whether her longing for Kyr has distorted her Dream. We agree with the South." Tovali glanced at Jolanya defiantly. "And we want to know what this 'secret mission' is. Has Jolanya invented it as an excuse to abandon her vows?"

Jolanya stared at Tovali in shock, feeling hurt and betrayed by her friend. She wanted to shout, "I am not a liar!" But she bit her lip and kept quiet, observing the protocol of Council. She would have her turn to speak. At this thought, her stomach twisted with fear.

"I speak for the East," said Dyrni, after exchanging brief glances with the two Elder Sisters. "Jolanya, you are still young, with many years to serve as Kailithana. It would be a great hardship on the Sanctuary to lose your services so early. We too agree with the wisdom of the South. What say you?"

Though angry at their dismissal of her Dream, Jolanya spoke calmly. "I understand your concerns, but I do not accept that my Dream is flawed. It is a true Dream." In the pockets of her robes, she clenched her fists. "I will *not* argue about it."

Her heart pounding in her chest, she knew she had to take a great risk. Even though her secret mission might be revealed, she saw no other way to avoid days of wrangling. Rising to her feet and mustering her courage, she said, "I ask that our Dark Moon Mother sense the truth of my claim."

A whisper of indrawn breaths rippled around the circle. Dyrni held up a hand to prevent an outbreak of comments. "Are you sure, Jolanya?"

"Yes."

A hush filled the Council Cave, vibrating with apprehension and expectation.

"Dark Moon Mother, I, Jolanya, ask for your favor. Please determine the validity of my claims."

Nothing happened. Jolanya clasped her hands to hide their trembling, fearing that her gamble had failed.

Then a deep quiet voice broke the silence. "I have been called." From the darkness in the North emerged a tall figure in silver-edged black robe and mask. She beckoned to Jolanya. "Come."

Taking a deep breath, Jolanya moved to the North to stand before the tall woman. The fathomless blackness of Dark Moon Mother's eyes captured her gaze. She felt as if she were falling through a starless night sky, and her knees started to wobble. But a strong, bony hand grabbed her arm and kept her upright.

With her other hand, Dark Moon Mother touched the round black sigil on her own forehead and then touched Jolanya's brow. From that touch, a syrupy blackness spread through Jolanya's mind. She nearly cried out, but forced herself to remain silent and endure the alien sensation.

"Ah?" breathed Dark Moon Mother, in surprise. "Ah." She let go of Jolanya and stepped back. "Confirmed." Light glinted off the silver edge of her mask as she bowed to Jolanya and to Dyrni. Then she turned and disappeared into the darkness of the North.

Jolanya sagged with relief. Dark Moon Mother had discovered all her secrets but revealed none of them, and had validated her Dream. She started to return to the West to sit with her friends, but she caught Tovali glaring at her, and stopped. Then she realized that she should stay in the North, Direction of Completion. She sank down onto one of the black cushions, glad that she had succeeded, and that she would be the one to fulfill the secret mission of the Kailithana at long last. She hoped and believed that would mean being reunited with Kyr. Who else could possibly be her partner in restoring the Sacred Balance? She shook her head slightly, smiling to herself. *No one.* But then she sighed, knowing that her victory would cost her a great deal: her friends, her community of sisters, her place at the Sanctuary, and her sacred work as the Kailithana.

Her sisters were murmuring to each other, upset and confused. Some cast angry glances at her, and Tovali raised her voice. "How can you let this happen? A Kailithana must not break her vows!"

Dyrni clapped her hands sharply, startling the sisters into silence. "Dark Moon Mother has spoken. Jolanya's Dream is true." The Full Moon Mother spoke firmly, quelling any argument with a fierce glare. "Now each of *you* must seek a Dream to discover if you are to be the next Kailithana. The Elder Sisters and I will assist you. This Council is concluded." She clapped her hands again, and started chanting, "Jeyal, gratharalai. We thank Thee."

The sisters settled themselves, and dutifully joined in. As Jolanya sang, her heart filled with a poignant blend of sadness, gratitude, and joy.

Part One ~ The Downward Journey

"May you travel in an awakened way,
Gathered wisely into your inner ground;
That you may not waste the invitations
Which wait along the way to transform you."

— John O'Donohue

Chapter One

Entanglements

The westering sun glimmered crimson on shallow ponds, and threw long shadows across the swales and hillocks of the marsh. Moss-draggled tree skeletons made black silhouettes against the sunset sky. An occasional red-caped blackbird perched regally on a tall reed, while a dozen teal gnat-catchers and a few purple swallows darted after the multitudes of flying insects hovering in the last of the daylight.

"Ouch!" Rajani swatted a bloodbug off his neck. "Last time I was through here, there were no birds. We had to gallop to get away from storm clouds of biting bugs. And the stench! Smelled like a hundred rotting corpses."

Kyr gave him a disgusted look. "Doesn't smell like flowers now."

Rajani laughed, and took a deep breath of the warm, fetid air. "And yet it's a tremendous improvement! The land and wildlife are starting to revive, now that the Soul-Drinker is dead — thanks to you, Kyr."

"Dauthaz was killing the land and animals too?"

"Yes! He weakened the very fabric of life by stealing the souls of the sacrifices, and keeping their zhan from returning to their soulkin. Thank the gods, the Soul-Drinker's blight never got as far as the Heart of the Forest, Ravenvale, or the Sanctuary." Rajani glanced at Kyr somberly. "Still, unless Zhovanya can be restored to Her rightful place, our land will never fully recover."

"When I was the Soul-Drinker's Slave, I had no idea that his evil was so... *poisonous*." He sighed, disheartened by this reminder of his former life. "By all the hells, I didn't even know that what he did was evil."

"That's right, Kyr: you did *not* know. Now stop blaming yourself for what the Soul-Drinker did. And remember: you are the one who liberated us all from that lethal nightmare."

"Gods, Rajani!" Kyr growled. "Stop making me out to be a hero, will you?"

"Never!" laughed the Warrior Mage, and gestured toward the west. "Isn't this sunset exquisite?"

Behind them, the healer Medari drove the lead wagon. Watching Kyr and Rajani, he noticed the similarity of the two men's postures and ways of riding. Except for their hair — Rajani's raven-black and Kyr's reddish gold — he thought they might be twins; although next to the muscular Warrior Mage, Kyr still looked too lean. Their banter and good spirits had enlivened the whole caravan, which moved along with an almost carnival-like cheer — except for the plodding, dusty prisoners at the rear and the Companions guarding them. The caravan was much smaller now, only eight wagons. Many Companions, villagers, and prisoners had been left behind at villages along the way. Only two dozen Companions remained with them now, those who planned to live in Ravenvale. The healer watched as Kyr leaned close to Rajani, pointing out something high above. A tawny eagle soared dark against a sky glowing rose and crimson.

Medari turned his eyes away from the sunset splendor, and clucked to his horses: "Get along, now." Kyr's dog, Friend, was curled up at the healer's feet, tired from chasing after Kyr all afternoon. Medari sighed heavily. By sundown the next day, they would reach Stonewell, his beloved village, where he'd have to face his empty house and the graves of his wife and children. Fresh grief struck his heart, and his face went rigid with his effort to hide it. Even Gauday's execution had done nothing to alleviate the healer's pain and anger. Only his desire to make amends to Kyr for his role in Gauday's tortures gave him a reason to keep on living.

That night, Kyr joined Medari and Friend at their campfire, sitting cross-legged on the ground, using pan bread to scoop up bean and bacon stew from his tin camp bowl. Kyr gobbled up most of his stew; but then he stiffened. "Gods, Medari, we reach your village tomorrow, don't we?"

Medari nodded and set his dish down, its contents half-eaten. "Here, Friend, this is for you." Eagerly, Friend jumped up and began lapping up the remaining stew. Kyr said nothing. He had no desire to mouth meaningless comforts.

Medari sat hunched up in silence for a moment, gathering his courage. Then he said, "I know I harmed you severely by going along with Gauday's vicious game, but I have a favor to ask. Will you come with me...to my house?"

"Of course. I never had a family, didn't even know what a family is, until you told me about your wife and children." Hesitantly, Kyr added, "They almost seemed like...*my* family."

Medari nodded, incapable of words. He stared into the fire, grief and rage a solid block in his throat. Kyr sat with him in silence while the fire burned down.

Long after Medari had disappeared into his wagon, Kyr sat by the dying fire, brooding over Gauday's treachery: how he had kept the two of them under his control by threatening to murder Medari's family if Medari didn't obey him and keep Kyr alive, when all the while Gauday already had ordered them killed. Kyr rubbed his face tiredly. The golden days of freedom at the start of this the journey away from Gauday's cursed fort faded away like a forgotten dream, and Gauday's nightmare rose up to haunt him again.

He stared grimly into the glowing embers, sullen-red like the light in that torture chamber at the fort; like the burning coals of his own buried anger. "Gods," he muttered. "I thought I had forgiven Gauday when I executed him." Then he shook his head. "No. I was under Zhovanya's influence, then. No, I'd like to kill Gauday again, very slowly this time." Sleep was impossible. He spent the night prowling the edges of the camp.

The next evening, the caravan reached Stonewell just as the sun slipped behind the western ridge-top. In the hazy, late-summer twilight, they made camp in the bow of a river named the Awanai. Leaving an unhappy Friend tied to the healer's wagon, Kyr and Medari crossed the stone-paved village square amidst a swirling crowd of people. Returning villagers fell into the arms of family and friends, hugging, kissing, and tenderly patting the faces of their loved ones. Meanwhile, a few Stonewell residents hurried through the crowd, anxiously looking for their relatives — in vain. Their wails of grief mingled poignantly with the joyous laughter of families and friends reunited.

Grim-faced, Medari led Kyr down a curving side street to a two-story graystone bungalow surrounded by spacious gardens of roses, lilacs, rosemary shrubs, and other aromatic herbs. Medari stood staring at his home for a few moments, then straightened his shoulders. "Let's go in," he said, dour as a soldier facing battle.

On the left of the small entryway, an open door revealed Medari's tidy infirmary. On the right, stairs led up to the second floor. The main room, downstairs, held comfortably padded chairs and a couch, a well-used oak-slab table and ladder-back chairs, and a scattering of stools and small tables. The hearth was cold and empty even of ashes, but before it sat a dark vase full of arching spikes of lush white flowers. Medari gave a sarcastic snort. "Nice of the headwoman to leave those. As if I need a reminder that my family is dead."

In answer to Kyr's puzzled frown, the healer said, "It's traditional: white flowers for a death in the family." Medari turned away, and Kyr stood quietly as the healer wandered around the main room, touching the top of a ladder-back chair, tracing the shape of a small, lumpy vase, picking up an embroidered pillow and setting it down. Tears dripped slowly down his face, unheeded.

Feeling helpless, Kyr stepped outside, giving Medari the respect of solitude. Sunset painted clouds scarlet fading to dusky purple as he paced the stone path of the small front garden. Roses red as blood still bloomed, but the lilac bushes offered only spindly brown skeletons of flowers among their dark-green leaves. Kyr followed the path around to the back of the cottage. Opening a gate, he entered a garden enclosed by a tall wooden fence. Untended sweet-berry bushes sprawled around the edges of the garden, with its raised beds of herbs and rotting vegetables.

It was too contained and crowded for the storm of emotions swirling in Kyr's heart. His grief and concern for Medari contended with his rage that the Soul-Drinker's nightmare of suffering seemed to endlessly engulf good and innocent people. Hoping for space to run off his pent-up fury, Kyr hurried through the back gate — and froze. "Merciless gods!"

Just before him lay four graves, each surrounded by low plants with fragrant white blooms. The four headstones were engraved with the names "Leanya," "Laro," "Franya," and "Mureya." It was Medari's family. The reality of Medari's terrible loss pierced his heart, turning his rage to heavy sorrow. Staring down at the graves, he whispered, "How could You let this happen, Zhovanya?"

But then he snorted to himself, knowing from his own dire experience that the Goddess did not protect even Her chosen Vessel from the worst evil. He shook his head like a bull stung by wasps, angry and baffled by the paradoxes of the Goddess, Whom he had witnessed at the Sanctuary dancing through all the wonders and horrors of life. She had forgiven him, and guided him to forgive Gauday; and yet She had done nothing to prevent such senseless slaughter. Unable to bear the sight of the four graves, he prowled back into the vegetable garden.

There, a sense that he had abandoned Medari crept over him, and he returned to the cottage, not knowing what to expect. Certainly, it was not to find Medari in his infirmary, meticulously wrapping bottles of oils and potions in cloth and packing them inside a wooden case designed to hold them.

"What are you doing?" Kyr blurted out in surprise. Medari set a bottle down, too carefully. Kyr could see grief and fury under strong rein in the healer's overly precise movements, the rigidity of his face.

With grim quietness, Medari said, "There's nothing for me here, now. May I come with you to Ravenvale?"

"Of course you can, but…. Are you sure that's what you want? To leave your home, your friends, your village?"

Medari's tone was deadly flat. "Yes."

Taken aback by his lifeless tone, Kyr asked carefully, "May I help you pack?"

"No, thank you. I must do this myself." Medari looked at him, a terrible anguish in his eyes. Kyr knew many kinds of suffering, but not *this* kind of devastating loss. He wanted to apologize for being the pretext for Medari's abduction, for the existence of such evil as men do to one another, for the possibility of such agony in the world.

Very gently, Kyr said, "I'll wait for you outside." Medari nodded and went back to his methodical packing.

Kyr returned to the small, somber graveyard and stood there in the soft evening light, fists clenched, furious that Medari should suffer so. His gut churned with loathing for Gauday and everyone who had carried out his despicable orders; and his scars flared up, pulsing with a craving for bloody retribution.

But then, in his mind, he heard Gauday laughing. Kyr shuddered, feeling the sticky strands of hatred and vengeance entrapping his soul. *No! I can't let him win! I can't leave the hard path — not after how hard I struggled to keep from hating Gauday.* He knelt before the graves, and once again strove to release his anger, to soften. He looked up at the night sky, now scattered with stars. "Zhovanya naralo," he whispered. "Zhovanya naralo."

"NO."

Kyr jumped, and looked up to find Medari standing over him. "No," the healer repeated in an implacable voice, "I can never forgive those who took my family from me for no reason. I cooperated with them, and kept you alive to endure hellish pain and degradation — all for *this,*" he growled, gesturing at the row of graves.

"Gods, Medari, I'm so sorry! I would rather have died than see this happen. Listening to your stories at the fort's infirmary, I imagined that *your* family was the one I never had."

"You're the only one who survived." Abruptly, Medari reached for something metallic at his waist.

Kyr froze. Medari stood over him, the knife in his hand glinting in the starlight. *Merciless gods! He must blame* me *for being the cause of this tragedy — for being alive when his family is dead.* Kyr choked back a sardonic laugh. *Am I to die now, after surviving all that Gauday did to me? Ah, why not?* Anguished with guilt, he bared his throat to the knife.

In the darkness before moonrise, Medari knelt by the graves of his wife and children, and asked, "Shall we be family for each other?"

13

"WHAT?" Kyr blurted out, shocked by this unexpected reprieve from death. It took him a moment to absorb what Medari was offering him, and then he smiled eagerly. "Family? Yes, yes! But how?"

"If we mingle our blood, we become family of the heart." Medari raised his knife a little.

Kyr took a breath to settle his jangled nerves. "I'd be honored and glad to be family with you."

"Very well," said Medari. "Then do as I do." He set his knife down and took off his tunic, baring his torso, so Kyr also shed his.

Medari took his knife, and lightly sliced his palm. Then he traced a palm-sized circle over Kyr's heart with the tip of the bloody knife, just barely breaking the skin. Then he handed the knife to Kyr, and Kyr gravely followed suit.

Medari placed his bleeding palm over the red circle on Kyr's chest, and looked into Kyr's eyes. "Son of my heart."

Holding Medari's solemn gaze, Kyr placed his palm on the red circle on Medari's chest, and said, "Heart-father." For a few moments, they stood with their hands pressed to each other's hearts, letting their blood mix, feeling the beating of their hearts coming into rhythm with each other. The bright pain of the shallow wounds released a little of their anguish.

Then Medari clasped their hands together and held them out, letting their mingled blood fall upon the graves of their family. Their appalling burden of sorrow and fury was no smaller; but, being shared, it was somehow easier to bear.

They rose and stood silently, taking a last look at the small graveyard. In the dark fires of their grief and rage, their hearts had forged a new bond. And Kyr now shared Medari's grief and anger in a more intimate way — as family. Yet he also felt an easing of his own hidden grief and fear: he was no longer alone in the world.

They put their tunics back on and went inside into the infirmary, where Medari cleansed their wounds and bandaged their hands. Then he said, "Now that we are family, I want to show you these." And he removed a stack of hand-sized rectangular objects from a satchel still sitting on his work table. "A patient of mine was an artist, and these were her way of paying me." One by one, he showed Kyr the portraits of his wife and children. Seeing their faces for the first time, Kyr's sorrow spilled over, and tears trickled down his cheeks. The two stood together for a few moments, grieving together for their lost family.

Then the healer said, "Let me show you my — our — home." Kyr wiped his face on his sleeve and nodded. Leading his heart-son into the main room, Medari showed Kyr the beautiful lace curtains that his wife, Leanya, had made, and the crude, three-legged stool that was his son's first handmade contribution to the household. Upstairs, Medari opened the first door on the right and explained, "This was Franya's room. She always kept it neat as pin. Each loved thing had its special place." Carefully arranged dolls sat on the neatly made bed. "Franya loved babies and looked forward to becoming a mother." Medari swallowed hard and stepped out of the room. Kyr followed him out and closed the door.

They moved down the hall to the next door. "And here is Laro's room," Medari said. "See, here is his bug collection. He was fascinated with bugs, the gods know why." In contrast to the neatly organized bug collection on the walls, a cheerful hodge-podge covered every flat surface: small wicker cages, string, pins, a red ball, twigs, stones, dried flowers. This bed, too, was neatly made, but that made it seem out of place in this room. "Laro loved being outdoors. He was always running off to the woods, or out playing with his friends." Medari gently closed this door and they went on to the door at the end of the hall.

"Mureya was my oldest," Medari began. "You can see, here, that Mureya loved books as much as Laro loved bugs. Never could get her to tidy up. Someone must have…." Medari choked to a stop, tears in his eyes. A shelf held a small collection of books. Quills, an ink bottle, and parchment sat neatly on a small desk. Medari resumed his narrative in a pain-filled voice. "She always had smudges of ink on her fingers and the side of her nose. She loved to write and draw. She was sketching all the herbs I use and writing down what they are good for. I hoped she would become a healer, too."

Kyr's heart ached, thinking of the lively children at the fort, or those who came along on this journey toward Ravenvale, racing about, shrieking and playing mysterious games. He detested the stillness of this empty home that should have been full of movement and laughter, according to the stories Medari had shared with him back at the fort.

Medari continued up the hall to the single door on the left. "This was *our* room, Leanya's and mine." Without another word, he stepped inside and gently shut the door behind him. Kyr sat down at the top of the stairs and waited, listening to Medari's muffled sobs. His heart was aching so badly that he could barely breathe. *Gods, is this what it means to have a family? This agony? It's worse than the Soul-Drinker's pain shocks.* Kyr sighed and rubbed his face tiredly. *Maybe it's easier not to love anyone. Which is worse: loneliness, or loving and risking this anguish?* But then he thought, *Would I give up my time with Jolanya to avoid the pain of losing her?* He shook his head slowly. *Never.*

After a time, Medari emerged, red-eyed but less tightly drawn. He sat down beside Kyr. "I now have some idea what a terrible thing I was asking you when I begged you not to die, after that night when Gauday left you out in the rain and you were so ill."

Kyr sighed, remembering his reluctant decision to give up his courtship of the Dark Lady, Death.

Medari went on. "Forgive me for saying this, but I wish I *had* let you die. Then I wouldn't have lived to see this day. And you would have been spared Gauday's most vicious games."

"The Goddess has other plans for us, it seems," Kyr said somberly. "I can't begin to fathom why any of this had to happen. But I must tell you, I am grateful for all you did for me — for saving my life, despite it all."

"Despite it all, I am glad you are here now, my son." Medari's last word rang through Kyr, touching him deeply. A startled gladness mingled poignantly with grief for Medari's family and a newly discovered but ancient grief for his own unknown father and mother. For a while, the two men sat together in the barren house that had once been a home.

"Kyr? Medari? Are you here?" Rajani's voice broke their sorrowing silence. "I'll go," Kyr told his heart-father, and went downstairs to greet the Warrior Mage, who stood just inside the open door.

"Ah, there you are, Kyr. I knocked, but no one answered."

"Sorry, we were upstairs."

"How is Medari doing? Is he settling back in?"

"No. Medari is coming with us."

Rajani glanced at the stack of wooden cases and cloth satchels in the main room. "Ah. He truly wants to leave his home?"

Kyr nodded. "There's something else you should know. He and I, we're family now." He held up his hand with its white bandage striped with red.

"I see." A surprised frown crossed Rajani's face, quickly replaced by a smile. "Well," he said, "that's one blessing to come out of this tragedy."

Kyr raised his eyebrows, wondering at Rajani's tentative tone. But just then Medari came downstairs, and Rajani turned to the healer.

"Medari, I'm glad that you will be coming with us. We need a good healer at Ravenvale." Rajani gestured toward the stack in the main room. "That's what you're bringing?"

Medari nodded.

"Would you like to eat before loading these on your wagon?" Rajani asked. "There's quite a feast at the square."

Medari shook his head, but Kyr said, "I need to eat."

"Alright," Rajani said. "I'll help Medari get these loaded onto his wagon."

A s Kyr walked back to the village square, an odd thought sent a pang through his heart. *This could have been my home, if I were really Medari's son.* He looked around forlornly. The square was paved with flat gray stones and surrounded on three sides by three-story wooden, richly painted houses with shops on the ground floor. On the fourth side stood a larger building by itself, in front of which was the beautiful well made of colorful, polished, and tightly fitting stones that gave the village its name. Torches on tall metal stands burned brightly in the calm air, lighting up the square.

Many of the villagers were gathered there, celebrating the return of loved ones and neighbors. Most stood around trestle tables loaded with food, eating, talking, and laughing all at once. Elders wrapped in warm shawls huddled on stone benches around a fire burning in the stone circle at the center of the square, their heads close together, chatting merrily, or snapping at the children who were racing wildly about the square playing tag, yelling and laughing: "Tag, you're it!" "No, I'm not! You didn't get me!"

Kyr hesitated at the sight of so many happy people, but a tall woman approached him, wearing a colorful turban. "Welcome! I'm Jaiyan, the head-woman of Stonewell Village. Are you hungry?"

"Yes," he said with a smile, liking her quiet friendliness. Kyr sat with Jaiyan on a bench by the fire, and ate spicy rabbit stew and buttery biscuits, washing it down with cool ale. After he had taken the edge off his hunger, Jaiyan asked, "How is Medari? We're glad he's returned."

"I'm sorry. Medari has decided to leave with us."

Jaiyan shook her head. "Such a terrible thing those cursed villains did to him. I can understand why he is leaving. But we will miss him and his talents as a healer."

"Yes, he is very skilled. He kept me alive despite.... Well, never mind." Kyr found his hands shaking and his throat too dry to swallow another morsel. He carefully set his plate aside, and drained his mug of ale. In a tight voice, he said, "Did anyone see who did it, who slaughtered Medari's family?"

"No, those monsters left that morning. We thought they were gone and were trying to get some sleep that night, after a quarter-moon of their 'fun and games.' When we heard the screams, we were all terrified, and kept inside with our doors barred." Jaiyan looked down in shame. "I'm sorry."

Kyr glared at her, thinking, *No wonder Medari wants to leave this place.* Enraged by Jaiyan's confession, he rose without a word and stalked off toward the caravan's encampment, his treacherous scars inflaming him into vengeful fury. *I'll torment those murderers until they scream for mercy, as Medari's children and wife surely did. But how can I find out who killed my family? Ha! There is one who must know.*

With his curse-scars beating a relentless demand for blood and pain, Kyr prowled around the perimeter of the camp until he came upon the prisoners, chained to the posts of a large corral under the watchful eyes of four Companions. Most of the prisoners were already asleep, curled up under their blankets. A few sat hunched up against the fence posts.

The four penitents, however, sat together unchained, chanting quietly. Kyr strode over to them. The four of them looked at him, the tentative hope in their eyes turning quickly to uncertainty and fear. Their chant faltered to a halt.

Chapter Two

Shadows on the Hard Path

Kyr glared at all the penitents, then turned his gaze on the redheaded one, Gauday's former sergeant. "You, Craith. You must know."

Quailing before Kyr's wrath, Craith asked, "Know what?"

"Who did it? Who murdered Medari's family?" Grabbing Craith by his shirt, Kyr hauled him up to demand an answer. Phantom-pale, the redhead made no resistance. Fighting against a desire to beat him to the ground, Kyr shook him instead. "You must have known. Who did it?"

"Gauday ordered it, but I passed on his orders," Craith admitted. "The men who actually did it...I told Rajani who they were, and he sent them to the desert prison."

"Gods damn it!" Kyr snarled in frustration. Thwarted of his desired victims, he turned on Craith. "You could have stopped Gauday! You could at least have countermanded his worst orders. You could have prevented the slaughter of Medari's family, and the gods know how many others. Gauday was too preoccupied with his 'experiments' to notice! Why the hells didn't you?"

Kyr's words fell on Craith like icy arrows, penetrating his heart. He could no longer bear Kyr's accusatory gaze and dropped his head, unable to speak.

Furious and frustrated, Kyr shook him again. Craith's ragged shirt ripped open, and Kyr suddenly let him loose as if he had turned into a dangerous snake. As Craith fell to his knees, his bared torso revealed a sinuous pattern of small scars similar to Kyr's, but less extensive. Their eyes met in mute recognition. Kyr stepped back in confusion and shock at this silent answer to his last question. "Gods damn it all to the lowest hell!"

Craith bowed to the ground, sobbing as never before since being abducted by the Master's Gatherers. The other penitents — Jorem, Kinar, and Zurano — looked at Kyr with hurt, bewildered eyes, crushed by their usually compassionate savior's condemnation. Jorem knelt by Craith's side and put a comforting arm across his back.

"Ah, gods and demons!" Kyr's rage fled before an onslaught of remorse and chagrin. *I can't do this to them, or I could throw them off the hard path before they've even had a chance at it.* He recalled again the fierce blessing of Zhovanya's gift of counsel — *"SOFTEN"* — and took several deep, shuddering breaths. He could find no words, but he sat down with the penitents, silently repeating *Zhovanya naralo* until he calmed down and his scars quit throbbing.

Craith's sobbing dwindled away, and the bewilderment faded from the others' eyes. Finally, Craith sat up, but he still couldn't look at Kyr.

"All of you, please forgive me," Kyr said. "I was just with Medari at the graves of his family — who are *my* family." Kyr took a breath, and added, "Medari is now my heart-father."

"Ah, gods!" Craith gasped, but Kinar and Zurano nodded in unison, and Zurano murmured, "No wonder you are so angry."

"Heart-father?" asked Jorem. The former Slave had little knowledge of the world beyond the Soul-Drinker's labyrinth. Kinar was sitting next to Jorem, and quietly explained what the term meant.

Kyr clenched his fists as his scars flared up, pulsing with the poisons of rage and vengeance. For a few moments, he sat with tense shoulders and bowed head, taking slow, deep breaths. When he felt more in control, he lifted his head. "I have to ask: did any of you kill Medari's wife or children, or stand by while it was being done?" He gazed at them one by one. Each man met his gaze straight on, and shook his head. Their eyes were clear of any deceit or doubt, and Kyr believed them. "I'm sorry. I had to be sure."

"But you are right," Craith said raggedly. "I c-could have stopped it, and I didn't. I n-never even thought to disobey, until that last day when Rajani and the Companions showed up at the fort. Gods, I am so sorry!" He buried his face in his hands, and groaned, "Maybe you should send *me* to the desert, too."

Kyr knew the pain of new-born guilt and remorse all too well. "No, no. We were *all* trained to obey without question. I understand why you didn't challenge Gauday. But now you must face the suffering you have caused by your blind obedience, as I had to. It's very painful, but it is part of the hard path. Can you do this?"

"You have done this, and so must we," said Jorem. Kinar and Zurano nodded, and Kinar said softly, "Yes, we must. It's the only way to cleanse our souls and be free of our evil deeds."

Kyr nodded, surprised by Kinar's wisdom. "That's right." Then, turning to the redhead, he said, "Craith, I am sorry for my cruelty. I let my anger get the better of me." He sighed ruefully. "As for sending you to the desert, the hard path you are choosing is much more difficult than rotting in prison." He paused for a moment, feeling the truth of this in his own experience. "Do you wish to continue on the hard path?"

Craith nodded. "Yes, no matter what. I've seen where it has taken you." Then, in an unsteady voice, he began singing, "Zhovanya naralo." In the deepening twilight, all five men chanted together, letting the power of Her song wash away rage, grief, shame, and pain. A deep cavern of loneliness in Kyr's heart was filled with the chanting of his brothers on the hard path.

It was far past moonrise by the time Kyr returned to the center of camp. Rajani rose from his seat beside the fire. "Ah, there you are. Are you all right? Medari was waiting for you. Where were you?"

"Oh, gods," Kyr winced with sudden guilt. "I had to, um, talk to Craith." He was too tired to explain. "Where's Medari?"

"He's gone to bed in his wagon. He looked drained." Rajani returned to his seat on the ground and leaned back against one of the logs ringing the fire.

Kyr sat himself on a log next to Rajani. "Was Medari angry with me for not being here?"

"He was just sad, and exhausted. And he drank a little too much of this," Rajani added, passing over a flask of brandy. Kyr took a good long swig. Then he stared into the fire, wondering what Medari would think of his spending time with the penitents. *Medari is furious at Gauday and his men, as he has every right to be. But, gods, I hope he can understand that the penitents need me too. And,* he realized, *I feel at ease with them. They are more like me, especially Craith. They are my brothers. But now, Medari is my heart-father.* He sighed, feeling torn between the two.

"Heya, my turn." Rajani nudged Kyr's ankle with his elbow.

"Ah, sorry." Kyr handed the flask down to Rajani, thinking, *And here's the man who was the* first *to claim me as a brother. Wonder how he feels about Medari and the penitents?* Kyr shook his head, perplexed. The liquor was softening the harshness of the day, and he slid down to join Rajani on the ground. Leaning against his log, he said in bemused wonderment, "I seem to be gathering a family of sorts along this road."

"Oh?" Rajani passed the flask back.

"Well, you said that we are brothers?"

Rajani nodded, but said nothing.

Kyr took another swig and went on, "Then there are the penitents. They are my brothers too. And today, Medari became my heart-father."

"I see what you mean," the Warrior Mage said, his eyes half-shut.

"The penitents need me to show them the hard path." Kyr sipped at the brandy, groping his way into this unknown territory called family. "Medari needs me. I'm his only family now. What if he doesn't like my helping them?" He sighed. "I've never had a family before. Is it always so complicated?"

Rajani's only answer was a soft snore. Kyr smiled ruefully and corked the flask. Nudging his "oldest brother," Kyr said, "Come on, let's get to bed."

The next morning, Rajani eyed the sun as it peered over the hills in the East. "Gods above, it's hot already." He tugged at the neck of his black tunic and turned to the penitents waiting to take down the command tent. "Craith, go wake Kyr. I've let him sleep as late as I can. When he's out, get that tent down. I'll be meeting with Jaiyan to discuss the new laws that are replacing the Soul-Drinker's tyranny."

Craith hesitated at the tent's opening, still shaky from the encounter with Kyr the night before, then stepped inside. Kyr lay half-covered, curled up on his bedroll with his back toward the door. As Craith stared at the marks of torment twining over Kyr's bare back, images of his own days of torture flashed through his mind, bringing the twin ghosts of desire and agony. Closing his eyes, he prayed, *Blessed Zhovanya, help me!* When he felt steadier, he went to kneel beside Kyr. "Sir, it's time to wake up."

Kyr twitched and moaned in his sleep, and didn't respond. Craith winced in commiseration. *Gods, I know those damn nightmares.* He risked putting his hand on Kyr's shoulder and shook him gently. "Wake up, sir."

Swimming up from dark dreams, Kyr woke slowly and turned over. Still half-dreaming, he reached out to lightly trace the scars showing through the rents in the redhead's torn shirt. Craith shuddered, and their eyes met. Kyr was seized by a longing to be held safe again in Craith's arms, as he had been twice at the fort. But then his scars began to pulse and burn, eclipsing the vision of comfort and replacing it with a surging desire to take Craith down into the dark ecstasy that Gauday had taught them both.

Dismayed, Kyr quickly withdrew his hand and sat up, wrapping his arms around his knees. "How long did it go on?" he asked, nodding at Craith's scars, and trying to ignore the dark desire throbbing through him.

"A half-moon," the redhead answered softly.

"Why did he stop?" *Gods,* Kyr thought. *It feels good to speak with someone who knows what Gauday did.*

Clutching his ripped shirt closed, Craith lowered his eyes to avoid Kyr's still-yearning gaze. "He wasn't so good at running the fort. The men were getting out of hand. He needed me back at work."

"Lucky for you," said Kyr, and the stark pain in his voice brought Craith's eyes back to his. Their perilous attraction charged the air with pent-up lightning. Kyr groaned and rolled onto his stomach. Through gritted teeth, he said, "You'd best leave now."

"Yes, sir, but…we need to take the tent down soon." Craith rose and hurried out.

"Merciless gods!" Kyr swore softly. Ashamed but aroused beyond bearing by his throbbing scars, he brought himself to climax. Afterward, he lay for a few moments, spent, fighting tears of despair, and feeling mired again in the Soul-Drinker's corruption, thanks to Gauday's cruelty. *Gods above and below, I hope Rajani's cleansing ceremony will work!* This thought gave him the motivation to at last quit his bed. Grabbing his towel and clothes, he headed for the Awanai River, desperate to feel clean, even if only outwardly. Friend barked as he rushed past, and Kyr untied her from Medari's wagon. "Come on, girl." She trotted after him, ready for an adventure.

When he reached the river, Kyr tore off his nightshirt and jumped into the clear water. He surfaced with a yell, welcoming the icy shock that drove all thought from his head. Barking excitedly, Friend splashed into the water and came swimming after him. Chest-deep in the water, Kyr dodged away, annoyed by her cheerful noise; but she kept after him, seeing it as a game.

A goldenfly came dancing around her head and she snapped at it. Her eyes got big with surprise when she actually caught it. Curling her lips in distaste, she opened her mouth and it zipped away, unhurt. Kyr couldn't help but laugh at her perplexed expression. Encouraged, she nabbed a floating stick and kept nudging him with it, trying to get him to throw it for her. Giving in to her enticement, he threw the stick in and out of the water for her until he was cold and tired, but he did feel relaxed and more at ease with himself. He dried off, dressed, rinsed his nightshirt in the river and wrung it out.

A flurry of activity greeted them back at the camp. The tents were down, wagons were being loaded, and horses and oxen hitched up. Lady stood waiting, already saddled. Kyr dug into his saddlebag for a tunic that the brawny Warrior Mage had given him. He was still gaunt from his ordeal at Gauday's fort, and the tunic hung on him.

Looking around, he spotted Craith helping to load one of the wagons, and hurried over. "Here, will this fit you?"

"You don't need to…."

"Yes, I do. Don't argue."

Craith tried it on, and it fit pretty well. "Thank you, sir."

"Gods, don't call me that! We are brothers on the hard path."

Craith's sudden grin lit up his face.

23

Kyr smiled back. "We better get that wagon loaded or Rajani will be snapping at us. He's dying to get home." Together, they finished the job, and parted.

Kyr looked around for Medari, and spotted him sitting on the driver's bench of his wagon, holding the reins of his two big chestnut horses, ready to leave. Kyr led Lady over to the wagon and tied her behind it. He boosted Friend into the back of the wagon, and went forward to climb up to sit beside his heart-father.

"Good morning, son. I missed you last night. And *you* missed breakfast."

Kyr winced. "Sorry I disappeared on you. I had some anger to deal with."

"Ah." Medari nodded but asked no questions. "Well, I saved you a couple of biscuits with bacon." Medari handed him the napkin-wrapped biscuits.

"Thanks." Kyr started eating, thinking sadly, *He's gotten older, like my teacher. Oh gods, I hope Dekani is all right. I miss him, but I can't bother him while he is fighting to protect me from the Soul-Drinker's smoke-beast and Gauday's curse. I'll talk with him after Rajani does the cleansing ritual…if it succeeds.*

Just then, Rajani rode by on Akbara, gesturing for Medari to start moving. The healer nodded and shook the reins, clucking at his team of sturdy chestnut draft horses. They leaned into their traces and the wagon started moving slowly, creaking in complaint. Friend shoved her way between the two men, putting her forepaws on the bench and leaning her head forward, panting happily.

"You are both rather damp," Medari observed.

"We went to the river for a bath." Kyr ruffled Friend's ears, smiling. "She caught a goldenfly. She was so surprised, she accidentally let it go."

Medari glanced at Friend, a brief flicker of a smile crossing his face. "She is aptly named."

"Yes," Kyr said, draping an arm over her shoulders. "She helps me, um, be here."

"Be here?" Medari asked, keeping his eyes on the road.

Kyr's face darkened. "You know — to forget…."

"Ah," Medari sighed. "That is undoubtedly helpful. So, you two went swimming this morning. And — last night? Where did you go?"

Oh, gods, here it is. Kyr took a breath. "I was angry, after leaving your house. If I am your heart-son, then it was *my* family too…. Then, in the village square, I asked the headwoman if anyone had seen who slaughtered your — our — family, and she said they all stayed inside their houses when they heard the screams. I got furious at their cowardice, and at those killers taking away the only family I might ever have." Kyr dragged his fingers through his hair, and shook himself, trying to calm down.

"What did you do then?" Medari asked stiffly.

"I went to see Craith, and demanded that he tell me who the killers were."

"Who *are* they?" Medari demanded in a murderous tone. "Who killed our family?" Disturbed, Friend pulled back and went to curl up on her blanket.

"I don't know. But Craith told Rajani who they are. And — fortunately or unfortunately — they are on their way to the desert prison."

The healer's hands on the reins shook with barely restrained fury, making the horses toss their heads uneasily. "And you believed him?"

"Definitely."

"Why?" demanded Medari. "Why would you believe any of those brutes? They'd all lie and turn on one another to save their own hides. It could have been any of them, even your so-called penitents."

Medari's fury inflamed Kyr's scars, fueling a resurgence of his own anger. He clenched his hands together, trying once again to calm his scars and release his fantasies of revenge. After a moment, he answered carefully, "You have every right to your anger, Medari, and I share it. Last night, I wanted to find those murderers and kill them — very slowly, as the Soul-Drinker trained me to do." Braving the healer's angry glare, Kyr said, "But Craith and the other penitents have assured me that they did not kill your wife and children."

"I know he's one of your favorites, but how do you know it wasn't Craith himself?" Medari demanded bitterly.

With an effort, Kyr kept his voice mild. "I've gotten to know the four of them well, this past month or so. They have awakened from the Master's vicious illusions and, like me, have chosen the hard path. Because of the pain and guilt they are experiencing as they realize what their lives have been, I trust them." He gave Medari a challenging glance. "Can *you* trust *me* on this?"

Shaking his head, Medari looked away. After a moment, his shoulders dropped and he blew out a noisy breath. "I'm sorry, son. I do trust your judgment. I just get so angry. Sorry I took it out on you."

"I can understand that." Kyr relaxed a little.

After a few moments, the healer asked, "What's this 'hard path'?"

"It's Zhovanya's way of forgiveness of others, and of oneself. For those of us who were Slaves — with so much to forgive ourselves for — it requires a life of atonement."

Medari reached over and placed his hand on his heart-son's knee. "That does not sound easy."

"No, it's not," Kyr answered softly, thinking of his most difficult penance — never to see Jolanya again. He looked away to hide his grief and pain.

"I'm not sure I could follow this path, myself. I hate this idea of forgiveness. What does this Goddess expect me to do, after all they have done to me and my family? Say it is all right and forget about it?"

25

"No, Medari. Forgiveness is something we do to free *ourselves* from the past. We don't forget, or agree that these evil acts are acceptable in any way. It's about realizing that hatred and anger take us captive and make our *own* lives miserable, and that the desire for revenge sinks us deeper into hell. I know you don't want to hear this, but Zhovanya taught me to see the hidden agony in the souls of those who harm us, even Gauday. This is the hard path I've been on."

Medari frowned, mulling over what Kyr had said, while his big horses plodded along at the caravan's slow pace. Watching their hindquarters bob from side to side, Kyr relaxed into the sway of the wagon, his eyes drooping. A slight touch of coolness whispered of Zhovanya's Presence, and blessed him with a sense of the rightness of this hard path he was following.

Medari broke the drowsy peace. "As a healer, I recognize the wisdom in what you say, Kyr. And I know you speak the truth, having witnessed your struggle myself. You have suffered more than anyone, and yet you still choose to follow this path. I honor you deeply for that. I don't know if *I* can follow your path, but..." Medari paused, looking inward for a moment. Then he heaved a deep sigh, and turned to look at Kyr. "Perhaps you can help me?"

Kyr's heart filled with a warm, airy brightness of unexpected joy. Smiling radiantly, he said, "Of course, heart-father! I'm so glad that you are willing to join me on this path!"

"Alright, then." Medari smiled; and, side-by-side on the wagon bench, they wrapped an arm around each other's shoulders in an embrace of deepened closeness and comradeship.

Then Medari sighed and rubbed his eyes. "Gods, I'm tired."

Kyr reached for the reins. "Here, I've practiced enough. I can handle the horses without you. Go lie down."

Medari handed Kyr the reins without argument, crawled into the back of the wagon, and sent Friend forward.

She climbed onto the driver's bench next to Kyr, where she sat happily sniffing the breeze, her pink tongue lolling to one side. Kyr smiled at her innocent enjoyment of the world, his heart gladdened by Medari's interest in the hard path. A smile lingered on his lips, and he felt affirmed in his choice: to follow this path, no matter how difficult it became. "Thank You, Zhovanya," he whispered. "Please show me how to help Medari follow this hard path, and bless him with Your Love."

The sun shone gently on the dusty road through the sparse forest of scattered oaks and bays. Kyr sniffed too, enjoying the sweet-spicy scent of the bay trees, glad that the caravan had left the marshy land with its scent of rotting vegetation behind.

That night, Kyr sat by their campfire eating supper with Medari and Rajani. The Warrior Mage looked disgustedly at his half-eaten bowl of bean stew and set it aside. "By all the little gods, I'll be glad to get home to Ravenvale, get some fresh food."

"Oh, no you don't." Kyr addressed Friend, grabbing the bowl to keep it away from her. She gave a little yelp of disappointment. "You want to sleep outside again? No beans for you, stinky girl!" And he polished off Rajani's leftovers, himself.

"Keep it up, Kyr," Medari smiled. "You're still too scrawny."

Kyr laughed. "Alright, heart-father, alright! I'm eating as much of this camp chow as I can. But I agree with Rajani. I'm looking forward to better food." He turned to the Warrior Mage. "How soon will we arrive at Ravenvale?" Despite the monotonous food, Kyr wasn't sure he actually wanted this journey to end, since he had little idea what being "home" would mean.

"In about three days, depending on how many damn wheels come loose or blasted axles break. Can't wait to get home." The Warrior Mage stretched and yawned. "I must say, another thing I'm looking forward to is sleeping in my own bed."

Kyr and Medari looked down, aware that neither of them had familiar beds to look forward to. After a short, uncomfortable silence, Kyr said, "I'm going to join the penitents for meditation and chanting. Would you like to come with me?"

"Sorry, Kyr," Rajani said. "I've got my rounds to do, then I'm heading for my lumpy bedroll." He bid them good night, and left to begin his nightly circuit of the camp. Medari remained sitting in grim silence.

"I know you are still angry at Gauday's men, heart-father. It might help you to remember that these men have suffered, too. Craith, Kinar, and Zurano were torn from their families as young boys to be literally whipped into becoming the Soul-Drinker's soldiers. And, like me, Jorem was tortured when he was a little boy into becoming the Soul-Drinker's blindly obedient Slave. He suffered the Soul-Drinker's punishments for many years, until I managed to kill our Master."

"I'm sorry, Kyr. It's hard to think of *their* suffering, right now. Even though your 'penitents' are not the ones who actually killed my family, still they followed Gauday's orders and harmed many people: kidnapping, stealing, enslaving."

"True. And for such men, choosing the hard path takes tremendous courage and humility."

"I guess that also makes them somewhat like you." Medari sighed. "And, as you said, forgiveness is a part of this hard path."

"It is the *hardest* part."

"Alright, I will go with you. But I don't promise to *stay*."

"Good enough." Elated that Medari was coming with him, Kyr prayed silently, *Dear Goddess, please bless Medari and guide him on the hard path.*

Together, they walked across the camp to the roped-off area where the prisoners were under guard. The Companion at the entrance waved them through.

They found the four penitents standing around a small fire in a corner of the prisoners' compound. Kinar and Zurano greeted them with tentative smiles. Craith nodded hesitantly, and Jorem regarded them with dark, enigmatic eyes.

"Brothers," Kyr said, "I'd like you meet my heart-father, Medari." Medari gave the group a stiff nod. Kyr continued, "Medari, you know Craith." The lanky, green-eyed redhead gave Medari a respectful bow.

Kyr gestured to a tall, swarthy man with dark eyes and straight dark hair tied in a knot at his neck. "This is Jorem, a former Slave. And these two are twins, Kinar and Zurano. I can never tell which one is which. They must have confused their commander quite often while they were soldiers." With twinkles in their pale aqua eyes, the light-skinned, white-haired young men bowed in unison to the healer.

"Let's begin," Kyr said. They all sat on the ground in a circle around the low fire, and settled in to meditate. After a few moments, Kyr noticed that his heart-father was frowning and clenching his fists. *Gods, he's about to bolt already! Maybe chanting will be easier for him.*

Kyr began to sing the forgiveness chant, "Zhovanya naralo, Zhovanya naralo, Zhovanya naralo." The penitents joined in quickly. After a few rounds, Medari seemed to be relaxing into the chant. Kyr smiled, glad to be singing the chant that had saved his soul with his heart-father and his brother-penitents.

Kyr's grief and anger over the murder of Medari's — now his own — family receded, and his heart warmed with quiet joy. "Zhovanya naralo, Zhovanya naralo, Zhovanya naralo." As he let the chant fill his soul, he sensed a subtle trace of Zhovanya's Presence, and his joy expanded, erasing all but the chant for a time.

Muffled choking sounds brought Kyr back to the circle of men around the fire. He let the chant soften into silence, and looked for the source of the disturbance. Medari was biting his own fist, trying to keep back his sobs.

The four penitents started to move away, but Kyr signaled to them to stay. He rested a hand on Medari's hunched back. Still in communion with Zhovanya, Kyr radiated compassion and love, murmuring, "Let go now, let go." Potent warmth flowed through Kyr's hand and penetrated the healer's heart, melting his rigid anger, thawing his icy grief, releasing a flood of tears. As Medari sobbed, Kyr and the penitents bore witness silently.

For the four penitents, it was torment. For the first time, they could actually *see* the suffering they had caused — not only to those they had harmed, but also to their loved ones. Remorse was a red-hot blade, searing their softened hearts. In addition, for Craith, Kinar, and Zurano, Medari's sorrow awakened them to their own grievous losses, when they had been torn from their families to become the Soul-Drinker's soldiers.

Jorem, however, had a stiff, puzzled look on his face. Kyr recognized that look. As a former Slave, the tall, swarthy man had been trained never to cry, nor did he understand the meaning of family. Kyr wanted to help him, but realized that words wouldn't mean much. *Jorem will have to learn what kindness, love, and family are through experience, as I did.*

Medari's tide of grief peaked and ebbed, and the healer's tears slowly subsided. Looking ancient, worn, and empty, he sat up with a groan and leaned into Kyr's embrace. "This is good," murmured Kyr. "It won't be quite so hard now." Kyr held his heart-father for a few moments; but then, at the physical contact, his curse-scars started to pulse. He sighed in frustration, and gently let go.

Medari straightened up, and saw the men whom he had reviled as brutal enemies sitting around the fire with him. "Sorry, I didn't mean to...."

"We thank you for showing us what we must see," said Craith. Jorem nodded, and Kinar and Zurano put their hands together before their hearts and bowed to him.

Medari shrugged in embarrassment, and gave Kyr an ironic glance. "Zhovanya doesn't ask much, does She?"

"Only everything you thought you could never endure." A sudden chill gave Kyr goose-flesh.

"What will She ask of us?" Kinar asked, his voice quivering with wonderment and dread.

"By all the hells, Kyr!" Craith snorted. "You make this hard path sound impossible. But your example shows us that we can follow it too. What you have endured and overcome is beyond belief, and still you have stayed on the hard path. You even found it possible to forgive your worst enemy, Gauday." Craith bowed to Kyr with great respect, followed by Jorem, Kinar, and Zurano. Medari, too, bowed, honoring the greatness of his heart-son's soul.

For once, Kyr was able to accept this honor with equanimity. With hands together before his heart, he bowed in return. "Thank you all for joining me on this hard path. It's less lonely now."

Part Two ~ A Place Called Home

"No matter how far he fled, what he fled from would always be with him, for it was within him, it was himself."

— Charles de Lint, *Wolf Moon*

Chapter Three

Ravenvale

A half-moon later, they entered an open, grassy valley with dark-green pines and blue-green spruce climbing the steep hills on either side. A creek dashed through the middle of the valley, rushing and tumbling over boulders and leaping in noisy cascades. At this sight, Rajani shouted exultantly, "We're almost home! Let's go!" He loosened the reins and Akbara broke into a canter. Kyr gave Lady a slight nudge, and she raced after the bright sorrel stallion. Leaving the caravan far behind, the two men followed a track alongside the creek. As they rode, the steep hills closed in on either side, while a dark barrier at the end of the valley rose higher and higher before them, and a deep rumbling shook the ground.

Rajani called a halt, and waved his hand upward. "Behold! Ravenfall!" Kyr looked up, shielding his eyes from the water spraying down on them.

Looming high above, dark cliffs blotted out half the sky. From the overhanging cliff top, an unbroken line of startling white plunged straight down into a cauldron roiling with magnificent, frothing fury. Even from this distance, thunder shook the ground, and a fine mist delicately patted their faces with a thousand tiny fingers.

"Whoa now, whoa," Kyr crooned as Lady pranced nervously, disliking the trembling of the earth under her hooves. The spray from Ravenfall was almost as heavy as winter rain. He shivered, reminded of the aching cold and lost faith of the night when Gauday had left him out in a storm. Feeling oppressed by this forbidding scene, he wondered what kind of place this "home" might be, with such a daunting entrance. But Rajani turned his face up to the waterfall's spray, smiling as if the wetness were a benediction.

Dark shapes wheeled and turned, appearing as they flew in front of the white cascade, disappearing as they entered the gloom of the dark cliffs. Puzzled, Kyr pointed them out. "What are those?"

"Ah!" Rajani smiled. "Those are Ravens, the guardians of Ravenvale. They are alerting the sentinels that we are approaching." Laughing, he brushed water out of his eyes. "We better get out of this spray. Don't want to look like soggy cats when we get home." He led them back out of range, and dug into his saddlebag. "Here." He handed Kyr a hooded rain-cape. The oil-cloth capes were large enough that they covered their gear and their horses' backs.

Some distance behind them, the caravan slowly ground to a halt. Jakar began shouting orders over the clamor of Ravenfall.

"Thank the gods for Jakar," said Rajani. "It will take them a while to get the wagons ready for the climb through the tunnel, but we don't have to wait. See that?" Rajani pointed to a darker line, not far from the waterfall. "That's the entrance to the tunnel. We can actually divert the waterfall over there to seal off the valley, if need be."

Kyr frowned. "Why would we need to do that?"

"Don't worry," Rajani said. "I doubt we'll ever need to, now that you've freed us from the Soul-Drinker and we've rounded up Gauday's men. Come on!" Rajani and Akbara trotted off toward the tall cliffs.

From under the hood of his raincape, Kyr peered ahead. Akbara's long blond tail flashed and disappeared into the dark fissure in the cliff. Kyr nudged Lady, and she minced forward reluctantly. He shared her lack of enthusiasm, wishing their time of freedom and travel was not ending. He had rarely been happier than during this journey, enjoying the freedom, continual movement, new sights, and moment-by-moment existence. He sighed and urged Lady up the trail and into the tunnel's dark mouth.

Ahead of them, Rajani rode through the upward-sloping tunnel, touching a lit taper to torches fastened by dark metal wings to the smooth stone walls. The torches flared wildly in the wind flowing through the tunnel, and orange light gleamed randomly from the water-sheened walls and floor. Water dripped sporadically from the roof, spattering Kyr's rain-cape.

Following Akbara, Lady clopped along, her iron-shod hooves clanging on the rough, ridged stone floor. Feeling the immense weight of stone enclosing him, Kyr's heart sank with the dread of being confined again. To occupy his mind, Kyr focused on what Rajani had told him of this new place. He had spoken often of its beauties, and of the new community coming to life in Ravenvale's safety. It sounded somewhat like the peaceful Sanctuary, but better protected. *Maybe I'll be safe here,* Kyr thought; but then he frowned. *Gods, I'll have to meet all these new people, and they're probably expecting some damn hero. They won't know, or want to know, anything about what I went through.*

The flickering carmine gloom of the tunnel reminded him of the bloody light in the Soul-Drinker's labyrinth and the red light of Gauday's torture chamber. Memories of what Gauday had done to him welled up and set his scars throbbing painfully, filling him with dark desires. He reined Lady to a halt. *Merciless gods! I can't bring Gauday's evil into Rajani's home! But where else can I go? Goddess help me! What am I to do?* Lady tossed her head, upset by her rider's confusion. Seeing her companion Akbara disappearing up the tunnel, she neighed in distress.

Rajani turned to look over his shoulder, and trotted back down the tunnel to Kyr's side. The horses whickered to each other as Rajani asked, "What's wrong? Why have you stopped?"

Kyr slowly straightened as if shouldering a heavy burden, and looked at the Warrior Mage with haunted eyes. "I can't go with you."

"By all the little gods, Kyr, why not?" Rajani demanded in alarm, fearing that his life's work was coming undone just as success was in reach; that all the sacrifices — his, the Circle's, and Kyr's own — would come to naught. "What happened to make you change your mind at the last moment like this? We're almost there!"

Kyr looked down in shame. "Gauday corrupted me. I can't bring that evil into your home."

"What are you talking about? You're not evil." Frustration and fear made Rajani impatient.

His face burning, Kyr said softly, "These cursed scars keep flaring up, driving me mad with craving for the kind of vicious pleasures Gauday inflicted on me. It's gotten worse since the smoke-beast from the Soul-Drinker's Crown infected me when I executed Gauday."

"Kyr, it will be all right. I'll do the cleansing as soon as I can. In the meantime..."

"Gods and demons!" Kyr broke in desperately. "Can't you see? I'm dangerous! I could hurt someone, even corrupt someone as Gauday has corrupted me. I can't risk it."

"You don't have to fight this on your own, Kyr. You have Medari and his potions, and," Rajani smiled, "Naran is here to help you."

"What?" Kyr looked up with sudden hope. "Naran is here, already?"

"Sorry I didn't tell you sooner. I thought it would be a nice home-coming surprise for you."

Kyr frowned slightly. *Gods, I'd be happy if I never had another surprise in my life!* Surprises, in his experience, tended to be nasty and dangerous. But then he nodded. "This *is* a good surprise. With Naran's help, I think I can keep hold until you do the cleansing." Kyr relaxed, his dismay and fear draining away. "Thanks for finding him, Rajani."

"After you asked for him, I sent someone to the Sanctuary. Fortunately, Naran was still there, and was eager to come here to help you." Rajani smiled. "Luciya and Devanyi are here too. We'll all help you any way we can, Kyr. You just have to remember to ask."

"I remember Luciya, of course, but who is Devanyi?"

"She was Tenaiya's assistant at the safe house in the City, and helped care for you after we rescued you from the Soul-Drinker's Watcher that was torturing you."

Kyr nodded, remembering a red-haired young woman tending to his wounds. He shuddered, also remembering his terrible craving for the vile ecstasy of the Soul-Drinker's sorcerous Rod. Devanyi had brought him kanna smoke to breathe, giving him blessed oblivion.

"Come on, Kyr. It's just a little farther. Then we'll be home safe."

"Promise me something, Rajani? Promise me that if I tell you I'm losing hold, you'll find somewhere safe to…" Kyr shivered but forced the words out, "lock me up."

"Alright, I promise. But I'm sure that won't be necessary." Rajani wanted to shake Kyr for giving him such a scare, but he merely nudged Akbara into a walk. With no encouragement from Kyr, Lady followed.

As they moved forward, Kyr resolved to do his best to keep hold, to prevent Gauday's evil from tainting Rajani's home. They went on, climbing upward at a steady slant. Ahead of them, a faint patch of daylight appeared, and Kyr sighed with relief.

The reddish light of the torches died into the welcome brilliance of sunlight. Kyr blinked against the brightness as they rode out of the dismal tunnel onto a wide ledge overlooking a large valley. Far behind, a cacophony of echoes told of the caravan entering the tunnel.

Rajani and Kyr halted to shed their rain-capes, and the horses blew noisily, as if glad to be out of the tunnel. Kyr agreed with them whole-heartedly. Following Rajani's example, Kyr shook out his cape. Though Akbara had taken this in stride, Lady objected to this noisy flapping thing by snorting and prancing. Kyr stuffed the cape under his arm and grabbed the reins with both hands. "It's alright, Lady. It's alright. Whoa now. Whoa now." Reassured by his voice and seeing that Akbara was not upset, she settled down.

Kyr rolled his cape up and offered it to Rajani, who said, "No, keep it. You'll need it when the rains come." Rajani winced, remembering how Kyr had suffered at the fort when Gauday left him chained outside in a rainstorm. "Sorry, didn't mean to bring up a bad time."

"Never mind." Kyr stuffed the cape into his saddlebag.

The Warrior Mage craned his neck to scan the sky. Kyr was about to ask what he was looking for when a loud, harsh cry made him look up. A huge black bird flew directly at him. Kyr ducked and Lady shied, ready to bolt at this second flapping thing. Kyr had to rein her in hard. He glared at the dark bird. It gave a short caw that sounded suspiciously like laughter, and veered over to land on Rajani's outstretched arm.

"Sorry, Kyr, she will have her jokes." Rajani sighed in affectionate annoyance. "This is Ra-Uka, matriarch of the Ravenvale Rabble." The raven eyed Kyr knowingly, as if she had taken his measure and knew his worth. "Ra-Uka, this is Kyr. He is my new brother." She bobbed her head and Kyr gravely bowed to her, sure that it was wise to show respect to such a powerful, crafty creature.

"Ha!" Rajani laughed. "Well-done, Kyr. That will get you off on the right foot with her." He looked at Ra-Uka, and she regarded him with dark, shining eyes. "Many new people are coming to live in Ravenvale. Will you tell the others of your Rabble to welcome them?" The raven tweaked his ear with her sharp beak and launched herself into the air with a short caw. Rajani laughed again, rubbing his earlobe. "Just had to show me who's in charge, didn't she?"

Amazed, Kyr asked, "You talk with her? She is your friend?"

"More to say, she is my co-regent," said Rajani. "And Raven is my soulkin, just as Eagle is yours."

"Ah," Kyr breathed, sensing the truth of Rajani's connection with Raven.

The Warrior Mage continued, "Our family has had a relationship with the ravens ever since we came here, hundreds of years ago. We help them, and they return the favor. If anyone bothers them, the ravens have their ways to let us know about the miscreant. Sometimes, the person has to leave Ravenvale. After all, it was *their* home first." He looked out over the valley, grinning. "Gods above and below, it's grand to be home! Let's go!"

As the horses picked their way down the stony path that twined down from the ledge toward the valley floor, Kyr marveled at the beauty of this hidden refuge. Tall cliffs surrounded a sizeable valley, enclosing and guarding it. Here and there, white trails of water poured down the cliffs to feed creeks and streams that wound their way across the valley floor. These, in turn, flowed into a large, shimmering lake near the center of the valley. On the northwest side of the lake rose a massive pile of gray stone.

Forests in various shades of green broke like waves, assailing the base of the valley's guardian wall. A patchwork of dark-green woods, wild grassy meadows in summer shades of green and gold, orchards, and hay fields filled the floor of the valley. Plumes of smoke arose from a scattering of cottages.

The valley, with its guardian walls, exuded serenity, protection, and peace. *Maybe here, I will be safe for a while, Goddess willing,* Kyr thought. But then he snorted to himself. *I thought I was safe at Her Sanctuary. Let me not forget: Zhovanya still requires that this "vessel" be "tempered by the fires of suffering."* Kyr sighed as his momentary hope evaporated.

"Welcome to Ravenvale!" Rajani smiled. "Isn't it beautiful?"

"Oh, yes," Kyr agreed, glad for the distraction. "This whole valley is your home?"

"Listen to me, Kyr. This is *your* home now, and forever."

Touched, Kyr looked down, longing to accept this gift that Rajani offered, this blessing of a safe and peaceful home. But his scars throbbed painfully, reminding him that he was still debased and dangerous. *I'll just have to keep to myself until Rajani does the cleansing ritual.* He looked back at Rajani somberly. "I hope the cleansing can be soon."

"As soon as possible," Rajani promised, saddened by Kyr's darkening mood. "Though I may have some things to deal with first. I've been gone a long time, and a lot has been developing here. I'll have to take care of the most pressing things beforehand, just in case…"

"Gods, Rajani, I need the cleansing badly, but…," Kyr's shoulders sagged. "If the ritual is dangerous for you, you mustn't do it."

"Of course I will, Kyr. Don't worry. We *must* clear you of the remnants of Gauday's curse and the Soul-Drinker's sorcery. I'll have to rest for a few days afterwards, but I'll be fine." He gave Kyr a grin. "Let's not think about that today, alright? Let's just enjoy being home, at last!"

Kyr smiled at Rajani's joy. "Alright."

"Come on!" Rajani whooped, and Akbara leapt forward, cantering down the dirt road that led across the valley. Catching Rajani's infectious joy, Kyr grinned and set Lady racing after him. In this moment, there was only the thunder of horses running, the warm wind in his face, and the exhilaration of speed.

A s they rode closer to the lake, the road, now paved with cobblestone, led in graceful curves up the hill toward the large outcropping of graystone that Kyr had seen earlier. Rajani slowed their pace and they walked their horses side-by-side. Rajani glanced at Kyr and smiled. "Welcome to Ravenhall!"

Kyr blinked. "Where?"

"You'll see."

And, indeed, in a few moments, what had appeared to be a mound of gray-stone now resolved into a cluster of buildings, all joined together by graceful arching walkways into a sprawling, multi-layered mansion. Curving terraces and hanging balconies were bright with orange and scarlet flowers in stone pots. Pointed arches held carved wooden doors or windows with wooden shutters. Dark-green vines starred with vivid pink flowers clung to walls and twined about the balustrades of staircases and terraces.

"By all the gods, it's so beautiful, Rajani!" Kyr had never imagined such a magnificent place, having spent most of his life in the gloomy, decaying lair of the Soul-Drinker. Since then, he'd seen inside at the safehouse in the City, the humble cabin in the woods, the remarkable home inside the Great Tree called the Heart of the Forest, and the modest Sanctuary. Only Zhovanya's small Temple there rivaled Ravenhall's beauty.

At the crown of the hill rose a massive oak tree, its thick branches spreading out protectively over the center of the mansion. Rajani came to a halt, and Kyr brought Lady to a stop beside Akbara. The Warrior Mage waved his hand toward the sprawling oak. "That tree is the Rookery, where the ravens roost to gossip, rest, and sleep. Ravenhall got its name because it grew up around the ravens' tree."

The tree flickered with the constant motion of ravens taking off or landing, or flapping from perch to perch in the tree, often jostling each other, with much croaking and squawking. Rajani laughed. "Thankfully, the Rabble isn't always this noisy. They're just excited by our arrival." Kyr stared up the hill at Ravenhall, his heart hoping that this could in truth be his first real home. The numerous buildings of Ravenhall climbed the hill in several layers, towering above their heads. Kyr gaped upward til he got dizzy and had to look away. "It's so tall."

"Yes, it goes up one to four levels, depending on which area you're in. The oldest levels are only one or two levels high. It takes a while to learn your way around. Don't worry. You'll have the time to get used to it, Kyr."

On the first level, wrought-iron gates stood open, revealing a wide stone-paved courtyard brimming with colorfully dressed and diverse people. Ravens circled above, cawing loudly over a surging murmur of many voices. Five broad stairs led up to a terrace in front of the main entrance to Ravenhall, with its tall, carven, oakwood doors. On the terrace, a row of people stood facing the crowd and the gate.

Rajani gestured toward the courtyard. "As you can see, a lot of people are waiting to greet us. They're especially excited to see you, I'm afraid."

"Merciless gods," Kyr breathed, thinking of all those staring eyes and reaching hands that he would soon have to endure.

"I know you don't care for this kind of thing, and I'll keep it as short as I can. But it's important. What you have brought about is a tremendous and astonishing transformation for all of Khailaz; and the people need to celebrate that, and you, to reassure themselves that it is real — that the long nightmare is really over."

"I'm not a goddamned hero," Kyr grumbled, frowning at the courtyard. "What the hells am I supposed to do in there?"

"After the people have cheered you, just say something like 'Thank you. I'm glad to be here.' Alright?" Rajani gave Kyr a friendly little shove. "And don't frown like that. You'll scare everyone into hiding!"

Kyr snorted. "Alright, alright." Together they rode through the wide gates into the stone-paved courtyard.

"Our Liberator! He's here!" cried a man in a loud voice, and the crowd erupted in jubilant cheers, startling Kyr and Lady immensely. She reared, but Kyr managed to keep his seat. As he worked to get her settled down, the cheering continued, with cries of "Welcome!" and "Goddess bless our Liberator!"

Kyr ignored all the noise, and softened his grip on the reins, crooning to Lady, "Whoa now, whoa now. It's all right. It's all right." Finally, Lady turned her ears back to listen to him, and stopped her stiff-legged hopping. She dropped her head and let out a big sigh. *Good thing Rajani warned me,* Kyr thought. *Too bad he didn't warn Lady!* He cast an annoyed glance at Rajani, who gave him an apologetic shrug.

On the terrace before the tall, oaken doors of the main entrance, Luciya and Devanyi watched Rajani and Kyr ride through the gates. Luciya was deeply glad that Kyr had survived the first two hells of the prophecy and was safe in Ravenvale; but she wondered what the third hell could possibly be. *Surely, no one here would hurt him. Look how happy everyone is to see him!* Setting this question aside, she joined in the cheering, laughing along when Lady reared. "Quite an entrance!" she exclaimed to Devanyi, who was standing by her side.

They were both dressed in their finest, as were most in the crowd. Luciya wore a russet tunic that brought out the highlights of her shoulder-length auburn hair, along with brown leggings and low brown boots. A gold chain around her neck held a golden key. Devanyi's flame-colored hair was pulled back in a bun, wispy curls escaping to frame her oval face. She wore a demure dress of dove-gray that, by contrast, only enhanced her reddish freckles and vivid green eyes.

"He handled his horse so well!" she remarked. "He never rode before, did he?"

"No. He must have learned a lot in the last few months." Watching Kyr dismount, and calm his black horse, Luciya frowned. "Oh, Devanyi! He was so open-hearted and happy when I last saw him at the Sanctuary. Now he looks tense and wary, like he's on guard against the world."

"And sad," Devanyi added softly, seeing the lines of pain and grief etched in Kyr's still-gaunt face.

"Almost like he never went to the Sanctuary at all." Luciya checked herself, and shook her head. "No, that's not right. He's not that depraved innocent Slave boy anymore, either. He's a man, now."

"I think he has traded innocence for wisdom." Devanyi's statement startled Luciya, and she looked at Kyr again, wondering what it was that Devanyi saw.

By now, the Warrior Mage had dismounted and handed Akbara's reins to a lanky boy with a mop of curly brown hair who was struggling to control the stallion. Akbara was prancing as if the crowd's ovation were for himself, alone. Another boy — compact, dark-haired, and dusky — grasped Lady's bridle and soothed her with gentle strokes along her neck. Kyr reluctantly handed the reins to the boy.

"Don't worry. I'll take good care of her, sir." Though startled by the boy's deferential manner, Kyr liked this young man's quietness. "What's your name?"

"I'm Grena, sir."

Kyr gave Lady's reins to Grena, trusting that his steed was in good hands. By now, the other boy had control of Akbara, and the two boys led the horses away. Behind them, Jakar and a half-dozen Companions arrived in a noisy confusion of horses, dust, and dismounting men. A tumble of boys and girls darted into the fray to lead their horses away.

The six Companions hurried over and got into formation behind Rajani and Kyr. At Rajani's commanding glance, the crowd melted aside, and they joined Luciya and Devanyi and other dignitaries awaiting them on the wide stone terrace before the grand carven doors of the entrance to Ravenhall. Kyr said nothing, but his face burned at being part of such a spectacle. The Companions stood behind Rajani and Kyr and the others on the terrace. Rajani raised a hand, the people grew quiet, and the ravens settled into their tree.

Pausing a moment for effect, the Warrior Mage proclaimed, "Our mission was a complete success. The Soul-Drinker's self-proclaimed heir, Gauday, was executed by our Liberator, and all Gauday's men are now prisoners, thanks to the Companions." The crowd greeted this proclamation with fervent applause. Then Rajani stepped to one side, placed his hands before his heart, and made a sweeping bow to Kyr. "All honor to Kyr, our Liberator, and Defender of Zhovanya's Sanctuary!" Rajani stepped back, leaving Kyr to face the crowd alone.

Wildly enthusiastic cheering burst forth from the crowd. "Thank you! Thank you!" they called out to him fervently. Some wept and smiled at the same time, looking up at this gaunt young man in tan riding leathers and dark-brown boots, his golden-red curls framing his face and somber brown eyes. Many of them tossed flowers up to rain down around Kyr. He flinched, but stood his ground.

Now Luciya cried out, "Goddess bless our Liberator!" And the crowd repeated her words in a loud chorus. At this, Kyr laughed sardonically to himself. *Thanks, but I have been thoroughly "blessed" by Her already. I don't know if I can withstand any more of Her fierce blessings.* His crooked smile, indecipherable to the crowd, only generated more tears and blessings. At a loss for words, Kyr bowed to them, which brought forth a great roar of acclaim.

Kyr felt like a rabbit surrounded by foxes. The people clearly wanted something from him. *What in all the hells am I supposed to do?* He glanced at Rajani in desperation. The Warrior Mage moved forward in response, and raised his hands for quiet. The people calmed down, waiting eagerly.

Kyr managed to say, "Thank you for...for your welcome. I'm glad to be here." Then he quickly stepped back, waving Rajani forward.

The Warrior Mage spoke over the perhaps somewhat disappointed applause. "We're very glad to be home, but we've had a long journey, and are looking forward to hot baths and good beds...quite eagerly!" He grinned and everyone chuckled. He continued, "Thank you all for your warm welcome. We'll see you at the feast tomorrow." The crowd applauded again and began to disperse, buzzing excitedly.

A dozen or so men and women wearing blue with black ravens embroidered on their tunics remained, and Luciya went over and began giving them orders.

Kyr frowned. "Are those people slaves?"

"Gods, no!" Rajani sounded a bit insulted. "We don't have slaves. Those are the current servers. Everyone takes a turn serving in the Hall, usually a quarter-moon every month. But that will be even less often as more people move here."

"Good," Kyr said, watching Devanyi disappear into the hall with three of the servers. "I hate slavery. It's evil."

Rajani nodded somberly. "You know this most of all, Kyr, but so do the rest of us who lived under the Soul-Drinker's rule."

Just then, Luciya rejoined the two men. "The servers will have your rooms ready in a few moments."

"Thanks, Luciya," Rajani said. "Kyr, I'd better warn you: tomorrow, there will be a ceremony for the returning warriors. That includes the Companions, me, Medari — and you."

"Me? Why?"

"Most certainly you, Kyr. You fought the hardest battle of all of us, against your worst enemy." At Kyr's frown, Rajani held up a hand. "No, don't argue on this. The ceremony is very helpful in making the transition from battle-readiness back into ordinary life."

"Alright," Kyr conceded doubtfully. "But I am hoping to find a bath and a bed sometime soon."

Rajani laughed. "Gods! Me, too. It won't be too much longer."

Rumbling and creaking, and trailing a cloud of dust, the caravan of eight wagons had almost reached the bottom of Ravenhall's hill. The same boys and girls who had taken the Companions' horses now ran down to guide the wagons to a nearby field dotted with shade trees. Kyr managed to spot Medari's wagon in all the commotion. "Luciya, see that first wagon? It belongs to Medari. He is my heart-father. I'd like him to stay close by me."

"Heart-father?" A startled frown crossed Luciya's face, but she quickly erased it with a smile. "Well, there's a story there, I'm sure." Luciya beckoned to a young woman in the servers' raven tunic and pointed out Medari's wagon. "Please send the driver to us, and take his wagon to a good spot." To a young man, she said, "Quickly, go prepare the room next to Kyr's." The two nodded and sprinted off in opposite directions.

In the near distance, Kyr could see Medari grabbing a couple of satchels out of the wagon, jumping down with Friend at his heels, and turning his wagon over to the young woman assigned to help. The healer and Friend pushed their way through the milling crowd, and joined the small party on the terrace. Kyr gave Medari a brief embrace, then knelt down to receive eager licks from an over-excited Friend. He petted her, murmuring endearments to calm her down.

Luciya glanced at Medari and nudged Rajani.

"Oh, yes." Rajani cleared his throat. "Luciya, this is Medari, the healer who helped Kyr survive at Gauday's fort." Luciya gave Rajani a puzzled glance, but at his slight shake of the head, she kept her questions to herself.

"Medari," he continued, "this is Luciya. She's our chatelaine, in charge of Ravenhall and, in my absence, all of Ravenvale." Medari gave her a formal bow.

She smiled, fingering the golden key she wore, symbol of her office. "I'm glad to meet you, Medari. Welcome to Ravenvale." She beckoned Devanyi forward. "This is our apprentice healer, Devanyi."

"Welcome, sir," Devanyi said shyly. "I'll be glad to be of any assistance you may require."

Medari smiled. "I'll be sure to take you up on that, young lady."

Luciya looked down at Kyr, still kneeling and petting the dusty dog. "I'm sorry, Kyr. We don't allow dogs in Ravenhall."

Kyr gave Friend a final pat and got to his feet. "Then I shall sleep elsewhere."

"Ah? Well, we can make an exception, if she is important to you?"

"This is Friend. She is *very* special to me. For a time, she was my only friend." Luciya and Devanyi exchanged concerned glances at his bleak tone.

"Alright, she comes with us," Luciya conceded, "but please don't let her run loose in the Hall."

Luciya opened one of the great carved doors, splitting in half its semblance of an oak tree and many ravens. As Kyr waited for the others to precede him, he felt sad to lose the freedom he'd enjoyed on the journey, though it also was mixed with relief at arriving in this safe, peaceful place. *Perhaps, here, I can leave behind the nightmares I've lived through and start fresh — if Rajani's cleansing magic can free me from Gauday's curse and the damned smoke-beast.*

His stomach clenched at the thought that the cleansing might not work. *Zhovanya, please let it work. Don't let the Soul-Drinker's evil spoil this place, too.*

Chapter Four

Ravenhall

Kyr stepped through the door into Ravenhall with Friend at his heels, and followed Rajani down a stone-floored hallway with wood-paneled walls, illuminated with golden light from hanging oil lamps. Colorful paintings of bejeweled women and richly dressed men lined the walls. The largest painting was set apart, the narrow table beneath it holding a silver vase of white flowers, and one white and one black candle in silver candlesticks on either side.

It portrayed a silver-haired woman and her piercing gaze brought Kyr to a sudden halt. She wore a blue robe glittering with small, clear jewels. From a silver chain around her neck hung a shining silver wheel embedded with tiny gems. The background was a night sky full of stars in strange patterns. Looking at her, an inexplicable chill ran down his spine.

"Kyr?" Rajani turned back to find him transfixed. "Ah, *there* you are. She *is* striking, isn't she? That's my grandmother, Lyriana."

"*Grand* mother? Well, she does look grand."

"Ah?" Rajani gave Kyr a puzzled glance. "Oh. 'Grandmother' means the mother of one's mother."

"I see." Kyr shook his head, marveling that he had never thought that a mother would have had a mother herself. "Gods, I still have so much to learn about ordinary life."

"Plenty of time for that here," Rajani said impatiently. "Come on, the parlor is just down this way. I can't wait for a decent meal. No more camp food!"

The "parlor" proved to be a wide, high-ceilinged room, with the same stone floors and wood-paneled walls as the hallway, and a stone hearth at either end. Near the hearth on the right stood a round dining table surrounded by stools. A long, waist-high cabinet stood against the inner wall by the door, holding stacks of blue plates and bowls, and mugs. Near the hearth at the left, on a faded blue carpet, sat low wooden tables and a pair of shabby but comfortable-looking couches. Light flooded in from tall windows and a wide-open double-door that led onto a stone terrace overlooking the lake. Sunlight flashed on the rippling water and cast sparkles around the room.

Kyr began to relax. He liked the quiet comfort of this parlor, and was glad to finally be alone with his friends. Friend sniffed around the room. Apparently, it met her approval too, for she promptly curled up on the carpet under one of the low tables and went to sleep.

"She must be tired," Kyr raised an inquiring eyebrow at Medari.

"Yes, she got away from me again, and ran ahead, trying to catch up with you." Medari shrugged. "I imagine she'll be glad the journey is over. Staying behind with me was not to her taste." He set his satchels down by the door, and they joined Rajani and Luciya, who awaited them in the middle of the room.

Devanyi smiled warmly at Medari. "I'm so happy to have another healer here in Ravenvale."

"Glad to be here," Medari answered politely, but his eyes were distant.

Devanyi's smile faded, and she continued in a businesslike manner. "Kyr, your bags have been taken to your room. Medari, I'll have someone take your satchels up to your room now, alright?"

"Thank you," Medari said, and Devanyi stepped into the hall to see to it.

Kyr's eye was caught by servers busily arranging things on a large, round table on the terrace. And then a shock of recognition ran through Kyr's body, and he hastened outside toward a gray-haired man standing by the balustrade, gazing at the lake.

Medari glanced at the Warrior Mage. "Who's that?"

"That's Naran," answered Rajani. "He was Kyr's Aithané at the Sanctuary. He helped Kyr to reclaim his soul and sanity from his hellish life as the Soul-Drinker's Slave."

"Ah, yes. Kyr told me a little about that." Medari frowned and looked away.

"Naran-ji! Thank the gods, you're here!" Kyr's voice was rough with choked emotions.

Naran turned to give Kyr a warm smile, and reached out to embrace him.

Kyr flinched away. "I'm sorry, Naran-ji. I, uh…it was bad. Gauday…."

"Ah," Naran said sadly, and lowered his arms. "Never mind, Kyr. I see we have work to do."

"Yes," Kyr murmured, his face tight and bleak. Then he shook himself and smiled. "But not for a while. I want to enjoy this new place and get settled in."

"Of course. Whenever you are ready."

Kyr met Naran's dark blue eyes. "Thank you for coming here. It means — so much." A wordless understanding passed between them, composed of their friendship and their work together at the Sanctuary to face and transform the burden of evil, pain, and remorse that Kyr had carried from his life as a Slave of the Soul-Drinker.

Then, Naran bowed deeply and said, in a surprisingly solemn and formal tone, "I've been asked to convey to you the profound gratitude of everyone at the Sanctuary. We honor your sacrifice most deeply, and want you to know that there will always be a place for you there."

Kyr's face burned with embarrassment. This honor was too much to take in, and he didn't want to think about the past just as he was entering this new life at Ravenvale. "Um, thank you, Naran-ji." He waved his hand in a dismissive gesture. "I couldn't let Gauday destroy Zhovanya's Sanctuary and kill my friends, could I?"

"No, *you* couldn't," Naran said softly. Together they went inside to join Rajani and Luciya in the parlor.

Devanyi joined the four of them after completing her errand. She looked up at Kyr with her beaming smile. "I'm glad you're home with us, Kyr." Her simple words held a world of warmth. Touched, he returned her smile.

"We all are," Luciya declared. "Oh, gods, Kyr, when you walked out of the Sanctuary...." At Rajani's quelling look, she bit her lip. "Well, you are the bravest man in the world."

"No, no," Kyr protested. "It was necessity, not bravery. There was no other choice." *As usual*, he thought, startled by his own bitterness. Putting this aside, he said, "Let's not talk about the past. Right now, I just want to enjoy this — my — new home, and being with old friends." With a smile, he added, "It's good to see you again, Luciya."

Without a moment's thought, she placed her hands on his shoulders, stood on tiptoes, and kissed his cheek.

"Don't!" Kyr gasped, as his scars flared up, sending a surge of violent lust pulsing through him.

Luciya jumped back as if stung. "Oh, I'm sorry! I shouldn't have...." Tears pooled in her eyes.

"No, sorry, it's just...," he mumbled, his face aflame. Friend jumped up and came to his side, her brow wrinkled in concern.

"Look at this feast!" the Warrior Mage interrupted jovially, and gestured towards the round table on the terrace. "The servers are finished, and everything is ready. Let's go eat." While the others filed out onto the terrace, he asked Kyr under his breath, "Are you all right?"

Kyr's face was still aflame. "I need a moment or two."

"Alright. We'll wait for you." Rajani assured him, and went out to join the others.

Kyr knelt to pet Friend, both to reassure her and to give himself time to regain his composure. Taking slow breaths, he silently repeated, *"Zhovanya nara lo,"* until his scars calmed down. When he rose, he noticed Medari still standing inside the parlor. "What's wrong?" he asked his heart-father quietly.

"These people..." Medari muttered. "They're all acting as if nothing happened. They'll never understand what we went through, what Gauday did to us."

"You may be right, Medari. But they are our friends, and this is our new home. We're safe here." He smiled. "You'll have to admit this is a vast improvement over that cursed fort."

"Ha! Very true." Medari nodded, and they stepped out onto the terrace.

Kyr cleared his throat, and said, "Um, could I say something?" The others turned toward them expectantly. "I want you to know that Medari is not just another villager who is joining us. He is my heart-father. He is a healer, and he helped me survive Gauday's little hell." Kyr turned toward Naran. "Medari, this is Naran, my Aithané from the Sanctuary. He helped save my soul from the Soul-Drinker's evil."

The two older men bowed to each other, and Naran said to Medari, "I'm grateful for all you did for Kyr."

"It was for my family," the healer muttered.

"Nevertheless." Naran's gaze was gentle and understanding.

Medari nodded uncomfortably, and turned to Rajani. "Thank you for allowing me into this haven of yours."

"We are blessed that you have joined us here at Ravenvale. Please consider this your home from now on."

Medari smiled, but grief for his own lost home and family shadowed his eyes.

"Well," Luciya said. "We're all here. Let's be seated."

Kyr took a seat between Naran and Medari. Devanyi sat next to Medari, and Luciya and Rajani were across from Kyr, completing the circle. Friend sat by Kyr's feet, looking up hopefully.

Kyr had never seen a table quite so luxurious. On the white cloth that covered the table, blue plates, white napkins, and forks and knives sat at every place. A small blue bowl in the center held a glory of purple, orange, and pink flowers, and was circled by an abundance of serving dishes. One white bowl held red apples, and another held green beans with golden mushrooms. Next to a basket of fresh-baked rolls sat a platter of nicely browned filets of fish.

A smaller blue bowl was heaped with spice cookies, Kyr's favorite treat at the Sanctuary. He choked up a little, touched by this small kindness, and nodded to Naran. "You remembered."

His former mentor laughed. "Who could forget? You could never get enough of these."

Then Rajani, Devanyi, and Luciya bowed their heads, and the others followed suit. "Zhovanya, naralo," Rajani said. "May we be forgiven." For a few moments, they sat in silence. Kyr wondered why *they* needed forgiveness, but then he smiled to himself: *Well, don't we all?*

"Zhovanya, naralo," said Luciya, and everyone echoed her.

Then Rajani exclaimed, "Ah, lake-jumpers, my favorite fish. Help yourselves, everyone." Luciya rose, picked up a stoneware jug, and filled everyone's mug with cool ale.

It almost seemed a sacrilege to touch such wonderful food, so beautifully presented. But Kyr's stomach insisted otherwise, growling loudly.

Rajani chuckled. "Gods, I'm hungry as a bear in spring…and I guess Kyr is too, from the sound of it." Everyone laughed along with Kyr, and began filling their plates.

Kyr looked around the table at his friends, remembering the last time he had eaten with a circle of friends — the dinner party he had hosted at the Sanctuary, so long ago, now. He looked down for a moment. His heart was glad to be with loving friends again — and yet sad for the one who would always be missing: his forbidden beloved, Jolanya.

Naran elbowed him. "I know the food is beautiful, but you *are* supposed to eat it."

Kyr laughed, and took a bite of fish. Its rich yet delicate flavor and tangy sauce awakened his appetite, and he began to eat. After the meager rations at the fort and the camp food on the journey to Ravenvale, he relished every delicious bite. He paused long enough to say, "Rajani, now I know why you were so eager to get home."

Pleased, Rajani grinned. "Nothing compares to Ravenhall food, thanks to Alenya, our wonderful Cook."

As they ate, Luciya and Devanyi told of recent events at Ravenvale, and Rajani filled them in on developments at the fort, which was now becoming a village and government center named Juradiché. Kyr gazed out at the spacious view of the sparkling lake, with shadowed cliffs rising beyond it. This all seemed like a fantastic dream to him, and he remained silent, half-afraid that by speaking he would break the spell and awaken cold and hungry in the dark prison at the fort.

But then, a cold nose nudged his hand. With a smile, he slipped Friend bits of the boneless fish. Medari and Naran kept him company in his silence. Comforted by these three friends, he helped himself to seconds of everything. At last, he pushed his empty plate away, and eyed the bowl full of spice cookies regretfully. Devanyi leaned toward him. "Take a few for later. You can wrap them in your napkin."

Surprised again by a small kindness, Kyr smiled. "Thanks, I will."

As servers cleared the table, Luciya took Rajani off to her office to confer about the current crisis at Ravenvale. Medari and Devanyi went into the parlor to sit on the comfortable couches and discuss herbs and potions. Friend followed them, plopped on the thick carpet, and curled up around her full tummy. Kyr glanced at Naran, and his stomach tightened. *Gods, he'll want me to go over everything that happened to me at the fort.* He cringed at the thought of baring his suffering and humiliation to anyone, even Naran.

"It's a lovely evening," Naran observed. "Shall we go outside?"

Kyr nodded, hiding his reluctance. Standing together on the terrace, they watched the dwindling of the day. The sun sank toward the western cliffs, sending long golden rays to gild the lake's gentle waves. Cool breezes brought the scent of the lake's clear water and muddy banks, while the ravens flapped about in the branches of their Rookery, muttering amiably amongst themselves as they settled down for the night.

Naran studied Kyr, noting his lean wariness and the haunted look in his eyes — and winced inside, asking himself again, as he had many times: *Why did I ever let him go through that gate into Gauday's hands?* He knew there had been no other choice, if the Sanctuary were to be saved from desecration and murder by Gauday's band of Slaves and soldiers. But his heart still was heavy with remorse and shame that he had not been able to protect Kyr from such grave harm. Naran took a moment to set aside his own feelings, and prepare himself to hear and hold Kyr's. Then he asked, "How are you faring?"

"Oh, gods, Naran-ji. It was...bad. I'm sorry...I don't know if I'm ready to face it all again with you yet."

Naran's heart clenched at the deep pain he sensed behind Kyr's words. In a soft but determined voice, he promised, "Whatever you need, as long as you need me." Naran smiled. "Or want me around."

"Then you shall never leave my side." Kyr's laugh was half a sob.

"All right by me...if you can put up with my snoring."

Kyr snorted. "I don't know. You do sound like a trapped goat." They both laughed. Then Naran said, "I have something for you. Let's go inside." Naran led the way over to the sideboard, opened a cabinet door, and handed a bundle to Kyr. "I brought you your things from the Sanctuary."

Kyr held the bundle gingerly. "Gods, Naran-ji. It feels like it belongs to some long-lost man." He sighed, then smiled at his friend. "Thank you for bringing it."

"Excuse me, everyone." Luciya, back from her conference with Rajani, crossed over to Kyr and Naran. Devanyi and Medari rose from the couch by the fire and joined the group.

"I'm sorry I took so long," Luciya said. "But I had to bring Rajani up to date, and it took some time to settle the issue. He's gone up to rest, and I'm sure you are also tired from your travels. Devanyi will show you your rooms now, if you like."

"Oh, yes," Medari replied. "It's been a long day."

"I'll come up with you," Naran said to Kyr. "My room is across the hall from yours."

"Across the hall? Good." Kyr chuckled. "I won't hear your snoring. Come, girl," he said to Friend, and they all followed Devanyi up a winding graystone staircase to the second floor, where a hallway opened on one side to rooms facing the lake and, on the other, facing the upper levels of Ravenhall as it climbed up its hill.

Devanyi opened one door. "Here's your room, Kyr."

Kyr peered in and gained a quick impression of polished wood furniture, a large bed, a sitting area, rich draperies and carpet, tall candles, and flowers. He croaked a slightly lunatic laugh. "Gods and demons! Are you sure this is for me? It's so...grand."

Medari poked his head in, too, and smiled wryly at Devanyi. "We haven't known such luxury for a quite a while."

"In my case," Kyr said, "never."

"Oh, Kyr! You deserve the best," Devanyi said seriously. "It used to be Rajani's brother's...." She broke off and a sudden frown darkened her face, but it was gone so quickly that Kyr wasn't sure what he had seen. In a brighter tone, she went on, "Medari is just next door on the right. And Rajani is next to you on the left."

"I'll be here if you need me," said Naran, opening the door to his room, which was directly across the hall from Kyr's.

"Thanks, Naran-ji."

"Sweet sleep," Naran said to everyone, and went inside, closing his door.

Kyr stepped into his room warily, as if entering unknown territory. He was surprised to see his dusty leather satchel sitting on the wide, soft bed. *Well,* formerly *dusty,* he thought. *Someone has cleaned it well.*

"I'm sorry," Devanyi said. "This satchel is all we could find of your belongings. Did you bring anything else? On one of the wagons, perhaps?"

"No, that's all I have," Kyr answered, and added dryly, "Gauday wasn't a... generous host."

Medari, still standing in the doorway, snorted at this, and Devanyi stammered, "Oh, oh, of course. I'm sorry."

"Never mind," Kyr said mildly. Friend shouldered past Medari and began sniffing around the room. Devanyi ushered Medari next door to his room, with a promise to be right back.

Kyr looked around, feeling lost in all this finery. A dark-blue carpet covered most of the graystone floor. Two padded chairs and a low, darkwood table sat near the stone fireplace to the right of the door. On the low table, a white bowl full of blue flowers emanated a subtle, sweet fragrance. Double-doors across from the main door stood open to a balcony overlooking the lake. Green curtains on either side of the doors swayed in a gentle breeze.

A four-poster bedstead of polished darkwood, green curtains hanging from its four corners, stood to the left of the door, along with a tall wardrobe. A green-and-blue quilt and matching pillows covered the plump mattress. Recalling the crude four-poster to which Gauday had chained him in that hellish room at the fort, Kyr shuddered.

When Devanyi returned, she found Kyr still standing in the middle of the room, clutching the bundle Naran had given him. "Please make yourself comfortable here, Kyr," she said kindly. "This is *your* home, now."

Startled, Kyr took a breath and dragged his attention back to the present once again. "Thanks, Devanyi."

She opened the door of the wardrobe. "You can put your clothes in here, and if anything in here suits you, it is yours. If you like, I could unpack your bags for you."

"That's not necessary." Kyr quickly set his pack from the Sanctuary in a corner of the wardrobe and closed the door, unable to bear any reminders of the man he had become there, or of Jolanya, who had healed and loved him. Devanyi gave him a puzzled look, but he turned quickly to open the satchel he'd brought with him from the fort, and began to unpack his clothes.

"Oh, dear" she said, "those are all rumpled. We'll take them to the laundry. They'll be ready for you in the morning."

Kyr looked at her in surprise. "Truly?"

"Of course." Devanyi collected his clothing in a bundle. "There's a laundry and bathhouse outside. And bathrobes, soap, and towels in here." She bent and opened a chest by the door.

"A real bathhouse, fed by a hot spring?" asked Medari, who just then reappeared at Kyr's door.

At the same time, Kyr asked, "Can Friend come? She needs a bath, too."

"Yes, the water is hot." Devanyi answered. "Medari, you can bring your dirty clothes to put in the laundry. And, yes, Kyr, you can give Friend a bath there, outside. I'll show you the way."

"Just what we need!" Medari rushed to his room to get his dirty laundry. Then he and Kyr collected robes and towels, and followed Devanyi down several flights of stairs, out a side door, and along a flagstone path through a night-dimmed garden to the bathhouse. Kyr took careful note of the way so he could find his room again.

Devanyi showed them how to operate the bathing pool. "Just put the plug in the drain hole, here. Then pull this lever down." She demonstrated, and hot water gushed from a ceramic pipe, rapidly filling the tub. "Now push this lever up to close the pipe. And please, when you're finished, don't forget to pull the plug out."

She dried her hands on her tunic. "Now for the laundry. You can each leave your clothing in one of these baskets. This one is yours, Kyr." She put the bundle of his clothing in a basket with a band of green chevrons. "And that is yours, Medari."

Accordingly, the healer put his clothing in the one with red stripes.

"I'll set them next door in the laundry," Devanyi continued. "The laundrymen will return your clothes to your rooms, cleaned and pressed."

"Am I dreaming?" Kyr shook himself. "Gods, this place is amazing!"

"I hope you will get used to it quickly. I did. It's wonderful here!" Devanyi laughed at her own enthusiasm. She opened the mop closet. "Kyr, here's a bucket and rags that you can use for washing Friend. Alright, I'll let you be. Can you find your way back to your rooms?"

Kyr nodded, and Medari said, "Thank you for all your help, Devanyi."

"Oh, one more thing. Breakfast is served buffet-style in the parlor, where we had supper. Come down whenever you wish. Sweet sleep." With that, she left them.

Kyr gave Medari a puzzled look. "Buffet-style?" He got back the same quizzical look people gave him when his ignorance of ordinary life showed.

"That means, food is set out and people come when they want and help themselves, rather than the meal being served at a set time," Medari explained. "Which means we can sleep late. And I, for one plan to sleep as late as I can!" He began stripping off his travel-dusty clothes. "Gods, it's good to be in a civilized place. A hot bath and a real bed!"

Kyr filled the bucket with warm water, took Friend outside, and gave her a good scrubbing. After toweling her mostly dry, he told her, "Be a good girl and stay here on the grass. Don't go getting dirty again, or you won't be able to sleep with me." This appeared to be enough of a threat, since Friend showed no sign of wanting to wander off. She roamed around the grassy area surrounding the bathhouse, then settled down to wait nearby, sniffing the myriad scents of this new place wafting to her on the evening breezes.

Inside the bathhouse, Kyr stripped down, glad that no one else was around. He hated the thought of anyone seeing the scars patterning his body — or worse, asking him about them. When he stepped down into the large stone tub set into the floor, his body shivered in surprise. "The water is so warm!"

Medari chuckled, already up to his neck in the water.

"Oh." Kyr laughed sheepishly, lowering himself all the way into the bath. "I'd forgotten what this is like." The last time he'd had a good soak was at the Sanctuary's hot spring. At the fort, he'd been lucky just to get a *cold* bath now and then. Only after that night out in the storm had he been allowed a warm bath and at that point, he hadn't been in any shape to enjoy it.

"I think we'll get used to this," the healer said with a blissful groan. The two of them soaked a while, not speaking. Medari's eyes closed, his face more relaxed than Kyr had ever seen, though he himself still felt as if any off-guard word would bring this heavenly hallucination to an abrupt end. He took some deep, slow breaths, and focused his mind on the wonderful sensation of soaking in the warm water, the slight sulfur scent in the air, the quiet rippling of the water. Soon his own eyes began to droop.

A splash broke the silence as Medari's nose hit the water. "By all the little gods!" he sputtered. "We better get cleaned up and dried off before we drown."

"Already?" Kyr said mournfully, but then yawned hugely. "Ah, I guess you're right,"

After a bout of scrubbing and rinsing, they dutifully pulled out the plug, clambered out of the water, and dried off. Wearing the robes they had brought from their rooms, they headed back toward Ravenhall. Friend, waiting for them outside the bathhouse, shoved her nose into Kyr's hand for a pat, then kept to his side as the two men followed the paved path. She, too, seemed a little overawed by this new place.

The soft, dusky night sky gave just enough light to see by, though the stars and Moon were not yet visible. A short distance from the path, oak trees whispered in the gentle evening breeze, amidst the steady creaking of crickets and the frogs' nighttime chorus. Ahead, the dark bulk of Ravenhall loomed up. Many windows glowed with warm yellow light like friendly eyes. Peace lay like an invisible warm mist throughout the valley, adding to Kyr's sense of unreality.

Entering through the side door that Devanyi had shown them earlier, they found only servers about — cleaning the floors, dusting, and tidying. The sound of someone playing a gentle tune on a stringed instrument echoed from somewhere within the depths of Ravenhall. A few oil lamps still illuminated the corridors and stairs.

In the hallway outside their rooms, Kyr paused and turned to his heart-father. "Medari, now that we're here in this safe place, I want to tell you that I am, after all, grateful to you for keeping me alive."

"Never mind that. You know I had to try to save my family." They exchanged a look of shared grief and love, and bid each other good night.

Used to austere accommodations or worse, Kyr felt lost in the spacious, luxurious room. Someone had lit several fat white candles while he was at the baths. *I guess one of the servers came in.* The thought made him uneasy. Locking the door, he relaxed a little.

Friend sniffed around briefly, then jumped up on the large bed and curled up. "*You* feel at home, don't you, girl? Wonder what will make *me* feel more at home?" Kyr looked around for a moment, then rummaged in his satchel for the driftwood and stones from his altar at the fort. On the low table by the hearth, he arranged the driftwood and stones in front of the bowl of blue flowers, and added one of the white candles from the mantel. He knelt on the blue carpet before his new altar for Zhovanya, and bowed his head. "Thank You for allowing me to come here. Please keep this place safe." No more words came, and he was too tired and relaxed to chant. He whispered, "Zhovanya naralo," and got to his feet.

From his satchel, he took out his patchwork quilt and small pillow, and shoved Friend aside so he could place them on the bed. She sniffed the quilt and promptly curled up on it with a happy sigh. He too sighed, feeling a little less lost, and stepped outside onto the balcony.

The Quarter-Moon's light shimmered on the glassy black water of the lake, and he could see stars swimming in its depths. Frogs were croaking in a steady, hypnotic rhythm, and wavelets splashed sleepily against the shore. It was so peaceful and beautiful that he felt as if he had gotten lost in some little god's heaven. Yawning, he went inside to bed.

As he drifted off, a kaleidoscope of images filled his mind; but this time, they were gentle and peaceful: scenes of Ravenvale's beauty, and his friends' welcoming faces. Feeling more hopeful than he had since he had walked out of the Sanctuary into Gauday's hands, he fell asleep.

Deep in the night, he woke with a shudder, his scars pulsing from a lurid nightmare. "Gods, no!" he whispered, fearing that he was back in Gauday's clutches. But then Friend's warm body and the frogs' steady croaking told him where he was. *Gods, I hope this isn't another false haven,* he thought, remembering being ripped away from the Sanctuary, and before that from the Circle's cabin in the woods, and before that from their safe-house in the City. From soul-deep fatigue, he begged, *Goddess, don't take this away from me, this refuge, these friends. Please, Zhovanya, have mercy.*

Chapter Five

A Strange New Heaven

A heavy weight pinned Kyr's legs to the soft bed. He bit his lip to keep back a moan of despair, not wanting to wake his cruel tormentor. *But the light. It's so bright. Where am I? What has Gauday done, now?* Cautiously, he opened his eyes. Strange light danced and sparkled across the ceiling. He looked down at his pinned legs, sagged into the bed — and laughed.

"Friend, get off me," he said firmly. "You're too heavy." She ignored him, so he slid her off his legs. With a sleepy protest, she settled herself next to him. He turned to hug her warm, solid body close to his chest, and heaved a sigh of relief, deeply grateful to be here in the safe haven of Ravenvale. *Only a few more days 'til Rajani does the cleansing ritual. Then I'll truly be free.* Treasuring this rare moment of peace and hope, he watched the mid-morning sunlight reflecting off the lake ripple across the ceiling.

A tap on the door woke Friend, who jumped down off the bed with a bark, then trotted over to the door and stood by it, wagging her tail. "Alright, girl, alright," Kyr laughed. Padding barefoot across the thick carpet, he opened the door. There, just as Devanyi had promised, was the green-patterned basket containing his clothes, now cleaned and neatly folded. Setting his clean clothes on an empty shelf in the wardrobe, he noticed that a lower shelf held a stack of clothing. On the floor of the wardrobe sat a pair of sandals, just his size. Touched by these gifts, he smiled. *New clothes for a new life.*

Kyr pulled on his own blue tunic and leggings, shoved his feet into the sandals, and stepped into the hall, more eager to face the day than he had been for many months. Spotting Medari heading toward the stairs, he called to Friend, "Come on, girl. Let's go!" And they hurried to catch up.

"Good morning, heart-father, how was your 'real bed'?"

"Perfect! I didn't notice it at all." Medari smiled. "How was your night?"

"Pretty good, except I forgot to ask for the sleeping potion."

"More nightmares?" the healer asked gently.

"Only one, thank the gods." Kyr hesitated a moment. "Would you give me a bottle so I won't have to bother you every night?"

Medari looked a little doubtful.

"I shouldn't need it much longer," Kyr added. "Rajani will do the cleansing ritual as soon as he can."

"Alright, just take two spoonsful at bedtime, and no more, promise?"

"Yes, I promise." Then, not wanting the lingering darkness of the past to sully this bright morning, Kyr commented, "This place is so big, so fancy."

"Yes, it's a bit overwhelming, isn't it?" Medari agreed. They shared a glance of understanding and comradeship, two hell-survivors at sea in this luxurious haven.

Downstairs, they found a small crowd out on the terrace, assembled around the table. Devanyi and Naran sat on the far side, talking together quietly. On the near side, Rajani, Luciya, and Jakar listened to a burly, ruddy-faced, sandy-haired man describing the condition of the livestock in the valley. In front of Rajani, a mug of tea and a plate of biscuits made islands in a sea of scrolls and folios.

Kyr sighed grimly. *It will take Rajani a month to deal with all this. Gods, what if I can't keep hold for that long?*

"Ah, the sleepy-toes are here!" Rajani looked up with a welcoming smile. "Good morning. Sleep well?"

"Mostly," Kyr answered.

"Like a stone," said Medari. "A good soak in the hot spring helped. Very civilized place you have, here."

Rajani smiled. "Thanks. You two know my lieutenant, Jakar. And this is Bru, the Steward of Ravenvale." Rajani nodded toward the burly man. To Bru, he said, "This is Kyr, and his heart-father, Medari — our new healer."

"Welcome to Ravenvale." Bru nodded respectfully to Kyr and Medari, and offered his hand to Friend to sniff. "And who might this be?"

"This is Friend." Kyr smiled proudly.

"Ah. Her name says it all." Bru smiled as Friend gave his hand a lick and wagged her tail politely.

"Sorry I can't join you right now, Kyr," Rajani added with a rueful laugh. "As you can see, I'm up to my ears in chores already. Just ignore us, and help yourselves to breakfast."

Medari and Kyr went inside to the buffet, where they heaped their plates with warm biscuits with butter and honey, scrambled eggs with bits of bacon, bowls of brambleberries with clotted cream, and mugs of tea. Kyr filled a small bowl with scrambled eggs for Friend.

Returning to the terrace, they joined Naran and Devanyi at the other side of the table. Luciya leaned back and spoke around Rajani to the healer. "Medari, as I mentioned, Devanyi is trained as a healer's assistant. She could work with you, if you like. And I'm sure she'd love to learn whatever you could teach her."

"I'll need some time to get settled in, but I'm sure we can work together." Medari nodded to Luciya, and turned to Devanyi. They began a quiet conversation about their work, while Luciya rejoined Rajani, Jakar, and Bru in their discussion of Ravenvale's many practical concerns.

Kyr started to pick up his fork, but a cold nose nudged his arm. "Alright, girl," he murmured, and set the bowl of eggs on the floor for her. She eagerly gulped them down as Kyr looked around, still dazzled by this wondrous turn of events. *Ah, Zhovanya, will You actually allow me to live here in this haven? Or am I dreaming?*

The Summer morning was clear and refreshingly cool. A breeze set the sunlight sparkling on the rippling waves, while ravens soared and dived after one another. Their croaking sounded like laughter, and Kyr smiled, sensing that they were celebrating the new day, as he was.

"Beautiful day, isn't it?" said Naran, echoing Kyr's thoughts. "Glad you got a good, long sleep."

"Thanks, Naran-ji. It truly is a beautiful morning, in many ways. One of the most beautiful of my life."

Naran smiled his understanding, and they began to eat.

"How long have you been here in Ravenvale?" Kyr asked, after finishing his biscuits and eggs.

"About a half-moon. The men Rajani sent to find me set a pretty good pace on the way here from the Sanctuary. My buttocks and legs are finally recovering." Naran laughed. "Not sure I ever want to get on a horse again."

Kyr winced in sympathy. "That's how *I* felt when we finally got to Gauday's fort. But now I love to ride my black Lady."

"You two made a spectacular entrance yesterday."

"We both got spooked by that crowd. By all the little gods, I wish everyone would stop trying to make me into a hero."

"Kyr, it's the truth. You *are* a hero. You freed us not only from the Soul-Drinker's horror, but also from the depredations of Gauday and his band. You can't expect people not to be grateful and admiring. It's been six generations since we had a hero — not to mention freedom, safety, and justice."

"I suppose you're right, but I don't *feel* like one, Naran-ji." Kyr looked down, frowning as his scars pulsed faintly.

"I understand. You've just done what you had to do. You weren't trying to be heroic."

"That's it, Naran-ji. I'm glad *someone* understands. Thanks."

"Of course. Let's make time to talk tomorrow. Today, there's the Warriors' Return ceremony, and a feast afterwards."

"Gods, I'm glad you're here." Kyr shrugged off his dark thoughts and smiled. "And I'm glad to be here in this beautiful, safe place."

Friend was standing on her hind legs with her forepaws on the balustrade, yipping at the ravens. A small, bright-eyed raven swerved and dove at her, squawking loudly, sending her into a frenzy of barking. Laughing, Kyr called, "Friend, come here!" After a few parting barks, she came over and settled down by his feet, watching the young raven soar away. "We'll go for a walk soon, girl. Maybe you two can play later."

He looked up to find Naran smiling at the two of them. "I see you have found a loyal companion, Kyr. How did that come about?"

"Very loyal." Kyr reached down to scratch Friend's favorite itchy spot behind her ear. "She adopted me at the fort. We've been friends ever since. I'll tell you the whole wretched story later. Right now, I am getting used to being here in this amazing place. How do *you* like it here in Ravenvale?"

"I'm enjoying the chance to take peaceful strolls by the lake, through the valley, or up in the foothills at the base of the cliffs. And it's interesting watching the community grow as new people arrive. Luciya has had her hands full. But I haven't had much to do."

"Peaceful strolls and nothing to do?" Kyr stretched his arms over his head and yawned. "Sounds wonderful."

On the other side of the table, Rajani brought up the question of where to house the new arrivals. At a pause in the conversation, Kyr leaned forward. "What will be done with the penitents? I need to meet with them for evening meditation, at least."

"For now, they'll have to be housed with the other prisoners in an empty barn down the road. I'll figure out something more appropriate for them tomorrow."

"They're not like the other prisoners," Kyr objected. "Can't you...?"

Rajani cut in a bit impatiently. "I'll do my best for them, but they're still prisoners, Kyr."

"I know," Kyr sighed. "But I don't want them to feel like I have abandoned them."

Luciya looked at them curiously. "Penitents?"

Kyr turned to her and said earnestly, "You remember when you told me about the hard path, Luciya?" She looked blank, and he continued. "At the safe house, you said something like, 'It's a choice everyone faces at some point:

to slide down the easy path of despair, greed, hatred, and fear; or to climb the hard path toward hope, kindness, love, and courage.'"

"Oh. Yes." Luciya smiled. "I'm surprised that you recall my words, after all you've been through. Rajani told me a little about that last night."

"Well, you were right," Kyr told her. "It *is* a hard path. But I have been doing my best to keep to it."

"Gods, Kyr, even through all that?"

"Yes. I haven't always succeeded." With a frown, he waved that away. "That's not what I wanted to talk about. A few of the prisoners from the fort have joined me on this hard path. I'm trying to help them."

Luciya blurted out, "You're helping these villains?"

He looked at her in confusion. "There hasn't been anyone else who could do it. I did the best I could, but now...." He looked up. "Maybe *you* could teach them?"

"Oh, Kyr, that's not what I meant. I was surprised that you're helping those who hurt you."

"These four men did me almost no harm." Kyr sighed. "I even forgave Gauday. No one seems to understand that. Doesn't 'Zhovanya naralo' mean 'the Goddess forgives us *all*'?"

Blushing, Luciya nodded. "Yes, it does. You never cease to amaze me, Kyr. As you have just shown, you make a much better teacher than I ever could be. But if there is something I can do to help you — or these penitents — I'll be glad to."

"Thank you, Luciya." Kyr thought for a moment. "We will need a place to meditate and pray."

Rajani held up a hand to forestall Bru's next question, and said to Kyr, "There's the Ravenhall chapel. Luciya, could you show it to him?"

"Surely," Luciya agreed. "I look forward to meeting these men you are helping."

"Let me see how they're faring here, first."

Devanyi spoke up, then. "Another thing we have to decide is where Medari can set up his new infirmary. The little room I've been using is small and hard to reach. I get worn out just running up and down all those stairs."

As the others debated this issue, Kyr sipped his tea and brooded about the plight of the penitents. It was better than worrying about how long it would be before Rajani was free to do the cleansing ritual.

"Alright, that should do it for now." Rajani dismissed Bru with a nod, and spoke to his lieutenant. "Jakar, please go ready the Companions for the ceremony." As Bru and Jakar strode off toward their duties, the Warrior Mage turned towards Kyr and Medari. "This afternoon, we have a ceremony to attend: a ritual to welcome returning soldiers home, help them shed the stains of duty and battle, and shift back into ordinary life."

"This is not the cleansing ritual you will do for me?"

"Sorry, Kyr. That will have to wait. This ritual is for all of us who have been hunting or fighting Gauday and his band: you, me, Medari, and the two dozen Companions who came with us to Ravenvale."

Medari scowled. "Not for me. I did nothing to fight Gauday. I just went along with his demands."

"You fought for Kyr's life in that ghastly situation all those months," Rajani said. "You need this as much as Kyr does, and more than the rest of us."

"No." Medari said flatly. "What I need is some time alone. I'll take Friend for a ramble, if that's all right."

"Well, you're the healer," Rajani conceded. "I suppose you know what's best for you."

That afternoon, Rajani led Kyr on a winding path through four curving hallways and up three staircases. As they walked, he explained, "This kind of ceremony is held in our outdoor chapel. It's at the core of Ravenhall and is a very old and sacred place." At last, they arrived at a wide door, which opened out to a small field of short, lush grass enclosed by a mossy graystone wall. Flowering bushes along the base of the wall added bright notes of white, orange, and yellow.

Despite the buzz of conversation, birdsong, and bee hum, Kyr sensed a deep silence permeating this holy place. The stone wall was carved with many cryptic symbols — some large and clear, some small, and some barely discernible for their coatings of moss. An aura of ancient power emanated from the symbols and stones, and Kyr shivered with a thrill of awe.

In the center of the left wall, a carving of the Sun radiated twelve rays; and opposite it, another carving depicted the phases of the Moon in an arc. Beneath each image stood low altars, with incense smoke rising from metal bowls — silver for the Moon, gold for the Sun. *Ah, Zhovanya and Jeyal are honored here, as They should be,* Kyr thought, remembering the mosaics of Jeyal and Zhovanya on the walls of the Kailithama at the Sanctuary, where he'd received such deep healing. He closed his eyes, allowing himself a moment to remember his sacred time there with Jolanya. Then he closed that memory away in his heart again, and came back to the present, feeling more at ease in this sacred place.

On the left side of the enclosure, branches of the Rookery tree arched over the wall. Some of the ravens lined the top of that wall in solemn silence, while others perched in the tree, still as stone. Kyr noticed Rajani smile at these usually raucous and restless birds.

Despite the warm sunshine, a low fire burned in a narrow trench in the center of the field. Around it, the two dozen Companions in their dark-green uniforms were assembled in a circle. Behind them, two men in silvery tunics and two women in golden ones beat a steady rhythm on a very large drum placed on half a dozen sturdy wooden legs. Beside them, a great gong hung from a blackwood stand. The drumbeat raised the hairs on Kyr's arms and neck, and he cast an apprehensive glance at the Warrior Mage.

"Don't worry," Rajani said softly. "This is for our healing." Kyr followed Rajani through the door, across a small terrace, and down four stairs to the lawn. There, they joined the circle around the fire. Kyr glanced at Rajani in surprise.

The Warrior Mage said quietly, "*I* need this ceremony as much as anyone." Then he added, "This ceremony will be led by Ylana, our Ritual Mage."

A stout, silver-haired woman in green robes stepped onto the terrace from the darkness of the hall. She radiated strength and peace, reminding Kyr of the Heart of the Forest, the Great Tree where he had been freed from the craving for the unholy pleasure shocks imposed on him by the Soul-Drinker's sorcerous Rod. Kyr shook off the memory and brought his attention back to the present, watching the Ritual Mage, liking her quiet solidity.

Ylana stood still until the Companions had ceased murmuring among themselves. Even the small birds and the bees quieted. In a voice like a deep, calm, powerful river, she announced, "Now we begin by asking for Zhovanya's guidance and protection." And she began to chant, "Zhovanya dagantalo, Zhovanya ganaralo."

Kyr's tense shoulders relaxed as he chanted along with everyone else. They sang quietly at first, but soon the chant gained in strength, growing louder and more beseeching. "Zhovanya dagantalo, Zhovanya ganaralo. Zhovanya dagantalo, Zhovanya ganaralo." Then everyone began stepping in place, in time with the beat of the drums. A deep yearning for Her protection and guidance welled up in Kyr's heart. But he knew all too well that Zhovanya's concept of "protection" bore little resemblance to what a mortal human would desire.

As the chanting reached a peak, the priestess raised her goldenwood wand toward the sky. Moving it around in a circle, she cried, "Shai-Rah!" Ethereal light bloomed above the outdoor chapel, and a light breeze swirled with the light, creating a subtly shimmering dome over the entire circle. "I call upon the clarity and truth of Air to help you see what you have done in this struggle. Look within and see. A'averalo!"

One of the drummers struck the gong, sending a deep tone reverberating through the circle, and raising the hairs on Kyr's arms and neck. Unbidden images of the torment and humiliation he had endured at Gauday's hands filled his mind, inflaming his scars with vile lust, and he flushed with shame. *No! Not now! Goddess, help me!*

The priestess glanced at him with eyes suddenly glowing golden, and a cool breeze wrapped him in Zhovanya's Presence. His scars quieted and the images in his mind shifted, showing him his own courage, compassion, and strength throughout his ordeal with Gauday. Even deeper, he saw that this all stemmed from an unknown place deep in his own soul, a place of pure love. He shook his head in denial, yet poignant tears trickled down his face. Confused and embarrassed, he wiped his tears away.

"Zhovanya naralo, Zhovanya naralo," sang the priestess, and everyone joined in, chanting quietly for a short time. Then she raised her wand and waved it above the fire in the trench.

"I call upon Fire to burn away all difficult thoughts and feelings remaining from this struggle, whether of anger, hate, revenge, resentment, or fear. Shai-yalo!" Pale golden flames engulfed them all in heat that did not burn, light that did not blind. The drum boomed out a rapid rhythm, and the ravens flew up, squawking and screeching, wheeling above the field in a black storm of darkly shining feathers and glinting eyes, sharp talons and snapping beaks.

Buried resentment, rage, terror, and vengefulness exploded in Kyr's core, and his scars flared up fiercely. *Gods and demons! I've got to do something or I'll go berserk!* Terrified that he would run mad and attack someone, he searched for escape. But then the circle of warriors burst into a fierce dance around the fire, yelling and screaming, jumping and stomping. "YAAAAA!!" Kyr let out a ferocious howl and joined the dance, shouting and whooping, whirling and leaping.

The dance brought Kyr close to the huge drum, halfway around the circle. Men and women were crowded around it, pounding out an ever-more-furious rhythm. A woman who was drumming stepped back and handed Kyr her drumming stick. He took her place and began hitting the drum in concert with the other drummers, beating out his heavy fury of rage and hatred, terror and vengefulness until he was dripping with sweat and breathing heavily.

Exhausted by the wild dancing and drumming, Kyr's fury cooled, his scars quieted, and he slowed the beat. The rhythm became the rhythm of the chant, and Kyr began to sing: "Zhovanya naralo, Zhovanya naralo, Zhovanya naralo." One by one, others matched his steady rhythm and joined the chant. For a time, they all chanted, eyes smiling at one another in gentle exaltation and deepening communion. The ravens circled above, silent except for the rush of wings beating in time with the drum.

At last the chanting dwindled away, and the last drummer let the beat go. One by one, the ravens settled onto their perches without a single squawk or altercation. Kyr sank to the ground along with everyone else, lying supine in blessed exhaustion. A few were weeping, or whispering prayers. The gong sounded again and Kyr felt the deep reverberations resounding in his bones and flesh, cleansing and healing.

But then he frowned. The tone of the gong now sounded distorted and dissonant. His scars flared up, throbbed against the rhythm of the gong's pulsation, poisoning the effect of the purifying sound. Kyr groaned. *Gods and demons! Does Gauday have to corrupt everything?*

Ylana lowered her wand to point downward. "I call upon Earth to help you release the pain and wounding you have suffered."

At these words, Kyr braced for a flood of the agony he had endured at Gauday's hands.

In a strong and resonant voice, she commanded, "Inorulo!" The earth beneath them rumbled and shook. Many gasped in alarm. But then the shaking dwindled to a deep and gentle vibration, like the purr of a giant cat. Around him, Kyr heard people sighing with relief or weeping quietly. The deep purring of the Earth rumbled through his bones, bringing a quiet surge of steadiness and strength. He felt some of his horror and agony draining away, and relaxed into the embrace of the comforting Earth, wanting nothing more than to remain forever in this blissful peace.

But Ylana spoke again. "I call on Water to cleanse and release all the stains of battle from your souls." She slowly circled the field, waving her wand in a flowing motion and singing, "Laralalo, Laralalo, Laralalo."An ethereal mist flowed from the wand and spread out over the field, drifting softly down to bless everyone. Some lay still, resting deeply, while others quietly sang along with Ylana, each in their own time. The soft chanting intertwined and flowed like a murmuring brook, deepening the spell of rest and cleansing.

Pleasantly limp, Kyr let the mist soak deep into his nerves, his bones, his soul. Water Essence flowed through him, damping down his scars, washing away a layer of the stress and defilement of his captivity, bringing him some ease and peace. He pushed away all thoughts and concerns, resting more deeply than he had since he walked away from the Sanctuary.

Ylana brought the chant to a close and went to stand quietly on the far side of the fire. Flames quietly crackling in the trench, oak leaves rustling in a slight breeze, and a few murmurs among the ravens deepened the tranquil silence. Kyr rested, relishing the warmth of the sunshine and the clean, wordless peace within his soul.

After a while, Ylana said to the group, "When you are ready, cross the fire and join us."

At this invitation, the Companions began to sit up, look around, and smile somewhat dazedly at each other. Rajani got to his feet and stood facing the priestess across the trench fire. Slowly, people gathered behind him, spontaneously chanting "Zhovanya naralo." Reluctant to lose this precious moment of peace, Kyr finally rose and joined them.

Ylana now stood on the terrace before the wide door through which they had entered the sacred enclosure. She raised her hands, and spoke with quiet gladness. "Return in peace, cleansed of the stains of battle, restored to yourselves and your families. Return in peace, knowing that this circle remains, and you may call upon any of us in need. Return in peace, knowing that Zhovanya loves and forgives us all."

"Zhovanya naralo," everyone repeated in a ragged chorus. Raising her wand, Ylana cried in a joyful voice, "Kaa'a-tay!" The wide door swung open, revealing a crowd of people waiting quietly inside the hall.

The Companions leapt across the trench fire by fours and fives. Cries of "Welcome home!" filled the air, and many were greeted with enthusiasm and love by family, friends, or even strangers. Kyr held back, unready for the hugging and back-slapping of the crowd. Rajani, Luciya, and Naran, however, were waiting for him on the far side of the fire.

"Come on, Kyr," Luciya called. "There's a grand feast waiting for us in the banquet hall."

The thought of the delicious food here was too tempting. Kyr smiled and jumped the fire.

As he joined his three friends, Luciya asked him, "I hope you feel better now?"

"Yes." Kyr returned her smile.

"Yes, I do too, thanks," Rajani said drily. Luciya flushed and looked away.

Naran said quietly, "You look much clearer, Kyr."

"These ceremonies always make me ravenous," Rajani exclaimed. "Let's go eat."

The banquet hall proved to be next door to the parlor where they had eaten earlier. This hall, too, had tall windows facing the lake, but no outdoor terrace. Large fireplaces filled either end of the long hall, but in the Summer heat no fires burned. A dozen long wooden tables and benches were filled with many people already eating. A cheerful clatter of cutlery and conversation filled the room, somewhat muted by banners hung between the ceiling beams and heavy tapestries on the walls.

"I'm afraid they've set a place of honor for you," Naran told Kyr, pointing toward a dais at the near end of the hall. Kyr looked up in dismay. On the dais sat a rectangular table with nine ornate chairs in a row facing toward the lower level where everyone else sat. Reluctantly, he followed Rajani, at whose smiling insistence he took the chair at the center of the row, with the Warrior Mage on one side of him, and Luciya on the other. Since no one else sat down, Kyr remained standing.

Rajani leaned close and whispered, "Just smile and nod. After a moment or two, take your seat." Then he pronounced, "Please welcome Kyr, our Liberator!" The people all stood and applauded. Smiling and nodding as instructed, Kyr endured their acclaim for a short time, then took his seat. The applause died away and everyone sat down. Kyr looked up and down the long table for his friends. On Rajani's far side was Ylana, the Ritual Mage, and beyond him, Naran, and then Devanyi. On Luciya's far side sat Bru, the Steward; and then a woman and a man Kyr did not know. But Medari was nowhere to be seen. Kyr frowned and turned to speak to Rajani about this, but just then servers set plates of food before them. Another filled their mugs with ale.

Raising his mug, Rajani called out, "To freedom and peace!" Everyone repeated his toast with loud enthusiasm, and took a swig of the ale. Kyr followed suit. Despite all the eyes watching him and his concern for Medari, the cool, fresh ale felt like a blessing to Kyr. For a time, they all ate intently, only murmuring about the delicious roasted chicken, spicy mashed carrots, sautéed green beans with mushrooms, and warm biscuits. Kyr especially liked the dessert, a creamy pudding with spice cookies around the edges of each bowl.

Then Luciya got to her feet, and raised her hands for quiet. "Thank you all for sharing this celebration with us. We're glad to welcome all newcomers to Ravenvale. We hope you will be very happy here." Motioning the slim, gray-haired woman next to Bru to rise, she began the introductions. "This is Alenya, the Head Cook, but everyone just calls her 'Cook.'" Alenya smiled, nodded, and took her seat.

Luciya nodded to the quiet, dark man at the end of the table, and he rose. "This is Grif, our Head Gardener," Luciya said. The man reminded Kyr of Maray at the Sanctuary, with his dark-brown skin and black curly hair; but this man's eyes were a startling green. The Head Gardener gave the assembly a silent bow, and quickly sat down.

Next, Luciya motioned to Bru to stand up. "This is Bru, the Steward of Ravenvale. He'll be happy to answer questions and solve any problems that arise." She smiled. "Won't you, Bru?"

The burly man laughed heartily. "I'll do my best." Luciya joined in with him, the camaraderie between them clear. Their laughter was contagious, and the audience joined in.

Luciya then briefly introduced Naran, Devanyi, and lastly, Ylana, who stood and raised her hands in benediction. "May Zhovanya bring you healing dreams."

Chatting together, people began leaving the banquet hall. Luciya and Cook headed to the kitchen to consult about tomorrow's menu. Grif and Bru refilled their mugs with ale and remained at the table, discussing plans for expanding the gardens to feed the growing population of Ravenvale. Ylana and Devanyi said their good nights and headed up to their rooms.

Rajani drained the last of his ale, and suggested to Kyr and Naran, "Let's go next door." The three of them made their way to the cozier parlor, and settled onto the couches by the fire that burned steadily in the hearth, now that the cool of evening had set in.

"Gods, it's grand to be home." Rajani slouched with his legs stretched out and his arms behind his head. Sated with delicious food and good ale, Kyr too leaned back and extended his legs.

"I can see why you love this place," Naran said, slouching a little himself, and resting his head against the back of the couch.

"Indeed I do, and I hope you both will love it here, too." The Warrior Mage glanced at Kyr. "How are you feeling now, Kyr?" he asked. "Did the ritual help you feel more at home, here? And in yourself?"

"Yes, the ceremony was helpful. I do feel more myself." Kyr sighed. "But my scars still bothered me."

"That monster!" Rajani growled. But at Kyr's disapproving glance, the Warrior Mage stopped himself from cursing Gauday again, and said instead, "I'll do the cleansing for you as soon as I can, but it might take me a month to deal with all the issues here."

"Oh, gods," Kyr said in dismay. "A whole month?"

"Maybe less, if Luciya and I work hard enough," Rajani said, "And I promise we will do our very best." Then he asked, "Naran is here for you. Will you be all right while I am busy?"

Kyr breathed out slowly, then gave his two friends a wry smile. "Well, I survived Gauday's little hell. I'll manage all right in this paradise." His smile faded, and he added, "Right now, though, I'm worried about Medari."

With a slight frown, Naran said, "Oh, he didn't come to the ceremony or the banquet, did he? Why not?"

"He felt that he didn't deserve to come to the ceremony, because he didn't fight against Gauday. He hasn't forgiven himself for going along with Gauday, and allowing me to suffer. Besides, he doesn't feel like celebrating...anything."

"He lost his entire family?" Naran asked.

Kyr nodded, his face going grim.

"Well, he's probably not ready to let go of any of that yet. He needs time."

"I guess so." Kyr got to his feet. "I'd better go see how he's doing."

"I'll go with you," Naran volunteered.

"I think he'd feel more comfortable with just me."

"Yes, I see. Let me know if you or he would like to talk."

Kyr knocked on Medari's door, eliciting an excited yelp from Friend. Then came Medari's voice: "That you, Kyr? Come in."

Friend was the first to greet Kyr, with wagging tale and eager eyes. Medari, on the other hand, was slumped in a chair by the window. But he raised a hand in invitation, and Kyr took the chair opposite the healer, who looked tired and disheveled, his usual meticulous tidiness vanished. *Gods, he looks terrible. I wish he had come to the ceremony.*

Medari took a nip from the flask in his hand. "Here," he offered.

Kyr accepted the flask and took a meager sip, then asked carefully, "How are you, heart-father?"

"Ah, a little drunk, my son. And you?"

"The ceremony was helpful. I feel more myself."

"Good."

"I'm sorry you didn't come."

Medari said nothing.

Not knowing quite what to do, Kyr directed his attention to Friend. "Come here, girl. Settle down." She huffed a sigh, but came over to him and curled by his feet. Stroking her head, he asked Medari, "Is your room, and everything, all right?"

"Room's fine. Not sure what these people are up to around here."

Kyr kept the frown off his face. "What do you mean?"

"Oh, gods, I don't know. Never mind. Just tired and trying to adjust to this whole...situation." Medari looked away, his eyes full of tears.

"Ah, gods, I'm so sorry.... I know you are grieving. Is there anything I can do?"

"They're dead!" Medari exclaimed. "There's nothing anyone can do about that, is there?"

"No," Kyr said gently. "We can't change what happened."

69

"Sorry, son. Here I am troubling you, when you suffered so much." Medari sighed heavily. "And I put you through that for nothing!" He took a swig from his flask, and offered it to Kyr, who waved it away.

"I don't need you to feel guilty on my account," he said firmly. "It was Gauday who trapped us both, and the Soul-Drinker who twisted and corrupted Gauday. The blame is theirs. We both know that."

At these words, Medari's face softened. "My heart-son," he slurred, smiling fondly at Kyr. "So wise and kind."

"Ah, heart-father…. I wish I could help you. You certainly helped me."

"Oh, my dear son! I have lost so much. I may never get over it. But it does help me a great deal to have you as my family now. Please remember that…," Medari smiled wryly, "even when I'm being an old grump."

"Alright," Kyr chuckled, but then said earnestly, "Whatever I can do for you, heart-father, just ask."

"Right now, you can get out of here. Friend and I had quite a ramble, and I'm heading for that lovely bed." From his healer's kit on the floor by his feet, Medari took out a dark glass bottle. "Don't forget this."

"Ah, the sleeping potion. Thanks! Sleep well, heart-father." Kyr took Friend next door to their room, still worried about Medari. *Gods, I hope he can find his courage for life again.* Bad memories swarmed through his mind, and he gratefully took a dose of the sleeping potion, hoping for a peaceful night's sleep. Exhausted from a long day, he and Friend went straight to bed, though the lazy Summer sun had barely set.

Part Three ~ Found and Lost

"The world is violent and mercurial — it will have its way with you....
We live in a perpetually burning building and
what we must save from it, all the time, is love."

— Tennessee Williams

Chapter Six

Found

Kyr rose late and eased into the morning, feeling cleansed and relaxed from the ceremony of the day before. He washed, dressed, and went out onto his balcony. Mystified but grateful, he stood marveling at the beauty of this strange paradise that he had somehow landed in. The lake was a serene blue, darker than the clear sky, and ravens soared silently in the mild air of this Summer morning. High above, a tawny eagle circled with slow grace. Enthralled, Kyr watched until his soulkin soared beyond the tall cliffs enclosing the valley, and disappeared from sight.

With a grateful sigh, he turned and went inside to kneel before his makeshift altar. "Zhovanya," he murmured, "thank You for this unexpected blessing, this beautiful home. May it be a place of harmony and peace for all who dwell here." Closing his eyes, he quietly chanted, "Zhovanya nara lo, Zhovanya nara lo." After a timeless while, he felt a breath of Her grace warm his heart.

And then a cold nose nudged his cheek. "Ah, my Friend," he said with a smile, giving her a hug. "Alright, girl, let's get you outside and then find some breakfast."

After a trip outdoors for Friend, they went inside to the parlor. No one was there, but covered dishes and a teapot awaited him on the sideboard. Taking his breakfast of tea, fresh herbed bread, and soft tangy cheese out onto the terrace, Kyr sat at the round table, soaking in the warm sunshine and enjoying this rare gift of peaceful solitude. Friend stood with her front paws up on the balustrade, sniffing the light breeze.

Sleepily sipping tea, he contemplated this new life in Ravenvale. *Maybe this will be a safe place, at last, Goddess willing. What will it be like without the Soul-Drinker, without the craving, without Gauday? Hard to imagine. I've never been free of such torments, except for my year at the Sanctuary.* Then, he remembered:

My time there was not easy, either. "Ah, Jolanya," he whispered, grief for his lost beloved weighing on his heart.

Stop it, he told himself. *I'm here now, and there's no going back.* Deliberately, he turned his mind away from the past, and tried to imagine what he would do in this new life. *I guess I could sculpt? Go for rides with Lady? Gods above and below! It's strange to think that I actually have the luxury of such choices.* He shook his head. *I could do those things now and then, but it's more important to help my family — my heart-father, and my brothers on the hard path.* With that, he drained his mug and jumped to his feet. "Come on, girl," he said to Friend. "Let's go find Luciya and see if we can locate a decent place for my brothers to live."

Having no idea where Luciya was, he asked a young server sweeping the floor in the hall where he might find her. The coltish boy smiled shyly, and silently led him to her workroom. Luciya sat at a wide desk covered with neat piles of papers, frowning at the paper in her hand. Behind her, an unshuttered window gave a view of the valley and the road leading back to the tunnel through which he, Rajani, Medari, and the rest of the caravan had entered Ravenvale.

She smiled at the boy. "Thank you, Greggo." The server grinned, gave Friend a pat, and darted back to his task. Then she said, "Good morning, Kyr. How are you?"

"Getting used to that extravagant bed. But I slept well, thanks to Medari's potion and the ceremony yesterday."

"How's our new healer doing?"

"He seemed to brighten up when I visited him last evening, but he needs more time to grieve. I think work would be best for him."

"You're probably right. I'll have Devanyi show him the building that I think will work for his infirmary. It's in the main courtyard near the gate, so it would be easy for patients to reach."

"Good." Kyr gave Luciya a grateful smile. "I'd like to visit the penitents today, see how they are doing. Also, could you show me the chapel that Rajani mentioned?"

"Let me show you the chapel first. Then we'll see what we can do for your penitents."

Luciya led him down a short hallway, and opened an oaken door carved with a radiant Sun. Kyr stepped into the chapel and stumbled to a halt, throwing out his arms. The midnight-blue stone floor, embedded with small silver stars, gave him the impression of standing on the night sky. Luciya caught hold of one of his arms. "Don't worry. Most people feel like they will fall, the first time they enter the chapel, but you won't."

Kyr gave a shaky laugh. "That *is* quite startling." He took a steadying breath, and looked around the spacious room with its high, vaulted ceiling. A few steps to their left, a large round window framed a striking view of the lake, and far beyond, Ravenvale's guardian wall of tall cliffs. Light reflected from the lake wavered across the high ceiling, splashing here and there on the pale golden walls and dark floor. Two steps led up to a dais below the circular window, where an altar of golden stone was polished to a warm glow. Above the altar, a darkened Presence Lamp hung from brass chains.

Luciya noticed the direction of his gaze. "Yes, the Lamps went dark all over Khailaz when you killed the cursed Soul-Drinker. I was so glad when his horrid red glare went out! My grandmother told me that when Zhovanya was with us, the Presence Lamps glowed with a beautiful iridescent light. The people of Ravenvale could see its light shining all night through that window, so they always knew She was here." She glanced at Kyr, a secret hope in her eyes. "Perhaps someday Zhovanya's Light will return to all the Lamps."

He nodded, preoccupied with his own concerns. Then he gestured towards the spacious, elegant chapel. "I'm sorry, but...it's so big."

"Oh, you don't like it? I love this chapel."

"No, it's not that," he said quickly. "It is quite beautiful, but this is too grand for the penitents and me. We'd feel lost in all this. Isn't there somewhere small and plain where we could meet?"

Luciya thought for a moment. "Well, there's a small building by the north gate. I'm not sure what it was used for, originally. And you and your penitents will have to clean it up. But in fact," she said suddenly, clapping her hands in delight, "maybe they could live there. Might solve two problems with one stroke."

"That sounds good."

"Let's go check with Rajani."

Rajani's only condition was that the penitents had to be kept under guard by a pair of Companions.

"But," Kyr objected, "that's not necessary. They have chosen the hard path, and they are my brothers."

"I'm sorry, Kyr. I'm already giving them special privileges by allowing them to live in this house. That's as far as I can go. They are still prisoners who must work out their penance like all the others."

"What about forgiveness, Rajani? Zhovanya naralo."

"I'm sure *She* forgives them, but the people they harmed do not. They — and you — will have to be satisfied with justice."

Kyr glanced at Luciya, but she said, "Rajani's right."

75

The building allotted for the penitents' house was bare and simple. Kyr sighed, wishing that he could live there along with them. As remarkable as Ravenhall was, its unfamiliar luxury seemed to him unmerited for one as corrupted by Gauday as himself.

Luciya was right: the long-unused building needed a thorough cleaning, and she had sent a server over with brooms, mops, rags, and buckets. After Craith assigned chores to Jorem, Kinar, and Zurano, Kyr said, "I want to help too."

"No, no," Craith objected. "You're our Liberator."

"None of that," Kyr growled. "I'm just a man like any of you. What can I do?"

"Alright, if you insist," Craith said. "You and Kinar take brooms upstairs, and sweep. Be sure to knock down the cobwebs." He tossed them each a couple of rags. "Tie one of these around your nose and mouth. It's dusty as an abandoned hell up there."

Upstairs, Kyr, having no experience in cleaning, carefully copied what Kinar did. They started at the back, sweeping the broom back and forth across the ceiling and down the walls, snagging dusty cobwebs and sending spiders scuttling for the cracks. Kyr's arms soon ached, the dust set him sneezing, and sweat mixed with the dust on his face, hands, and arms in a gritty paste.

At first, he found it odd to be doing this kind of work. Then he snorted to himself, realizing that this was due to his experience as a Slave. In the Soul-Drinker's hell, women called "drudges" had done all the cleaning. Yet as tiring and dirty as it was, he found this work satisfying in a new way. Working with his brothers to cleanse this house and to create a chapel for them all to meditate and pray together gave him a fulfilling sense of belonging and purpose that warmed his heart. But then his scars pulsed in angry opposition. Kyr frowned, fervently wishing he could cleanse his body, mind, and soul of Gauday's corruption as easily as they were cleaning this house.

When the upper room was clean, Kinar and Kyr joined the other three penitents downstairs. There was still much to do, but Kyr went outside for some fresh air. The two Companions assigned as guards sat playing dice under a shady oak tree in front of the house. Tired and dirty, Kyr grabbed an empty bucket from Jorem, who was on his way to the nearby well, and stalked over to the guards. "We need water. Please fetch it for us."

The smaller guard frowned and started to protest, but the larger glared at him, and said, "Of course, *Liberator*. Glad to help you."

The smaller one said, "You go on, Chavri. I'll keep watch."

Chavri got to his feet and took the bucket. "Your turn next, Nyx." He chuckled at Nyx's scowl, but all Nyx said was "Yes, sergeant."

With the guards' help hauling water as needed, the cleaning work went faster. Kyr and the penitents scoured the kitchen, scrubbing the grimy walls and stone floors, and cleaning the dented pots and pans, rusty kitchen tools, and chipped mugs and bowls. Then they turned to the small room that would be their chapel and scrubbed it clean, taking special care with the small glass window. A dusty brown carpet covered its stone floor, but after a good beating, it proved to be a good, thick rug, only slightly moth-eaten.

Just as they finished cleaning, a server arrived leading a donkey pulling a cart loaded with four straw pallets. Kinar's eyes lit up. "Such luxury! No more sleeping on cold, hard ground." Once they hauled the pallets upstairs — no easy chore — the four penitents spread out their bedrolls on the pallets, and set their packs by the wall.

"Gods above and below!" said Zurano, looking at their clean, comfortable dormitory. "I can't believe we actually have a place like this." He bowed to Kyr. "Thank you!" Craith, Kinar, and Jorem followed suit.

"You're welcome." Kyr took a moment to search for a truth that these men, who looked to him for guidance, might need to hear. "The hard path doesn't mean we always have to be uncomfortable. The work of cleansing our souls is hard enough."

When the entire house was clean, they gathered in the kitchen, filled the tub with water, and took turns washing up. Then Craith looked around, grinning. "Well now, this looks like a home for people instead of ghosts." The brick fireplace, now cleared of old soot and ashes, occupied the wall common to the newly designated chapel. The kitchen came equipped with a dented metal washtub and two sagging shelves that held a kettle, stewpot, and frying pan on one, and a half-dozen chipped brown plates, bowls, and mugs on the other. A collection of well-used kitchen utensils hung from pegs on the wall. Six rickety stools surrounded a scarred and dented table. Kyr smiled. "These things are as battered as we are."

Jorem snorted, Kinar and Zurano laughed, and Craith said with a grin, "It's better than squatting by a campfire."

"I figure we can fix things up pretty good," said Kinar, and his twin, Zurano, added, "We worked in the kitchens and woodshop a lot as boys at training camp, before we were old enough to start training as soldiers."

Kyr looked around. "We need some firewood, candles, and food. I'll go talk to Luciya."

Returning to Ravenhall, he found Luciya still in her office. He asked her for what they needed, and added, "I'd also like something to serve as an altar in our little chapel."

"Alright, I'll send someone with candles, wood, and a low table for your altar."

"Thanks, Luciya. This means a lot to me. Oh, and thanks for sending the pallets. My brothers appreciate all you are doing for them."

"Anything *you* want, just ask."

Kyr frowned. "They are as deserving as I am."

"*They* did not free all of Khailaz from the Soul-Drinker, or — "

With an abrupt gesture, Kyr cut her off. "As I keep *telling* you, *I* did not kill him. Some god or demon took me over and used my hands to choke him to death."

"Nevertheless, you deserve whatever we can do." Her tone seemed more somber and weighty than her words, but then she smiled, and added, "I'll ask Cook to send over supper for tonight, and supplies so your men can cook for themselves."

"Thanks, Luciya. I need to get back now. I'll be there until late."

Wondering again what mysteries she and Rajani were hiding, Kyr climbed the stairs back to his room, and collected the driftwood and stones from his makeshift altar. They would be more at home in the penitents' simple chapel than in this lavish room.

Next, he tapped on Medari's door.

"Enter," the healer called.

Opening the door, Kyr stepped inside. "Heart-father, the penitents and I will be consecrating our little chapel in the house Rajani assigned them. It would mean so much to me if you would join us."

"Alright, son. I'll be down later. I promised to meet Devanyi here for supper and a lesson on the use of herbs."

When Kyr returned to the penitents' new home, he found a fire crackling in the hearth, and the four men perched on the unsteady stools around the battered table, with mugs of ale before them. They looked pleased and a little dazed at their new and, for them, unusually comfortable situation.

With a smile of welcome, Craith said, "We're about to eat the supper Cook sent over. Will you join us?"

"Gladly. I never knew what hard work cleaning is, before."

"Neither did I," Jorem groaned. The former Slave added, "I'm starving!"

"Tendertoes," Craith teased. He and the twins — former soldiers who were well acquainted with such work — chuckled.

Smiling, Kyr took a seat on one of the stools, far more at ease with his friends in this humble kitchen than he had been at last night's formal banquet. Zurano lifted the lid off the pot, and they all widened their eyes at the delicious scent of chicken stew. Zurano ladled the stew into bowls, while Kinar passed around a basket of warm biscuits. Used to camp food, they ate in reverent silence, except for a few little moans of pleasure. When every morsel was gone, Craith licked his fingers. "I think we've fallen into some little god's heaven, with food like this!"

"Glad you enjoyed it," Kyr replied. "But I hope one of you is a good cook. You'll be cooking for yourselves, after this."

"Gods help us!" Jorem sighed.

But Zurano smiled. "I love to cook. The rest of you will have to do the washing up."

"All depends on how good a cook you are," Craith joked. "If it's horrible, you will have to do your own washing up."

"I'll bet he never has to," Kinar answered.

"Good to hear," said Jorem.

Kyr smiled, bemused by their joshing — something he had never experienced before — and pleased to see them enjoying each other and their new home.

At sunset, all was ready for the inaugural chapel service. Kyr looked into the small room, overjoyed to help create a chapel for Zhovanya with his brothers on the hard path, and with his heart-father. The bricks at the back of the hearth radiated warmth into the chapel, the now-clean brown rug softened the stone floor, and the low table that Luciya had promised was already in place as the altar, covered with a white cloth that she had thoughtfully provided. Together, Kyr, his heart-father, and his brothers had planned a simple ritual to consecrate the room, now to be their new chapel.

He smiled, and returned to the kitchen. Here, he and the penitents awaited Medari's return from his room, where he had gone to fetch the cleansing herbs he needed for his part in the ritual. The five of them remained silent, each preparing for this sacred moment in his own way. When Medari returned, they all quietly moved next door.

Kyr knelt to arrange his driftwood and stones on the altar. Medari circled the room, gently waving a bowl filled with smoldering herbs, wafting sweet-smelling smoke to all corners. Jorem, the desert tribesman, followed him, reverently carrying a bowl filled with fresh lake-water, which he sprinkled lightly onto the walls and floor. Kyr moved back while Kinar and Zurano surrounded the altar with fresh-cut pine branches, which added their sweet-pungent scent to the air. Craith placed a short, fat white candle on a chipped saucer on the altar, lighting it with the flint striker from the kitchen. The golden light softly graced the curves of the driftwood, and sparkled in the tiny crystals embedded in the river stones.

For a time, they sat in silent meditation. When the quiet in the chapel deepened, Kyr began to pray. "Zhovanya, we give thanks for allowing us to reach this safe haven. We ask for your blessing on this chapel, on Ravenvale, and all of the land, soulkin, and people of Khailaz. May Your Love heal the evil wrought within our souls by the Soul-Drinker and by his crippled servant, Gauday." Kyr cringed inside, feeling that very evil within him rising now against the sacred peace of the new chapel as his curse-scars started to pulse. *Merciless gods, not now!* Silently, he begged, *"Dekani, help me!"*

Quickly, Kyr began the chant. After a moment, the other men added their voices to his. As they chanted, Kyr felt Dekani's strength steadying him. With his teacher's help and the power of the chant, his curse-scars calmed and the Soul-Drinker's sickening malevolence subsided, enabling him to relax into the chant.

"Zhovanya naralo, Zhovanya naralo, Zhovanya naralo, Zhovanya naralo."

Hearing his brothers and heart-father all singing strongly with him, tears came to Kyr's eyes. *Maybe it was all worth it. The Sanctuary is safe, and we are here — my heart-father, my brothers on the hard path, and I. Ah, Zhovanya, maybe it was worth it. But, dear Goddess, why did Medari's family have to die? Why do You allow so much suffering?* Grief and anger swelled up, choking him into silence. For a few moments, he could not sing, and sat with his head down, biting his lip.

But then came the memory of Zhovanya as he had first seen her, dancing through all the wonders and horrors of death and life. He heaved a deep sigh and, murmured, "Ah, Zhovanya, forgive me. You know all of our suffering. And I should know by now that I can never comprehend Your purposes." He raised his head, took a breath, and resumed chanting.

As they continued to chant, the small room filled with harmony and peace. All the men, burdened with grief or guilt, hard-ridden by life, felt a tentative hope that here, in this safe and lovely valley, they might find soul's ease. What Kyr had known of Zhovanya's Love and Forgiveness came back to him now, caressing his heart lightly, and his voice soared in reverence and in gratitude for his deliverance from Gauday's madness.

Medari was stunned by Kyr's surrender into adoration; but after a moment he sighed and let himself go into the chant more than ever before. Craith and Jorem let their hearts open to the Goddess, putting all their longing for forgiveness and healing into the chant. Hearing Zurano's soft, soul-touched weeping, Kinar put an arm around his brother's shoulders and continued to sing. For a time, all were lifted upon the wings of Kyr's full-voiced worship into wordless communion with Zhovanya.

At last, Kyr let the chant die away, gently returning them to earth. They all remained in a meditative silence, even as they rose and bowed good-night to each other.

Walking back to Ravenhall with Kyr, Medari broke the silence. "Perhaps we can, after all...," he swallowed a sob, and continued, "...begin again."

"I hope so," his heart-son said softly. "I'm glad you're here with me. This" — Kyr made a sweeping gesture that included Ravenhall and the entire valley — "is all so strange, after what we went through."

"That it is, son. I keep feeling that I am lost in a fantastical dream."

"Me, too. I fear that if I say the wrong word, I'll wake up back there at the fort." Kyr shrugged. "But here we are. How are you holding up?"

"I will always grieve for my family." Medari's sounded voice sad and weary. "But having you in my life gives me a reason to go on."

Kyr smiled, but a weight settled on his heart: grief for Medari, and a sense of responsibility for his heart-father's happiness.

A quarter-moon had passed since Kyr had arrived in Ravenvale. Even with Medari's sleeping potion minimizing his nightmares, and Dekani containing the smoke-beast and damping down the pulsing of his curse-scars, Kyr still found it difficult to believe in this strange phenomenon called "ordinary life." Worse, his friends, along with many other denizens of Ravenvale, were eager to offer small kindnesses: fresh flowers in his room; a warm muffin from Cook; a comforting word when painful memories made his face go dark and tight.

After months of brutality, each act of thoughtfulness hurt sharply, a painful reminder of how little gentleness he had experienced in his life. He accepted these kind gestures warily, watching for hidden motives. Gauday had often been "kind." Only with the penitents and with Medari — those who knew what he had suffered — did Kyr feel somewhat at ease. Yet this lovely dream of safety, rest, and peace was beginning to feel a little more real to him.

Today, he was on his own. Naran had found himself in demand as a counselor to new arrivals, some of whom were bewildered by the upheavals in their lives caused by the end of the Soul-Drinker's reign. Medari and Devanyi were busy setting up the new infirmary in a building just inside the gate to Ravenhall. Craith and the penitents were at work in the fields, orchards, or gardens with the other prisoners. Rajani, Bru, and Luciya were immersed in the plans and details and complaints and problems and decisions of Ravenvale's rapidly expanding community.

Alone and free of responsibilities, Kyr grabbed the chance to take Lady out for a ride. Together, they ambled along the path around the lake, with Friend trotting beside them. Warm sunshine soaked into his shoulders, and the spacious beauty of the lake and the valley spread out around him. He sighed happily, greatly relieved to be away from everyone's eyes. The residents of Ravenvale looked at him with unnerving reverence, and his friends were either overly attentive or seemed to rely on him for wisdom and support. "Ugh!" He shook himself, and nudged Lady into a trot, then a canter, leaving Friend to catch up later. In this valley she was safe, and could always find her way home. *Home,* he thought, *home. I'm beginning to feel what that might mean.* And his heart lifted.

The fresh breeze in his face and the rhythm of Lady's strong body swept away the cobwebs in his mind. He grinned as they thundered by the sparkling lake on his right and golden hayfields on his left. "Keeeyaaa!" he yelled out of pure joy in solitude and freedom, safety and peace.

"Kyeerr!"

Throwing his head back, Kyr laughed to see a tawny eagle soaring through the empty sky, and his heart soared higher on wings of hope.

That night, pleasantly tired but sore from his long ride, Kyr bade his friends an early good night. After giving Friend a good scrubbing, he soaked in the baths, more relaxed than he could remember. Upon returning to their room in Ravenhall, Friend curled up in her spot on the bed and went to sleep, worn out from their long, lovely day.

Kyr went out onto the small balcony of his room. Stars were coming out, one by one, and the summer-night chorus was rhythmic with croaking and chirping. He found himself thinking of his teacher. *Gods, I haven't talked with Dekani since the beginning of the journey here. I got mad when he wouldn't tell me about my parents. But perhaps he has a good reason. Still, I wish I knew. I seem to be the only one who has no idea who his parents were — or are. Gods! What if they're still alive?* Startled by this new thought, Kyr tried to imagine what it would be like to meet his parents, and failed. He realized sadly that he had no idea what having a real mother and father might be like. *Well, Dekani's been sort of like a father to me, and I miss him.* He heaved a deep sigh. *I'll just have to forgive him for keeping secrets from me. Perhaps he will be able to talk with me for a short time, despite having to keep control over the smoke-beast.*

The night breeze made Kyr shiver, and he went inside to bed. Lying there, with one hand resting on Friend's back, he turned his mind toward his teacher. *"Dekani? I'm sorry I stayed away so long. May I visit?"*

Kyr found himself on the path to his teacher's cottage, but that was all he could see clearly. The meadow and forest were ghost-like. Frowning, he hurried into the cottage. There was no fire in the hearth, and his teacher was not sitting in his usual chair. *"Dekani?"*

"In here." Dekani's voice came from his bedroom, a place Kyr had never entered. *"Come in, son."*

Kyr shoved the curtains to one side. The simple room contained only a narrow bed. Dekani lay atop the covers wearing his changeable robes, though now they were unusually dark. Dekani's white hair was wispy, his skin finely wrinkled.

"Gods, what's wrong, Dekani? You look so pale." Kyr knelt beside the bed.

"You are safe now, in Ravenvale?"

"Yes." Worried, he reached to take Dekani's hand in his own.

"STOP!" Dekani croaked. *"Remember, in this realm, we must not touch."*

"Sorry, Dekani. I forgot. Tell me what's wrong. Are you ill?"

"No, no. Not ill. Just very old." From a pocket in his robes, Dekani took out a red, heart-shaped gem that sparkled even in the dim light. He set it over his heart, and placed both hands over it. Closing his eyes for a few moments, he took three slow breaths, breathing in strength and vitality from the red stone. Then he got to his feet, looking more like his usual self, and said, *"Come, let's go sit by the fire."*

They stepped into the front room and took their seats by the hearth. Dekani whispered *"Shai'ya!"* and a smokeless fire sprang to life in the hearth, crackling quietly. He stared into the fire a moment, and then said, *"Kyr, I need to tell you something."*

"What is it?" Kyr asked, alarmed by Dekani's somber tone.

"At some point, I'll be moving on."

"What do you mean? Are you leaving me?" Kyr's heart pounded in his chest. *"No! You can't. You're my teacher, my protector. Without you, Gauday's curse-scars and the smoke-beast will drive me mad!"*

Dekani nodded soberly. *"That's why it is imperative that Rajani does the cleansing for you as soon as he can. I don't know how much longer I will be here. But for now, I'm still protecting you as much as I can."*

"Oh gods, this is my fault, isn't it? I'm sorry I was angry with you. I should never have ignored you for so long. I promise I'll never be mad at you again. Just don't go away!"

"No, no, son," Dekani protested. *"This has nothing to do with that. And I'm sorry I can't tell you what you want to know about your parents. No, this isn't about you at all. It's just that my time is coming to go home to Zhovanya's justice, as we all do when our life force is spent."*

"Merciless gods!" Kyr gasped. *"You mean you're dying!"* He sat stunned by the thought of losing his life-long teacher, his steadfast guide through so

much torment. Even when they hadn't seen each other for long periods, he had known that Dekani cared for him and would help him as much he could. Now, with the foundation of his life suddenly crumbling out from under him, Kyr panicked. *"Don't leave me here alone!"*

"You are not alone, son," Dekani said firmly. *"You are safe at home in Raven-vale with Rajani, just as you should be. And you have other friends, too. Naran is here, isn't he?"* Kyr nodded, and Dekani smiled kindly. *"You will be all right now. You'll see. Everything will work out fine."*

His heart stone-heavy, Kyr bowed his head. With a quick, stealthy wave of his hand, Dekani sent him a gentle flow of blue kailitha, which eased his grief and numbed his fear.

Kyr sighed and looked up. *"Can't you use your healing magic to stay with me?"*

"I'm sorry. I have staved Death off as long as I can. Now that you are safe in Ravenvale, I can feel the Dark Lady approaching, and this time, She won't be denied." Dekani sounded weary — and glad.

Kyr choked back another useless plea, his heart sinking at the finality of Dekani's tone. *"Gods, Dekani, I don't know how I'll survive without you. You're the one who helped me keep my sanity through two hells: all those years in the Soul-Drinker's compound and these past months in Gauday's clutches. I'd be dead or a vicious madman, if it weren't for you."* He knelt before Dekani. *"Teacher, in case I don't get another chance, I want to tell you how grateful I am for all your help and guidance. All I can say is…thank you."* Choking up, he buried his face in his hands.

Quickly, Dekani held his hands above Kyr's bowed head, and again sent a flow of soothing blue to calm Kyr's mind and heart. Then he said, *"Get up, son. It's I who should kneel before you. Go on, now."* Kyr resumed his seat, and Dekani smiled at him, now radiating golden kailitha, enveloping him in love and blessings. *"You have done so well, my son, so well, even during the times we didn't see each other. Don't doubt yourself. You are a truly remarkable man, and have done immeasurable service for our land and people — and for the Goddess. I am so proud of you. Always remember that I love you. And for now, I am still with you. Rest well, my son."*

Dekani and his cottage faded away, and Kyr slept deeply until morning.

The next day, the conversation with Dekani seemed like a dream. Kyr felt sad that someday Dekani would be gone; but for now, his heart glowed, warmed by his teacher's love and praise.

Chapter Seven

Too Raw

Friend nosed around the orchard looking for fallen apples, after a morning of exploring the gardens surrounding Ravenhall with Kyr and Naran. The two men lounged on a blanket in an open spot, enjoying the late-summer sunshine. Bee hum and squirrel chatter filled the air, and many birds twittered and chirped in the leafy trees.

Naran looked ruefully at his scratched hands. "Maybe we'd better ask Bru for some gloves and gardening tools." The ornamental gardens were still shaggy and untended, though the vegetable gardens had been restored to help feed the growing population of Ravenvale. The two men's knees and hands testified that they hadn't been able to resist pulling quite a few weeds.

"I forgot how much work weeding is." Naran lay back, his hands behind his head, but Kyr sat fidgeting with the edge of the blanket, and frowning at the ground.

"What's on your mind, Kyr?" Naran suppressed a sigh. He'd been ready to doze off in the peaceful warmth of the afternoon.

"Naran, you know that I went riding with Rajani yesterday on his tour of Ravenvale to meet the new residents and check on their needs and contributions?"

"Yes. Did you enjoy that?"

"I loved riding Lady through the valley. And it was amazing to see how Rajani dealt so easily with all kinds of people, and their questions and demands." Kyr sighed and looked down. "But I'm not sure I'll ever get used to the way they look at *me* — like I'm a little god or something."

"I'm afraid you'd better get used to it." Naran smiled. "You *are* special, Kyr. People are in awe of you for freeing us from the Soul-Drinker. Now they revere you even more for protecting the Sanctuary, though they have little idea what a terrible sacrifice you made to do so. Beyond all that, your forgiveness of your tormentors is beyond many people's understanding, and seems god-like to them."

"I wish they would understand that I'm just a miserable ex-Slave, redeemed by you, Jolanya, and the Goddess." He shook his head. "It wasn't me. All that I did — it was Zhovanya working through me, using me." He bit his lip at the bitterness that had crept into his tone.

Friend showed up then, panting happily. Kyr grabbed her gently by the ears and put his forehead to hers. "*You* don't think I'm special, do you, girl? *You* aren't going to look at me like that, are you?" She shook her head, ears flapping, and Kyr laughed.

Naran watched as Kyr fondled and played with Friend. He knew it was best to start the clearing work with Kyr as soon as possible, but his heart quailed at the thought, knowing that it would be a dark and difficult task for them both. In addition, Naran couldn't shake an irrational feeling of guilt over not protecting Kyr from Gauday. But he took a breath and plunged in. "Can you tell me something of what you went through at the fort?"

Kyr let go of Friend and stared at Naran. "Gods and demons! Already?" He started to shake at the mere thought of facing the reality of what he had suffered. Friend whined uneasily, and he gave her a hug. "It's all right, girl. Go play." She licked his face a few times, and he gave her a gentle shove. "Go on, now. Go find your raven." She wagged her tail and bounded off toward the lake. Kyr hunched over and wrapped his arms around himself, trying to stop shaking.

"Take a few deep breaths," Naran said gently.

As Kyr complied, his trembling subsided, and he sat up with his hands clasped tightly in his lap.

"Remember, Kyr, you don't have to talk about anything until you're ready. We will go at a pace you can handle, and can stop whenever you want."

"I don't…. Isn't it too soon?"

"You don't want to carry this pain any longer than you have to, do you?"

"Gods, no," Kyr groaned. "But…. " He sighed and bowed his head. "Alright, Naran-ji. I'll try." He stared down at his clasped hands, noticing distantly how white his knuckles were.

"Good. Now, just start at the beginning and we'll do a little bit every day. How was it when you left the Sanctuary and turned yourself over to Gauday?"

"When I went out that gate, I thought — hoped — I'd be able to go back into the ice." He smiled grimly. "But I couldn't. So I had no refuge from pain anymore."

"I am so sorry, Kyr! We stripped you of your armor, and sent you back into hell. I don't know how you can ever forgive us." Overcome with remorse and sorrow, Naran buried his face in his hands.

Kyr laid a gentle hand on his friend's shoulder. "Naran-ji, we both know it was the only way to protect the Sanctuary." With a faint tinge of pride, he added, "Besides, *you* didn't send me. I *chose* to go. So you see? There's nothing to forgive."

Naran sighed and raised his head. "Thanks, Kyr. You're right, but I...." He shrugged. "Well, never mind. I shouldn't let my feelings get in the way of our work. Shall we go on? I'm ready," he added wryly, "if you are."

Kyr nodded and clenched his hands together in his lap again. "At the Sanctuary, Zhovanya asked me to be Her guardian, but I didn't know what She meant. When Gauday threatened to destroy the Sanctuary unless I turned myself over to him, I knew *that* was what She was asking of me." He smiled crookedly. "I hoped Zhovanya would protect me somehow. When I asked for Her help, She gave me one word of counsel. 'Soften,' She told me."

"That's *all* She gave you?" Naran exclaimed. "What use was that?"

"It was good counsel. Resisting what I had to endure would have only made it worse." He gazed blindly down the row of trees, failing to see the red apples glowing amongst the verdant leaves. "It was hard, keeping to that word She gave me. Sometimes I hated Her for it. But it helped me endure. That and the forgiveness chant kept me from losing myself in hatred or despair. Well, most of the time, anyway."

Naran winced at Kyr's bleak tone. "I'm so sorry."

Kyr glanced at his Aithané with a slight smile. "Zhovanya's gift of counsel wasn't my only defense. I had all the healing and lessons that you and Jolanya gave me at the Sanctuary, and I knew Zhovanya's forgiveness and love. It took me a while, but I finally realized what an advantage that gave me."

"Advantage?"

"Yes. Gauday only knew the Soul-Drinker's vicious path of rage and cruelty. I know the reality of healing, kindness, friendship, and love. I have received Zhovanya's forgiveness. These were my *true* shields against Gauday's madness, not the false protection of anger and hatred." Kyr gently blew a small red bug off his arm and watched it fly away. He sighed and returned his gaze to his tightly clasped hands. "But gods be my witness, it was still...difficult."

The two men sat silently for a few moments. Kyr felt his scars pulsing faintly, and took some deep breaths, trying to keep calm. Then he went on. "Without all these gifts, I'd have been quickly lost in Gauday's madness. What he did to me was so familiar, so much like what I grew up with in the Soul-Drinker's hell."

"What was that like, being at the mercy of Gauday's madness?"

"Mercy? Ha!" Naran's question ignited a burning ball of fury in Kyr's core, and he snarled, "What do you *think*, Naran-ji? His men were crude and brutal, and did everything they could to debase and humiliate me. Gauday was more subtle and vicious." His scars flared up, pulsing raggedly. "Merciless gods! Why are you making me look at all this, when I've just gotten to this haven? Can't I have a moment's respite?"

Hot-eyed, he jumped up with clenched fists, wanting to punch Naran; but he knew that his scars and the smoke-beast were pushing him toward madness. Calling on his iron discipline, he stalked off down the aisle of trees.

Naran frowned, alarmed that Kyr's eyes had turned red; but let him go, sensing that Kyr needed time alone.

Kyr paced up and down the orchard for a while before coming to a stop, and stood rubbing his aching head. Then he shook himself, took some slow deep breaths, and deliberately relaxed his tight fists and shoulders, working to calm his scars and regain control. At last he walked back to Naran and sat down under the old apple tree, facing his Aithané.

Naran breathed a sigh of relief. Kyr's eyes had returned to their usual topaz brown. "Um, Kyr, did you know your eyes turned red just now?"

"Oh, gods, did they? Gauday's eyes did that when he used the scrap of sorcery he got when the smoke from the Soul-Drinker's Crown invaded him. He used it to inflict pain on others' heads. Made your brain feel like it was being burned and twisted." With a grimace of disgust, he added, "And now that cursed smoke is in *me*." Then he paled with shock. "Merciless gods! Did I hurt you like that, Naran-ji?"

"No. I'm fine." Naran had many questions but kept them to himself. Kyr had enough to deal with at the moment.

"Thank the Goddess!" Kyr shook his head. "This is bad news. I don't want to hurt anyone. I've got to stay calm so the smoke-beast and my curse-scars don't get stirred up."

"What do you need right now, Kyr?"

Kyr closed his eyes and took a couple of calming breaths. "Let's chant for a while."

Naran nodded, and began. "Zhovanya naralo, Zhovanya naralo, Zhovanya naralo." Kyr joined in, his voice husky and low. As they sang on, Kyr felt a gentle flow of serenity quieting his scars. After a while, he let the chant go, and they sat together in silence. Kyr focused on the warmth of the sunshine, the slightly rotten sweetness perfuming the air from fallen apples missed by the gleaners, the rustle of the apple trees' withering leaves.

"Alright, Kyr, do you want to continue?"

"Let me try to finish giving you the summary of what happened. I want to get that over with." Kyr took a breath and shrugged to loosen his tight shoulders. "At first, Gauday kept me chained to the whipping post in the courtyard. I was fair game for anything the ex-Slaves wanted to do to me, as long as it didn't seriously damage or kill me. 'No whips, no knives,' Gauday said. He even banished Viro for breaking those rules."

"What did this Viro do to you?"

"Beat me with a flail. That got me a few blessed days in the infirmary." Kyr shook his head. "So strange. Even though he hated me, Viro did me two favors."

"Two?"

"Viro is the one who led Rajani to the fort."

"Ha! Bless the god of unintended consequences."

"Never heard of that one." Kyr's brief smile flickered out and he went on, his hands gripping each other, his words fast and clipped, his voice a bleak monotone. "You see, for the first few months, Gauday let the Slaves do his dirty work, while pretending to pity me and doing me little kindnesses. When that didn't work, he locked me in a lightless cell for a long time. I very nearly went mad. Only the chant saved me from despair. Later, he chained me up outside again, and one night he left me out in a storm. I got so cold...." Kyr shivered. "I got very sick, lost faith in Zhovanya, in everything and everyone."

He fell silent, his nails making bloody crescents on the back of his clasped hands, but then forced himself to go on. "Gauday waited until I was begging the Dark Lady for death. Then he promised to 'protect' me, took me into his own quarters. I was glad to be indoors and warm, eat decent food, even allowed to wear clothes. Then he started in...."

Kyr choked to a stop as his scars flared up again, pulsing and burning viciously. He found himself becoming aroused. "Merciless gods!" He hit the ground with both fists in disgust. "I can't do this, I can't!"

"What's happening, Kyr? We've been through a lot together. You know you can tell me anything."

"My scars are driving me mad!"

"What scars? Why...?"

"Curse it!" Kyr tore off his tunic, and Naran stared in shock at the livid scars patterning Kyr's torso. They were engorged, a dark purplish-red, and pulsing slightly in a most disturbing way. "Gods and demons, Kyr!"

"Talking about all this is stirring up the spell Gauday cast on me. It makes these damn scars flare up...." Kyr groaned as the scars pulsed savagely. Gritting his teeth, he dragged his tunic back on. "Rajani is going to do a cleansing ritual for me soon. If it succeeds, my scars and the smoke will no longer bother me. I'll be able to talk about all this, then."

"Alright," Naran said reluctantly. "I'm here anytime you want to talk about anything. You can wake me in the middle of the night, just like at the Sanctuary."

Kyr nodded and, calling for Friend, fled back to the flower gardens, where he lost himself in ripping out weeds as if they were his tormentors.

Naran remained standing in shock and confusion. *Goddess, this is so much worse than I imagined. What did Gauday do to him? How did that smoke from the Crown get into Kyr?* Lost in a swarm of questions and fears, he trudged over to the penitents' house, and entered their simple chapel to pray for help and guidance.

Chapter Eight

Lost

Deep in the night, Kyr awoke. Something wasn't right. Tense and wary, he listened for whatever had disturbed him; but all he heard was the usual chorus of frogs and crickets outside the open door to his balcony. Friend slept on peacefully. *Must have been a nightmare, though I don't remember it.* He sighed and relaxed, and then he heard it.

"Kyr, Kyr."

"Dekani!" Instantly, Kyr found himself outside the cottage, and hurried in to Dekani's bedside. His teacher's skin was nearly translucent and drawn tightly over his bones, his eyes filmy, his changeable, shining robes gone dark and dull.

Dekani quavered, *"My son, it is time to say good-bye. I've done all I can."*

"Oh, gods, Dekani! So soon?"

"You must get Rajani to do the cleansing immediately. Promise?"

"Yes."

"Promise me one more thing: stay here in Ravenvale until it's all over, no matter what."

His heart heavy as stone, Kyr bowed his head, tears trickling down his cheeks. *"I promise."*

Dekani gave a great sigh as if an onerous burden had been lifted from his soul. *"I am so proud of you."* The old man's voice sank to a whisper. *"Forgive me."*

"Forgive you? For what? For helping me so much?" But there was no answer. A strong, golden light swirled up, and a deep sound reverberated through Kyr, blinding and deafening him. Yet he thought he heard Zhovanya whisper, *"WELCOME, BELOVED!"*

When Kyr could see and hear again, there remained no trace of Dekani, and the cottage was fading away. In the next instant, he was back in his room on his bed. Too stunned to cry, he curled up around Friend's sleep-heavy body

91

and hugged her to him. She settled against his chest with a gusty sigh, smacking her tongue sleepily. But her warmth couldn't touch the icy void in his heart. He stared thoughtless and dry-eyed into the darkness. Once and again, he tried to go back to Dekani's cottage, but the way there would not open. His life-long refuge and protector were gone.

Without Dekani's protection, Kyr's scars pounded in a malevolent rhythm, and surges of hatred, lust, vengefulness, and despair swirled through the emptiness in his mind. But grief and loneliness outweighed them all, crushing him to the bed, sending him crashing down into a black pit of nothingness.

The next morning, Rajani lounged on his favorite couch in the parlor, enjoying the warmth of the fire crackling in the hearth, sipping hot spiced tea and relishing its aroma of cinnamon and cloves. Rather than hurrying through breakfast and rushing off to deal with some problem or decision, he was waiting for Kyr to show up. At last the demands upon his attention had settled down, and he felt he could leave the estate in Bru's capable hands for a while.

He finished his tea, and rose to pace back and forth by the tall windows. A strong breeze sent white-cap waves dancing across the dark blue lake, while puffy clouds scudded by above, their shadows racing over fields and cliffs. "Where is Kyr?" Rajani muttered. "He's never been this late." With a worried frown, he stood still, closed his eyes, and murmured, "Ganarali ya zhanto Kyr."

"Gods and demons!" He dashed out of the parlor, took the stairs two at a time, and knocked on Kyr's door. Friend started barking, sounding distressed, but Kyr made no response.

The door was locked. Rajani snapped, "Kaa'a-tay!" The door swung open and he went in. Friend wriggled loose from Kyr's grasp and ran to the Warrior Mage, whining anxiously. He hurried to Kyr's bedside. "Kyr, what's wrong?"

Kyr lay staring at nothing. He looked devastated, as cold and stiff as he had when they'd first rescued him from the Soul-Drinker's hell. Remembering what it had taken to get Kyr to respond back then, Rajani commanded, "Tell me what's happening, right now."

Kyr blinked, focused on Rajani, and groaned, "Merciless gods." Strange colors swam in his eyes, and he began shaking. "The cleansing," he croaked. "Now!"

"But I have to prepare." Rajani sputtered in dismay. "I can't just...."

"NOW!"

Kyr's desperation shocked Rajani into action. "Goddess help us! Alright, we'll do it at noon, when the Sun is at Her strongest. Can you make it until then?"

"Get Medari." Kyr closed his eyes and grabbed his upper arms, digging his nails into his flesh.

Rajani turned and found Naran standing at Kyr's door, looking concerned. "What can I do to help?"

"Stay with Kyr. I have to find Medari, and take Friend to the stables until this is over." He headed for the door, commanding, "Come, Friend." Reluctantly, she followed him.

Naran stepped into the room, and closed the door. Feeling menaced, he glanced around. Seeing nothing unusual, he hurried to Kyr's side. "What is it? Those scars?"

"Out of control," Kyr grated. He clenched his jaw shut and squeezed his eyes tight against the bloody illusion of Naran as sacrifice, as prey. Struggling against the sickening malevolence assaulting his mind, Kyr could barely keep from attacking his friend.

"What can I do?"

"Chant."

Naran grabbed a chair and began the chant. "Zhovanya naralo, Zhovanya naralo." The threatening atmosphere in the room increased, and an ominous force tightened his throat until he could barely sing. Frowning, he called on his faith and strength, and changed the chant, calling on Zhovanya for guidance and protection. "Zhovanya dagantalo, Zhovanya ganaralo. Zhovanya dagantalo, Zhovanya ganaralo." Slowly, the menacing force began to ebb, and he sang in a stronger voice. It ebbed further, until he could sing full-voiced.

But Kyr still lay curled up in a tight ball, moaning. "ohgods, ohgods, ohgods." With all his strength, Naran begged — no, commanded — Zhovanya to shield Kyr's mind. "Zhovanya da'agantaloro ya Kyr!" Drained, he fell silent. And so too was the room — too silent. Naran's eyes snapped open. "Kyr? What's happening?"

Kyr lay in a slumped huddle. "Oh gods, no!" Naran breathed.

The door flew open. Medari barged in with his healer's kit. Quickly, he examined Kyr and checked his pulses.

"Is he still alive?" Naran asked, his heart thumping erratically.

"Yes. What are his symptoms?" Medari demanded.

"Let's talk over here." Naran drew the healer across the room and quietly described what he'd witnessed and experienced.

"He relaxed when you asked Zhovanya to shield his mind? That means this is due to the smoke-beast or his curse-scars, or, gods help him, both." Medari grabbed his kit, set it on the table by the window, and began mixing a potion.

The Warrior Mage strode into the room, tensed for disaster or battle. "What's happening?"

Naran again explained, and added, "Medari is making him a potion now."

With Naran and Rajani to help, the healer got the potion down the unconscious Kyr's throat. After a few moments, Kyr opened his eyes and whispered, "That's a little better. Thanks."

"Kyr, I have to go prepare for the cleansing now. Naran and Medari will stay with you. Hold on." Kyr nodded once, and closed his eyes. Rajani glanced at the other two men and rushed off.

With Medari's potions and Naran's steady support, Kyr managed to cling to his sanity as he battled the tides of unbridled evil surging through him.

At noon, sunshine blazed through the grand chapel's circular window, making the goldstone altar glow as if it held a spark of the sun itself. Reflections off the rippling lake danced over the alabaster walls and ceiling, and sparkled on the silver stars of the dark floor, filling every corner with light.

On the chapel's night-sky floor, twelve moon-shaped white candles on round silver salvers formed a large circle. At each of the cardinal points, Kyr's four friends stood barefoot, wearing full-length robes: young Devanyi in the East, wearing the rose-gold of dawn and Spring; Naran in the South, in the leaf-patterned green of noon and Summer; Luciya in the West, in the deep amethyst of evening and Autumn; and Medari, the eldest, in the North, wearing the midnight-blue of night and Winter.

Ylana, the Ritual Mage, occupied the center of the circle, in a shimmering white gown embroidered with golden suns and silver moons. She held a golden bowl and her goldenwood wand. Beside her stood the Warrior Mage, his raven-dark hair flowing loose over his shoulders. A sleeveless black robe patterned with silver arrows and golden swords revealed his muscular arms. Around his upper arms, he wore gold and silver armlets embedded with fiery opalescent gems. He faced the altar, his arms raised with his blackwood wand lying across his palms, allowing the wand to drink in the golden sunshine.

Fists clenched, head down, Kyr stood before the altar, wearing only a loincloth, his engorged purplish scars pulsing and burning with relentless agony. Shivering and twitching, he gritted his teeth to keep from moaning. He stared unseeingly at the floor, unable to look at his friends. With the madness of the Soul-Drinker's smoke-beast swirling in his mind, his own friends looked to him like wild-eyed demons leering and sneering at him. Only by fiercely focusing on the soothing warmth radiating from the golden altar behind him and the coolness of the stone floor under his feet could he keep from attacking them or fleeing.

"Kyr, please join me here," Rajani said.

The smoke-beast howled, and Kyr found himself turning to run from the chapel. "No!" he growled. Rajani looked at him in alarm. Kyr turned back and forced himself toward the center of the circle. Fighting for every shambling step, sweaty and trembling, he reached Rajani's side.

Ylana said quietly, "Kyr, you must remain within the circle, no matter how difficult it may be. To break the circle before the cleansing is complete puts all our lives at risk. Are you ready?" Kyr gave her a stiff nod. Then she glanced around the circle. "Everyone, you also must remain in the circle no matter what, and follow my instructions exactly." Devanyi nodded, looking frightened but determined. Somberly, Naran, Luciya and Medari also nodded.

Ylana tapped her golden bowl with her wand, and a beautiful tone rang out. When its reverberations died away, she began to chant, "Zhovanya dagantalo, Zhovanya ganaralo," and the others joined in. Amplified by the vaulted ceiling, their blended voices filled the chapel with rich harmonies.

For Kyr, it was agony. His scars pounded an antagonistic rhythm, and he could barely hear over the howling of the smoke-beast within. Singing was impossible. He clamped his jaw and sealed his lips to keep in the screams and curses filling his mind, and silently, desperately, repeated the chant, begging Zhovanya for help. Yet in his heart, he knew this torment was part of the tempering She required if he was to be Her Vessel. And no help came.

Ylana raised her hand to bring the chant to a close. After a few moments of silence, she spoke in slow cadence, her voice echoing with power. "Allow yourself to be as solid and steady as the cold stone under your feet. Send your zhan down deep in the Earth to the bedrock beneath us. Feel the patient, abiding strength of Earth and Stone. Let that strength flow upward, filling your bones." She aimed her goldenwood wand downward, and commanded, "Inorulo."

A flow of strength and substance rose from the Earth into Kyr's bones, filling him with steadfast resolve and courage, and giving him the strength to force back the smoke-beast and quiet his scars. He straightened and settled more solidly onto his feet.

Then Ylana spoke in a lighter tone and quicker pace. "Allow yourself to be as clear and pure as Air. Pay attention to your breath. Breathe in through your entire skin. Let the air touch you, flow into you. Breathe out from your whole body, and release all thoughts, all fears, all distractions. Send your mind soaring into the vastness of the sky. Let its limpid purity and spaciousness fill you with serenity." Raising her wand above her head, she commanded, "A'averalo."

Kyr didn't dare breathe deeply for fear of setting off the smoke-beast and his curse-scars. Instead, he focused on memories of his soulkin, the Eagle, soaring on the winds above the earth. Longing for the Eagle's freedom filled his heart, and fired his determination to be free of these last remnants of the evil sorcery that had plagued him for so long. But the pulsing of his scars grew so strong that he dug his nails into his forearms, and had to fight not to tear off his own skin.

Ylana resumed in a quieter, more fluid tone, "Be as fluid and vital as Water. Pay attention to your heartbeat. Feel the life-blood flowing in your veins. Send your mind flowing with the streams and rivers, lakes and seas that nurture the earth, bringing life everywhere. Feel the power of Water that wears away all obstacles, that brings cleansing and renewal. Let the life-giving force of water move you to the rhythm of hearts filled with grace and strength." She waved her wand in a flowing way, and began chanting, "Laralalo."

In the wavering, watery light of the chapel, the Warrior Mage began to move in a slow, powerful dance, and his four assistants started dancing around the circle, each to their own heartbeat. Kyr stood frozen, his scars pounding a heavy rhythm that shook his whole body and drowned out his heart's true tempo. His friends seemed like evil enchanters dancing his death.

He closed his eyes against the terrible illusion, and began to silently repeat the chant that had saved his soul and sanity so many times: *Zhovanya naralo, Zhovanya naralo, Zhovanya naralo.* Though the smoke-beat howled and his scars flared, he focused ferociously on the chant, shutting out all else. *Zhovanya naralo, Zhovanya naralo, Zhovanya naralo.* And then he began to sway slightly to his own heart's rhythm.

Together the Warrior Mage and his four helpers wove an invisible pattern of grace and flow around the circle. Now Kyr sensed Water flowing within him, soothing the fires of the smoke-beast and his curse-scars. Slowly his rigid body softened, and he heaved a deep sigh of relief. The dance came to a natural close and, for a few moments, they stood in silence.

Then Ylana continued. "Let us all be as ardent and potent as Fire, which gives us light in the darkness, warmth against the cold. Feel the warmth of your own body, sense the Fire that burns in your core: the Fire of your will to live, to love, to laugh. Let its brilliance fill your spirit with joy and faith." She raised her wand high and waved it in a circle. "Shaiyalo!"

Reddish-gold flames burst to life on the white candles, growing taller and taller — far beyond the reach of an ordinary candle flame — and the golden altar glowed more brightly. Luciya, Rajani, and even Medari smiled, while Devanyi and Naran laughed with delight as the flames danced, shaping themselves into slender trees, women, or firebirds. But Kyr broke into a sweat, his curse-scars blazing up with frantic brutality. It took all his strength not to scream and he crumpled to the floor, curling up in a knot of agony.

"Dagantalo!" Ylana shouted, pointing her wand at the nearest flame, then waving her wand toward Kyr. The flame broke free of its candle and flew down, spreading wide wings to envelop Kyr. He flinched but instead of burning, the flame felt like a silken caress. Yet its gentle light and warmth were so potent that the pounding of his scars and the howling of the smoke-beast dwindled to a low ebb. Kyr gasped and shook, the relief was so great. Then, with a deep sigh, he stretched out and lay still, just breathing, and recovering his strength.

"Fire, we thank you," said Ylana. "Ji tal." The flame enveloping Kyr flowed back to its candle, and all the flames shrank to their normal height. Ylana stepped out of the circle of moon candles and walked slowly around the circle, chanting, "Vaa'a lan ti," commanding the circle to be whole. When she returned to her starting place before the glowing altar, she said, "The circle is complete. I am its Guardian." And behind her rose an ethereal white egret with wings spread protectively over the ritual circle. Then the Guardian said, "You may begin, Warrior Mage."

Kyr started to get up but, at Rajani's gesture, he remained stretched out in the center of the circle. The Warrior Mage took two large, clear crystals from his green leather satchel with its magical symbols, and placed one on Kyr's chest over his heart, and one on the floor near the crown of Kyr's head.

Looking around the circle, Rajani caught everyone's eye with his intense blue gaze. "I will be sending my spirit into Kyr's inner world, where, Goddess willing, I will uproot Gauday's spell and the remnants of the Soul-Drinker's sorcery, and expel them into this crystal." He pointed to the one on the floor. "You should see it turn smoky, then dark.

"Your duty is to sing this chant: 'Zhovanya dagantalo. Valanera moruba le zhanto.' It means 'Zhovanya protect us. Dissolve the evil that binds this soul.' It empowers and protects Kyr, and me while I am in Kyr's inner realm. Listen to me until you have it, then begin. The four of you must keep this chant going until Kyr and I wake up." He added somberly, "Don't do *anything* else until then, *no matter what happens.*"

Luciya frowned at this, but Rajani gave her a stern glance. She sighed and nodded, as did Naran, Medari, and Devanyi. Then the Warrior Mage began the new chant that empowered this cleansing ritual. After a few repetitions, his four helpers joined in. "Zhovanya dagantalo. Valanera moruba le zhanto."

As soon as they began to chant, Kyr's scars began to flame and pulsate in a hectic, conflicting cadence. Drawing on the strength and steadiness of Earth, he managed to remain still and quiet.

The Warrior Mage fell silent, but his four assistants continued chanting. Quietly murmuring "Zhovanya, ganarali," Rajani began to weave his blackwood wand in an intricate pattern above the crystal resting on Kyr's heart. The crystal began to sparkle, then to hum in thin, high overtones. The eerie crystalline sound swelled to a peak, and Rajani's wand was drawn like a magnet to the apex of the crystal, sending him spiraling into Kyr's inner world.

Fire! There was nothing but fire: sheets of flame contorting and twisting angrily. Pain beat against Rajani's mind in the same demonic tempo, and he could find nothing to hold onto, nothing to stand on, no way to withstand the terrible cadence of agony. Panic surged and instinctively, he called out to the one who had always aided him in such situations. *"Lanir! Help me!"*

Chapter Nine

Cataclysm

A hand reached through the flames and beckoned. Rajani took a step toward the hand. The next instant, he was standing in a meadow, next to a tall figure, dark and indistinct against the writhing and twisting flames that surrounded the meadow at a short distance. *"Gods! Thanks, Lanir! I never expected anything like that!"*

"Who is Lanir?"

An icy shock speared through Rajani at the sound of the familiar voice. *"Kyr? Is that you?"*

"Yes." Kyr frowned suspiciously. *"Who is this Lanir?"*

"Your inner guide, your teacher."

"You mean Dekani?"

"Is that what you call him? Yes, that makes sense: 'Dekani' means teacher. Where is he?"

"He died. How the hells do you know about Dekani?"

"Died!" Rajani gasped. *"When? How?"*

"Just last night. He said his life force was spent. Now tell me how you know about him."

"Gods, Kyr, we'll have to talk about this later. We've got to complete the cleansing."

Kyr crossed his arms over his chest, and the pale sky over the meadow darkened. *"No! Something is going on that you're not telling me. I've wondered before, but now I know it. There's no way you should know about Dekani, but you do."*

"Let's not discuss this now, Kyr," Rajani pleaded. *"I promise I'll tell you what I can after we finish here. You want to be cleansed of the last of the Soul-Drinker's evil, don't you?"*

"Yes. But you must keep your promise afterwards."

"*I will.*" Rajani hastily changed the topic. "*Alright, tell me how the smoke-beast appears in this realm.*"

"*It usually takes the form of fire, as you can see. When challenged, it becomes a huge black dog with blazing red eyes.*"

"*A hell-hound. Goddess help us!*" The Warrior Mage glanced at Kyr. "*If it's in the form of fire, I won't be able to kill it. We have to make it take its beast-form. Since it is after only you, Kyr, I think you need to be the rabbit.*"

"*I lure it out, get it to chase me, and you kill it?*" Kyr frowned. "*Something doesn't feel right.*" He shook his head in frustration, unable to put his finger on what was bothering him. But he shrugged. "*Well, I don't know what else we can do.*"

"*Alright, then. Here's the plan.*"

Rajani was nowhere to be seen. Kyr sat with his head bowed in dejection, mumbling, "*Gods damn Gauday. Hadn't done enough to torment me. Had to go and curse me with these damn scars just as I was getting free of him. How can Zhovanya let these things keep happening to me?*"

As Kyr voiced his doubts, the flames raged up, and his scars began pulsing with agonizing fire. He fell back on the grass, writhing and groaning. The circle of flames narrowed around him, and his scars beat more heavily than ever, sending spikes of pain stabbing into his core. He bolted to his feet and ran toward the flames, screaming like a demented soul, "Gods curse you! Stop tormenting me! Stop it! Stop it!" The flames condensed and blackened — and turned blazing red eyes on him. The hellhound stood as tall as himself — a beast of smoke and flame, yet somehow massive and muscular. It stepped toward him with menace in every movement, its deep growl reverberating clear into Kyr's bones.

Every instinct told Kyr to run. And his mind, too, insisted that he keep to the plan and lure the hellhound toward Rajani. But something kept him frozen where he was.

He closed his eyes, closed out the hellhound, closed out the pulsing agony of his scars, prayed for his Goddess's help, and *listened.* Zhovanya whispered one word. "*LOVE.*"

Kyr sat down and began to chant. "*Zhovanya naralo, Zhovanya naralo, Zhovanya naralo.*" The black dog jumped back and stood snarling and slavering. Kyr continued to chant. The hound lunged forward, growling, and snapped its jagged fangs at Kyr's head.

"*NO!*" The Warrior Mage started to run toward Kyr.

But Kyr held up a hand to stop him. "Look *at it, Rajani. It's not touching me. Give me a moment more.*"

With great effort, Rajani stood still, trembling with battle fury, while Kyr returned to chanting. *"Zhovanya naralo, Zhovanya naralo, Zhovanya naralo."*

The hound shook its head and pawed at its ears, whining and snarling. *"Zhovanya naralo, Zhovanya naralo, Zhovanya naralo."* The hellhound glared at Kyr with baffled red eyes and paced back and forth, its head weaving in frustration. Rajani stood glowering, doubtful and uncertain; but then his face cleared, and he began chanting in harmonious counterpoint, *"Zhovanya, valanera moruba le zhanto. Dissolve the evil that binds this soul."*

Kyr opened his arms to this furious, confused creature and began singing, *"Zhovanya loves you. Go home to Her. Zhovanya loves you. Go home to Her."* The hellhound howled, a piercing, heart-breaking sound of agony and longing. As the two men kept singing, the dim light of the fire surrounding the meadow slowly began to brighten and soften from angry red to gentle gold.

The hellhound looked over its shoulder, gave a joyful bark, and took off running toward the golden light that now surrounded the meadow. As the black dog ran, it shredded into many wisps of smoke, all rushing toward the golden light, and dissolving into it.

No trace remained of hellhound, baleful flame, or smoke. The golden light coalesced into a sun shining down gently upon the flowery meadow that now spread out all around them. Birds began to swoop and sing, bees to fly and hum.

Kyr looked at his friend with a luminous smile, his eyes glowing with golden radiance. *"They are free."*

"Who?"

"The souls of those who were sacrificed to create the Soul-Drinker's sorcerous Crown."

"Ah. Kyr, you have astonished me again. Sitting there with that beast! How did you know to do that?"

"As always, it was Zhovanya. She gave me a word of counsel."

"That must be a very powerful word!"

"It is." Kyr met Rajani's eyes, his gaze still golden. *"The word She gave me was LOVE."*

"That's all? And with that, you faced down a hellhound," Rajani said in amazement. *"You are wise and brave — a warrior of the soul."*

Kyr's eyes dimmed to topaz, and he shook his head. *"I'd still be a Slave or dead, if not for you — and the Goddess."*

"Zhovanya guides us all, despite our wishes," Rajani laughed wryly.

Kyr raised an eyebrow at the edge in his friend's tone. *He sounds bitter toward Zhovanya for some reason. Why? What is he hiding?* Kyr was about to demand answers from Rajani, but the Warrior Mage said, *"Well, that's not all*

101

we have to do. We still have to break Gauday's curse, and silence those damn scars. How are they, now that the smoke-beast is gone?"

"I still feel them pulsing, but they are a lot weaker."

"Perhaps I can break the curse now." Rajani stood up, drew his wand, and commanded, "Ta'a Kor!" Instantly, he was holding a silver sword. With another command, "Shai'ya!", his sword began to shine with a red radiance.

"Gods, Rajani!" Kyr groaned. *"Stop!"*

"By all the hells! Why?"

"My scars are flaring up badly. Please stop!"

Reluctantly, Rajani said, *"Ji Tal,"* and now held his blackwood wand again.

"Gods. That was bad." Kyr panted with relief as his scars subsided. After a moment, he added, *"My scars flare up when I see or feel anger, fear, pain, or violence — whether in my memory or in reality."*

"I see. Attacking the curse will only strengthen it. We'll have to find another way." Rajani thought for a while, then asked, *"How was this curse made?"*

"I am not sure. Give me a few moments." Kyr sought for the serenity to cast his mind back to the time he had suffered so much. But the mere thought of doing so inflamed his scars. *Merciless gods! Will I ever be cleansed of this torment? I can't live like this!* His fear and anger only inflamed his scars further. He groaned and clawed his nails into his forearms. *"Goddess, help me,"* he pleaded. *"Please! Help me see how to free myself from Gauday's corruption, from his curse."*

And then, with a feather touch to his eyes, Zhovanya blessed him with the cool detachment of and clear vision of his soulkin, Eagle. Dispassionately, Kyr examined what Gauday had done to him as it unfolded in his mind's eye.

After a time, he sighed and opened his eyes. *"What Gauday used to make this curse was pain and seduction, pleasure and domination. Underneath all his rage and cruelty, he was blindly seeking love in the only way he knew."*

"That means we will have to undo Gauday's curse with love, just as you did with the Soul-Drinker's sorcery, doesn't it?"

Kyr frowned doubtfully. *"But in that case, I knew the smoke-beast was made of souls in torment, just as the Soul-Drinker's Rod and Collar were. Those souls were desperate to be free and to move on to whatever awaited them next. When I executed Gauday, I saw a brief flash of joy in his eyes just as he died. Didn't his soul move on, then?"*

"It can't — not completely: part of his soul is invested in this curse. But I'm not sure how to proceed."

"Let's ask Zhovanya." Kyr smiled. *"She helped me with the smoke-beast. Maybe She'll help us now."* He settled into meditation pose and began. *"Zhovanya ganaralo, Zhovanya ganaralo, Zhovanya ganaralo."* Rajani quickly joined in.

When Kyr reached a state of receptive tranquility, he placed both hands on the grass-covered ground in front of him. *"Zhovanya, please show us how to end the curse Gauday laid on me. Take this burden off Gauday's soul, and free me from the torment and corruption this curse causes me."* Kyr fell silent and bowed his head, waiting. Rajani sat watching, envying the depth of the younger man's connection with the Goddess.

After a few moments, Kyr looked up, smiling, and again his eyes glowed with a golden light. *"Zhovanya, narali. I forgive him. I forgive Gauday."* Then he nodded to Rajani.

Rajani couldn't choke out those words, at first. He took a deep breath, and whispered, *"Zhovanya ganarali."* The cool green of the meadow cleared his mind, and compassion touched his heart. For the first time, he could see Gauday not as his enemy but as just another of the dark innocents corrupted and twisted by the Soul-Drinker. He smiled. *"Zhovanya, narali. I forgive Gauday."*

And then, with clear mind and compassionate heart, the Warrior Mage knew what to do. He turned to sit facing Kyr. With his wand, he conjured a sphere of blue-green light between himself and Kyr, and commanded, *"Ravalo, ya zhanto abaharo. Ravalo da libaralo. Come forth, lost soul. Come forth, and be free."*

A shapeless darkness appeared in the turquoise light, writhing from side to side, seeking escape.

"Ravalo, ya zhanto abaharo. Ravalo da libaralo."

The darkness took shape as Gauday's tormented face, his mouth open in a silent wail.

"Narali," Kyr declared firmly. *"I forgive you."*

"Narali," said Rajani gently. *"Naralai. We forgive you."*

As they softly chanted *"Naralai, Naralai, Naralai,"* the dark remnant of Gauday's soul grew quiet and still. Slowly, its agonized grimace became a look of sadness, and relief. *"Kaa'a ta lak!"* it mouthed. The blue-green light flared, blinding the two men for a few moments.

When they could see again, there was no sign of Gauday's dark soul, nor the sphere of blue-green fire.

Kyr jumped up, blazing with joy. *"He broke the curse! It's gone!"*

"How can you tell?" Rajani got to his feet more slowly, looking pale and drawn.

"I feel so clean! Ever since Gauday cursed me, it felt like a slimy worm was crawling around in my brain, slithering in my gut. I couldn't quite notice it before, but now that it is gone, I can clearly feel the difference. It was there and now it is gone. Thanks to you and the Goddess!"

"What about your scars?"

"Look!" Kyr held out his arms. His scars were no longer the engorged purple they had been, but simply the slightly ridged red of old scars. He shouted jubilantly, *"I'm finally free!"* Clapping his hands over his head, he began to stamp and leap around the meadow. Laughing, Rajani joined in his dance of victory and joy.

After a few moments, they both sank to the ground, smiling but exhausted. Rajani heaved a sigh. *"Gods, I'm worn out."* The cleansing had drained both of them nearly empty. He stretched out and closed his eyes.

Kyr sat quietly, warily sensing inside for any sign of the curses he'd been under for so long. He found no trace of either the Soul-Drinker's sorcery nor of Gauday's curse. Eagerly, he thought, *I've got to tell Dekani the good news. He can rest now.* But a cold tide of sadness swept over him, as he recalled that he could never tell Dekani anything again.

And then that cold tide turned to fire.

"Wake up, Rajani!" Kyr snarled.

"What?" The Warrior Mage looked up, bleary-eyed.

"Tell me how you know about Dekani."

"Gods, Kyr, not now. I need a few days to recover. We'll talk after that."

Kyr took a firm grip on his anger. *"Tell me one thing, Rajani. Have I earned your respect?"*

"Of course. You have shown extraordinary courage and endurance...."

"Then why won't you tell me the truth? Who was Dekani, whom you call 'Lanir'? What do you have to do with him? Who are you?"

"I'm sorry," Rajani choked out. The oath bind was nearly strangling him.

"Gods damn it!" Kyr growled, his voice low and furious. *"All this time, I thought you were my friend. But now I can tell that you know things about me that I don't know."* He loomed over Rajani, suddenly large and menacing. *"Tell me what you're hiding!"*

"No," Rajani croaked.

"TELL ME!" Kyr grabbed him by the shoulders, determined to shake the truth out of him. At this contact — soul to soul, with no barriers of flesh, no mental masks — all boundaries dissolved, and memories poured from each mind to the other.

"Ka'a ta lak!" the Warrior Mage cried with the last of his strength, breaking their connection.

In the chapel, an ominous wildness surged up, filling the ritual circle. Rajani's two large crystals began to whine, the pitch going higher and higher.

With a sudden sharp scream, they shattered, sending tiny shards flying in every direction. Naran, Medari, Luciya, and Devanyi gasped and jumped back, breaking off the chant. "Goddess, help us!" Luciya exclaimed.

Fitful breezes tugged at their hair and clothes. The candle flames flickered wildly. Waves crashed against the windows, and even the earth beneath the chapel trembled.

"What's happening?" demanded Medari, starting toward Kyr and Rajani, who were lying in the center of the circle, still as death.

"Halt!" commanded Ylana. "The Elements we invoked are out of control. We have to end the ritual as properly as we can. Quickly, get back in your positions." They all stepped back into their places around the circle of moon candles.

"Alright, everyone repeat after me: Powers of Earth, Air, Water, and Fire, we apologize for the disruption. Naralo."

"Powers of Earth, Air, Water and Fire, we apologize for the disruption. Naralo."

"Depart to your homes with our thanks. Ganaralo vida!"

"Depart with our thanks. Ganaralo vida!"

"Kaa'a-tay!" Ylana tapped her golden bowl with her wand three times. The tones resonated throughout the chapel, dissipating the baleful tension that had filled the room, and she declared, "The circle is open." Her soulkin, Egret, could no longer be seen. For a moment, everyone stood frozen, stunned by all that had just happened.

Then Ylana shook herself and bent down to blow out the round white candles, and gestured for the others to do likewise. By the time the last one was snuffed out, the chaotic breezes had dispersed, the lake was calm, and the earth was still again. The altar no longer glowed like a small sun. Ylana set her wand and bowl on it, and sat down on the edge of the dais, pale and trembling. "That was a near thing," she whispered, wiping her brow. "I must go rest. Tend to your friends." She got to her feet and made her way back into Ravenhall.

Medari quickly knelt beside Kyr's motionless body and shook him by the shoulder. "Kyr? Wake up!" There was no response. Frowning, the healer took hold of Kyr's wrist and felt his pulses. "Kyr's alive, but his zhan is weak and erratic."

Devanyi looked up from checking Rajani's pulses, her face pale. "Yes, Rajani too."

"Luciya," Medari commanded, "we need stretchers to get them to their rooms." Luciya nodded and headed back into Ravenhall to summon help. Medari, Devanyi, and Naran gathered around the two fallen men.

Devanyi wrapped her fingers around Rajani's wrist, and pressed inward. "Tenaiya taught me this. It may help stabilize their energy." Medari did the same for Kyr. Naran knelt by Kyr and placed his hand over Kyr's heart, quietly singing, "Zhovanya naralo. Zhovanya naralo."

They all knew better than to speak their fears aloud when near unconscious patients, so they said little. While they waited, Medari tended to the small cuts everyone had from the flying shards of the two crystals. Soon Luciya returned with four strong men and two stretchers.

Part Four ~ Baleful Truth

"Someone I once loved gave me a box full of darkness.
It took me years to understand that
this, too, was a gift."

— Mary Oliver

Chapter Ten

Star-Cursed

"**K**yr, wake up *now*," Medari pleaded. "I love you, son. Don't leave me!"

Kyr fought against the light, the glaring, vicious light. Stabbing flashes of memories not his own tumbled through his mind: a circle of stones, dark against a flaming sky; a nude, shining woman; guttural chanting; a sword slashing down; Luciya weeping; Dekani....

"NO!" He shouted himself awake.

"Kyr! You're with us. Thank all the gods!"

"NO! NO!" Kyr stared around wildly, and struggled to get up. Medari set a restraining hand on his shoulder. "What's wrong, son?"

"NO! Oh gods, no!" Kyr struck Medari's hand away, sending the healer reeling back, wide-eyed.

Naran hastened forward. "Let *me* deal with Kyr," he said. "Luciya and Devanyi need help with Rajani." And he quickly steered Medari toward the door. The healer started to object, but the harsh sound of Rajani's agonized scream sent him rushing to his room next door.

Naran pulled a chair up to Kyr's bedside. "I'm here, Kyr. You're safe in Ravenhall. Try to calm down, now. I'm here. Look at me."

The familiar, kindly voice gave Kyr an anchor in the maelstrom. His eyes clung to Naran's. "N-Naran-ji?"

"Yes. Can you tell me what's going on?"

"Rajani...I saw... Merciless gods, no!" Kyr turned over and buried his face in his pillow, trying to not think, not feel. *Oh gods, if only I could find the ice!* He tried desperately to bury himself in his old blank numbness, but the swirling memories fell relentlessly into place, bringing many mysteries into horrifying clarity. He wanted to scream but he couldn't take in a breath, couldn't move. It took all his strength just to fend off the pain of truth.

"Kyr, do *not* do this," Naran said sharply. "Don't cut yourself off from me now. You clearly need help with whatever happened in that chapel. You know it will only get worse until you tell me."

"Worse?" Kyr choked. "Oh gods, worse!" His half-crazed cackling tore at the air. He glared at Naran. "*Nothing* could be worse than what I found out from Rajani. And," he added spitefully, "I hope he enjoys what he got from *me*."

"Gods and demons, Kyr! What *happened*?" Even the usually unshakable Naran was aghast at the change in Kyr.

"I *told* you the gods are merciless!' Kyr snarled. "Stay away from me." Throwing himself off his bed, he shoved Naran aside and bolted out of the room, heedless of Naran crashing down and striking his head on the stone floor.

Next door, in Rajani's room, the Warrior Mage screamed and thrashed on his bed. Medari dug frantically through his satchel, searching for a tranquilizing potion, while Devanyi and Luciya struggled to keep Rajani from hurting himself. To get the powerful sedative down the tormented man's throat, Medari had to clasp Rajani's head with both hands, while Luciya lay across his chest to keep him still, and Devanyi dribbled the potion bit by bit into his mouth, then clamped her hand over his mouth and nose until he swallowed. It was a long, exhausting process.

When the Warrior Mage at last went slack and silent, they all collapsed, panting and terrified. They huddled together in Rajani's room as they waited for Naran to report back to them on Kyr's condition, speculating about what had gone so terribly wrong. But Rajani, drugged into insensibility, could tell them nothing.

Like a wounded animal, Kyr sprinted down the stairs, out the main doors, and across the courtyard, dodging residents' surprised questions and reaching hands as he raced heedlessly away from Ravenhall. On and on he ran, until a painful stitch in his side brought him to a halt. Gasping for breath, he bent over, hands on his knees. When the pain eased, he straightened up to find that his feet had taken him to the penitents' house.

At this time of day, all the prisoners, including the penitents, were at work in the fields. Trembling and nauseated, Kyr staggered inside, desperate for a place to hide. The kitchen was too public, and the chapel seemed like a cruel joke, so he trudged upstairs into the dim, quiet dormitory, flung himself down on Craith's bedroll, and curled into a hard, tight ball. Arms wrapped tightly around himself, he rocked back and forth, as he had long ago during his vicious training to become a Slave of the Soul-Drinker, now feeling as bereft and forsaken as that small boy.

All he wanted was oblivion, and he tried desperately to block out the foreign memories that had invaded his mind when he had grabbed the Warrior Mage in the inner realm. Now he knew why Dekani had always forbidden any touch in that realm. But it was too late: he couldn't stop the flood of Rajani's memories from engulfing him.

No matter what, the Soul-Drinker had to be destroyed before he sucked the life out of the people, their soulkin, and the land. And now it was clear that the demands of the Star-Seer's Prophecy could no longer be avoided. Rajani passionately hated this foretelling that ruled his life; yet he was responsible to ensure that the damned Prophecy was fulfilled. And, like it or loath it, the oath-bind would ensure that he did.

He had fought for years to find another way, as they all had. But they had failed; he had failed. The Circle had tried everything, sacrificing many people in vain. No one could get through the Soul-Drinker's sorcerous defenses, not even the best mind-masker. When assassins had managed to get past the tyrant's red-eyed Watchers, the Soul-Drinker had always detected them, and laughed while he slowly tortured them to death. Despite all their efforts, the Circle had come to the very point they had tried so hard to avoid.

They would have to resort to what they despised most — black magic — and now they had it. From far across the Sand Sea, Lavilya had returned, wild-eyed and raving. At nearly the cost of her sanity, she had brought them the terrible ritual and the sorcerous oil that would make this deadly magic work. Two sacrifices were required. Lanir had volunteered — and indeed, he was the best choice: a Healer Mage and an excellent mind-masker. Brave Alytha, their strongest mind-masker, had volunteered to be the vessel.

And now, there was no more time. The most stalwart men and women of the Circle had gathered on a clifftop far north of the Soul-Drinker's lair to carry out the despicable ritual. The Firebird spread its starry wings across the top of the heavens, and the Dire Cross was almost complete. Six of the seven Wanderers were in position. This pattern occurred only once in a thousand years. If the star-cursed babe was to be born, the ritual had to take place this night. In another thousand years, Khailaz would be an empty wasteland of dust and ghosts.

Within a ring of boulders carved with runes of protection and containment, the participants stood in a circle, awaiting the signal to begin. Incense burned in brass pots set at the cardinal points, sending out clouds of smoke that wreathed around the circle of stones. In the center crouched a low altar of raw stone, where a woman lay unclothed, her body shining with oil.

As the sun sank, spreading swaths of flame crimson and violet across the sky, Rajani stood by the altar, gritting his teeth to keep from screaming, "STOP!" He watched Lanir strip off his robe, and stand steady as a rock before Tremonya, an ancient priestess and long-time member of the Circle. Protected by leather gloves so that she would not get even a drop on her own skin, she carefully brushed his body with the sorcerous, arousing Oil of Tramantha. It smelled of summer flowers. Rajani hated it even more for that.

Outside the circle, musicians huddled over their instruments. As darkness spread over the clifftop, the drummers began pounding out a heavy rhythm. Twanging kythera and wailing jaroon added a strident melody. At Tremonya's signal, Rajani raised his blackwood wand and pointed it at the keystone in the West, and commanded, "Shai!" The runes on the keystone flared to life, glowing with eerie silver light, which spread around the stone circle, igniting the runes on every boulder. From them arose a shimmering dome of magical containment.

The people began swaying in time with the drums, and chanting, "Kyah ghar zho. Ozh rahg hayk. Kyah ghar zho. Ozh rahg hayk." Even Luciya was chanting, though tears trickled slowly down her cheeks. Rajani unwillingly joined the tuneless chant. "Kyah ghar zho. Ozh rahg hayk. Kyah ghar zho. Ozh rahg hayk. Kyah ghar zho. Ozh rahg hayk."

The words merely meant "Two into one. One becomes two." But the guttural chant — the heavy drum beat — the plangent music of kythera and jaroon — the lovely, odious scent of the Oil — the thick, sickeningly-sweet smoke that writhed around the circle as if it were a living thing — all these wove together to create a vicious, viscous spell that vibrated ominously within the containing dome.

Tremonya watched the heavens intently, tracking the Moon in His slow arc toward the position that would complete the Wanderers' Dire-Cross. The other six Wanderers burned steadily in their positions under the Firebird's wings. At last, the Moon reached His place, and the heavens shivered with power. "Now!" croaked the ancient priestess.

Lanir mounted the altar and gazed into Alytha's eyes, caressing her cheek gently. At her nod, he thrust himself into her. Their passion was driven to an extreme by the Oil. Each touch, each sensation was exquisitely amplified and echoed in each other's bodies. They lost all sense of themselves as separate beings, and melded into the prolonged and perilous bliss brought by the Oil of Tramantha.

Woodenly, the Warrior Mage stepped forward. He opened his mouth to cry NO! But his throat was frozen. The grip of the oath-bind was irresistible. Of its own accord, his arm rose up and plunged his sword into his brother's back, piercing his heart. Unwillingly, Rajani shouted, "Ozh rahg hayk, Ukaiyeey!" With this sorcerous command, Lanir's mind and soul were buried deep within the soul of the child who had just been conceived.

As the years passed, Luciya, the Circle's chief spy in the Soul-Drinker's labyrinth, kept Rajani informed of the progress of their plot. Alytha, pregnant with the child who harbored Lanir, gave herself up to the Soul-Drinker's Gatherers. Hiding her pregnancy behind her impenetrable mind-mask, she endured repeated rapes by the Soul-Drinker's chosen Slaves, always under close observation by the red-eyed Watchers. But when her pregnancy was obvious, she was left alone. She bore the child in the "cow barn," as the female breeders' quarters were called. It was a boy, and she named him Kyr after the lonely, fierce cry of the eagle. For four years, she nursed and loved the child as best she could. Then Kyr was taken into the boys' quarters to be trained as a Slave. Only boys bred and born in the cow barn could become Slaves of the Soul-Drinker. Dauthaz would trust none other. After Kyr was taken from her, Alytha quietly hung herself, as breeders often did.

"Merciless gods!" Kyr gasped, nauseated with gut-churning horror. *Dekani — Lanir — was my* father! *And I was* created *by evil sorcery and by gods-cursed brother-murder.* Body and being, he felt drenched in his own father's blood, permeated by the treacherous Oil of Tramantha, and fouled by utter evil. *Oh, gods, what have they done to me?* His red rage washed everything in bloody light, and he beat his fists against the floor. *How could they? How could they do this to me? Gods curse them all!*

The Sun was going to Her rest. That meant the prisoners could, too. Craith, Zurano, Kinar, and Jorem trudged wearily back from the fields toward their dormitory, under the eye of their bored guards. Craith wiped sweat out of his eyes, his shoulders aching. He shook his head in disgust at his former arrogance toward those who worked the fields and orchards, as he did now.

In his eagerness to get home, he got a little ahead and entered their house first. He stepped into the kitchen--and froze, instantly on sentry alert. A thumping sound came from above. Warily, he climbed the stairs. At the top, Craith paused for a moment to let his eyes adjust to the dim light. The thumping had stopped. But a dark figure lay curled up on his bedroll, rocking slightly back and forth, moaning, "No, oh gods, no."

Craith hurried to the man's side. "Gods above, it's Kyr!" he whispered. Taking a calming breath, he knelt beside Kyr, and asked gently, "Sir, what's wrong?" Kyr froze and made no answer. "How can I help you, sir?"

"Sir?" Kyr snarled. "Curse the gods, don't call me that!"

Craith stared at Kyr in shock. Then he heard the others coming into the kitchen below. "I'll be right back, Kyr. Don't...." He broke off, unsure of what he feared Kyr might do if left alone, and hurried down the stairs into the kitchen. Kinar and Zurano slumped tiredly on stools by the table; Jorem was cutting carrots into their perpetual stew. Alarmed by Craith's grim face, Kinar and Zurano straightened up, and Jorem tensed, instantly holding his kitchen knife like a weapon. "What's wrong?"

"Kyr is upstairs, and he's in some kind of trouble. I'll try to find out what's going on. Just stay down here until I come back, alright?"

"What can we do for him?" Zurano asked.

"Kinar and Zurano, you go into the chapel and start the chant. That will probably help him more than anything. Jorem, you stay here, in case I need help."

Craith sprinted back up the stairs, taking them two at a time. He found Kyr sitting hunched up, arms around his knees. Sitting down to face him, Craith asked very gently, "What is it that has hurt you so? How can I help?"

"Hurt me? Oh, yes." In a turmoil of rage and hatred for his tainted, unnatural life and all those who had hurt and betrayed him, crazed with self-loathing and despair, Kyr craved physical pain to blot out the pecking agony of thought and memory. "Oh, gods, yes! *That's* what I want. You know how, Craith. Gauday taught you." He poked Craith in the chest, and kept poking. "Come on! Hit me. Do it!" At Craith's horrified expression, a wild-eyed Kyr scrambled to his feet and headed toward the door.

Craith jumped up and grabbed Kyr's arm. "No! Don't leave. Let me help you." At this, Kyr finally lost hold after years of utmost restraint. He lashed out, battering Craith with punches and kicks. But the sergeant only shielded his face, refusing to fight back. A wicked gut punch knocked him to the floor. He curled up on his side, bruised and bleeding.

"Craith!" Startled out of his frenzy, Kyr dropped to his knees beside his friend. "Gods and demons, what have I done?" Blood clogged Craith's nose and mouth, making it difficult for him to breathe. Kyr grabbed a blanket from the nearest bedroll. Balling it up, he gently tucked it under Craith's head and spread another blanket over him. Then he tore off his tunic and gently wiped the blood off Craith's face as well as he could. "I'm sorry, Craith. I'm so sorry."

Forcing his one good eye open, the redhead struggled to say a few words through his puffy, bleeding lips. "I deser'e id--'ee awrigh." It took Kyr a moment to understand the mangled words. "I deserved it. I'll be all right."

"Oh, Craith, no! You don't deserve this. You, least of all." Kyr shook his head and clambered to his feet. "Got to get you some help," he muttered. "Medari, yes. He'll help you. I'll go get Medari."

Shaking and soul-sick, Kyr headed downstairs. *Look what I've done! I am evil, made and born of evil, an evil despicable* thing! He stumbled down the last few steps into the kitchen. Barely able to stand, Kyr stuttered, "C-Craith is hurt. I hurt him. G-got to g-get Medari."

"Goddess, help us," whispered Jorem, getting to his feet. "Come sit down, sir. You're in no shape to be going anywhere. We'll get Medari, don't you worry," he promised, ushering Kyr to a stool. "Here, now. Sit down."

Kyr slumped onto the stool. "You'll g-get M-Medari?"

"Yes. I'll go ask one of our guards to fetch the healer. Now, don't move. I'll be right back." Kyr nodded and leaned his elbows on the table.

"Zhovanya naralo, Zhovanya naralo." The chant of forgiveness rang from the small chapel.

Kyr groaned and covered his ears against the sound that had once promised salvation, but now echoed derisively in his star-cursed soul.

On his way outside, Jorem poked his head into the chapel to tell Kinar and Zurano, "Go stay with Kyr. He's in the kitchen. Don't let him leave." The twins broke off their chant and hurried into the kitchen, while Jorem ran upstairs to see what shape Craith was in. He pulled back the blanket covering the huddled form on the floor.

As a former Slave of the Soul-Drinker, Jorem was well-versed in the shades of violence, and could see that though Craith was badly beaten, he was not in danger of dying. With a huff of relief, Jorem hurried downstairs and went out to the porch, where their guards, Chavri and Nyx, sat playing dice, as usual. "Sirs," Jorem told them, "Craith is hurt. Would one of you go to Ravenhall and ask the healer to come here right away?"

"What the hell happened?" demanded Nyx, a badger-like man who tended to be belligerent.

"Craith got into a fight. He's beat up pretty bad."

Chavri, the heavy-set, affable sergeant, intervened. "You go fetch the healer, Nyx. You're faster. I'll see what's going on." Outranked, Nyx grumbled to himself, but sped off toward Ravenhall.

In the kitchen, Chavri glanced at Kinar and Zurano, who were hovering around a hunched figure sitting at the table, but he couldn't see who it was. He followed Jorem upstairs.

Medari hurried into the penitents' kitchen with his healer's satchel, and stopped dead. "Kyr! What are you doing here?" Kyr slowly raised his head from his hands and stared at the healer.

"Merciless gods!" Medari had last seen that look of utter despair the night Gauday left Kyr out in the rain. "What happened? Where's Naran?"

"Sir," Zurano interrupted. "Kyr is not injured. It's Craith. He's hurt pretty bad."

"He's upstairs," added Jorem. "Follow me."

With a worried glance at Kyr, the healer went up to tend to the injured man. He cleaned Craith's abrasions with an astringent, smoothed a salve on his bruises, and gave him a good dose of pain-killing potion. Then he and Jorem got Craith settled into his own bedroll. Medari handed Jorem the bottle of the pain-killer. "This should help him sleep. Give him another dose whenever he needs it, whether he asks or not. Don't let him play the tough soldier."

When Medari returned to the kitchen, nothing much had changed, there. Kinar and Zurano looked up with identical worried frowns. "Don't worry," Medari told them. "Craith will recover. He just needs to rest for a few days." The twins sighed with relief. The exhausted healer shooed Kinar off the stool next to Kyr and sat down, himself. "Let me talk with Kyr," He said, glancing toward the doorway.

"We'll pray for them both." Kinar said, and the twins disappeared back into the chapel.

Someone had made tea, but Kyr's mug sat untouched. Medari took it and swallowed half the tea in one gulp. "Ah, that's a help." He sighed and rubbed his face. Then he gently took Kyr's wrist to check his pulses. Finally he asked, "What's going on, son?"

In a lifeless voice, Kyr asked, "Craith will be all right?"

"Yes, he'll be fine," said the healer, masking his alarm at Kyr's wildly erratic pulses. "Come on, let's get you back to your room. You need to rest. We'll sort this all out in the morning."

"No!" Ravenhall was the last place Kyr wanted to go. But then a slight smile briefly curved his lips, though it did not touch the bleak emptiness of eyes. He shrugged. "As you wish."

Star-cursed, star-cursed. As he trudged up the path to Ravenhall beside Medari, the words drummed through his mind in rhythm with his footsteps. *Star-cursed, star-cursed. Look what I did to Craith, all the people I sacrificed for the Soul-Drinker. Even Svahar, the Tree Warden, died from helping me. I'm a star-cursed monster. Dangerous, poisonous, evil!*

116

In Kyr's room, they found Naran sitting on the floor, holding his head. He looked up. "Ah, there you are, Kyr. Are you all right?"

Kyr stared at him, and turned away in shame. *Oh, gods, I hurt him too.* He dropped down on the rug by the cold hearth, while Medari knelt by Naran and examined him. "What happened to you?"

"Fell and hit my head. Head hurts. A little dizzy. I've had worse bumps. This is not too bad."

"Your pupils are even and your pulses are pretty strong," the healer reported. "A night's rest will do you good." Medari dug in his bag. "Here's something for the pain." He gave Naran a bottle. "This is my next-to-last bottle of prepared pain-killer. Don't overdo it, alright?" Naran nodded. "Could you wait in your room until I get Kyr settled?"

"With a little help." While the healer got Naran across the hall to his room, Kyr stared at the dark ashes in the hearth, his heart growing colder by the moment. He didn't look up when Medari returned.

"Alright, Kyr, let's get you to bed." Medari helped a listless, silent Kyr shed his boots and curl up under the covers. "Here, now, this will help you sleep." The healer gave Kyr two swallows of sleeping potion, replaced the wax plug, and started to pocket the bottle.

Kyr frowned, and quickly reached out both hands toward the healer. "I love you, heart-father. I'm sorry for all this trouble."

With tears in his eyes, the healer set the bottle on the nightstand, and gladly grasped Kyr's hands. "I love you, too, son."

"I think I'll be all right after a good sleep. Thanks."

"Good to hear. We'll talk in the morning." Reassured, the distressed and nearly overwhelmed healer hurried out to check on Rajani.

Kyr stared at the bottle, a dull fire burning in his heart, a heavy ball in the pit of his stomach, his mind whirling.

My mother killed herself. Gods! She may have been the wisest one in this whole cursed mess. He scrubbed tears from his eyes. *I wish I remembered her.*

But then, fury flamed up. *Dekani — no, I'll never call him that again —* Lanir *is my damned* father! *He used me unmercifully, lurking inside me, letting me be tortured into becoming an obedient Slave, then sweeping me aside so he could kill the Soul-Drinker. All his supposed love, protection, and guidance were just tricks to control me. How clever of him to die just in time to escape facing me now. Gods curse his soul!* He slammed his fists into the bed. Howls of rage swelled up, but he clamped them down to keep from alarming Medari.

Rajani and Luciya too. Liars! Traitors! They're all worse than the damned Soul-Drinker. At least he *didn't pretend to be anything good. Luciya helped with that demonic ritual, and Rajani, by all the hells,* murdered *my father to make me into this…this* shell *for Lanir to hide in. What they did to me is unforgiveable!* He got up and stalked back and forth, grinding his teeth.

Ha! Let the weapon they made me into turn on them now! I'll kill them! Then he shook his head wildly. *No, no. That's too good for them.* A slow, sinister smile twisted his lips, his fury gone as cold as the lowest hell. *I know much better ways to make them pay. Wasn't I the Soul-Drinker's Favorite?* He imagined torturing Rajani in the ways he had learned so well, keeping his victim alive for days. He imagined making Rajani watch as he tortured Luciya, and laughing at him for pleading, *"Stop! Take me instead! Leave her alone!"*

Kyr laughed, but his gut was twisting with a dreadful sick feeling. "Gods and demons! I *am* evil, evil since before I was born!" In this dark light, his life took on an even more baneful aspect. *I am not like anyone else. Even the other Slaves, wicked as they were, were not* created *out of black sorcery and murder. I'm just Lanir's mask, the Circle's weapon to end the Soul-Drinker's reign.*

But — if that's all I am, why didn't Lanir just let me die and take over my body, after he killed the Soul-Drinker? And why has Rajani done so much to keep me alive since then? Why bring me to Svahar, and the Sanctuary? Why rescue me from Gauday? Why bring me here to Ravenvale? "Oh, by all the hells!" he gasped, freezing in his tracks. "The Circle plans to use me for something else!"

A deep chill of frozen rage filled his body, heart, and mind. It was almost like the ice, his old haven — and he welcomed it. With cold clarity, he saw what his best revenge would be. He straightened up and, through stiff lips, whispered, "Enough! I won't let Rajani or his Circle use me anymore. No more of this false life. No more!"

Chapter Eleven

Dark Nights

Medari applied a salve to Naran's bruised forehead, and helped him into bed. He looked around the room. Naran had made himself at home. His clothes were draped on the couch by the hearth and over the washstand. The open wardrobe revealed a winter cloak on a hook and various satchels on the shelves. The low, round table in front of the couch held wilted wildflowers in a pottery vase, and a scatter of feathers and stones. "Naran, would you have a mug around here, somewhere?"

"Oh, over on the washstand. Sorry it's such a mess in here."

"Never mind." Medari picked up the tunics covering the washstand, shrugged, and added them to the pile of clothes on the couch. Peering into the pitcher, he said, "Ah, good," and filled the errant mug with water from the pitcher. Then he gave Naran another dose of the painkiller, and handed him the mug. "Now, drink up. You need extra water for a few days. You should also take it easy, but then you should be fine."

"Thanks, Medari." Naran handed him the empty mug, and lay back against the pillows, eyes drooping closed.

"If your headache gets worse, let me know right away. Otherwise, sleep well."

"Alright," Naran murmured drowsily.

The weary healer returned to Rajani's room, and checked on the Warrior Mage. He was, thankfully, deeply asleep.

Luciya and Devanyi were collapsed on the couch by the hearth, and Medari joined them, taking one of the two padded chairs that flanked the couch. All three of them were worn out, and chilled more by the inexplicable events of the day than by the cool Autumn evening. Devanyi had built a fire, and they all leaned close, needing its warmth.

"I'm starving," Luciya said, pushing herself up to her feet. "I'll send for some supper." She tugged on a braided leather strap hanging by the hearth. At Medari's questioning look, she explained, "It's a bell-pull. It rings down the hall at the server's station."

Very shortly, someone tapped on the door and Luciya went to speak to the server, then returned to her seat. Glaring at the two healers in frustration, she demanded, "What in all the hells went wrong with that cleansing ritual?"

Devanyi sighed. "My head hurts from trying to figure it out."

"I have no idea." Medari said, "And I'm too tired to think about it. Best if we get some rest, and discuss it in the morning with Ilanya."

"But...."

A tap at the door cut short Luciya's objection. Two servers brought in trays laden with a supper of cold roast chicken, bread, cheese, apples, and, best of all, hot vegetable soup. A large basket held extra bread, cheese and apples for Rajani, Kyr, and Naran if they awoke hungry. The servers set out the food on the low, round table in front of the couch. Luciya thanked them and sent them on their way.

Then, turning to Medari, she conceded, "I guess you're right. I can't think, either." The three of them ate in silence, the only sounds the crackling of the fire and Rajani's heavy snoring. When everyone was done eating, Medari said, "I don't want to leave any of my patients alone all night. I'll stay with Kyr. I suggest that Luciya stay here with Rajani, and Devanyi with Naran, alright?"

The two women nodded. "There are winter blankets in the wardrobes." Luciya offered. "We can use those."

"Good." Medari got to his feet. "Call me if they wake or if you need any help. May we all have a peaceful night."

Numb with exhaustion, Medari trudged down the hall, carrying his healer's satchel, muttering. "What a terrible day! Just have to check on Kyr, then I can get some sleep." He reached the door to Kyr's room — and froze, listening intently. "Oh, gods!" He burst through the door, and found Kyr lying on his bed, mouth hanging open, snoring loudly, raggedly.

"Kyr? Wake up!" Medari shook him hard, but there was no response. He checked Kyr's pulses, eyes, breath. "Gods and demons!" He patted his pocket, then looked around frantically. A bottle lay on its side on the floor, and he grabbed it and sniffed it. "Curse it, I thought I took that with me!" His eyes narrowed. "Damn it, Kyr! You did that on purpose."

Cursing himself for a fool, he dug in his satchel for the purgative. It was long, hard, and messy work to force the potion down Kyr's throat, then hold him over the pisspot as he vomited or shat. Kyr remained nearly unconscious and limply unresisting, except for a few feeble protests.

When Medari judged the danger to be past, he cleaned Kyr up and got him settled in bed. He immediately sank into a heavy but more natural sleep. Medari sagged with relief and exhaustion, then found the bell pull and got a server to take the pisspot out to the latrine while he went to the kitchen to prepare a restorative tisane. When the healer returned to Kyr's room, the clean pisspot was beside Kyr's bed, and a robust fire burned in the hearth.

Medari set the teapot near the fire to keep it warm, took a blanket of heavy green wool out of the wardrobe, and pulled a padded chair over next to Kyr's bed. Wrapping himself in the blanket, he settled into the chair, determined to stay awake to watch Kyr; but exhaustion soon overtook him.

Kyr ached all over. His head felt as if it were being used for a blacksmith's anvil, his throat and stomach were stripped raw, and his guts hurt. For a few moments, that was all he was aware of. Then it hit him. *Ah, merciless gods! No, no, no. Oh, gods, no!* Kyr could barely breathe for the bitter anguish welling up inside him. *She wouldn't take me. Even the Dark Lady has no mercy for me.* He had to fight to keep from wailing aloud, from flailing about like a demented thing. *Why do You force me back into this terrible life of mine, Zhovanya? Do You hate me so much?* A sob escaped him, causing Medari to jerk awake.

"Ah, you're awake. Good." He got up and poured a cup of the tisane he'd left by the fire. "Here, son, drink this. It will help."

Kyr's eyes were icy. "*You* did this!" he croaked. "You dragged me back into this life, didn't you?"

"I couldn't stand by and watch you die!"

In a raspy whisper, Kyr ranted, "You, of all people, know what I have suffered! You know how I longed to die at the fort. But I endured Gauday's hell — for the Sanctuary — for your family — for *you*. And *this* is how you repay me? You have no idea what you've done to me, now." Kyr turned away and closed his eyes, clutching his arms tightly together to refrain from attacking his heart-father.

"I'm a sworn healer. You know I can't give the Final Grace except in the most extreme circumstances. I never even considered it, even at the fort, except when Gauday was about to enslave your soul. You are young and strong. Here, you have the chance to heal, to begin to live a good life. I couldn't let you throw that away."

Kyr remained curled up, his back to Medari, tight with furious despair. *Gods damn him! Medari has betrayed me into living — again. I can't forgive him, this time.* Kyr had never felt so alone. He had no inner teacher to run to now, no

121

friends to rely on, no Goddess to beg for help. *Ha! I don't even have my crazed brother Gauday to fight with. By all the hells, I wish I were back there at the fort, playing his vicious games with him. It would be better than this!* The forgiveness chant sounded in his mind, a mocking reminder of all he had lost.

"Son? Tell me what happened. Please!"

When Kyr made no response, Medari groped blindly for the chair and slumped down onto it, slow tears sliding down his lined and weary face.

A ray of morning sunlight crept deeper into Rajani's room and pawed gently at Luciya's face. She woke with a groan, wondering what she was doing in a chair instead of her bed. "Oh, gods! 'Jani!" She jumped up and leaned over to check on Rajani. He was still asleep, but twitching restlessly, his brow deeply furrowed, his teeth clenched. She turned and checked: no one else was in the room. She leaned close to the fallen Warrior Mage. "Rajani, you must get better! I can't fulfill the Prophecy by myself. You're the only one who knows what needs to happen next." Rajani tossed and moaned, his eyelids flickering. She sighed with relief. "Good, you're waking up. I'll go get Medari."

Luciya hurried to Kyr's room. As she opened the door, a sickly odor wafted forth. Stepping inside, she saw Kyr curled up on his bed, his back to Medari, who sat hunched up in the chair nearby, face buried in his hands. Her heart shrank with dread. "Goddess, help us! What's happened now?"

The healer looked up blearily. "I… so much happening last night…got distracted…left it…the whole bottle…." His voice trailed off.

"What bottle?" Luciya demanded.

"Sleeping potion…he drank it…the whole thing." Tears started to trickle down the healer's face.

"Gods damn it, man, is he alive?"

"He's…alive…," Medari murmured.

"Yes, he's alive," snarled Kyr, sitting up suddenly. "Thanks to his dear heart-father." He glared at Medari, then turned his icy glare on Luciya. "But he's not going to be part of your cursed Circle's little plans anymore."

"Wha…what did you say?"

Kyr sprang off the bed and stalked toward her, fists clenched. Luciya stumbled back a few steps, and Medari shouted, "Kyr! Don't hurt her!"

Kyr cast a disgusted glance at the healer, but loosened his fists. Leaning forward, he snarled into her face. "Rajani couldn't handle the kind of torment I live with, and made a big mistake. He called out for help from your old lover, Lanir. Rajani wouldn't tell me the truth, but I shook it out of him. Your gods-be-damned plot isn't a secret anymore."

Luciya paled and moaned, "Oh, no!"

"Oh, yes! I know all about the gods-cursed ritual you used to make me. I know how you used me as your damned cat's paw to kill the Soul-Drinker. What I can't figure out is why you and Rajani and the rest of your blasted Circle have gone to such lengths to keep me alive. What are you planning to use me for next?"

Luciya looked at Kyr in dismay, shaking her head, while Medari stared from one to the other, perplexed and alarmed.

Kyr laughed caustically. "Well, never mind, it doesn't matter. Whatever you had planned, it won't happen. I'm done being *anyone's* plaything: the Circle's, Gauday's, the Soul-Drinker's — or Zhovanya's."

"But Kyr, we need you!" Luciya clutched at him, pleading, "You have to help us!"

"NO!" He shoved her onto the bed, wanting to shake her until every bone in her body shattered; but then Craith's bloodied face swam before his eyes. He snatched his hands off her. "If you know what's good for you, you will stay away from me, you and your entire gods-cursed Circle." He strode toward the door, then turned around and hissed, "By the way, your precious Lanir died yesterday."

"No! Oh, no, no, no," wailed Luciya, overwhelmed by new and ancient grief.

"Good riddance to my two-faced, lying *father!*" Kyr stalked out, slamming the door. He had learned well how to be cruel. Gauday had been a good tutor.

But his vengeful words and Luciya's grief gave him no satisfaction. He stamped down the stairs, and fled the foul luxury of the snare called Ravenhall.

K yr stood on the path by the lake, his head aching fiercely. His rage-fueled strength drained out of him in a rush, leaving him weak from the purging that Medari had forced on him. Clouds darkened the lake's sparkle, and a chill breeze made him shiver. He was barefoot and wearing only his breeches, but he refused to return to Ravenhall for anything. *I've got to get away from Rajani's so-called home, false haven that it's turned out to be. I want nothing more to do with him and his Circle, that nest of liars and betrayers. And, gods curse it, I can't go back to the penitents' house — not after what I did to Craith. By all the hells, I have nowhere to go.* He shrugged. *Well, it hardly matters. So long as it's away from here.*

He turned north, head and guts aching, and trudged along the path beside the reedy lakeshore. Red-caped blackbirds clung to the reeds, singing melodiously. The clouds drifted away, and sunlight sparkled on the open water beyond the reeds. Lost in numb misery, Kyr was vaguely surprised that the entire world had not turned to ashes.

The path veered away from the lake and into a shadowy forest. Tall pines hid Ravenhall from view at last, and he slowed to a plod, barely able put one foot in front of the other. In the midst of the forest, he reached a sunny green meadow, dotted with orange and pink flowers. He started across it, hoping for a warm, dry spot to rest; but with each step, his bare feet sank deeper into the cool, soggy meadow. "Blast it! Too damn wet."

He started to retreat, but a green jay flashed by, landed on a large, flat-topped boulder next to a tall pine, pecked at something, and flew off. Kyr squelched across the boggy meadow to the big rock, clambered atop it, and stretched out. The warmth of the sunshine and the sun-warmed stone felt good to his aching, exhausted body, but did not penetrate the coldness of his soul. He lay on his stomach with his chin on his hands, gazing down at the small, white, star-shaped flowers huddling around the base of the boulder. Soon, despite it all, his eyelids drooped closed.

"CAW, CAW!"

Kyr jerked awake. A raven perched on a low branch of the nearby pine, turning its head side to side, examining him. Seeing that it had his attention, it bobbed its head, hopped to the ground, and started to waddle away. Glancing over its shoulder, it could see that Kyr hadn't moved. "Caw, caw!" It hopped back toward Kyr, then turned and waddled away again. When Kyr still did not move, the raven repeated this performance, cawing impatiently. "Alright, alright," Kyr muttered, and sat up. "Might as well follow you. I have nothing better to do." With no hope of returning to the oblivion of sleep, he climbed down off the boulder, and followed the raven back to the forest trail.

A short while later, the babble of a creek made him aware of his raw, parched throat, and he hurried around a bend in the trail. There, he saw the raven taking a sip from a small brook next to the trail, tilting its head back to gulp the water down. Kyr knelt by the creek, splashed some water on his face, and drank from his cupped hands. The icy water soothed his throat, but woke growls of hunger from his stomach.

"Caw!" The raven flew a short ways down the trail, lit on a branch, and looked back at him.

"Alright, alright," grumbled Kyr, getting shakily to his feet and starting onwards. The dark bird kept ahead of him, flying from tree branch to rock top, leading him along. The trail wound through the trees and emerged at the lake's edge again. Kyr saw a smudge out in the middle of the lake. At first, all he could see was shifting veils of fog. But then the fog thinned, revealing an island.

"Wish I could get there," he told the Raven, who was strutting along a low grassy ridge. It bobbed its head as if in answer, and hopped back and forth on the ridge, cawing loudly. Having learned to trust his strange guide, Kyr examined the low ridge, and discovered that it was the peaked roof of a narrow shed, covered by living grass and shrubs. "Is this what you wanted to show me?"

The raven bobbed its head, hopped to the ground, and began tugging at the brush in front of the shed. "Alright." Kyr pulled back the brush covering the opening and peered inside. Something made of smooth, polished wood gleamed in the invading sunlight. As his eyes adjusted, he saw that it was a small, narrow boat. He straightened and looked at the Raven. "It's a boat. What about it?" The raven cocked its head, then launched itself in the air and flew toward the island, then circled back.

"Oh." He hauled at the boat, slipped, and fell back into the shallow water, while the boat slid smoothly forward and slipped into the lake. The Raven's cawing sounded suspiciously like laughter. Glaring at the bird, Kyr managed to clamber aboard without capsizing the boat. Inside, he found a coil of rope, a neatly folded blanket, and a long pole. Without thought, he picked it up and started poling toward the island, in too much despair to notice the unnatural skill with which he did this new thing. "Awrk," said the raven in a satisfied tone, and flew off.

Kyr briefly wondered what he might do if the water got too deep for the pole, but shrugged once more. *If Zhovanya refuses to let me die, I have no need to worry about that sort of thing.* The thought brought a bitter smile to his lips. Indeed, the water remained shallow, and he reached the island just as the sun began to sink behind Ravenvale's distant guardian wall. A huge tree with scant, drooping foliage overhung the water. Kyr tied the boat to a limb of the tree. Darkness was spreading swiftly. Exhausted beyond measure, Kyr wrapped himself up in the blanket and lay down in the boat. The lapping of the water against the hull and the gentle rocking of the boat soon soothed him into a deep sleep.

Silent as a dream, a tawny eagle lit weightlessly upon the prow of the boat, emanating a soft, golden-red radiance that kept the cold mist away, and radiating a healing warmth that soaked into Kyr's slumbering body.

"Tlonk, tlonk, tlonk." Kyr pulled the blanket up over his eyes, but the boat rocked with his motion, startling him awake. Dismay at still being alive was sharp as a sword in his gut. For a few moments, he lay curled up in a tight knot, desperate for the forgetfulness of sleep. But it was hopeless. His body ached, and his bladder demanded relief.

"Tlonk, tlonk."

125

Gods, what is that noise? Angrily, he pulled the blanket down and slit open his eyes to see swirls of gray mist twisting in the branches of the drooping tree. On a branch overhead sat the Raven. "Tlonk," it said.

"Damn bird!" Kyr sat up and glared at it for disturbing the sweet oblivion he'd found sleeping in the boat on the breast of the lake.

"Awrk," said the Raven.

Moving carefully, Kyr clambered out of the boat, drank some of the slightly muddy lake water, and waded onto shore, soaking himself to his waist. Wanting nothing that Rajani had given him, he shed his wet breeches and dropped them on the ground. Shivering in the cool morning mist, he grabbed the blanket out of the boat. Clutching it about himself, he followed a half-overgrown path away from the shore. The raven kept flying ahead and returning to examine him with its dark, shining eyes.

Kyr shuffled blindly along, blank with despair. Abhorrence at what he had learned from Rajani's memories numbed all thought, but his feet automatically kept to the trail that wandered through a forest of white-barked trees. *Star-cursed, star-cursed, star-cursed.* The malignant truth of his origin cut like a knife with every breath. Stones and stickers bit at his bare feet, but he welcomed the distraction. Weak from Medari's purging, shaken to his core, he trudged on and on, with no goal except the exhaustion that might bring back the oblivion of sleep.

"Curse it!" Stepping unawares into icy water shocked him out of his daze. He hopped out of the rivulet that crossed the trail, knelt beside it, and drank water from his cupped hands, then sank back against the nearest tree trunk, body and soul drained to the dregs. He dried his feet with a corner of his blanket, curled up under it on the soft, thick layer of tan and yellow leaves covering the forest floor, and closed his eyes. Instantly, he found what he longed for: deep, dreamless sleep.

Raven perched on a branch above his still body, mantling her wings protectively, muttering cryptic incantations.

Chapter Twelve

Devastating Memories

"No, no!" Rajani cried out, thrashing on his bed.

Medari's eyes snapped open. "Rajani! Wake up. It's only a nightmare. Wake up!" The Warrior Mage subsided into restless somnolence, twitching and moaning. Medari was dismayed to realize that he had fallen asleep on the chair next to Rajani's bed. They were in the Warrior Mage's austere room, so at odds with the rest of Ravenhall. Instead of a handsome, carved-wood bedstead and feather mattress, Rajani slept on a narrow cot. A small, square table and two wooden chairs sat by the hearth. Beneath the uncurtained window, a low, scarred table squatted before a shabby couch. A small wardrobe, sized for a boy, stood in a dark corner. Otherwise, the room was bare, almost as if Rajani were purposely denying himself any comfort.

Medari stood and stretched, groaning as his stiff joints protested. The past two days had been grueling, and the healer was exhausted from his grim and perhaps futile fight to save Kyr's life, as well as tending to Rajani. Thankfully, Naran was back on his feet, and Luciya had recovered her composure enough to take command of the search for Kyr. No one knew what had become of him since he had fled Ravenhall.

Devanyi came into the room, looking tired but freshly washed and dressed, and carrying a breakfast tray with warm apple muffins, crisp bacon, and tea. "Good morning, Medari." She set the tray down on the table in front of the couch. "How is he?"

"It wasn't so bad this night. Gods! I hope he's coming out of whatever nightmare he's been trapped in since that damn ritual." Medari bent down and placed his fingers on Rajani's wrist, feeling his pulses. "Ah. Seems to have gone into a natural sleep, at last."

"That's a blessing."

They both took seats on the couch, and Devanyi filled their mugs from the teapot.

"Thanks." The healer took a sip of tea. "Ah, chyma and vortan, just the thing." He took another sip. "Don't know what I'd do without you. You've been a steadfast support to us all. How have you managed to remain calm and collected through all this?"

"It's what I can do to help. You don't know how scared I am, inside." She gave him a shaky smile and offered him a muffin, then took one for herself.

"Aren't we all?" Medari sighed. "Any news?"

She shook her head. "They still haven't found Kyr."

"Where could he have gotten to? Seems like he's disappeared into thin air."

Luciya rushed into the room, her hair escaping from its braid in wild wisps, her dark gown rumpled as if she had slept in it, dark circles under her reddened eyes. "That's right. We can't find him anywhere. We really need Rajani. He knows this place better than anyone. Is he any better? Can we wake him?"

"Let's keep our voices down," Medari admonished. "He's sleeping naturally now. It would better to let him come out of this — whatever it is — on his own."

"We don't dare wait," Luciya objected, more quietly this time. "We have no idea what's happening with Kyr. We must find him!" She clasped her hands tightly, and whispered, "Oh, Goddess! He's got to be all right!"

Puzzled by Luciya's outburst, Medari said, "I'm worried about Kyr too, Luciya. But he's either succeeded at killing himself by now, or he's hiding. Maybe he just needs some time to come to terms with whatever happened in that cleansing ritual."

"You don't understand," Luciya snapped. "There's more at stake than just Kyr's life." She raised an imperious hand to forestall his questions. "No, I can't tell you more, except that we've got to find him. Please, wake Rajani now."

"We don't know what harm we might do to him," the healer said, crossing his arms.

"He would agree with me. He's taken many risks for Kyr, more than you know. Wake him!"

Medari stared at Luciya for a moment, then capitulated. "Alright, but this goes against my advice." He looked through his healer's kit, took out his smelling salts, and waved them under Rajani's nose.

"Gaahh!" The Warrior Mage shoved the healer's hand away, and looked around blearily.

"You're back with us, thank all the gods!" Luciya exclaimed.

"What happened?" Rajani asked, then groaned, "Oh, gods! Kyr!" A grimace of guilt and pain crossed his face, and his eyes began to close.

"Rajani, look at me!" Medari commanded, taking his patient's wrists in a firm clasp, and nodding to Devanyi. She began pressing points on Rajani's head and torso to help him stay conscious.

"Don't go, Rajani! Stay here with us," Luciya urged. "We need you." She leaned forward and put her hands on his cheeks, forcing him to look at her, and said sharply, "Rajani, listen to me. Kyr is lost. You've got to help us find him."

"Lost?" Rajani stared at her. "Oh, Goddess, NO!"

"Yes. Kyr has run away. We've searched but we can't find him anywhere. You know Ravenvale better than anyone. Can you tell us where else to look?"

"'Can't find him anywhere,'" Rajani repeated, recalling where he and Lanir had been when others had said this of them long ago. They had escaped to Granmere's island in the lake, her sanctum where she studied the stars in her tall, crystal-domed Tower. She would sometimes allow them to visit the island when the pressures of their training to carry out her Prophecy became unbearable. With conjured illusions, she had kept the island hidden from unwanted eyes, though of course the Ravens saw right through her magic. Rajani and his brother had run free there, playing, roaming, or lazing about. He sighed, hating even now to reveal the island's existence, his private symbol of escape and freedom.

With his last scrap of will, he forced himself to speak. "Granmere's Tower on island in lake...in fog illusions...boat on north shore." He sagged back, surrendering to his oldest enemy, guilt.

Luciya sighed sadly, gently caressed Rajani's cheeks, and whispered, "It's not your fault, 'Jani. Not your fault."

But he whispered, "Yes, it is."

She shook her head sadly, stepped back from Rajani's cot, and turned to Medari. "Take care of him. We've got to search the lake." She hurried out, calling orders to the servers awaiting her in the hallway.

After Luciya left, Rajani lay moaning and twitching, lost again in nightmare. Devanyi looked at Medari in dismay. "Isn't there something else we can do?"

"Not when he's unwilling to come back to us. Let's sit and have some breakfast." Medari, gray with fatigue and grief, trudged across the room, and sank down on the couch by the window.

Naran came in just then, looking all right except for the purple-and-yellow bruise on his scarred forehead. "What's going on? Have they found Kyr yet?"

"Here, sit down," Devanyi commanded. Naran took a seat next to the healer, while Devanyi took up the teapot and filled three mugs, adding dollops of honey.

While Naran sipped his tea, Medari brought him up to date. "After he told us about the island, Rajani seemed to give in to the nightmares," he added, "almost as if he welcomed them. I just don't understand what happened in that ritual. It seems to have driven them both mad. Whatever it is, it's beyond my skills." The healer sighed. "At least, now Luciya has an idea where to look for Kyr."

"Kyr didn't seem mad when I last saw him, just very angry and disturbed." Naran paused, frowning thoughtfully. "I don't know how, but from what little Kyr said, it seems like he must have taken knowledge or memories from Rajani that made him furious and frantic. I suspect something similar happened to Rajani. He may have taken in *Kyr's* memories, which would be enough to drive any man — except Kyr — mad."

"That makes some sense." Medari said. "But why is Rajani so much more affected by what happened than Kyr?"

"Kyr has had a lot more experience of this kind of thing. He was subject to mental invasion by the Soul-Drinker. Then Gauday tried to mind-bond him, and nearly succeeded. And he's had more practice than anyone at coping with suffering of many kinds. He's the strongest soul I have ever met."

"Yes, he is that. Gods above and below, what happened to him in that ritual must have been more devastating than we can imagine!" Medari turned away, wiping his eyes.

"Poor Kyr!" Devanyi exclaimed. "The gods *are* merciless to him!" She clutched her hands together in her lap, and took a deep breath. "Sorry. I'm trying to stay calm, but...."

Naran placed one hand on top of hers. "You're doing remarkably well. We're all upset. This is a great challenge for everyone."

"What can we do to help Kyr when we find him? Do you have any idea?"

"Yes," Naran answered. The two healers looked at him in surprise.

"We need the Kailithana. She's the only one who has the skills for the kind of mind-and-soul healing Kyr and Rajani both need. She normally would never leave the Sanctuary; but for Kyr, I think she will come. And she might be able to help Rajani, too."

At the midday meal, Naran and Medari found Luciya in the parlor, eating a quick lunch of soup and bread. Naran told her his idea. "Jolanya is a powerful healer, not just of physical ills, but also of mental, emotional, and spiritual wounds. She has skills and magic that no one else has. If she's willing, I think she could help Rajani recover, as well as helping Kyr when we find him."

"Excellent idea, Naran. I'll send a squad of Companions to fetch Jolanya immediately."

"I'm afraid Jolanya would object to being 'fetched,'" Naran demurred. "As the Kailithana, she has her sacred duty to fulfill, and she is quite dedicated to it. *I'll* have to go. She'll listen to me. Just lend me a couple of Companions for protection."

"You must rest for one more day," Medari said adamantly.

"That's fine," said Luciya. "It'll take me 'til morning to get things arranged, anyway."

Chapter Thirteen

Tower of Reflection

The path through Dekani's meadow had changed. It was stony and steep, now. Kyr shambled along it, yearning to reach the cottage and huddle up in his old chair before the fire. But it was taking much longer than it should. Kyr finally looked up, and stopped in dismay. This was not the inner realm he had shared with Dekani.

Instead of a meadow edged by forest under a misty sky, here there was a steep path winding up toward craggy hills under a wide, lavender sky. A sharp cry made Kyr scan that strange sky — and there high above, soared a tawny eagle. The Eagle's sublime freedom and the immaculate sky mocked his own vileness. "Gods and demons! Zhovanya, must You taunt me so?" Heart aching for the purity and clarity he could never know, he watched Eagle soar out of sight.

A pattering sound brought Kyr out of the dream. An earthy, forest scent filled his nose, and he was now dry and warm. He opened his eyes but could see nothing but golden light. *Did the Goddess have mercy on me at last?* But his aching head and ravaged throat convinced him that he had not been so lucky.

With a groan, he sat up. A rustling cascade of golden aspen leaves poured off him, leaving a few clinging to his green blanket. The bare branches of the tree above him sketched dark lines against a gray sky. The tree had shed all its leaves and buried him in their papery golden abundance. He puzzled over this for a moment, but cold touches on his bare shoulders made him shudder. "Merciless gods, it's raining."

Cloaking himself with his blanket, he looked at the trail winding upward through the forest of white-barked, golden-leafed trees. *It must go someplace where I can get out of this cursed rain.* Exhausted and half-starved, he plodded up the steep trail, barely noticing the trees thinning, until at last the open sky spread wide above him, pale blue with scattered gray clouds sending down random showers. Now he could see that the trail continued to the top of the hill, where a dark tower pointed toward the heavens. As he looked up at this welcome prospect of shelter, the early evening sun pierced the clouds with golden rays, setting the top of the Tower shining and sparkling like nothing he had ever seen. The astonishing sight stopped him in his tracks, and a sense of wonder broke through his despair.

But then, cold rain flurries spat and hissed, hounding him up the slick, steep path. Desperate to reach cover, he pushed himself to his limit, keeping his eyes on his feet as he climbed the wet, slippery trail. And so he failed to see the vivid rainbow arching across the sky.

At last, he reached the top of the hill and clambered over the waist-high stone wall that surrounded the Tower onto a graystone courtyard. He stood there gasping for air, his heart pounding, his vision darkening, his knees quivering. Abruptly, he sat down on the stone wall and put his head to his knees. When his heart slowed and he could breathe normally, he straightened and stared upward.

Tall and slender, the graystone Tower loomed dark against the rose-hued evening sky. Impossibly far above, its crystal dome still sparkling with the last of the sunlight. It was a magnificent sight, even to his darkened mind. But rain spattered his back, riding a sudden cold wind, and he hurried across the courtyard to the Tower's portico. Two columns, one black and one white, upheld a narrow roof over a small terrace before the door. Kyr leapt up the two steps and stood before the blackwood door, which, patterned with points of crystal, looked like the night sky. But there was no knob or handle. "By all the hells," he muttered. "After all it took to get here, this door better open!"

He put his hand in the dark area in the middle of the star pattern, and shoved. The door didn't budge. But tingling warmth embraced his palm, and the crystal stars swam into a new pattern, one that seemed hazily familiar to him. Before he could decipher it, the door swung open. Not caring if he met his death at the hands of a resident demon or sorcerer, wanting only to get out of the cold rain, he stepped inside. The warm tingling expanded to envelop his whole body as he crossed the threshold, but vanished as the door swung silently shut behind him.

No sorcerer or demon, but a cozy, round chamber greeted him. To the right of the door, in the eastern portion of the room, a richly hued carpet covered the stone floor, and a divan piled with colorful cushions sat before an empty hearth. A stone ledge curved along the wall, holding a scattering of covered baskets and carved wooden boxes. To the left, cabinets, shelves, and a counter lined the curving western wall, with a small round table and three stools in front of them. From the center of the room, goldenwood stairs ascended in a spiral, casting shadows over the northern area behind the staircase. Small round windows were set high in the thick walls of the Tower, one at each of the cardinal points. The western window glowed dimly with fading sunset, but the others were dark.

"Thank the gods!" he sighed, dropping his wet blanket on the floor. But then he snorted. "Which gods should I thank? The ones *I* know are merciless." Shaking with chill and fatigue, he crossed over to the divan and sank down into its comforting depths. A fire blazed to life in the raised hearth, though he could see no wood for it to burn. He blinked at the eerie blue-green flames. The mage-fire warmed him soft and kindly, but he took no notice. Heavy with despair and loathing, aching in body and soul, he welcomed the empty blackness that engulfed him.

As he slept, soft sighing and subtle movement swirled around him. The frown slipped from his face as gentle dreams drifted through his slumbering mind, accompanied by a silent chant: *Zhovanya naralo, Zhovanya naralo.*

Dawn-light shining through the eastern window gently brought forth the shapes and colors of the small round chamber. At first, no thought crossed Kyr's waking mind. There was only a quietness, an enfolding warmth, and a silent whisper. *"BLESSINGS, BLESSINGS, BLESSINGS, MY BELOVED."*

Then he blinked, and shuddered. "Merciless Goddess," he groaned. "I can't bear any more of Your blessings!" He curled up among the pillows of the embracing divan and remained there until thirst and an aching bladder became a torment. Dully resentful, he rasped, "So You curse me to live another day."

He rose, wrapped his now-dry blanket around his torso, and headed outside. Ignoring the beauty of the translucent, empty sky, he followed Rajani's memories down the flagstone path, around the Tower, and down a few stone steps to an outhouse screened by tall bushes with prickly dark-green leaves and pale berries.

On his return, he noticed a roofed well on the west side of the Tower, and stopped to crank up a bucket heavy with water, setting it on the edge of the well. Shaking from the effort, he sat next to the bucket, resting his pounding head in his hands for a few moments. Then he looked up and spotted a tin mug chained to one of the posts holding up the well's roof. Dipping it into the bucket, he filled the mug, and drank. The icy water made him shiver, but it felt good to his parched mouth, ravaged stomach, and aching gut.

Setting his blanket aside, he splashed himself unmercifully with the rest of the icy water from the bucket, scrubbing away the last remnants of his illusions about his life, and his hope of becoming the man whom Jolanya had loved. Roughly, he rubbed himself dry with his blanket, draped it over his shoulders, and went back in to the Tower.

More awake than when he had first arrived, he examined this providential shelter. Among the baskets and boxes on the eastern ledge, he found a large basket of clothing. He sorted through it, ignoring the fine tunics and leggings, and instead chose a thick brown woolen robe, shabby and unpretentious; a patched gray tunic and leggings; and gray woolen stockings. A pair of worn leather slippers lay on the floor beneath the basket. Everything fit well enough, and provided warmth and comfort. For a moment, he felt grateful to whoever had left this refuge and these things for him to find.

Hunger made his stomach rumble. "Well, Zhovanya," he muttered, "You insist that I live, so I suppose there must be food here, somewhere." And, indeed, in the kitchen, he found stone crocks sealed with beeswax. One held unshelled nuts; another, ration sticks of dried berries and meat; and a third, dried apple slices. He also found stoneware mugs, bowls, and plates, and other kitchen utensils. He took a pitcher out to the well and filled it, then went back into the kitchen, where he set a few sticks of jerky to soak in a bowl of water. Overlaid by Rajani's memories, everything had the strange familiarity of a recurring dream.

He perched on a stool at the small table, chewing dried apple slices, and looked around uneasily. *It's so quiet. Of course, I'm alone here, but…..* Frowning, he washed down the apples with a swig of cold water. *Something's missing. Oh!* He set his mug down with a thump. "By all the hells, no one is plaguing my mind!" Cautiously, he probed his awareness for any presence but his own, but there was none. *The Soul-Drinker is dead, Gauday dead, Dekani — curse it! I mean Lanir — dead.*

No one was invading his mind with punishments and pleasures, or healing and guidance. No one was manipulating him into fulfilling their mysterious schemes. The empty silence within was such a strange freedom that his body kept shivering and relaxing, shivering and relaxing, each time more deeply than the last. He sat on the stool with his elbows on the table and his head in his hands until his body calmed. Then, worn out, he went back to the divan and curled up in the nest of pillows.

All that mattered now was to be alone, where no one could use him and he could hurt no one. The quiet isolation of the Tower was the best he could hope for. "Hells, maybe I'll stay here until You deign to allow me to die." He huffed a mordant laugh. "But I should know by now, You'll never be that merciful."

For the rest of the day, he simply existed in a state of thoughtless exhaustion, sleeping on the divan before the strange fire, accepting without question the odd magic of this Tower.

His second day in the Tower waned to a close, and the shadows of night crept into the round chamber, the only light coming from the eerie aqua flames. Kyr thought about lighting the candles that were scattered around the chamber, but the gloom better suited his mood. Sitting before the inexplicable fire, memories — his own and Rajani's — stung and bit, driving him to jump up and pace around the chamber. As he paced, he passed by the northern side of the staircase, looked up it, and wondered where it led. Too tired to explore, he turned away — and froze. His heart thudded with painful recognition. "Zhovanya!"

In a niche below the northern window sat an altar draped in purple velvet. One white and one black candle set in golden candlesticks framed a golden figure. She was poised on one foot, dancing in front of black draperies encrusted with random swirls of tiny crystals. "Ah, cruel Goddess, I can never escape You, can I?" He laughed bitterly, turned his back on Her, and resumed his restless pacing. *Star-cursed, star-cursed, star-cursed.* The words kept time with his footsteps.

In the dire light of his unnatural, star-cursed birth, his entire existence seemed to be nothing but a nightmare of torment and betrayal: his boyhood at the mercy of the cruel Trainer, kept sane by the false comfort and guidance of Lanir, his teacher, father, and betrayer; becoming a Slave and then the Favorite of the Soul-Drinker; enduring his Master's capricious punishments and terrible favors, and in turn coldly torturing innocent people to death to feed the Soul-Drinker's insatiable greed. *Curse his empty soul! If it weren't for him, none of this would have happened, and I would never have been created by that evil ritual. What better blessing could I ask for?*

Instead, my own father *brought me into this life to suffer the Soul-Drinker's tortures; and taught me how to go into the ice so I could endure it all — pretending all the while to love and care for me. Ha! All he cared about was shaping me into the weapon he could use to kill the Soul-Drinker. And* then *he leaves me alive to endure the Watcher's tortures. Worse, he wakens me to the reality of love, leaving me alone to face my guilt and remorse at the Sanctuary. Curse Lanir to the deepest hell!*

He strode over to the altar, and stood staring at the golden figure of Zhovanya, shaking with outrage. "My own father did this to me! My own *father!* *He* cursed me to this terrible life. *Now* I know why he asked me on his deathbed to forgive him. Ha! Not even You can expect me to do *that.* I could forgive Gauday. He was my Slave brother, lost in the Soul-Drinker's madness. But

Lanir knew exactly what he was doing to me. I cannot forgive him his false, devious 'love.'" Kyr choked to a stop, his throat aching fiercely. In a harsh whisper, he added, "By all the hells, he was the one I turned to for help and guidance. Fool that I was, I thought he loved me!" Sharp pain stabbed through his heart, and he crumpled to the floor. Beating his fists on the carpet, he sobbed, "Damn him, damn him, damn him!"

The mage-fire flared up in flames of green and gold, white and red, dancing quietly in the hearth, emanating soothing warmth. Kyr slowly calmed down, and crawled over to the divan. Climbing into the nest of pillows, he curled up, feeling heavy and drained, and slid into a deep sleep. The Full Moon sent His silvery light flooding through the east window, and a whisper of weeping shivered the still air of the Tower.

S ilvery light yielded to darkness, and darkness to the pale light of dawn. Kyr woke in a calm, detached mood. Taking the water pitcher, he stepped outside. "Hells!" he cried. The day was cold and blustery, with dark clouds threatening storm. He paid a quick visit to the outhouse, filled the pitcher at the well, and ducked back inside the Tower just as the rain began pelting down. After a breakfast of nuts, dried apple, and cold water, he returned to the divan, draped his blanket over his shoulders, and sat in meditation pose, determined to face the reality of his star-cursed life.

It wasn't just Lanir who forced me into this cursed life. The Circle *performed that evil ritual, and* Rajani *murdered his brother — my father — to send Lanir into my soul. Gods and demons, what a cruel pair, Rajani and Lanir! Merciless as the gods, those two.* Kyr shook himself and rolled his tense shoulders, trying to remain calm.

Then Rajani, Luciya, Tenaiya, and their Circle rescued me from the Watcher before I could die in peace; pretended to care for me; and taught me to believe in "kindness" and "friendship." Ha! What a joke. Bitter anger overrode his calm detachment.

Blasted Warrior Mage! Why did he always manage to come to my rescue too damn late, leaving me to suffer the "favors" of the Watcher, and then of Gauday? Probably part of manipulating me to fulfill this cursed Prophecy he's oath-bound to fulfill. What is *this damn Prophecy? What does it have to do with* me? *What is he trying to use me for next? Curse it! I didn't get those memories from him. He cut our connection too quickly.* Bereft of answers, Kyr set that trail of inquiry aside, and returned to reviewing his life.

Even Tenaiya and Svahar are a part of Rajani's damned Circle, using their skills to heal me and free me from the craving. They went to so much trouble! Svahar even died to help me. Why? Why? It makes no sense. Lanir had already used me to kill the

Soul-Drinker. Khailaz and all its people and soulkin are free! He shook his head, baffled and frustrated.

Let's not forget Luciya. She persuaded me to choose this cursed hard path. He glanced over at the altar. "Goddess, did You laugh when I made that choice, knowing what I would suffer?" He jumped up and stomped over to stand before the altar, fists clenched.

"Am I just Your puppet, Your plaything? Yours, and Lanir's, and the Soul-Drinker's, and Rajani's, and Gauday's, gods damn them all!" An anguish of betrayal and loathing wrenched his gut, and he dropped to the floor and curled up in a tight ball, refusing this time to give in to the tears of his soul.

But he no longer had the ice to numb all thoughts and feelings. No longer could he call up the forgiveness chant to soothe and calm him. No longer could he meditate or pray. What god or Goddess would listen to the prayers of a star-cursed creature made from evil and murder? All he had now was the iron discipline tortured into him by the Soul-Drinker's Trainer.

Kyr drove himself up and outdoors, glad to find that the clouds had passed on. The stone courtyard glistened wetly. He kicked off his slippers and looked around. "Ah." Grabbing two heavy stones that had fallen out of the courtyard wall, he began the grueling regime of exercises he'd had to learn in order to avoid his Trainer's vicious punishment. Holding a stone in each hand, he jogged in place, lifting the stones up and down, yelling curses at all his false friends from the Circle.

Still weakened by Medari's purging, and having eaten very little over the past few days, he was soon sweating and breathing hard. He forced himself to go on until he was shaking, and the stones dropped from his trembling hands. He leaned over, hands on knees, panting. The anguish in his gut had condensed down to a hot ember. "Why?" he panted. "Why have they kept me alive, put me through all this? What in all the hells do they want out of me?"

He straightened up with a groan. And there was the Raven, sitting on the wall, cocking its head, examining him with dark, enigmatic eyes.

"Damn bird, what do you know? Will you share Rajani's secrets with me?"

"Rawrk," said the Raven. Somehow, its remark sounded sympathetic.

"Hmph." Kyr shook his head, but a slight smile touched his lips. Exhausted but calmer, he went inside. Delving deeper into the stores in the kitchen, he found hard biscuits and honey to add to the jerky, apples, and nuts. After his meal, he took a long nap. But as soon as he woke, his mind returned to its relentless quest for the truth, and he sat on the divan with his knees up, and his arms wrapped around his shins.

Who else has been using me? Betraying me? Who else is part of the cursed Circle? Medari, Craith, and the other penitents? No, they are innocents caught up in this madness. Naran-ji? Jolanya? He sucked in a breath. *Merciless gods, were they part of the Circle too?*

Let it not be true! Naran and Jolanya helped me so much. Kyr sifted through the memories he'd absorbed from Rajani. *Ah, I see. The Circle highly valued the Sanctuary and protected the secret of its existence, but that's all.* Sagging with relief, he dropped down onto the carpet to sit before the hearth. *Naran and Jolanya and the others at the Sanctuary did their best to help and heal me.* His heart ached with melancholy gladness: the two to whom he had entrusted his soul were not part of the deceit and manipulation by the Circle. Naran and Jolanya were truly his friends.

Now his time at the Sanctuary seemed more precious than ever, the one good year in his entire life. And his most cherished moment was Jolanya whispering her love to him just before he turned himself over to Gauday. Bitter-sweet tears filled his eyes. "Ah, Jolanya, perhaps you did truly love me, then."

To survive the hell he had been through with Gauday, he had buried his memories of her deep in his heart, safe from Gauday's madness. Now, at last, he could let himself fully remember his forbidden beloved: her deep healing wisdom, courage, strength, and kindness; her luminous dark eyes and lush woman's body; her dark river of shining hair; her passionate, gentle love-making; and her powerfully healing hands. Knowing what he truly was, a star-cursed creature born of evil, he could never keep his promise to become a man worthy of Jolanya's love. In fact, he had *never* been worthy. "Jolanya!" he cried out, his heart shattering, his iron control breaking. He bowed his head to his knees, wracked with deep, harsh sobs.

As soft shadows of evening crept across the floor, his sobbing waned, leaving his face tight with dried tears. His arms ached to hold Jolanya, but he was sure that great blessing would never again be his. Then he thought of holding *Friend* close, as he had at the fort and since, and groaned with a deep ache of longing for the comfort of her warm, solid body, and her wordless affection. *Gods, what happened to Friend? I haven't even thought of her since that cursed "cleansing" ritual. I hope she's all right.* He raised his head, glanced over his shoulder toward the statuette of Zhovanya, and muttered, "Cruel Goddess, have You taken even my dog from me? Will You allow me no consolation at all?"

Lost in a desert of grief, loneliness, and despair, he stared dully at the hypnotic dance of the mysterious turquoise flames. Slowly, a strange lethargy erased all thought, all feeling.

After a night of restless dreams, he woke feeling edgy and tired. The round chamber seemed to be closing in on him, and he fled outdoors into a cool, clear morning. After visiting the outhouse and splashing icy well-water on his face, he felt wide-awake but no less edgy, and began his Trainer's punishing regime of exercises again. As he jumped up and down and ran in place, a huge wave of rage swelled up from his gut, and he roared out, "Gods damn you! Gods damn you all! And gods damn You, Zhovanya! How could You *do* this to me?"

He stormed inside and stood before the altar, fists clenched at his sides. "'Beloved,' You called me," he snarled. "'Be my guardian,' You said. 'Live,' You insist. Why? Why all this? It would have been kinder if You had just used me as ruthlessly as Gauday or the Soul-Drinker. Why not let me destroy Your enemies without all this cursed 'kindness' and 'love.' Why let the Circle 'rescue' me from the Watcher? Why send me to the Sanctuary, let me feel forgiven, let me think of myself as a real person, even imagine I could be a good man?"

There was no answer. "Cruel, lying Goddess!" He shook his fists at Her, stalked over to the divan, and slouched down against the pillows, legs out straight, ankles crossed, and arms folded across his chest. *If I'd never gone to the Sanctuary, I'd have still had the ice. It would have been so much easier to endure Gauday's little hell.* Slamming his fists into the divan, he growled, "You didn't *want* me to have the protection of the ice, did You? Learning of love and kindness made what Gauday did to me so much worse. Unnatural creature of evil that I am, do You *want* me to suffer? Do You enjoy it, like the Soul-Drinker did?"

He saw it then: the baleful truth. Through stiff lips, he murmured, "By the evil sorcery and brother-murder that created me, I am not even one of Your children, am I, Zhovanya? Who better to use as your weapon for regaining Your sovereignty over Khailaz than a creature You despise? *That's* why You keep me here in this cursed life." Everything was clear now; exquisitely, agonizingly clear. He slumped back against the pillows, giving in to bone-deep weariness and utter desolation, while the eerie fire flickered white and blue, gold and green.

Chapter Fourteen

Eagle's Gift

He was chained to Gauday's bed. No, it wasn't soft enough to be Gauday's. Opening his eyes to the vast dome of blue sky, Kyr tried to get up, but ropes bound him hand and foot to a flat stone. A rustling of wings filled the air, and a dark shadow cut him off from the sky. "Kyyyyrrr!" A great Eagle hovered over him. Fierce golden eyes stared down at him, and a harsh voice demanded silently, "Tell me who you are."

"I'm the star-cursed beast created by evil sorcery and murder."

The Eagle swooped down and snatched Kyr's right arm. "Tell me who you are."

"Why are you doing this to me? Do you, my soulkin, hate me too?"

"Tell me who you are," The Eagle demanded implacably.

"I'm a weapon the Circle used against the Soul-Drinker, a broken weapon."

The Eagle swooped down and snatched Kyr's left leg. "Tell me who you are."

"I'm Zhovanya's pawn, her tool to regain her ascendancy over Khailaz."

The Eagle swooped down and snatched Kyr's left arm. "Tell me who you are."

"Stop it! Stop it! I'm nothing, no one! Leave me alone!"

The Eagle swooped down and snatched Kyr's right leg. "Tell me who you are."

"I'm Gauday's executioner, protector of the Sanctuary."

The Eagle swooped down and snatched Kyr's guts and pelvis. "Tell me who you are."

"I'm Naran's Aithané, Jolanya's kailithos."

The Eagle swooped down and snatched Kyr's ribcage and spine. "Tell me who you are."

143

"I'm Kyr! Kyr! Is that what you want to hear?"

The Eagle swooped down and snatched Kyr's head. "Tell me who you are."

Black emptiness. Soundlessness. Nothingness.

Yet in this void, a golden spark flared, a steady rhythm pulsed.

"Tell me who you are."

"I am who I choose to be."

"Kyyyrrrr!"

Deep in the night, he woke empty of all feeling, his mind quiet and contemplative. It was a strange but welcome relief from his storms of fury and grief. He rose and went to the outhouse. On the way back, he stopped to stare up at the tiny, mysterious lights which had cursed him to this terrible travail. *What are these stars, that they rule my fate?* There was something fascinating about their cold, distant resplendence.

"Gods!" he gasped as a large, silent shape flew in front of his face, its soft wingtip brushing his cheek.

"HUU, HU HU, HUU." The soft sound came from overhead. Looking up, Kyr spotted the large bird sitting hunched on a low branch of a tree that stood near the tower. The tree was so tall that it reached to the Tower's crystal dome. From its size, he thought the bird was a Raven, but then it turned its head and looked at him with large, round, golden eyes. Rajani had named it Owl one night long ago, on their trip to the Sanctuary.

Launching itself upward, Owl flew to a branch near the top of the tree, and peered into the dome. Kyr noticed rays radiating upward from the dome, shining with the cold light of the stars themselves. "What in all the hells is up there?" Going back into the Tower, he went over to the staircase spiraling upward into the darkness, and began to climb.

After two turns of the spiral, he emerged into a round room with a bed on the west side. Opposite that, a padded chair and a low, round table sat before a hearth, where another blue-green fire sprang to life. Several large chests sat under the northern window. The bed looked inviting, but Kyr continued on. As he climbed, the pale light from the bedroom mage-fire faded, leaving him in pitch darkness; but he kept climbing, feeling for each step with his toes, keeping one hand on the cold smoothness of the stone wall. A slight groove was worn into the wall just where his hand touched. He wondered how many others had climbed these endless stairs before him.

Several times, he had to sit and rest. The darkness was not oppressive; rather, it was somehow soothing, even friendly. The stairs wound upward far longer than seemed possible, given the apparent height of the Tower as seen from outside. But at last, an ice-blue glow appeared above him. He hurried up the last turn of the stairs and entered a room with no ceiling. Dizzied by the dark and endless sky above, Kyr stumbled to a stop. Closing his eyes, he focused on his feet standing on the solid floor. Then he looked up. There was, in fact a ceiling. A clear-crystal dome arched over the room, with the stars shining through it, close and bright. Narrow beams from each star shot down onto a round table. Its black surface reflected each one, mirroring a perfect map of the heavens.

Kyr stood entranced for a long while, watching the slow crawl of the stars across the blackness above the dome, and below, on the star mirror. At first, the patterns on the dark table seemed to gleam at him malevolently; but after a time, he sighed, realizing that the stars were merely what they were: as impersonal and uncaring as fire, rain, windstorm, or — as it seemed to him now — the Goddess.

A faint "HU HU" from the tree outside drew Kyr's attention across the chamber. Owl was still there in the tree outside the crystal dome, peering right at him. For a timeless moment, their eyes met, and Kyr was startled by an odd sense of consolation and encouragement. Still, he was glad when the bird turned its disconcerting stare downwards.

Following its gaze, he saw a wide table, stacked with books and papers. Owl hooted softly again. "Alright," Kyr said, crossing the chamber to the table. There, he discovered that the papers depicted star patterns similar to that on the star-mirroring table.

The first one showed a star-pattern of a great bird with its wings outstretched, over a cross indicated by seven larger circles, each a different color. With a shock, Kyr recognized this pattern. It had appeared on the door of the Tower when he first entered. And it was the star pattern under which the vile ceremony that had created him had been performed.

The drawing on the parchment seemed to vibrate with omnipotent menace. *Gods and demons,* this *is what has cursed me to this wretched existence!* Horrified and fascinated, heart thumping, he picked up the parchment with trembling hands, expecting a jolt of lightning, hoping perhaps to be blasted into a heap of bone and ash.

But after a moment, he snorted. It was just a drawing on parchment. It had no power in itself. "Who drew this chart? Who cast me into this terrible life?" he muttered. "Ha!" In Rajani's memory, it was a Star-Seer who had pronounced the cursed Prophecy that the Circle followed. *Must have seen my fate in the stars with this blasted star-mirror.* "Gods curse it!" he growled, tempted to smash it to pieces. But then he sighed. "Too late now."

Outside, Owl hooted sadly, and flew silently away.

The next morning, Kyr stood on the steps of the portico, looking out over the stone-paved courtyard into the dawn sky's pale vastness. High above, a tawny eagle soared. Kyr gasped, recalling, now, the powerful dream of Eagle tearing him to pieces. "Gods and demons! That seemed so real!"

Watching the eagle spiral higher and higher, envy stabbed Kyr's gut — envy of the eagle's freedom and serene neutrality. He, in contrast, felt filthy with blood and black sorcery, sick with shame and self-loathing. Gripping his upper arms, he dug his nails into them, just barely keeping himself from ripping his skin off. With a sudden gasp, he let go of his arms and stood watching in wonder as the eagle plummeted, swerved, and flew toward him. Passing overhead, it circled once above the courtyard before rising again. Lifting his arms toward his soulkin, Kyr begged, "I don't know who I am, what I am, what I should do. Please, please grant me the ability to see with your eyes."

A cool breeze feathered across his face and into his heart. Sensing within, he discovered that the raging anguish in his core had calmed to glowing embers. As the eagle soared out of sight, he placed his hands together before his heart and bowed, whispering, "Thank you."

He entered the Tower and sat cross-legged on the divan, back straight, hands resting on his knees. He felt ready, now, to face Eagle's dream question, "Tell me who you are."

"My last answer — and the one that Eagle accepted — was 'I am who I choose to be,'" he murmured. "But gods and demons, how can that be true? When have I ever made my own choices?"

All I knew under the Soul-Drinker's command, he mused, *was obedience. I had no idea that choice was possible. And after the Circle took me, I made no choices until we got to the cabin. There, I chose the hard path, though I had no idea what that meant.* He shook his head, perplexed. *Why the hells did I?* He tried to sink back into the mind of the dark innocent he had been then, remembering what it had been like when he had first emerged from the Soul-Drinker's realm of evil and suffering, and encountered the strange thing called kindness.

Ah, I see. Despite their hidden motives, Luciya, Tenaiya, and Rajani treated me kindly. Watching how they treated each other showed me a new way of life — so different from anything I had ever known before. They obviously wanted me to choose the hard path of healing, hope, and love. And deep down, my soul was desperately hungry for this strange new life. That's why I chose the hard path, and ever since have tried to follow that path. With the eye of his soulkin Eagle, he saw that everything else stemmed from this choice.

What was my first step on the hard path? Ah, yes. Agreeing to go to the Heart of the Forest with Tenaiya; hoping the Tree Warden, Svahar, could rid me of the craving. Not much of a choice. The thought of a horrible death from the unchecked craving was unbearable. Bless his soul, Svahar did save me from that.

When he died right after cleansing me of the craving, I felt so much remorse, so guilty for causing his death and the deaths of all those I had sacrificed to the Soul-Drinker. I wanted to do penance; and with Rajani's encouragement, I chose to go to the Sanctuary. But instead of the punishment I expected — the kind of agony the Soul-Drinker inflicted — my penance was to face all the harm I did as a Slave, and all that I had suffered, myself. With Naran's help, I freed myself from much of my guilt and remorse, and from being an obedient Slave. And what Jolanya — the Kailithana — did for me is precious beyond telling. She helped me become…human.

"Ah gods, I made a promise to her, didn't I?" Vividly as if it were happening that moment, he recalled hearing Jolanya telling him that their work together was at an end, and adding, "*The Goddess not only forgives us. She loves us. To honor Her, honor yourself and others with patience, love, and kindness. Promise me this.*" In deep grief over the ending of his time with Jolanya, and with immeasurable gratitude for all she had done to heal him, he had knelt and bowed to her, saying, "*I promise.*"

Bitter-sweet tears now filled his eyes at this precious memory. "Jolanya," he whispered, "I will always love you. To honor you, I will try to keep this promise. But — oh my beloved! — I don't know if I *can*, star-cursed and born of evil as I am." Then he recalled his promise to himself to again become the kind of man whom Jolanya could love, even though he would never see her again. At that time, he had decided that this would be his way to honor her and the love they shared.

But now, he shook his head. *I'll never be that kind of man again. Maybe I never was. Maybe I was deluding myself and everyone at the Sanctuary, even Jolanya.* At this thought, his heart ached so badly that he could barely breathe.

Hunching up with his arms around his legs and his head on his knees, he couldn't keep from imagining Jolanya's horror if she learned that he had been created out of dark sorcery and murder. *How can I be kind and good when I'm drenched in blood and black sorcery, and have spent most of my life as a Slave to evil incarnate?* For a time, he rocked a little from side to side in grief and despair, bereft of all solace.

The light through the eastern window dimmed, and the western window began to gleam with afternoon sunshine. Glowing blue-green, the mage-fire's subtle warmth eased Kyr's heart; and with a deep sigh, he raised his head and straightened up. His stomach grumbled loudly.

Getting to his feet, he stretched and went into the kitchen. As he cobbled a meal together, he again recalled his dinner party at the Sanctuary, when he had thanked his friends for all their help and given them his small handmade figurines as gifts. The contrast between that convivial feast and this lonely, meager meal brought tears to his eyes. He set down his mug of water and stood leaning on the counter, choking back sobs.

After a few moments, he drank some water, swallowing his grief as best he could, and sat at the small table to eat. Though his throat was tight, he managed to choke down enough nuts and dried apples to take the edge off his hunger. Then, returning to the divan, he sat cross-legged and continued to review his promises and choices.

I made another promise to Jolanya and Naran-ji: to pass on the gifts I had received at the Sanctuary to those who crossed my path in life, especially to my transgressors. But then he burst out, "By all the hells! How can someone born of evil and murder be expected to carry out these impossible promises? It's ridiculous!"

He jumped up, rushed outside, and began pacing around the courtyard, the Eagle's question still burning in his mind. *Who am I? Am I the man I choose to be, or just a puppet of this star-curse?* He stalked back and forth for a while, until his frustration and anger cooled. Then he paused and looked out over the surging green sea of wind-tossed treetops down the hill from the Tower. He breathed in the cool, late-Autumn air before returning to examining his life.

What else have I chosen? I chose to protect the Sanctuary by turning myself over to Gauday. His skin crawled at the thought of all that he had suffered as a result of this choice. *Would I still make that choice?* He nodded slowly. *Yes, I would do anything to protect Jolanya, Naran-ji, and all the good people there, no matter the cost to me.* He stood a little straighter and began pacing again, rubbing his arms for warmth.

What next? Ah, yes. At Gauday's fort, I tried to fulfill my promise to pass on the blessings I received at the Sanctuary. I failed to reach Gauday and most of his men; but I did help the four penitents and Medari. I created a chapel at the fort where many people came to chant and meditate. And I did manage to forgive Gauday. He sighed, feeling as if a door had started to open. *Perhaps these promises are not so impossible. Perhaps I can be kind, despite the star-curse.* He straightened his spine and lifted his chin. A tentative whisper of pride touched his heart, but he flinched away.

Clouds covered the sky, and a cold breeze whipped through the courtyard, sending him inside to sit by the fire again.

Am I the man I have chosen to be? Or am I just Zhovanya's cat's-paw? After all, my Trainer tortured obedience into me, beginning when I was four. For most of my life, that's all I knew. Perhaps all I have done is to obey one master after another: the Soul-Drinker, Lanir, Rajani, Naran-ji, Jolanya, and Zhovanya.

Fire shot through his veins. *Gods and demons! Why didn't I see this before? Zhovanya is my master, now. That night on the ledge above the Sanctuary, when She came to me as the Firebird, I pledged to serve Her with all my heart, even though She demands that I suffer until I somehow become this Vessel She wants me to be. And when I was near to giving in to Gauday's mind-bonding, I wanted to submit myself to him to end the torment; but instead, I begged Her to accept my submission.*

With a dark sense of relief, he rose and crossed over to the altar, where he knelt and bowed his head. "Ah, Zhovanya!" he whispered. "I am your dog. I gave you my submission, and must accept whatever You decree for me, no matter how painful." It was so familiar, this giving up responsibility to a more powerful being. The world seemed to make sense again, though he had an uneasy feeling that it had shrunk somehow, with no spacious skies in which his soul might soar.

Remembering dancing in sweet surrender to Zhovanya in Her Temple at the Sanctuary, he yearned hopelessly for that innocent joy, and grieved for all that he had lost since that time. He crouched there, dreading a life of endless submission and suffering.

Ponderously, he got to his feet and retreated to the divan once more, staring into the blue-green fire. "What do You want me to do, Zhovanya?" he whispered bleakly. At first, there was no answer. But as he looked into the changeable fire, an image came to his mind of Medari as he had last seen him, looking devastated and heart-broken. *Ah, hells! Medari!* Sharp remorse bit his heart. *First he loses his beloved wife and children because of me, and now I revile him — for what? Only for saving my life. Without me,* he *may have nothing to live for.*

But — can I forgive him for dragging me back into this terrible life? He brooded over this for a few moments, then shrugged. *Well, it is* Zhovanya *Who demands that I live. Medari was just Her instrument. Besides, he had to keep to his Healer's Oath. And I chose to take him as my heart-father. He and I are family. But what does that mean now?* Kyr sank back among the pillows of the divan. *Surely it doesn't mean abandoning him. I must forgive him and go back to be as much of a son to him as I can.*

But — oh, hells! — if he learned that I am star-cursed and drenched in blood and evil magic, even he would revile me. Telling him the truth would be as bad as deserting him. Either way, he would lose me. I must keep silent for his sake and tell no one else, for they might tell him. He snorted. *Though I doubt Rajani or his cronies will tell anyone what they did to me.*

Thinking of the members of the Circle reminded him of Lanir, and the death-bed promise that Lanir had exacted. *He made me promise to stay here in Ravenvale "until it's all over, no matter what." Until what is all over?* Kyr sat up and brushed his tangled hair out of his eyes. *Well, it doesn't matter. I have to stay here in Ravenvale to be a son to Medari — unless he wants to leave. Gods, I hope so!* With a vindictive laugh, Kyr thought, *If he does, I will gladly break my promise to Lanir, my heartless father.*

He curled up amongst the pillows on the divan, gripped with a fierce longing to remain in the Tower forever, or flee from Ravenvale; to break all his promises and abandon the hard path. But with Eagle's gift, he could see that this was the easy path, and would lead only to a chaos of lostness, regret, blame, and anger. With a brief, pain-filled laugh, he straightened up.

I chose the hard path. Dishonoring that choice would make me nothing but the product of the Circle's evil ritual — of all the evil I have suffered. Gods, no! His gut revolted at the thought of such a barren, meaningless life.

Staring into the mage-fire in the hearth, he found a small flame of love still burning deep inside his soul — and also a spark of defiance. *Why should I let this star-curse, or the Circle's evil ritual, define me when I refused to let the Soul-Drinker or Gauday do so?* He slowly raised his head, a fierce look in his eyes. That small spark of defiance blazed up brightly, and he nodded once, definite and strong. *I won't abandon Medari to his grief, or toss aside the precious gifts of healing and love that Naran and Jolanya gave me. It may be impossible, but I will try to keep my promises, try to be the kind of man Jolanya would love.*

That small flame in his heart brightened, glowing gentle and golden, and his mind was at last at peace.

In the morning, he woke feeling calm and settled. For a few moments, he lay still, enjoying this inner quietness. With his painfully earned iron will, he was determined to do keep to the choice he had made the night before. He rose and stood before Zhovanya's altar. "Despite all You have done or may do to me, I will keep my promises, return to Medari, and try to become again the kind of man Jolanya would love — or at least, to act like one. But I must keep to myself. I'm Your dog, Your tool and weapon in Your quest to reclaim Your place as Goddess of Khailaz. I'm tainted with evil, and You want me to suffer, so I will not allow myself anything beyond my duty to Medari."

His serenity evaporated at the thought of what awaited him at Ravenhall, and he returned to the divan. *What am I going to say to Craith and the other penitents?* Remorse for what he had done to Craith was bitter in his mouth, and he cringed with shame at how he had failed his brothers on the hard path. *Gods, what about Naran-ji? He'll want me to tell him everything. I couldn't bear to see the revulsion in his eyes if I told him how I was created. And Zhovanya wouldn't want me to receive his kindness and help. I'll have to shut him out, somehow. And how in all the hells am I going to deal with Rajani and his cursed Circle? I don't know if*

I can ever forgive them. The best I can do is to avoid them all. If I see them, I don't know if I can keep hold. Curse them all!

This path seemed the hardest of all, harder than suffering the Soul-Drinker's tortures, harder than facing his remorse and guilt at the Sanctuary, harder than enduring Gauday's torments. "Merciless Goddess!" he groaned. "How will I bear it?"

He sat on the edge of the divan, wishing he could stay on the island alone until Zhovanya relented and let him die. But the faded scars on his forearms reminded him of all he had endured at the fort — and the difficult lessons he had learned there. *Curse it! Lanir's teachings are valid despite his treachery. What difference does it make if it is Gauday torturing me or Zhovanya? It's still the same problem. If I think about the past or the future, I will lose hold and go mad, hurt someone like I did Craith.* Kyr laughed harshly, appalled that he had to use the gifts of his worst betrayer — his teacher, his father — to endure the star-cursed life that this same traitor had forced upon him.

Dreading what he must endure, he watched the sunlight from the eastern window crawl slowly across the faded carpets and up the purple altar cloth, and gleam from the golden image of the Goddess dancing there. He rose and went to kneel before the altar in somber acquiescence. "Please...," he began, longing to beg for Her help. But the memories of the evil ritual that brought him into being filled his mind, and he could not do it, convinced that She loathed him, despite calling him Her "Beloved"; despite Her desire that he become Her Vessel; despite Her promise that passion, peace, and love would fill his days.

He placed his hands over the burning anguish in his core. "Zhovanya, I offer this to You." He felt Her Presence descending toward him, but he could not bear it. Shaking his head, he rose to his feet. "I am only Your dog, Zhovanya. No more of Your pretended love, Your cruel blessings."

Wearing the shabby brown robe, patched tunic and leggings, and old slippers he had found, and cloaked in his green blanket, Kyr left the Tower and started down the stony path. In the ordinary sunshine of this new day, he felt trapped by his choices and promises, ensnared in a life of evil, betrayal, pain, and despair. But in honor of the tiny golden flame of love in his heart, and in defiant submission to his cruel fate, he went on.

Part Five ~ Defying Fate

*"Out of suffering have emerged the strongest souls;
the most massive characters are seared with scars."*

— Khalil Gibran

Chapter Fifteen

Tears of the Fire

K yr trudged down the path from the Tower, keeping his attention on his breath and what was around him. At first, the path led across a wide swath of smooth, dark stone. Small pools from the recent rains glistened in its depressions and crevices, attracting hovering insects and small, darting birds that flashed green or purple as they dove and twisted in the air, chasing the insects. The immaculate serenity of the rain-washed sky reminded him painfully of his own defilement, and he kept his eyes on the steep, stony path.

Yet, as he warmed with the exercise, he felt stronger and moved with more confidence — and discovered a grave consolation in returning to his chosen path, hard though it was. For the first time, he felt entirely his own man.

As Zhovanya demanded, he would endure life — but on his own terms, now. He would defy the forces of deceit and defilement by keeping to the choices and promises he had made, even though that meant he would have to endure whatever suffering the Goddess inflicted. With this choice — although his mind and heart were weighed down with sadness, anger, and dread — his soul was at peace.

I will keep to the hard path. But I have no idea how I can forgive Rajani and his Circle. His jaw clenched, and he tripped over a root but managed to stay on his feet. Refraining from cursing, he took this as a reminder of the cost of dwelling on the past, and the need to let go of everything that was not here and now. He forced his attention back to his footsteps, his breath.

Raven appeared overhead, cruising silently above him or flying ahead to light upon a branch until Kyr caught up. This time, the bird had no cryptic comments but merely regarded him with its bright dark eyes.

The path entered the shady forest, leaving the open field of rocks behind. Kyr sighed with relief to be away from the taunting purity of the sky. The air was colder inside the forest, and he pulled his blanket closer round him. A hidden bird sang an echoing, melancholy refrain, in melodic counterpoint to the creek that chuckled along beside the path.

A short while later, he passed between two tall golden aspens that arched toward each other over the path, and entered a small vale dappled with sunshine that sifted down between the aspen leaves. *Don't remember seeing this place on the way up,* Kyr mused, *but of course I wasn't paying much attention then.*

In this vale, the creek trickled through the roots of a large pine tree into a small, dark pool, forming a miniature waterfall. The peacefulness of the place lured him to a stop. Hungry and in need of a rest, he left the path to sit on a log by the small pond, and dug in his pocket for the handful of dried fruit and nuts he had brought from the Tower. After making this his meal, he leaned over to cup some water from the tiny waterfall in his two hands. The water tasted of stone, leaf, and earth, and his body avidly absorbed its cool grace and vitality. He drank his fill, then slid down onto the earth and leaned back against the log. Following his breath in and out, he relaxed, melding with the stillness of this modest, blessed place.

Wordlessly, he regarded the little pond, noticing the way the water trickled quietly between the roots of the great old pine. Graceful ferns leaned over the edge of the pond, and tiny fish flashed silver, darting in and out of the pond's tree-shadowed depths. A sense of abiding Presence, smaller and more earthbound than that of the Goddess, crept upon him; and he became aware that he was no longer quite alone.

A moss-bearded man, sad and old, peered out at him from a knotted pine root. *"Yes, life is difficult,"* he seemed to say, *"but we go on. We do our duty."*

Then a silent giggle drew his attention to a round-faced boy visible in a large stone embedded in the far bank of the pond. *"Oh, poof, don't listen to the old man. Life is an adventure!"* Kyr smiled a little at the boy's irreverent enthusiasm.

A hunch-backed, big-nosed driftwood woman paused in her journey, standing in the rivulet that slid smoothly from the pond down toward the distant lake. He caught a glimpse of a smile on her face; but when he looked at her more closely, she was somber again. *"There's nothing to do but follow your nose,"* she murmured. *"Let your nose tell you what smells right."*

Kyr's head nodded onto his chest, and he slept. When he woke from this short, refreshing nap, the man, boy, and old woman were now nothing but root, rock, and driftwood. Nevertheless, he rose and bowed to the root-man and the rock-boy. "A difficult adventure, indeed." Then he bowed to the old woman. "Thank you, Grandmother, I will try to follow my nose."

Bemused but reassured that he was on the right path, he continued downwards toward the shore, thinking of the spirit beings who had spoken to him by the pool. *Did I dream them, or were they actually there? Well, it doesn't matter. It was kind of them to share their wisdom with me.*

A rustling sound startled him out of his reverie. He glanced down to find that he was wading ankle-deep through crackling drifts of gold. The aspen trees had cast their leaves in heaps across the path, and he shivered at the thought of the oncoming season of rains.

When he reached the shore, he found the boat that had brought him here still tied to the willow tree. Exhausted by his long walk and having nothing left to eat, he knelt by the creek that had tumbled after him down the hill, and filled his stomach with its gift of clear water. Then he shed his clothes, wrapped them in the blanket, and tossed the bundle on board to keep them dry. With a shiver, he waded into the chilly water and clambered aboard the boat.

Too tired to pole back across the lake, he dried himself off with a corner of the blanket, donned his clothes, wrapped himself in the blanket, and curled up in the bottom of the boat. As he listened to the lapping of the water against the hull, the rustling of the breezes through the nearby forest, and the faint cawing of ravens tacking back and forth above the treetops, he gladly returned to the sweet oblivion with which the lake had first blessed him upon his arrival at the island. Unbeknownst to him, the ethereal Eagle's radiant red-gold light again warmed and soothed him throughout the misty evening and cold Autumn night.

"Can you see anything, Bru?"

A familiar voice echoed across the misty lake, startling Kyr out of peaceful dreams. *Merciless gods, that's Luciya. They're hunting for me.* Praying they would not find him, he lay still, barely breathing.

"Not a damn thing," a deeper voice answered her. "This mist is impossible. We'll never find the island like this, rowing back and forth. We're just chasing illusions."

"We've got to find Kyr. Let's try *that* way. I think I see something."

"It's useless." But Bru's grumble was followed by a rhythmic clunk and splash, which slowly faded into the distance.

Kyr waited until he could no longer hear the splashing of Bru's oars. Then he silently untied the boat, stood, and began poling toward the mainland. The boat slid silently through the mist as if in a dream.

He blearily began to consider what came next. *There's only one reason I'm going back: to be a son to Medari. Can't go near Ravenhall or the penitents' house. I'll just go straight to the infirmary, wait for him there.*

Thinking of the long walk back from the boat house, he muttered, "Gods, I wish I knew how to go straight there, instead." He looked around, hoping for some landmarks, but mist obscured every direction and he had no idea which way to head. *Ha! Here I am trying to follow my path — and now I'm lost.* He set the pole aside in the boat, and sat down with guilty relief. *Perhaps She has abandoned me to die out here on this peaceful lake.* He smiled ruefully, sure that this was a forlorn hope. "Zhovanya, if you wish me to live, guide me where you want me to go." He sat, eyes closed, listening to the lapping of the water against the hull; and, after a time, he reached a deep quietness.

A loud caw broke the stillness, and Kyr smiled. *Ah, my guide has returned.* Appearing out of the mist, a Raven flew close by, heading purposefully in one direction. "Thank you for showing me the way," Kyr murmured, and began to pole in the same direction. Soon, the slim boat slid out of the mist into midday sunshine.

Behind him, the mist covered most of the lake and hid the searchers from sight. Squinting against the glare of light on the water, Kyr followed the Raven across the lake. Sooner than he would have liked, he saw the great tree of the Rookery showing over the horizon, followed by the gray bulk of Ravenhall.

Reaching the stone terrace that edged the lake, he tied the boat to a docking ring embedded in the stone, folded up the familiar blanket, and left it in the boat where he had found it. He climbed onto the pier and headed for the infirmary. Noticing two Companions squatting by the gate playing dice, the eternal game of bored guards, Kyr frowned and came to a halt.

Curse it! I don't want anyone to know I am here except Medari. But then, looking down at his shabby clothes and muddy slippers, and thinking of his scruffy beard and dirty hair, he chuckled to himself. *Who could imagine the "great Liberator" would look like this?* Hunching over, he limped toward the gate, keeping his eyes downcast.

The older guard looked up from their game of dice. "You one of the new ones from the fort?"

Kyr nodded.

"Where you headed?"

"My foot...." Kyr muttered, and pointed toward the infirmary.

The talkative guard waved his hand, impatiently. "Go on, then." He grabbed the dice. "My turn."

Kyr limped through the gate into the courtyard, and turned to the right, thankful that the infirmary was just inside the gate. He pushed its door open and went in, glad to reach the quiet, orderly infirmary. Closing the door, he straightened up and glanced around.

The low-ceilinged room was cozy and warm, with white-washed walls. To the right of the front door, a large pine table and six chairs stood by a window overlooking the lake. Further back, two comfortable armchairs and a plump couch sat in front of a stone hearth, where a low fire crackled quietly to itself, though the room was empty. From the rear wall, a staircase led upward.

Kyr took off his heavy robe and hung it on one of the cloak hooks to the left of the door. Walking past a pine cabinet that held stacks of blue-pottery mugs, plates, bowls, and a clutter of boxes and baskets, he came to the door of Medari's workroom and went in. On the wall opposite the door, several crowded shelves held baskets, bottles, and jars of herbs, potions, and salves. Beneath the shelves, two stools stood by a long plank table. At the far end of the room, locked cabinets framed a window with a view of the lake. Though a mortar and pestle stood ready on the table, along with bundles of dried herbs, Medari was not there.

At the other end of the workroom, a door opened to a short hallway. Kyr glimpsed three doors that stood open to small sleeping rooms for patients. He trudged down the hall, but found all the rooms empty except for two cots with neatly folded blankets and pillows. He shrugged. *Well, I'm sure Medari will be back here sooner or later. Gods, I'm tired.* He stepped into the first of the small, chilly rooms, curled up on one of the cots, and pulled the blankets up over his head.

The sound of the door scraping on the stone floor pulled Kyr out of a deep well of slumber.

"Hello," he overheard, "I'm the healer. The guards told me that someone had gone into the infirmary and needed help. Are you ill? Hurt?"

Kyr shivered a little at the sound of Medari's familiar voice. *Now it begins — this new life I've chosen.* He pulled the blanket down and sat up. "I'm…just tired. No need to play the healer with me."

"Kyr!" Medari gasped, dropped his healer's kit on the second cot, and sat down on the cot with a thump. "Gods, Kyr, I am so glad you have come back! Are you all right? What can I do for you?"

"I'm glad to see you, too, heart-father." Kyr smiled faintly at the healer's anxious questions. "I'm all right, but I *am* looking forward to some good food."

"Where have you been? What happened to you? You look so thin, and sort of…hardened."

Kyr's face darkened. "I'm not ready to speak about all that now. Maybe later."

Medari looked at Kyr with eyes full of guilt and remorse. "Did you flee because of what I did to you?"

"It wasn't because of what you did, Medari." Kyr fought back a rush of longing for the oblivion of death — so often denied to him — and watched his breath until he could speak calmly. "I know you had to keep to your Oath. And I must keep to mine. We are family now. It was selfish of me to abandon you. I won't do that again."

"You don't hate me for keeping you alive?" The older man's voice quavered like a scared young boy's. "You still want to be my son?"

"Yes, heart-father," Kyr said warmly. In a somber tone, he added, "It is Zhovanya Who demands that I live, no matter what. She used you to keep me from dying. So you see, it's not your fault."

Overcome by Kyr's forgiveness, Medari sobbed into his hands.

Kyr moved to sit by his heart-father's side, thinking of his terrible grief for his wife and children, a deep sadness that he often hid under his calm healer's demeanor. Both Kyr's own life of suffering and Medari's terrible loss seemed incomprehensibly cruel. Sadly, quietly, Kyr asked, "Why won't She just take us Home, Medari? Why must we continue to live, when it hurts so?"

Medari slumped back against the wall with a heavy sigh. "By all the hells, Kyr, I have no answers for you. With all that we have been through, I have little faith left. Perhaps the gods *are* merciless."

Kyr gave a painful laugh, wishing that he could comfort his heart-father. But he, too, could see no solace in all the world.

The healer reached into his tunic pocket and pulled out a small flask. He took a swallow, himself, then handed it to Kyr. "*This* is my answer when it gets too hard. It's called Tears of the Fire."

Furrowing his brow, Kyr asked, "Not another potion, is it?"

"No, son. No magic, no healing properties." Medari smiled sadly. "Just numbs the pain a bit. Can't indulge too often. Pretty potent."

Kyr noticed that Medari's speech was less crisp than usual, but he took a cautious sip. Golden sunshine flamed down his throat. "Ah!" He took another, bigger swallow and handed it back. "I'm sorry I left you for so long, Medari. It's just been so...."

"Never mind, son. You have had your own trials, far more than your share." He straightened up. "You look starved, son. I'll let the others know they can stop searching for you and fetch us some supper. Will you be all right here for a little while?"

"Gods and demons!" Kyr's face went hard. "Medari, I don't want to see anyone from Ravenhall, especially Luciya and Rajani. Keep them away from me."

"I don't understand. But whatever you say, son. You don't have to worry about Rajani. He's still not recovered from whatever it was that happened in that cleansing ritual. But I'll tell Luciya to stay away." Medari frowned, imagining how poorly this would go over with her.

"What happened to Rajani?" Kyr asked in vengeful curiosity.

"We don't know exactly, but it seems as if he got lost in some terrible nightmare. Naran thinks you two exchanged memories during the ritual."

"Ah, gods! Perhaps there *is* some justice, after all!"

Concealing his shock at Kyr's harsh comment, Medari rose. "I'll be back as soon as I can."

Kyr nodded, and slouched down with his head and shoulders propped up against the wall, and his legs stretched out in the narrow space between the cots. *No wonder Rajani didn't want me to touch him when we were in the inner realm. I guess that's how we traded memories.* He snorted in bitter amusement. *Well, at least, he is paying for killing my traitorous father and cursing me to this wonderful life of mine.* Kyr found some sour satisfaction in these thoughts. He crossed his arms on his chest and noticed the faded scars on his forearms. They reminded him to keep his focus on the present. He sighed and counted his breaths for a few moments, but kept losing track.

It had seemed simple back on the island, when he had decided to abide by his choices and promises. But now that he had returned to Ravenhall, everything seemed difficult and confusing. *To live here, I must accept food and shelter from those who cursed me before I was born. Merciless gods, it galls me! But I have no other way to survive here. Ah, Goddess, Your torments are subtle, various, and unending.*

With a sigh, he tried again to bring his attention into the moment by looking around the small room, with its two cots against opposite walls, a small table between them, and a narrow gray rug on the floor. When he spied the flask sitting on the floor where Medari had left it, he shrugged and bent forward to pick it up. He took a sip and sat back, savoring the potent taste of the golden liquor. *Amazing! It's like sunshine on ripe hayfields.* He took a few more sips, giving each one his full attention.

The liquor spread throughout his half-starved body, numbing his pain and anger but making him feel dizzy and slightly nauseated. Regretfully, he set the flask aside, thinking of what Medari had told him. *Rajani is lost in my memories? I'm not sure even he deserves that.* Exhausted and inebriated, he slid into a doze.

Chapter Sixteen

Communion of Sorrow

"**W**hy did you follow me here?" Medari demanded of an angry, disheveled Luciya. They were standing in the hall just outside the patients' rooms. "I told you, Kyr doesn't want to see you. And he's exhausted. Leave him alone, Luciya."

"Get out of my way!"

The sound of Luciya's raised voice startled Kyr awake, his heart pounding. Fear turned to rage as he realized who it was. *She's as guilty as Rajani, gods curse her!* He sat up, back to the wall, knees up, his arms wrapped tightly around his shins. Head bowed, he battled against the desire to charge out of the room and throttle her.

Ignoring Medari's protests, Luciya barged in, and slammed the door in Medari's face. He pounded on the door, demanding entrance, but she leaned against the door to keep him out; and after a moment, he stopped.

"Gods, Kyr, where *were* you?" Luciya cried. "You had us all so scared! Please, don't go running off like that again!" Hunched up on his bed, head down on his knees, Kyr made no response. She took a breath, trying to calm herself. "Are you all right?"

As soon as he raised his head, his fierce, accusing glare stabbed through her, and all the color drained from her face. Unable to look away, she sank to her knees. "P-please, Kyr! We had to...there was no other way. We tried but...." Her pleading voice trailed away under the continued assault of his gaze.

Kyr dug his fingers painfully hard into his calves, longing to spit curses at her, to condemn her and the entire Circle to the deepest hell. *I am star-cursed, a dangerous weapon that could turn on its masters. I could cut her with cruel words, beat her, rape her.* An image of her kneeling before him, bruised and bloody, begging for his forgiveness, made him shudder. He gritted his teeth, and remained still. *Or I can be the kind of man Jolanya would respect.*

Taking a deep breath, he made himself see Luciya's distress, shame, and remorse. Nevertheless, he could find no kindness or forgiveness for her in his heart. He lowered his head to his knees again, shutting out the sight of her. It was the best he could do.

Luciya, released from his fierce stare, climbed unsteadily to her feet and steeled herself to speak. "I won't leave until you promise me you won't disappear again. It's important, so very important. Promise me." Without looking up, Kyr jerked his head in a nod of assent, just to get rid of her. He was already bound to stay by his tie with Medari.

"Good. Thank you. Is there anything you want? Anything we can do for you?" Kyr rose and stood there glaring at Luciya, fists clenched, shoulders hunched. His silent rage and rejection burned like red-hot coals, and sent her out of the room, brushing hastily past Medari without a word.

The healer hesitated just outside the door to Kyr's room, and asked cautiously, "Kyr, what happened? Are you all right?

Kyr muttered through clenched teeth, "Give me a little while to cool off." And shut the door brusquely. Perplexed and concerned, Medari called, "I'm here if you need me." After a moment, he sighed and retreated to his workroom.

Alone in his room, Kyr growled, "Gods curse her! Gods curse them all!" and hit his door with both fists. "Ow, gods dammit." He snorted at himself and rubbed his sore hands on his thighs. Then he huffed out a breath and shook his head. *I need to calm down. Don't want to be any more trouble to Medari.*

Accordingly, he sat on his bed in meditative position: cross-legged, back straight. Bit by bit, he regained his focus on his breath and began to relax, partly from sheer exhaustion. Grim and quiet, more sad than angry now, he saw how the Soul-Drinker had trapped the Circle into evil in their efforts to end his horrific reign. *Perhaps the people in the Circle are just Zhovanya's tools, like me?* He shook his head, confused and angered by this thought, still unwilling to forgive them.

After a while, Medari opened the door. "I brought supper. Come, let's eat by the fire. It's cold in here." Kyr followed him into the main room, where the table and two stools sat by a crackling fire in the hearth. Two plates held bread-crusted fish, mashed carrots, green beans, fresh bread, and spice cookies. Kyr raised an eyebrow. *As if cookies could make up for what they did to me.* But hunger pushed aside all other concerns, and he gave his entire attention to the delicious food and the warm chyma tea Medari had brewed for them.

Medari forbore to disturb Kyr's dour silence. He knew from his own grief and rage that his heart-son needed no questions or idle talk. They ate together in the quiet. Afterwards, they moved the table and stools back under the window, and sat in the high-backed padded chairs by the fire. As the evening wore on, they occasionally sipped Tears of the Fire, handing the flask back and forth, saying nothing. Kyr discovered that there was some solace, after all, in this silent communion of sorrow.

L ate the next morning, Kyr woke with a fierce headache and sick guts. "Gods!" he groaned, "What new torment is this?" He shambled out to the latrine in the back of the house, then returned to the main room, and slumped into one of the chairs by the fire.

Medari emerged from his workroom, carrying a mug. "Here, son. You'll need this after last night." Without opening his eyes, Kyr reached out, and Medari placed a cup in his hands.

He gulped the potion down. "Gagh! That's awful."

"I know, but it's effective," the healer promised. "Give it a few moments. You'll see."

Medari was right. After a while, the headache subsided, his guts calmed, and Kyr dared to open his eyes. The sight of the breakfast tray made his stomach growl. "Gods, that blessed potion *is* effective." They quietly shared the purpleberry muffins, coddled eggs, and tea that Medari had brought from the kitchen. Kyr, in fact, was still ravenous and ate three of the four muffins. Then he went off to the bath house for a direly-needed wash.

Kyr returned much cleaner, but his hair and beard remained shaggy.

Medari looked up from rolling up strips of cloth for bandages. "Feel better?"

"Yes. I could have soaked in the hot spring the whole rest of the day."

"Those baths are one of the blessings of this place. Ah, you're keeping the beard long?"

"I am not that boy, anymore," Kyr snapped.

Medari blinked. "No, you're not." He continued rolling up bandages.

Kyr watched him work for a few moments. *Here's a man who lost his whole family to wanton savagery, whose heart is bleeding; and yet here he sits, preparing to help others who are hurt. He is a kind, good man whose life was devastated because of me.* Respect and affection for this man who had become his heart-father through shared torment and sorrow softened Kyr's tired heart.

"Can I help with that?" he offered.

Medari looked up with a smile. "Thanks."

Kyr set to work. It helped, having something mindless to do. He could keep his focus on what he was doing, and on his breath, and that kept tormenting thoughts and memories at bay.

After lunch, he returned to his cot, worn out by the light work he had done with Medari. Satisfaction at having been of help to Medari brought a faint smile to his lips. As he drifted off, he prayed humbly, expecting nothing.

"Zhovanya, tainted and cursed though I am, please allow me to make myself useful by being here for Medari, helping him as I can."

Kyr woke with a start at a tap on the door, wondering muzzily who had found his hideout at the Tower.

Medari opened the door and stuck his head in. "Time for dinner. Shall we go?"

Rubbing his eyes, Kyr realized where he was, and sat up. "Oh, it's you. Go where? To Ravenhall?" Medari nodded, and Kyr frowned. "You go on. I'll not be setting foot in there again."

"Ah, I see." Medari looked puzzled but asked no questions. "I'll go fetch our supper, then."

While Medari was gone, Kyr kindled a fire in the hearth of the main room, and sat by it. The warm yellow-and-orange flames seemed friendly and humble after the eerie turquoise mage-fire at the Tower. *Medari didn't even question me about refusing to go to Ravenhall. He is so kind and loyal.* Kyr cringed inside. *He wouldn't be so loyal if he knew what I really am. Is it fair to me to be here, pretending to be the son he wants me to be, when I am just Zhovanya's star-cursed dog? Gods, it's so confusing! What is it I am supposed to* do *in this life that She insists I live?* Kyr sighed. *One thing is clear. I mustn't add to my heart-father's burden of grief.*

Medari returned with a covered tray. "Dinner was already served, so Cook made a quick supper just for us." He set out their meal on the table by the fire. Kyr ate every bite of his mushroom-and-bacon omelet and bran muffins. He even eyed the untouched muffin on Medari's plate.

"Here," Medari laughed. "What the hells have you been eating while you were away — acorns and grass?"

"It wasn't that bad," Kyr said with slight smile. "Jerky, nuts, dried apples, hard biscuits, honey."

"Your hideout was well-supplied, then."

With a frown, Kyr nodded and looked away.

Medari quickly changed the subject. "Can't have you cluttering up the patients' rooms. There's a residence upstairs for the infirmarian and his family. That's me and you, son. Shall we move up there?"

"As you wish, heart-father."

The next day, Medari went to their old rooms in Ravenhall to collect their belongings, and returned along with four servers carrying their satchels, and a supply of rags, mops, and buckets. They set the satchels down and disappeared upstairs to clean and dust the long-closed second-floor residence.

"These two are yours," Medari said, handing Kyr his satchel from the fort and the one that Naran had brought back from the Sanctuary. To Kyr, they both seemed to belong to some other man, some other life. He set them aside without inspecting them. *Wonder what has become of Naran. Probably went back to the Sanctuary. Good thing if he has. Won't have to deal with his questions and offers of help.*

After the servers left, the two of them went upstairs to explore their new home. All the rooms were furnished with plain pine furniture, well-used and homey. There were five bedrooms, and the library full of healing texts made Medari's eyes light up.

Medari took the room at the front by the stairs, where he could hear and reach late-night patients easily. And Kyr, feeling more at ease here than he ever had at Ravenhall, chose a back room for himself. It contained a small wardrobe, a washstand with pitcher and bowl, and a shabby padded chair by the hearth. Opposite the hearth was a bed, large enough for two, but small and plain compared to the extravagant bed in his room in Ravenhall. The only other furnishings were a small square table and two stools below the window. He opened the shutters, and was glad to see only a view of the forest-clad hills and the distant guardian wall of Ravenvale. He desired neither a view of Ravenhall, with its reminders of treachery, nor of the lake, with its temptation to escape back to the solitude of the island.

As he took his clothes out of his satchel from the fort and placed them in the wardrobe, he thought of changing out of his worn brown robe, patched tunic, and leggings from the Tower. He stood holding the tan riding leathers the Warrior Mage had given him, remembering the freedom and hope he had felt at the beginning of the trip to Ravenvale, eons ago. He snorted. "What a fantasy that was!" Shaking his head, he shoved the leathers and all the other things Rajani had given him onto the bottom shelf. He did not want to be wearing any of his betrayer's gifts.

In the satchel that Naran had brought him, he found the clothing given to him by those at the Sanctuary for the winter: a thick brown woolen tunic and leggings; three finely woven woolen undershirts in shades of gray and tan; and sturdy fleece-lined boots. Grateful for this unremembered, untainted gift, he quickly dressed in the warm clothing.

At the bottom of the satchel, he found his heavy black cloak. Feeling its rough, familiar texture, he was reminded of his difficult yet hopeful days at the Sanctuary. Aching with loss and sorrow, he picked up the folded cloak and held it close.

Something hard pressed against his chest.

Carefully, he set the cloak on his bed and unfolded it. Inside it, in a rag-wrapped bundle, he found three of the figurines he had made at the Sanctuary, the ones he had left with Gaela for Tenaiya, Devanyi, and Seranu. "Curse it all, I'll never be able to give these to them now. They wouldn't want them, anyway, if they knew the truth about me." Brushing tears away, he quickly set the rest of the clothes and the figurines on shelves in the wardrobe, and closed the door.

In the following days, as Kyr regained his strength, Medari taught him to help with small tasks around the infirmary: washing and sweeping; filling small bottles with the potions Medari mixed; and rolling endless bandages. From the parade of patients who came to the infirmary, Kyr came to understand that even ordinary life includes much suffering.

Resigned to a life of isolation and torment, Kyr kept secret even from himself the humble peace that he found in helping Medari. Seeing the lines of grief in his heart-father's face lessen, and the quiet gladness in his eyes as they worked and ate together, was all the reward Kyr dared hope for in this life that Zhovanya demanded he live. For the rest, there was the discipline of keeping his focus on the present.

But sometimes — when his concentration failed and his mind clutched at the painful, treacherous past or bleak future — he retreated in despair even from Medari, remaining in his room, refusing to eat or speak for a day or two.

The healer, however, refused to abandon him to his despondency for longer than that, and insisted that Kyr drink the soothing potions he brought, coaxed him to wash and dress, and to come for meals in the parlor. Bound by his promise to be a son to his heart-father, Kyr dredged up his iron will, forced his desolate thoughts back, and obeyed.

Chapter Seventeen

Renunciation

One chilly, clear evening, Kyr stood by the window of the infirmary, looking out at the night. The silvery light of the second Full Moon since his return from the Tower shimmered on the rippling waters of the lake. Feeling restless and despondent, Kyr took his heavy cloak and headed down toward the lake. After being cooped up in the infirmary for days by Winter's early storm, it felt good to be outdoors and moving; and he walked for a while, taking deep breaths of the fresh, cold air. His aching muscles told him that he needed exercise, and he resolved to make a habit of walking at night when the risk of meeting anyone was low. A soft "Huu Hu Hu Huu" reminded him of Owl at the Tower, and he slipped into the strange state of detachment he had found there. For a time, there was nothing but movement through the darkness and the play of silver light on the dark, restless lake.

But then a faint sound brought him back from the quietness he had found. He listened more closely, then shivered with dismay. The penitents were at their evening meditation, singing the Zhovanaya chant.

Unable to find forgiveness in his heart for the Circle's wicked ritual, and believing that Zhovanya would never forgive him his evil origin, he could no longer bear to sing or even hear of Her forgiveness. Though he was also sure that the penitents would not forgive him for what he had done to Craith, he continued onward, drawn by a tremendous longing for the companionship of his brothers on the hard path. As he neared their house, he came to a stop, struck by a painful realization. *Ah, gods, I must apologize to all of them, and offer to make amends somehow. Let them punish me if they wish.* He smiled bitterly. *I'm sure that would please You, Zhovanya.*

Reaching the penitents' house, he looked around for the two guards, hoping to avoid their notice, but they were not in evidence. *Must be in the kitchen keeping warm.* As he knelt in the shadows on the cold ground outside the small chapel, listening to his brothers' serene voices uniting in harmony, his heart ached painfully; and he yielded to this torment as part of the suffering that Zhovanya demanded.

Inside, the penitents brought their chanting to silence and settled into meditation, as their mentor Kyr had taught them. But a strange sound from outside disturbed the peacefulness of their little chapel, and at Craith's nod, Jorem went out to investigate. Engrossed in a card game at the kitchen table, the guards Chavri and Nyx ignored him, assuming that he was going out to the latrine.

Jorem circled around to the side of the chapel. There, he discovered someone bowed to the ground, unrecognizable under his cloak and hood, both hands over his face, muffling his sobs. "Sir," Jorem said, "how can I help you?"

Recognizing the penitent's voice, Kyr froze in mortification. But after a moment he steeled himself and sat up, wiping his eyes with the hem of his cloak. "I'm sorry, Jorem. I didn't mean to disturb you. I just...." He shrugged helplessly and looked down.

"Come inside, sir. It's too cold out here."

"Gods, Jorem, please don't call me that! After what I did, I deserve no respect."

"Come inside." Jorem rose and took Kyr's arm in a firm grip. "Craith would never forgive me if I left you out here alone."

Kyr clambered stiffly to his feet, dreading having to face Craith. They went in through the rarely used front door that led directly into the dimly lit chapel, Kyr following Jorem with lowered head and downcast eyes.

"Who's this with you, brother?" asked Kinar.

Kyr raised his head, pushed back his hood, and looked at them, his face burning.

"Kyr!" Craith exclaimed. "You've come back, thank all the gods!" And he jumped up and approached him — not with angry fists, but with smiles and friendly greetings, as did Kinar and Zurano.

Startled and confused by their warm welcome, Kyr stood by the door like a frightened deer tensed to flee at any moment. "No, you don't understand," Kyr faltered. "I...can't stay. I just came to...to apologize to you, Craith, and to all of you...for letting you down so badly."

"Don't worry," Craith reassured him. "We're very glad to see you. Come, let's all sit down." He took Kyr's arm and gently steered him to a seat on the floor, and they all settled into a circle.

Kyr stared at the floor, at first unable to speak. Then finally he said, "I'm terribly sorry for hurting you, Craith. If there's a way I can make amends to you, to all of you.... Whatever you want...."

"Kyr, please, look at me," Craith said.

Kyr looked up and met the redhead's gaze, fearing his angry chastisement, or worse — deep disappointment.

But Craith looked at him kindly. "No need to apologize, Kyr. We've all cracked at one time or another, and taken it out on someone. I hold no grudge against you. If you need my forgiveness, you have it."

"But I dishonored everything I taught all of you," Kyr protested. "How can you…?"

"Truly, there is nothing to forgive," said Kinar firmly. "You are a man like us, and you were in grave distress, though we don't know why. We all have made terrible mistakes, as Craith said."

"We understand the kind of pressures that can drive a man to violence," Jorem said somberly.

And then quiet Zurano spoke. "What you taught us most of all was to forgive, and we forgive you, Kyr." Craith, Kinar, and Jorem murmured their assent.

Bittersweet tears pricked Kyr's eyes, and he looked down again. Not wanting to reject their offer of forgiveness nor deter them from the hard path, he bit back the protests of unworthiness that rushed to his lips. As true children of Zhovanya, *they* could earn Her love and forgiveness, though his own path, he now believed, led only into endless bleakness. Steeling himself, he raised his head and nodded. "Thank you, my brothers."

The four men smiled, but Craith sensed Kyr's wariness and despondency. "Kinar, why don't you fetch us some tea? Kyr looks half-frozen." Kinar jumped up and went into the kitchen, and Craith continued in a conversational tone, "How long have you been back? We don't get much news, here."

"A couple of months. Sorry I waited so long to come apologize."

"Where have you been keeping yourself?"

"I'm staying with Medari in the infirmary." Kyr breathed a sigh of relief when Kinar returned with mugs of tea for everyone, glad to not be the center of attention any longer, and quickly asked for their news. He listened as each of them shared his difficulties and successes keeping to the hard path, and nodded in acknowledgment, but said nothing. As soon as he could without being rude, he said, "Thank you for the tea, and…your kindness. I'd better get back. Medari will be wondering if I fell into the lake."

With a mere tilt of his chin, Craith sent the others into the kitchen, and said to Kyr, "I hope you will be joining us for evening meditation?"

"I'm sorry. I can't. Please, don't ask me why."

"You are welcome here anytime," Craith said. "My friend, we have all forgiven you. Now you must forgive yourself. Zhovanya naralo."

With an abrupt nod, Kyr slipped out the front door into the cold, star-haunted night, and trudged back toward the infirmary. The kindness of his brothers and his longing to be one of them again weighed heavily on his heart, but he shook his head. *I can't come here again. They'd despise me if they knew of my star-cursed origin. It would destroy their faith, and they'd abandon the hard path. I mustn't let myself forget the truth, mustn't let myself become close with them.*

He stopped and looked at the full Moon low over the lake, making a shining path across the waters. *Cruel Goddess, your torments grow ever more subtle. You want me to suffer, so You surround me with kind friends.*

One morning, a half-moon later, Kyr and Medari were sitting at the table under the window in the infirmary's main room, rolling bandages. In a dull daze after a sleepless night, Kyr was trying not to think about anything at all.

"Ah, look who's coming." Medari nudged Kyr and pointed out the window. And there, bounding across the courtyard, came Friend, followed by Grena, the stable-boy who had been taking care of her all this time. "I asked Grena to bring her over. I thought you would be glad to see her."

Grena opened the door. Friend bounded in and ran straight to Kyr, wagging her tail wildly. He knelt and embraced her, burying his face in the ruff of her neck, and whispered, "Gods, girl, I'm so sorry I abandoned you." She licked his face, wriggling with joy. Kyr took her gently by her ears and put his forehead to hers, hiding his tears. *Zhovanya wants me to suffer. How can I allow myself the comfort of having Friend with me? But she will be so sad if I send her away. Ah, hells!*

"She's missed you terribly, sir," said Grena, smiling to see Friend's joy.

Standing up abruptly, Kyr turned away, staring blindly out the window. Then his shoulders slumped. *I must not defy Her will.* Stiffly, he said, "I've not thought of her. Thank you for bringing her for a visit." Medari and Grena stared at Kyr's back in shock.

"Don't you want her with you, sir?" asked Grena.

Medari protested, "She can stay here, Kyr. It's fine with me."

"No, I can't...." Kyr choked to a stop, whirled, and raced up the stairs to his room. Friend started to follow him, but Grena grabbed her by the collar, looking at Medari in confusion as Friend barked and struggled to get loose.

"I'm sorry, Grena. I thought he was ready. Would you mind taking care of her for a while longer?"

"I don't mind. She's a great dog." He pulled a length of rope out of his pocket and knelt to knot it onto Friend's collar. "But she won't like this at all." And indeed, Friend fought and wriggled so much that Grena had to pick her up and carry her out of the infirmary. Kyr returned only when he heard the front door close, and crossed the main room to stand by the window. Halfway across the courtyard, Grena set Friend down, and she slunk along at the end of the rope, head and tail drooping.

Watching Friend leave, Kyr felt a part of himself shrinking into the distance, too. *My soul is going with her.* He shivered with frigid shock at a new thought. *If I ever had one. Gods, maybe the only soul in me was Lanir's.* He felt cold inside, cold and entirely alone.

Medari came and stood by his side. "Why, son? Why not let her stay here with us?"

"I made her no promises," said Kyr in a soft, wretched voice. When Grena and Friend disappeared from view, he retreated to his room again. Kneeling on the floor, he bowed down so that he was half-resting on his bed, head pillowed on his arms. "Goddess," he whispered, "You ask too much. I cannot do this, live this lie, pretend I am a good son, a friend, a real person. By Your will, I live, but that is all I can bear." He grabbed his pillow to stifle the harsh sobs that tore up from his gut.

Chapter Eighteen

Web of Ashes

It was a rare balmy day in early Winter, and Medari had the infirmary door propped open to welcome in the fresh air. Hearing the sound of several horses clattering onto the stone paving of Ravenhall's courtyard, he abandoned his mortar and pestle, made sure that the dangerous potions were locked up, and hurried out to see what was happening.

In the sunny courtyard, four travel-stained riders were dismounting from weary, dusty horses. Medari recognized Naran, and surmised from their dark-green uniforms that the other two men were Companions. But the woman with the long dark hair was unfamiliar to him. "Must be that Kailithana Naran went for," he breathed. "Maybe she can bring Kyr out of his despair. Gods know, nothing *I've* tried has worked."

While the two Companions led the horses away, Luciya and Bru swept Naran and the Kailithana into Ravenhall. Medari sped after them, and caught up with them in the parlor overlooking the lake. Naran welcomed him with a tired smile. "Ah, good to see you, Medari. This is Jolanya, the Kailithana from the Sanctuary." The indigo-robed woman regarded him with gray eyes that spoke of wisdom hard acquired. Naran continued, "Jolanya, this is Medari, the healer I told you about. He is Kyr's heart-father."

Medari bowed to Jolanya perfunctorily, his worry for Kyr overriding politeness. "Welcome, lady. I'm glad you're here. Kyr truly needs your skills. In the past half-moon, he's given up, gone into deep despair. It's as bad as the worst time at that gods-forsaken fort, maybe worse."

Jolanya frowned in concern. "Is he eating?"

"Yes, he does what's required to stay alive, but that's all. Hardly says a word, just hides in his room at the infirmary. We live upstairs there."

"I'd like to see him right away," the Kailithana declared, and started for the door.

But Luciya intervened. "No, my lady, he's not in immediate danger. You will do better if you take a little time to rest and refresh yourself. Let me show you to your room. While you rest and freshen up, we'll have a quick luncheon prepared."

Jolanya sighed. "You're right. I *am* tired, and hungry." She turned to Medari. "I'm sorry. I'll be there soon, if someone will show me the way?"

Naran stepped to her side. "Whenever you're ready." The Kailithana nodded, and the two of them followed Luciya upstairs to their rooms.

Medari returned to the infirmary, wondering if he should tell Kyr that the Kailithana had arrived. Upstairs, he checked on his heart-son again. Kyr lay unmoving except for the rise and fall of his chest. Unsure of how he would take the news, Medari said nothing.

L ate that afternoon, Naran and Jolanya entered the infirmary. Medari rose from his chair by the window. "Good, you're here."

Dispensing with formalities, Naran said, "What can you tell us about how Kyr has been since he returned to you?"

"At first, he was just grim and quiet," Medari said. "He didn't want to see anyone. But once he gained some strength, he helped out with chores around here, and seemed to be recovering. He even seemed peaceful, in a somber way. Then one night he went for a walk outside. He was upset when he got back, but wouldn't talk about it."

Then the healer rubbed his hands together anxiously. "I may have made a mistake," he admitted. "The next day, I had the stable-hand who has been caring for Friend bring her here." He glanced at the Kailithana and she nodded. Apparently, Naran had told her about Friend. Medari continued, "I thought Kyr would be glad to see her. I think he was, at first; but then he sent her away. That's when the heart went out of him. It's even worse than the time he got so ill after Gauday left him out in the storm. Although this time, he's not ill — physically."

"Thank you, Medari. May I see him now?" Jolanya kept her face serene but she was puzzled and concerned.

Medari led the way upstairs, and opened Kyr's door. "Son," he said from the hallway, "there's someone here to see you."

Kyr made no response, but lay on his bed, inert and uncaring. He could hear the door closing and the visitor pulling the padded chair over by his bed and sitting down. Too tired to struggle against another temptation, another painful snare of kindness, Kyr wished whoever it was would go away. But the person merely sat quietly, making no demands, offering no help. Kyr found this soothing, and let himself drift back into his only refuge, the oblivion of sleep.

Opening herself to the Flow of kailitha, Jolanya studied Kyr with both her outer and inner senses. She saw lines of pain etched into his grim, gaunt face, and sensed that his zhan pathways were murky and stagnant. It seemed as if the only thing that kept him on the earth was the weight of his despair. Recalling the vibrant, strong, open man he had become at the Sanctuary, she had to fight back tears of dismay and sorrow.

Goddess, what is Your purpose with this man? Jolanya cried out silently. *Can there be any justification for the suffering he has endured in this one life?* Then she sighed at these fruitless questions, and sought to regain the equanimity she needed. *Forgive me, Zhovanya. Forgive me, Jeyal. Please, I beg You, help me bring him peace and healing once again.* She prayed wordlessly until she felt the subtle vibrations of the kailitha in her hands. Then she took a breath, and said, "I'm here, Kyr."

He smiled in his sleep, but did not awaken. She spoke again: "Brave one, I'm really here. Wake now."

Kyr opened his eyes to see gray eyes looking lovingly into his. "Jolanya!" he breathed.

Jolanya's heart leapt up as she sensed the joy flickering like sheet lightning through his entire being and blazing from his golden eyes.

But then his eyes went dark. "Oh, Goddess! Not this too!" He jerked away until he was sitting hunched up against the wall, bitter anguish in his eyes.

Startled by Kyr's reaction and hurt by his rejection, Jolanya bowed her head for a moment to regain her equanimity. Then she looked up and nearly gasped aloud. She had never seen such soul-wrenching agony. *Gods above! What is this? What did that damned Gauday do to him?* She took a steadying breath. "Naran brought me here to help you recover from what Gauday did to you, and whatever went wrong in the cleansing ritual. Brave one, will you let me help you?"

For Kyr, this invitation was the worst torment he could imagine: opening himself to her in the Kailithara, and then losing her again. He stared at Jolanya in utter dismay, and had to clench his jaw tight to keep back moans of anguish. *No, Zhovanya, not this, not this. Please, please, not this.*

"Kyr, it's just me. Tell me what's upsetting you so."

"P-please go away, Kailithana. I...I c-can't...bear this." Closing his eyes, he clasped his arms around his middle and held on tight. *Ah, Goddess, You are truly cruel. Now you taunt me with the one I long for with all my heart but cannot have.*

"I've come to heal you, Kyr, not hurt you. Please, won't you tell me why you don't want me here?" Tears sparkled in her eyes.

The last thing he wanted was to hurt his beloved. "I-I'm sorry, Jolanya. I... It's not that... Oh, gods! Don't cry, please, don't! It's just that this is...impossible. You're the Kailithana...and I..." *Want you more than anything.* He kept silent these words that ached in his heart, sure that she could never be his, especially now that he knew what he was.

But he had to say something to make her leave before she found out the truth about him. Desperately, though he had little hope that she would listen — she never had let him avoid any difficult challenge during the Kailithara, before — he tried. "Please, go away. Forget about me." He buried his head on his knees. "Go back to the Sanctuary, where you can help someone...worthy."

"*No one* is more worthy than you, Kyr. No one! I will *not* abandon you to suffer the consequences of your sacrifice. I won't let the very woundedness that I came here to heal stop me from doing my work." In a softer tone, she added, "I'm here to see you whole and strong again, no matter how long that takes."

He looked up, saw the determination in her eyes, and knew there was no escape. *She will insist that I open up to the kailitha...and she will find out what I am. Then she will despise me and leave. I will lose the comfort of even* remembering *her love for the man I thought I was at the Sanctuary. I will be left for all time with only the disgust in her eyes for what I really am.* Bitterly, he addressed the Goddess in his thoughts: *Perhaps* then *You will be satisfied, and allow me to end this torture You call life.* Staring at his unattainable beloved in longing and dread, his shoulders sagged in defeat.

Jolanya saw him wilt, and insisted, "Brave one, you know I can help you as I did before. Will you allow me to begin to heal the harm that has been done to you?" With the kailitha surging potent and beneficent in her hands, she reached toward him. "Please lie on your stomach."

In hopeless submission to his cruel fate, he turned over, reminded of the many times he had lain helpless under the cruel hands of the Watcher, and later, of Gauday. Now, he wished that *their* cruelty was all he had to face. His clenched jaw ached and burned.

The Kailithana placed her hands gently on his back, and he shivered all over.

"Zhovanya ganarali, Jeyal ganarali. Zhovanya, Jeyal, guide me," she whispered. Kyr shuddered again — this time, with silent, bitter laughter.

The Kailithana placed her hands on his back. At first, Kyr lay braced for battle, but there was nothing but a golden flood of kailitha, warm and gentle. It felt so good, so right, that he couldn't fight it. With a deep sigh, he sagged into the bed and yielded himself up. The Flow carried him to a quiet place where no thoughts moved, nothing hurt, and he found a deep repose.

Jolanya nearly gasped aloud as his need for healing pulled the kailitha through her hands more strongly than ever before. Closing her eyes, she watched the kailitha flow bright and golden into his zhan pathways — and then disappear. *Gods and demons! There's a black hole draining the kailitha, without healing or closing. It's like a piece of his soul has been torn out.* As she continued to study his zhan, her dismay deepened. *Goddess help him, that's not all. His zhan pathways are twisted and broken, as if they were being forced into an unnatural, perverted pattern, especially around his sexual energy. What the* hells *was Gauday doing to him?*

Fiercely, she demanded, *Zhovanya, Jeyal, You must grant me the ability to heal this man, if no other ever again.* In all her long, difficult life, she had never before made such a claim on her Gods. Though frightened by her own audacity, she knew she would dare Their eternal wrath to see Kyr whole and well again.

For a long while, she cautiously attempted to find a way to seal the black hole; but something resisted her efforts, undoing whatever she tried. Feeling too tired and uncertain to continue, she lifted her hands from Kyr's back, got to her feet, and murmured, "Sleep well, brave one."

Kyr turned onto his side, deeply relaxed and nearly asleep, and unthinkingly whispered what was in his heart: "Don't leave me."

Jolanya stood looking down at him as he subsided into a deep sleep. His words echoed her own longing, and at last, unable to resist his command, she lay down facing him. He frowned as he dreamed, and the tears that he kept locked in his heart during the day slipped out while he slept. Sensing his terrible lostness and desperation, her own tears trickled down her cheeks. But soon, exhaustion overcame her, and she too slipped into sad dreams.

In the middle of the night, Kyr woke suddenly and jerked up to a sitting position, in the process nearly tumbling Jolanya down onto the floor. Her heart pounding, she struggled to catch her balance and sit up. "Gods! What's wrong, Kyr?"

"Are...are you...all right? Did I...hurt you?"

"Yes, I'm fine. Just startled. What's wrong? Was it a nightmare?" It was dark in the little room, but Jolanya recalled seeing a candle and striker on the small table by the bed. She fumbled for them and managed to get the candle lit. In the warm yellow light, she could see that Kyr was hunched up against the wall again, looking at her warily.

"Why are you here with me, Kailithana?"

"You asked me to stay with you as you fell asleep."

"I'm sorry! I shouldn't have done that." Burying his head in his hands, Kyr whispered, "Goddess forgive me!" Then he gave a brief, bitter laugh at his own foolishness.

The Kailithana put her hands on his shoulders. A fine tremor shivered through his body, like a panicked horse held still by a hard rein. The kailitha surged up through Jolanya and took her deep into her working trance. "Lie face-down, kailithos," she commanded. "We must work now."

There was no arguing with her when she sounded like that, and so he did. She placed her hands on his back, and he felt the soothing warmth of kailitha, bringing comfort and calmness. He let go and began to drowse.

Carefully, the Kailithana felt her way into his distorted and broken zhan pathways. She had to work with slow caution, and found herself growing more uneasy with each passing moment. *Ouch!* She nearly jerked her hands off Kyr's back. *What stung me?* Taking a deep breath, she made herself relax and refocus. Now, she saw an ash-gray web that entangled Kyr's zhan pathways and surrounded his core. Even the lightest contact with the web stung her; but she steeled herself, and sent the kailitha deeper, delicately exploring this strange ashen web without trying to change anything. After a few moments, she sighed heavily. *I don't understand what all this is: the black hole; these broken, twisted pathways; this gray web. There's so much damage,* she lamented, *I'll never be able to heal him!* And she started to take her hands off Kyr.

Wait! What am I doing? I can't give up now; I've barely started. What's going on?

She looked around Kyr's inner world, and saw that she was standing at the edge of a dank swamp surrounding a black pit, with gray vines tangled in dead reeds. *Oh, I understand now. This gray web is emanating Kyr's despair and self-loathing, and it almost infected me. No wonder he is acting the way he is!* Her heart ached for him, but she gave herself a mental shake. *I must be more aware of the moods and auras in here. How could I forget? It's the first thing I learned.* More determined than ever to free Kyr from such desolation, she turned her attention back to her work.

As she carefully explored the ashen web, she discovered that it had three layers: one older and deeper; one more recent but similar to the oldest one; and one very recent, which somehow tied into the first two and bound them all together. With gentle touches of kailitha, she sensed the nature of each layer, despite the stinging pain the web inflicted. *Ah, now I see. The deepest layer is what he suffered in his childhood, what the Soul-Drinker did to him. It's the foundation. Everything ties back to it. And the next layer must be what Gauday did to him.*

But this recent layer echoes with horror, and betrayal. Dimly, she sensed that this layer had deep roots, deeper even than the oldest layer. *It's as if this recent experience, whatever it was, confirmed this horrible web as the truth. Dear Goddess, I don't understand.*

The Flow of kailitha began to wane. Mystified and exhausted, she gently withdrew her awareness from Kyr's zhan pathways, and removed her hands from his back. Still deeply asleep, he turned on his side, facing her. She smiled to see him sleeping peacefully. Then she blew out the candle and lay down facing him, taking one of his hands in her own, and slept. All the while, the kailitha flowed gently, keeping away any dream of hurt or horror.

Kyr woke with the dawn and tensed: someone had hold of his hand. Opening his eyes, he found Jolanya facing him, sound asleep, her hand clasping one of his own. Though he was certain that the Goddess wanted no comfort for him, it was beyond him to let go of her hand. Instead, his grip tightened, and Jolanya murmured and stirred.

He watched her wake, greedy for every tiny flicker of expression on her beautiful face, every slight motion or sound. Her fathomless gray eyes opened, and she smiled. He thought his heart would burst. Though he'd had to bury his longing for her deep within, he had yearned through many dark and painful days to see those eyes, that smile. And he knew he always would. He lowered his own eyes, unable any longer to bear the sight of the one who had loved him into a wholeness now lost forever.

Hazily, he felt he owed the Kailithana an apology, and in a halting whisper he tried to explain. "I'm so sorry, Kailithana. I lost…everything…all the blessings…. Gauday ruined it all…all the healing …re-opened old wounds…dug them deeper." Kyr paused, fighting for breath against the anguish in his heart. "And here in Ravenvale, I found out…what I am. Your gifts are so precious… but I was never worthy." He had to close his eyes, close out the sight of her concerned, loving face. He tried to pull his hand away but she wouldn't let go. "You shouldn't be here. I shouldn't let you…."

"This is *exactly* where I belong." Tenderly, Jolanya brushed his hair out of his eyes and kissed his forehead. "Brave one, you have nothing to apologize for. You saved the Sanctuary at the cost of unimaginable suffering. With Zhovanya's grace, you will be healed once again."

With a look of despair and bitterness, he muttered, "No, that's not…my fate."

"Kyr, why do you say that? I am glad to offer you the healing of the Kailithara again."

Kyr looked at her, then looked away. "I know. But She doesn't want…"

"Who doesn't want what?"

181

He tugged his hand out of her grip and sat hunched up, arms around his shins, head on his knees. "Never mind, Jolanya. Please, just leave me alone."

The Kailithana sat up to face him, sitting cross-legged on the bed, and studied his energy. She sensed exhaustion, and a deep shame and hopelessness. Her heart ached for him, and she wanted cry out, to deny this madness. But she took a deep breath and let it go slowly, saying only, "Kyr, what are you thinking? Do you believe that Zhovanya wants you to suffer?"

Shocked that Jolanya had divined his secret, Kyr raised his head to stare at her but remained silent.

"Ah, Kyr! I can see why you might think that, after all you have been through. But just because you have had to suffer so much doesn't mean She wants you to *go on* suffering. You experienced Her forgiveness and love at the Sanctuary. You know they are real, too, just as Her fierceness and cruelty are real."

Kyr looked down, refusing to meet the Kailithana's kind and concerned gaze. *Forgiveness and love may be real for you, for Zhovanya's true children — but I am not one of them. No,* he realized, *I can't say that to Jolanya. I can't bear to tell her the truth of what I am, and then have to watch her concern turn to revulsion. Gods, what a coward I am!*

Jolanya waited for him to speak; but when he said nothing, she went on, trying to find a way through to him. "Zhovanya is both kind and terrible. We often cannot understand Her ways. In your case, at least it is clear that your suffering had a purpose. You destroyed the Soul-Drinker, who would have continued to oppress and torment our land and people for many more generations, if not for you. And you protected Her Sanctuary from desecration."

Love, respect, and admiration poured from her eyes, stabbing into his heart, his bones, his soul; an agony worse than any he had suffered before. "You don't understand!" he snarled. "Every time I think it's over, something worse happens. Every time I have a chance to end this nightmare life of mine, She won't take me Home, no matter how much I beg. She *wants* me to suffer."

Jolanya started to protest, but Kyr interrupted. "No, don't mention the Sanctuary. She brought me there so I could taste something besides suffering — peace, wholeness, happiness — and so I would let the ice melt. That way, I could *truly* suffer at Gauday's hands, with no refuge from the pain and degradation, all the while knowing that life can offer kindness, healing, friendship to some...." He choked up, unable to name the worst gift of all: love.

Softly, the Kailithana said, "Most people wish to reject Her cruel gifts of suffering and keep only the gifts of Her love and forgiveness. You are simply doing the opposite. You diminish Her by rejecting Her love and forgiveness, just as they denigrate Her by rejecting her more painful gifts. How can we dare to reject *any* of Her gifts, when She is the One Who gives us Life?"

"NO! Zhovanya did not give *me* life," he burst out, driven beyond all caution. "It was the Circle, with their unholy ritual. *I* was born of the blackest sorcery and brother-murder. I am an evil abomination. *That's* why She scourges me so, and won't let me die. *Now* do you understand? You must forget me!"

Seeing the shock in Jolanya's eyes, Kyr turned away and curled up in a small ball. To him, it seemed that the very air he breathed reviled him, hating to enter his body. He froze, unable to think or move, waiting for the worst torment to begin.

"Kyr, what are you talking about?" Jolanya asked.

Though she waited, Kyr remained silent, biting his lips until they bled to keep from crying out for her help, her love.

"I don't understand what you are saying, Kyr. But after the deeply intimate time we shared during the Kailthara, I know *you* heart and soul, and I *know* you are *not* evil. All your actions show your courage and goodness. Please, tell me: What Circle? What ritual?" She gently touched his shoulder, but he brusquely shrugged off her hand, walling himself off from her.

"Alright, Kyr, I will wait. If you want to tell me what happened, I'm here." The Kailithana settled herself, closed her eyes, and focused on her breath until she felt calm. *Zhovanya, Jeyal, I pray for your help and blessing for this man who has suffered so much and served You so well. Help me to help him.* She prayed for a long time, but Kyr remained silent, tense as a wildcat in a trap.

Feeling frustrated and helpless, Jolanya finally rose. "I need to talk with Medari and Naran. I'll return soon, brave one."

She trudged wearily down the stairs to the infirmary's main room, where she joined Naran and Medari at the table by the window. Medari filled a mug with tea and passed her the honey. The cinnamon scent of warm honey-and-nut muffins set her shaking with hunger. She grabbed one and gobbled it down. Then she noticed Naran and Medari regarding her with slight smiles.

"Oh, sorry!" She blushed. "My work with the kailitha always makes me ravenous."

"Have another," said Naran. "And whatever else you need, please take or ask."

"Right now, another muffin and this lovely tea will do." She added honey to her tea, wrapped her cold hands around the warm mug, and gratefully gulped down some of the hot, sweet liquid. Then she consumed another muffin.

As she was licking the sticky honey off her fingers, Medari asked, "How is he?"

"Goddess help me, I don't understand what is going on with him. He's quite bitter, and believes that Zhovanya wants him to suffer endlessly. He said something about an 'unholy ritual' by some sort of 'Circle' and about being born of 'black sorcery and murder.' But then he went silent and shut me out." She looked at the other two and saw her own mystification reflected in their eyes. "I see you know nothing about this?" They nodded, and she sighed in frustration.

"Gods and demons," Naran swore. "The Kailithara can't succeed if he is keeping secrets."

"That's right," Jolanya sighed.

"What can we do?" Medari asked.

Jolanya looked at the two men thoughtfully. "Perhaps if the three of us work together, we can convince him to tell us what he's hiding. What if we sit with him, and tell him we won't leave until he tells us the whole truth? Won't he eventually break down?"

"Might take a while," said Medari. "He can be incredibly stubborn, as Gauday found out to his utter frustration."

"Any other ideas?" Jolanya asked, but neither of the men had any suggestions. They took a little while to discuss what to do, while finishing off the muffins and tea.

Then they all headed up the stairs to Kyr's room. The Kailithana seated herself on the padded chair, and the men brought over the two stools from the table under the window.

Kyr sat hunched up on his bed, body aching with a terrible tension. *Now it begins,* he thought: *a torment of kindness by my truest friends.* He had never felt such bleak dread. *I have to tell them. I'm just trying to hold on to these kind friends under false pretenses. Trying to evade Zhovanya's will once again.*

Chapter Nineteen

Dark Revelations

I t was Naran who spoke first, in a voice both stern and kind. "Remember the Sanctuary rules: no violence, no secrets, no lies? You know the healing process cannot succeed without the truth. We're here for the secrets you are hiding, Kyr."

Jolanya added, "We're prepared to wait as long as it takes. We all care for you deeply, and will not abandon you to your suffering, nor allow you to do that to yourself." Medari nodded; and his look of grief and concern hurt Kyr's heart worse than their words.

Kyr's heart shrank at the thought of seeing their love and concern turn to abhorrence. *I'll tell them, and they'll see that there's no point in wasting time on me. I'll make them understand that even if they* do *help me somehow, Zhovanya will only find new ways to torment me. I must let them go, let them get on with their lives.* Tears choked him painfully, but he made himself to sit up cross-legged and straight-backed. In a tight voice, he said, "As Zhovanya wills, I must endure this too. During the cleansing ritual, I found out the truth of what I am — not the hero you think I am, but a monstrosity created through evil sorcery. I will tell you what I learned, and then you *must* abandon me to my fate. I am Zhovanya's to do with as She wills." He ignored their murmured protests.

"After Rajani did the cleansing, I was finally free of the last traces of the Soul-Drinker's and Gauday's sorcery. But something Rajani had said during the cleansing made me suspicious and angry, and he refused to answer my questions. You're not supposed to touch, on the inner plane, but I grabbed him, and Rajani's memories — those that answered my questions — flooded my mind." Kyr swallowed hard, and closed his eyes for a moment before forcing himself to go on. "I learned who my parents were, and what I truly am. I saw the evil ritual that brought me into being." Feeling drenched in his traitor-father's blood and suffocated by the lovely scent of the dreadful Oil of Tramantha, he started coughing.

Medari jumped up and filled a mug with water from the pitcher on the washstand. Kyr gulped the water down, took a deep breath, and went on.

"Long ago, a Star-Seer created a secret Circle to destroy the Soul-Drinker and restore Khailaz to Zhovanya's Hands. Rajani and Luciya were — *are* — part of it, have been since they were children. They and their Circle follow the Star-Seer's Prophecy, and Rajani is oath-bound to ensure that I fulfill it. It foretold that there would be a moment of opportunity — the only one for a thousand years — to create the weapon that would destroy the Soul-Drinker: when the Wanderers formed the Dire Cross under the star-pattern called the Firebird. That's when I was created, through a ritual of the vilest sorcery."

Kyr glared unseeingly at his friends. "Gods and demons! How could they!" He slammed his fists into the bed, and snarled, "At the moment I was conceived, Rajani killed my father and sent his soul to hide inside me. Curse them both!"

As healers, his three friends battled not to show their shock and horror. After a moment, Naran asked quietly, "For what purpose?"

"My father was the weapon. I was the sheath that hid the weapon from the Soul-Drinker's mental invasions. My damned father kept me on the path that the Circle chose for me: to be born and trained as a Slave of the Soul-Drinker, and then to become his Favorite, the only one allowed to get near him physically. Just after I became the Favorite, Rajani and the Circle attacked the Soul-Drinker's labyrinth, distracting my Master, as I thought of him then. As soon as he sent his last two Watcher-bodyguards away to fight, my father rose up inside me, swept me aside, and choked the supposedly immortal Soul-Drinker to death, using my hands."

He darted a quick glance at Naran. "I always told you it wasn't *me* who killed the Soul-Drinker." His throat ached fiercely, but he choked out, "It was my father — Rajani's own brother, Lanir — whom I knew as Dekani."

Naran gasped. "Your inner teacher?"

"Yes," Kyr spat. "My revered teacher, my only guide and helper through the Soul-Drinker's hell, and Gauday's."

Naran was appalled, and greatly saddened for Kyr. But he only said, gently, "You must feel so betrayed."

Kyr gave a harsh bark of mirthless laughter, and steeled himself to say what had to be said. "This is why Zhovanya abhors me: I am not Her child like all of you — just Her star-cursed tool, created from evil sorcery and kin-murder. So, you see, I am not worthy of your concern. You must forget me; go on with your own lives." Bitterly, he added, "You don't have to worry about me. Zhovanya apparently has plans to use me again: She won't let me die, no matter how much I beg." He looked down, unable to face the revulsion and hatred he expected to see in their faces.

Glancing at his fellow healers, Naran saw that Medari and Jolanya were stunned speechless by Kyr's story, and by the depths of his despair and self-loathing. The gray-robe searched within himself for the best way to approach this raw and wounded soul. Quietly, he said, "No matter what ritual brought you into the world, Kyr, you have shown over and over that you *are* one of Her children."

Kyr shook his head angrily. "Didn't you *hear* me? I just told you! I was created by black magic and brother-murder!"

Naran looked down, sensing inside for any doubt or fear about Kyr's dark revelations. But all that came to him was Kyr's valiant struggle to face his crimes and his own suffering, and the light that shone forth as he cleansed his soul. Then Naran looked up to meet Kyr's angry, despairing gaze. "It makes no difference to me," Naran said, his voice quiet but definite. "When we worked together, I got to know you very well. Despite a life of horror and suffering, you faced every challenge bravely and became a loving, kind, courageous man. And I have never seen or heard of a braver, more compassionate act than when you turned yourself over to Gauday to protect the Sanctuary."

"Oh, gods," Kyr groaned. "No, no. It was Zhovanya! I'm just a tool — or weapon! — that She uses for Her own purposes. Can't you see? I'm a star-cursed abomination. *She* doesn't care what I suffer. Neither should *you*."

Naran took a breath and tried again. "Seeing this terrible ritual through Rajani's memories must have been horrifying, but it has *not* determined who you are. By your own willingness and courage, you have become a man I love, honor, and respect."

"That's right, Kyr," said Medari. "I, too, got to know you at that damned fort, and what Naran says of you is true. You even showed compassion toward Gauday, your worst enemy — a man who tortured you unmercifully!" He leaned forward, trying to catch Kyr's eye. "I love you, son. I have *seen* evil — its name was Gauday — and that is *not* what you are, not even close."

Kyr kept his eyes averted, unable to bear his heart-father's affectionate, caring gaze. *You're wrong, heart-father. Gauday was not my worst torturer. It is the three of you!* Their kind, loving words seemed like acid dripping into open wounds. He hunched up again, burying his head on his knees, desperately trying to think of some way to make them go away.

"Brave one, you must listen to us," Jolanya said. "We three know you better than you know yourself. You *are* one of Her children. You showed that when you walked out of the Sanctuary to protect us, and in so many other ways. You are noble and brave and kind, despite being surrounded by evil most of your life. I — we — love you."

Kyr jerked as if struck in the heart by a heavy fist. *Oh, gods, don't let her say that. She didn't, she mustn't!* Only that small change from "I" to "we" kept him from flinging himself at her feet, lost forever between Zhovanya's demands and his heart's forbidden longing.

"Please, Kyr," Jolanya pleaded. "Hear us, look at us. See that we speak the truth."

It took him long moments to find some courage; but at last Kyr raised his head and looked at them. Braced to see only horrified disgust, he was stunned. He could not deny the love, concern, and respect in their eyes — a banquet set before a starving man; a feast he was forbidden to touch.

He began to tremble, feeling as if his heart were being clawed out of his chest. "Oh, Goddess, please," he whispered. "Please, make them understand." But he could see that they did not, and would not. Pale and wild-eyed, he begged, "Please, please, stop! Oh gods, please — leave me alone!"

Jolanya saw that he was at his limit. "Alright, brave one. We'll give you some time to rest, now. But do not think we have given up on you."

Medari murmured his agreement, adding, "Thank you for telling us your secrets. It took a lot of courage. And don't worry, we will keep them private."

"Jolanya is right," said Naran. "We will not abandon you to your suffering. One of us will be outside in the hall. Just call if you need anything, or want to talk."

The three healers went out and closed the door to Kyr's room. In the hall-way, Naran said, "Kyr is likely to flee, if his history is any guide. That's why one of us needs to stay out here."

"I'll stay. Just give me a few moments." Medari fetched a chair and blanket from his room, and settled himself to keep watch. Naran and Jolanya headed downstairs.

As soon as the door closed and he was alone, Kyr threw himself face down on his bed, and grabbed his head with both hands, digging his nails into his scalp. *"Please, please, no more of this, no more! Zhovanya, please have mercy! Send them away!"*

Invited, Her Divine Presence came close and hovered like a great bird with huge, soft wings. *"BELOVED, OPEN YOUR HEART."*

"Open my heart? You'd like that, wouldn't You? Open my heart, love my friends, my beloved; watch them turn away in horror or disgust. Or worse, pity me and keep trying to 'help' me. Merciless Goddess, do You want me to lose hold completely, attack them as I did Craith?" Suddenly furious, he clenched his fists, and slammed the

bed. *"NO!* That *I will never allow! I will fight You forever before I harm Jolanya in any way!"* He gave a bitter snort. *"And pardon me for begging Your mercy."*

He heard something like a patient sigh. And those great, soft wings enfolded him in velvet darkness.

While Medari kept watch upstairs, Naran and Jolanya sat together at the table in the main room. Naran glanced outside, amazed to see late-afternoon shadows darkening the lake. Jolanya stared unseeingly out the window, brushing away slow tears. To give her time, he fetched the teapot from the hearth, and filled mugs for them both.

"Thanks, Naran." She wiped her eyes, accepted the mug he offered, and blew on her tea to cool it. "It's so sad to see Kyr like this. He was so strong and clear...." She choked to a stop.

"I know," Naran said sadly. "But now he is drowning in shame, anger, and despair." He frowned as he stirred a dollop of honey into his tea. "It sounds like he has turned the blame on himself. Since he sees himself as a 'star-cursed abomination,' then perhaps he thinks that is the reason he has suffered so. It may seem to make sense out of his life."

Jolanya frowned and said slowly, thinking aloud, "If he believes he is not Zhovanya's child, that he's this star-cursed monster, then perhaps he can believe he deserves all this suffering, and that She is right to inflict it?"

"Hmmm." Naran thought for a moment. "Let's see. If he is an innocent, then he has no explanation for and no defense against the horrors he has been through, but if he is an evil monster... Yes. I've seen it before — been through it myself, actually. We hold onto our guilt and self-hatred as a sort of barrier against the weight of our loss and pain."

Jolanya nodded abstractedly, thinking about what she had sensed of Kyr's zhan. *Yes, that gray web is made of his guilt, shame and self-loathing, and, to make it worse, that black hole is an unhealing wound.* She took another sip of the hot, sweet tea, grateful for its soothing effect. "I keep sensing a strange, twisted pattern in his zhan. It seems to be having a bad effect on him. Do you know what that is?"

"It could be related to the pattern of scars Gauday that inflicted on him."

"What scars?"

"Gauday burned and cut a pattern of scars all over Kyr's torso, upper arms, and thighs. They were a part of the sorcery Gauday used to try to mind-bond Kyr. Before the cleansing ritual they were livid, and they pulsed in a sickening way that disturbed Kyr badly at times. But the cleansing ritual seems to have calmed them down. From what I saw just now, they are quiet and faded, like old scars."

189

"Oh, gods," Jolanya whispered, "He's suffered so much!"

"Yes, and I don't understand Zhovanya's purpose, at all." Naran glared out the window toward the dark bulk of Ravenhall, where the yellow light of oil lamps shone from many windows. "Something's going on that Rajani and Luciya know about. Luciya won't tell, and Rajani still isn't talking to anyone."

He turned to look at Jolanya. "Ah, I've been meaning to ask: will you be able to help Rajani, too?"

"I have to help Kyr first." Jolanya turned her clear, gray gaze on Naran. "*You* have great skill in helping transgressors face their guilt and suffering. You could work with Rajani."

"What?" Naran stiffened. "No, no. I'm too angry at him for what he's done to Kyr." But then he shook his head. "Ah. You're right. That's what I need to be doing." He sighed heavily. "First, I'll have to ask Zhovanya to help me forgive Rajani."

"Well, if you're as tired as I am, maybe we'd better get some supper and rest now."

"You go on. I need to tell Craith and the others what's going on, and pray with them."

A short while later, Naran sat with the four penitents in their kitchen, sharing their stew and bread. "How are you all doing?"

"We're all right." Craith shrugged that aside. "We're concerned about Kyr."

"Will he be all right?" Jorem demanded.

"The Kailithana is here now. It may take a while, but she will help him return to himself, and to us. The best we can do is to pray for them both." Kinar and Zurano nodded, but Craith and Jorem still looked worried. Before they could ask more questions for which he had no answers, Naran asked, "May I join your meditation tonight?"

"Of course," said Craith. After they finished supper and cleaned up the kitchen, the five of them went into the small chapel. Zurano lit the candle on the low altar, and they all sat cross-legged on the carpet, facing the altar in a semi-circle. Kinar began the chant. "Zhovanya naralo, Zhovanya naralo." They chanted for a time. Then, as the silence deepened, they began to silently meditate or pray, each in his own way.

But Naran could not find peace. He struggled with his anger at Rajani and the Circle for their heartless use of Kyr. *How could Rajani do this? Kyr's suffering is beyond anything imaginable. Serves Rajani right, experiencing Kyr's memories!* He winced at this punitive thought, and reminded himself that Zhovanya had forgiven his *own* monstrous crimes. Memories of that time crowded his mind.

Long ago, he had been an ordinary slave in a wealthy merchant's household. When he was given a mate and allowed to have children, he had been happy, and felt that his master cared for him. But when the merchant tore his mate and children from him and sold them for a handsome profit, Naran was enraged beyond thought or care. Waiting until his master's entire family was gathered for a feast, he had poisoned them all, even the babes in arms, and then escaped.

But his revenge had curdled in his soul, and, after years of regret and self-loathing, he had been guided to the Sanctuary, where he went through his own purification, just as Kyr had. Deeply grateful for his liberation, Naran stayed on and became an Aithané to help others reach Zhovanya's forgiveness.

Now, knowing that Zhovanya loves and forgives even the worst sinners such as himself, Naran bowed his head. *Zhovanya, if You wish me to aid Rajani, please help me release my anger and forgive him.* He straightened his spine and rested his hands on his knees, palms up, and began to silently repeat the chant. *Zhovanya naralo, Zhovanya naralo.*

Remembering his redemption by Zhovanya's Forgiveness, he continued repeating the chant until, with a feather-touch of Her Love, his heart softened and his anger drained away. *Rajani and the Circle did the best they could in an impossible situation. For the good of all Khailaz, they brought forth the only one who could end the Soul-Drinker's horrendous devastation of the people, the land, and the web of life itself. Kyr deserves all healing and blessings. But Rajani, too, deserves my help.*

The velvet darkness faded slowly away, stranding Kyr gently on the shore of wakefulness. Feeling deeply rested, he remained peaceful and still in the pale light of dawn. But then he remembered revealing his odious secrets to his three friends, and his futile attempt to make them abandon him. *Hells! What do they expect from me?*

His own question came back to him. *Yes, what do they expect of me?* In the stillness of early morning, he considered this. *They expect me to believe that they care for me, and that they "refuse to abandon me to my suffering." And they expect me to believe that I am not cursed, not evil.* "Oh, gods," he whispered, "they will never leave me alone." He didn't know if he was angry or glad.

Then he remembered Zhovanya's brief visitation, and the gentle blessing of restful, nightmare-free sleep She had given him. *Why does She keep calling me "Beloved"? How can I be that to Her, when I was created by evil magic? How can She love me and yet let me suffer so?* He felt on the verge of something profound, but the realization eluded his grasp. He sat up on his bed and leaned back against the wall. *Gods, I'm so confused!*

Zhovanya asked me to open my heart, he recalled, wincing as he remembered his caustic words. *I was so bitter and hateful to Her! I'm veering off the hard path into despair, bitterness, and anger. I've got to stop or I'll fall into Gauday's traps, after all.* He snorted. *Can't waste all my hard work avoiding that.*

Longing for the somber clarity he had reached at the tower, he sighed and straightened, sitting cross-legged on his bed. *What have I chosen? To submit to Zhovanya's will; to follow the hard path; to be a good son to Medari; and to refuse to let others' evil define me.* He laughed aloud at the impossible tasks he had set for himself. But he knew all too well the alternative; Gauday had shown him in excruciating detail. He sighed. *If I could survive that hell, I can do this. At the least, I must try.*

He bowed his head. *Goddess, forgive me for resisting Your will. What is it You are asking me? Open my heart to what?* He could think of no answer, so he turned the question around. *What is it I am closing my heart to?* And then he sighed. *Ah, yes, to the love these friends of mine insist on offering me.*

"Merciless gods," he murmured, fearing the pain that was sure to come from yielding to their concern and care. Yet he raised his head and returned to the discipline of watching his breath. Unseen by anyone, and unknown to him, his eyes glowed with the fierce, golden light of the Firebird.

A rap on the door brought Kyr back from the deep silence of meditation. He brought his hands together and murmured, "As You will, Zhovanya." Dreading this new travail of opening his heart, he called, "Enter."

Naran carried in a tray. "Brought some breakfast. Hope you're hungry, but you need to eat, in any case." He glanced pointedly at Kyr's gaunt frame. "You're enough to scare the ravens — or should I say, *not* enough."

Kyr lifted an eyebrow, appreciating Naran's matter-of-factness. Sympathy or pity would certainly send him fleeing back to the Tower. Naran set mugs and plates on the small table by the window, poured the tea, and uncovered the plates. The two men sat down to the sight and scent of browned sausages, golden scrambled eggs, and warm apple muffins. "Thank you, Naran-ji."

"Thank Cook next time you see her. I'm just the mule who carried this over here. That tray was heavy."

"Mule?" Kyr snorted. "Yes, you can be stubborn, all right. You've never given up on me, no matter what."

"No, Kyr, and I never will."

Kyr washed down a bite of muffin with a swig of tea, and set his mug down. "Naran-ji, I realized this morning that it's wrong of me to try to keep my heart closed to my friends. But..." His face burned and he couldn't look at Naran. "I *am* star-cursed: poisoned by the Circle's cursed ritual; tainted by what Gauday did to me. I don't think there is anything anyone can do for me now."

"The Kailithana can help you." Naran spoke with adamantine certainty. "Her powers come from the Goddess *and* the God, Zhovanya *and* Jeyal. Nothing is more powerful than that."

"But I can't go on...with her." Kyr swallowed, trying to ease the ache in his throat. "I could try to talk with *you*, Naran-ji. But not her."

"I cannot untangle the damage you've suffered. Only the Kailithana can do that."

"But..."

"But you still love her," said Naran gently. "And you fear having to let her go again, when the Kailithara is complete?"

Without looking up, Kyr nodded.

"Will you let fear of *possible* future pain condemn you to a life of certain suffering?"

Possible? Beyond all reason, Kyr's heart leapt. "Doesn't make much sense, the way you put it. But truly, I couldn't endure that — opening up to her, and then letting her go again. It was hard enough the first time. I'd go mad, at last." He sighed, knowing he could expect no pity from his fiercely compassionate Aithané. "Gods, I should never have left that island."

"Kyr, I know this will be difficult, but you have chosen the hard path in this life. Going through with the Kailithara is the next step on that path." With a slight smile, Naran added, "And you don't really know where it will lead."

"No, I don't," Kyr agreed. But he knew there was no escape from this torment of love and grief. *I must stop resisting. It's Zhovanya's will that I suffer.* He looked up, eyes bleak. "I yield, Naran-ji."

"Good. I'll send the Kailithana up." Naran collected their empty plates and mugs and set them on the tray, then looked at Kyr. "Please let her help you."

After Naran left, Kyr retreated to his sheltering posture on his bed, hunching up against the wall, clasping his knees to his chest, resting his forehead on his knees. There would be no avoiding any form of torment for him.

Part Six ~ Sweet Surrender

"Your past is just a story. And once you realize that,
it has no power over you."

— Chuck Palahniuk

Chapter Twenty

Confronting Innocence

Wearing the indigo robes of the Kailithana, Jolanya came into Kyr's room. Out of respect, he straightened up and sat cross-legged on his bed, as tense as if facing his executioner. She pulled the padded chair over and sat facing him, noticing his tension and despondency.

"Good morning, kailithos." She kept her face and voice calm, playing her role as Kailithana, yet privately filled with joy and excitement that Kyr had agreed to go through the Kailithara with her again.

Kyr's throat was dry as parchment. "I'm sorry," he whispered sadly, hoping to forestall her well-meant efforts. "I can never be the man you thought I was at the Sanctuary. I lost it: everything you and Naran helped me become. It's gone. Gauday destroyed it all...if it was ever real...."

"Brave one," the Kailithana broke in, "what you found at the Sanctuary was *most* real. It was your own spirit, your authentic essence; and that can never be lost. We'll free you from this quagmire of Gauday's, and you'll find it again. I promise."

"But..."

She leaned forward, concern and kindness on her face. "What is it you fear?"

"That you..." Kyr glanced away, and cleared his throat. No, he could not betray how much he feared to lose her again. Instead, he said, "That all the healing I might gain with you...could be ripped away again. It was different at the Sanctuary: Then, I trusted Naran-ji, you, and Zhovanya. But now...I know that She will use me again, quite ruthlessly if it suits Her purposes." He looked down, adding softly, "She always has."

The Kailithana didn't know what to say. *Goddess, guide me. He's right. How can he trust You now? You have used him so hard! What can I say to him? How can I help him?* Finally, she said the only thing she knew to say, though it seemed entirely inadequate, even cruel. "I can't answer that for you. The Goddess is ruthless *and* merciful, fierce *and* kind. It is up to us to forgive Her."

"What? Forgive *Her*? No, Kailithana, that's madness! She is the *Goddess*. She is the One Who forgives *you*."

"Her purposes are beyond my understanding. But I know She will allow me to heal you again, if you want me to. Can you trust me on this?"

He glanced at the Kailithana with a sad smile. "I trust *your* kindness. I can't trust *Hers*." In his belly arose a writhing viper of rage at Her terrible demands, a worm of blame for Her callous use of him. He gripped his hands together tightly and reminded himself: *Zhovanya is my master now. I must submit to Her. And that means going through the Kailithara with Jolanya, even if it is useless, and unendurable.* But he couldn't help trying one more time to avoid this worst torment of all. "Perhaps you can heal what *Gauday* did to me. But how could anyone reverse the star-cursed ritual that made my blood and bones, my mind and heart out of evil and murder?"

"Until I try, I won't know what I can do about the star-curse. You must trust Her, despite everything."

Kyr shuddered and closed his eyes. "I don't know that I can recover from any of this — or that I dare to...."

"What do you mean?"

He was silent for a while, gathering the courage to speak the truth of his heart. Striving to show only respect and to demand nothing, he spoke in a restrained, formal tone. "Kailithana, I fear I don't have the courage to go through this with you; to open myself to you as completely as I must to heal, and then," his voice quavered, "lose you again."

The Kailithana knew that he needed his own reason to fight for healing, for life, for himself, and not just to try to gain her love; so she too answered with formality. "It is Zhovanya's will, and Jeyal's, that I heal you. They shaped me for this, just as They shaped you to rid Khailaz of the Soul-Drinker and protect Her Sanctuary. They knew you would need me." Her clear gray eyes met his grief-laden gaze. "Please, let me help you."

Kyr trembled with the urge to flee back to the island. But he knew that his kind friends would never leave him alone until they had tried their best to help him. Dread and grief were twin firesnakes coiling in his belly, gnawing at his heart. Yet he bowed his head and said, "Alright, Kailithana. Let us begin."

Tense as a deer facing a wolf, he lay down on his bed, the Kailithana on her chair facing him. She settled herself and sat quietly for a moment. Bowing her head, she prayed, "Zhovanya, ganarali. Jeyal, ganarali. Guide me in my work." Then she reached forward and placed her hands on Kyr's chest, opening to awareness of his zhan and the Flow of the kailitha.

Again, she saw the dark swamp of Kyr's zhan, surrounded by the tangled gray web. Delicately, she sent the kailitha to probe the web. It stung her, but she ignored that and sent the kailitha deeper. At last, it broke past the web. Instantly, she heard a sound that she hadn't heard before. Somewhere in this inner swamp, a small boy was sobbing hopelessly.

"Kailithos, will you tell me how you are feeling now?"

Kyr moved restlessly. "I don't know...feels like...I deserved it...all this pain. Like I did something terrible, long ago. Can't remember what it was... but it was when I was...little...before I was taken for Training."

Jolanya asked gently, "You were only four when the Trainer took you. What terrible thing could a child have done, a child as young as you were?"

"No!" Kyr cried out, as the unrelenting kailitha brought forth his most deeply buried memory:

> It was a rainy day but he wanted to go outside to play, to fly his little wooden bird around the courtyard. Momma had given it to him for his fourth birthday, just the day before. "Wait, Kyr," Momma said, "you can't go outside without your cloak. Here, put it on."
>
> "NO!" he shouted. He just wanted to go outside.
>
> Momma knelt in front of him and began putting the cloak on him. "It's cold and wet today. You have to wear your cloak."
>
> "No, no no!" As Kyr struggled against the offending garment, his flying elbow hit his Momma's nose.
>
> "OW! You hurt me!" Momma let go of him to hold her nose. Intent on escaping outdoors, he tucked his little bird in his tunic pocket and ran toward the door. Without warning, the door opened and a tall, old Slave shoved his way inside.
>
> "Ah, just the pup I was after," the man said in a voice colder than the rain. He grabbed Kyr by the arm in a painful grip. "Come with me, whelp."
>
> "Kyr!" Momma ran to kneel beside him. "This is a Trainer. You're a big boy now. You must go with him." She hugged him tight, then held him from her, looking into his eyes. "I love you. Do what the Trainers tell you, no matter what." Tears trembled and fell from her eyes and he saw how sad she was, and hurt and angry.
>
> "I'm sorry, Momma," Kyr pleaded desperately. "I'll be good. Don't make me go away!"
>
> But she let him go and just knelt there, shoulders slumped, head hanging. "I'm terribly sorry, Kyr. Forgive me." She buried her face in her hands.
>
> The Trainer tugged him toward the door. He struggled hard to get away but it was no use. "Momma! Momma!" he screamed.

The Trainer slapped his face. "Shut up!"

Seeing the mean man's hand poised to strike again, Kyr stopped scream-ing. The Trainer walked fast, half-dragging him. Momma! Momma! Kyr wailed silently. But she never came. Secretly, he stroked the little wooden bird in his tunic pocket.

In a bleak monotone, Kyr told the Kailithana what he had remembered. Then he said, "I never saw my mother again. I learned from Rajani's memories that she hung herself after the Trainer took me away."

Jolanya kept the kailitha — a soft, creamy white — flowing steadily, gently. "What do you see about all this, now?"

"I was very young when the Trainer took me away and started my Train-ing — no — it wasn't 'training.' What he did was *torture*!" His eyes widened in surprise.

"By all the hells," he breathed. "I see it now. I thought all the punishment, the torture, was because I hurt my mother, because I was bad. I thought she was mad at me, hated me. Why else would she never come and take me away from the Trainer?" A rush of grief and a deep sense of abandonment brought tears to his eyes.

Jolanya nodded. "Yes, you had no other way to explain it, did you?" The kailitha, now aquamarine, flowed gently to surround Kyr's heart.

"Gods, I was so young; I didn't understand anything." An unthought-of tenderness for his young self softened his heart, leaving him feeling vulnerable and shaken. In silent sadness, the two of them contemplated the little boy who had been torn away so abruptly from all love and comfort, and had blamed himself for it. The blue-green kailitha flowed more strongly, penetrating Kyr's heart.

He stiffened.

"What is happening, Kyr?" Jolanya asked in concern.

He was silent for a moment, looking back to that long-ago day. "She kept insisting I wear my cloak — because she didn't want me to be cold." His body tensed further as he fought a deep, old pain in his heart.

"What do you see, Kyr? Don't block it. Tell me now."

"Oh, Goddess," he murmured, softening. "She loved me. My Momma loved me." Eyes full of sad wonder, he looked at the Kailithana. "She did love me, despite the Circle's cursed plan. I remember now. She cared for me as well as she could in that horrible place."

"Yes, Kyr, your mother loved you. And you were not bad; you were just a little boy who wanted to go out and play with his new toy. Can you see your innocence and helplessness?"

A dark, shapeless terror made him stiffen again, and he shrugged off Jolanya's hands. "NO!" he said in a young, panicked voice. "I *was* bad — star-cursed from before I was born. Don't you see? This is hopeless! We have to stop this."

"Alright, Kyr," Jolanya soothed, knowing that this earthshaking revelation — that he had a mother who had loved him, and that he had been an innocent child — was fundamental to his whole sense of himself and crucial for his healing. "I know that this is a lot to take in. We'll stop for now. Try to calm down. Remember, we will only go as far and as fast as you are able to." Standing up, she told him, "We'll see what we can do tomorrow. Rest easy tonight. I'll ask Medari to bring you something, if you like."

Kyr wouldn't meet her eyes, only muttering, "Thank you, Kailithana."

Jolanya closed Kyr's door gently and descended the stairs. She found Medari in his workroom, bandaging a cut on a man's arm. After the injured man left, she joined the healer by his work table. "Kyr's pretty upset. Do you have something to help him relax?"

"Yes, I have a calming potion. I'll take it to him now."

"Thanks, Medari." She was grateful that he asked no questions.

The healer selected a small blue bottle from his shelf of prepared potions, and headed upstairs to Kyr's room.

Jolanya sighed, tired but glad that she and Kyr had begun the arduous work of clearing and healing the extensive damage to his psyche and soul. Filling a mug with tea from the pot on the hearth, she sat down at the table by the window overlooking the lake, still and gray under a gray sky. She added honey and sipped her tea, pondering Kyr's reaction to her question. *Why can't he see his own innocence as a child? Everyone knows what little children are like — sweet and innocent.* Jolanya sucked in a breath. *Oh, Goddess!* Not *everyone. When has he* ever *had a chance to see this? I'll bet he's never spent any time around infants or little children. I guess it's about time he did!*

The next morning, Kyr returned from the bath house and entered the infirmary. He stopped short in the doorway at the sight of two strangers in the main room. Medari, Naran, and Jolanya sat at the table by the window, with a plump, brown-haired woman holding a blanket-wrapped bundle close to her heart. A little boy crouched by the hearth, poking at the flames with a stick.

"Ah, Kyr, there you are," said Jolanya. "Want some tea?" She poured Kyr a mug as he warily crossed the room and took a seat by the table. She gestured to the new woman. "This is Nyvali."

Nyvali smiled, blue eyes crinkling kindly at the corners. "Good morning. I'm glad to meet you, Kyr." With a glance toward the hearth, she said, "That's

Jonir there, my oldest boy." She held up the bundle in her arms. "And this is my youngest. His name is Beran." Kyr peered hesitantly at the small, perfect, though rather undefined, face, noticing the baby's smooth, glowing skin, and the wisps of dark hair on his head. Big blue eyes looked back at him, and the baby made an odd, meaningless sound.

"Uh, hello." Kyr had a sudden urge to touch the baby's cheek, wanting to feel that unmarred smoothness; but he refrained, feeling too corrupted to touch such purity. "He's, uh, very small."

"He's only a few weeks old. Ah, Jonir," the mother said. "Stop playing in the ashes!" She held Beran out toward Kyr. "Here, hold him for a moment." Startled, Kyr's protest stuck in his throat — and then the baby was in his hands. Awkward and stiff, he held the warm, squirming bundle away from him.

Seeing Kyr's discomfort about to turn into panic, Medari leaned over, smiling. "Here, like this. You need to support his head and bottom." The healer began to move Kyr's hands into a better position, but Kyr resisted.

"You take him, Medari. You know what you're doing. Besides, I shouldn't be touching him." Kyr held the baby out to Medari, but the older man shook his head.

"No, Kyr, you can do this. It's all right." The healer moved the baby into a comfortable position so he was safely cradled in Kyr's arms. "That's it. Now hold him close." Medari grinned. "He won't bite yet. No teeth."

Kyr held the baby, staring down at the little round head and the miniature hands kneading the soft blanket. "He's so tiny, and...perfect!" he whispered.

Softly, Jolanya said, "You were once this small, this helpless and innocent, Kyr."

A shiver ran through his body and lodged painfully in his heart.

Meanwhile, Nyvali crossed over to kneel by the little boy. "Jonir, stop it. You're getting your hands dirty."

"No, Momma!" Jonir protested angrily. Kyr tensed, sure that the adult would punish the child, just as the Trainers always had done to him.

But Nyvali merely said, "Come, Jonir, let's get you cleaned up. Then you can have a nice warm muffin, alright?" Jonir nodded, sniffling.

His mother took him over to the washbasin and wiped his hands clean with a wet rag, then gave him a muffin, as promised. The little boy sat in her lap, tears forgotten, happily eating the muffin, scattering crumbs all over her dress and the floor. Again, there was no punishment. Kyr looked at Nyvali in bewilderment and awe.

Medari was also watching Nyvali and Jonir, admiring her gentle, loving nature. *She is very good with the boy – like Leandra was.* With a pang of grief, he cried out silently, *Oh, my dear wife, I miss you so!*

Nyvali smiled at Kyr. "Beran likes you. See, he's asleep." Kyr looked down. The blue eyes were closed and the little mouth was curved in a tiny smile. The sleeping infant's warm, trusting weight touched something deep in Kyr's heart, and tears sprang to his eyes. He kept his face down to hide them, until he could blink them away.

Handing Nyvali a small bottle, Medari said, "Here's the potion for Jonir's sniffles. I made it with spearmint and honey so it will taste good. Give him two spoonsful three times a day." Tucking the bottle in her pocket, Nyvali smiled her thanks. Dazzled by her quiet radiance, Medari smiled back.

Ah, look at that! Jolanya smiled to herself. *They like each other.*

"Time to go, Jonir," Nyvali said. The little boy jumped off her lap. She rose and held out her arms to Kyr. "Thanks for holding him." Reluctantly, Kyr handed Beran back to his mother. His arms felt strangely empty.

The little boy was almost out the door. "Wait a moment, my boy," Nyvali called. "What do you say?"

Jonir turned around and gave a quick little bow. "Thank you for the muffin."

Everyone laughed, except Kyr. Overcome with a confusion of feelings, he fled to his room.

As Medari watched Nyvali and her two children leave, tears of grief and loneliness filled his eyes. He busied himself at his worktable, putting things to rights.

Jolanya went to the healer's side before going to Kyr's room. "Nyvali is a widow, you know. Her husband was killed in the rioting after the Soul-Drinker's death. Luciya found her, pregnant and alone, trying to survive and take care of Jonir, and had her sent here along with others who needed protection." She put one arm around his shoulders, and gave him a quick hug.

After Jolanya left, Medari stood staring down at the vial of spearmint oil in his hand, struggling with his grief and a new torment called hope. *No,* he thought, attempting to put Nyvali from his mind. *I can't betray Leandra.*

But then he thought he heard his wife's best no-nonsense voice: *"Oh, don't be silly, you old man. You can't betray me. I'm dead. Go on with you, now. Get on with your life. Do you think I want you moping around forever?"* He could almost see her, flapping her apron at him to shoo him out of her kitchen as she used to do.

And over the following days, Medari found that the image of the widow and her two young children would not leave his mind.

Jolanya returned to Kyr's room, and found him on his bed, hunched up against the wall again. She took her chair facing him, and waited quietly.

After a time, he said softly, "They are so little…and they know nothing of evil, do they?" Kyr glanced at Jolanya. "How old is that little boy?"

"He's four. The age *you* were when that Trainer dragged you away from your Momma."

"Are all little children like that?"

"Yes, they are. And so were you, Kyr."

"Are you sure?" he demanded, suddenly angry. "What about the Circle's damned ritual? What about being star-cursed?"

"Think of that little baby, Beran. Could he be evil?"

Kyr felt ready to flee or fight some unknown, dangerous foe. Yet he slowly shook his head, and whispered "No."

"You were just like that when you were born. You could *not* be evil. No newborn can." She saw Kyr's skeptical look and insisted, "No, if anyone was evil, it would be those who performed that cursed ritual, those who harmed you — never you. You were born innocent, Kyr. Like every child of Zhovanya."

Her words struck Kyr like a whiplash. He sat bolt upright, rigid with rage. "How can you *say* that to *me*? Look at my life! I was cursed before I was born, and condemned to the Soul-Drinker's hell. Lanir — *my own father!* — was absolutely ruthless. He was my only source of comfort, whispering encouragement for what he wanted me to do: endure terrible pain, learn to live in the ice so I could commit the horrible crimes the Soul-Drinker demanded. Merciless gods! I tortured, raped, and killed many innocent people. Curse Lanir, Rajani and their entire Circle!" Kyr gasped in a ragged breath before storming on.

"If *that* wasn't enough, I had to endure months of Gauday's viciousness. When I finally begged Dekani — I mean Lanir, gods curse it! — for death, he *refused*; just kept using his false kindness to keep me from going mad, or succumbing to Gauday's sorcery." Kyr shook with rage. "Gods and demons! Every kindness he ever did me was cruel trickery." He hit the bed with both fists, and leaned forward, glaring at Jolanya.

Frightened by his intensity, she silently pleaded, *"Jeyal, ganarali! Please guide me!"* A subtle silver flow of strength and serenity permeated her heart and soul, and she relaxed, knowing now that she could be present for the full force of Kyr's pain and rage.

"I am *not* a child of the Goddess!" he snarled. "I'll tell you what I *have* been: the Trainer's victim; Lanir's puppet; the Soul-Drinker's torturer; the Circle's weapon against the Soul-Drinker; the Watcher's plaything; Gauday's prisoner, whore, and nearly his damned mind-slave. Can't you see? I *am* star-cursed. Tainted, crippled, evil!"

"Crippled and tainted, perhaps," the Kailithana said, "but that can be healed. Evil? No, Kyr, you're *not*." She spoke with the calm strength of truth.

Ignoring her, he snapped, "And I am *still* dangerous. Look what I did to Craith. By all the hells, don't you see? Gauday is dead, but his mark is deep in me." He turned red, and growled, "I still have nightmares about what he did to me. Even though his curse is broken and my scars are quiet, any kind of pain or violence arouses me, thanks to him." Kyr roughly swiped the sweat off his face. "How in all the hells do you expect me to go on as if I'm some sort of ordinary man that I've *never been*? May all the gods be damned if I can see how!"

In the face of his wrath and despair, the Kailithana looked at him steadily and asked, "What else, Kyr?"

"Isn't that *enough*?"

"What else?" she repeated, undeterred.

Kyr glared at her, fists clenched, every muscle tense, and a flood of bitterness burst forth. "How *could* She let this happen? How could She demand so *much* from me? Zhovanya has used me worse than all the rest! You have no idea how often I have begged Her for death. And, by all that's unholy, She won't even let me *die*." He laughed harshly. "*Goddess*, HA! She's a vicious *demon*, laughing at my faith in Her!" He abruptly fell silent, stunned by his own words. He glanced at Jolanya, expecting shock, disapproval, rejection.

But the Kailithana's gray eyes showed only acceptance of his virulent bitterness. "Zhovanya forgives you, even for this blasphemy. Despite it all, you *are* Her child."

Kyr glared at her in furious bafflement — and she returned his gaze with gentle understanding. Time seemed suspended as their eyes met. In that eternal moment, the towering wave of his rage and pain broke against the rock of the Kailithana's compassion, and he dissolved into the bewildered sobs of the lost child, found.

She moved from her chair onto his bed, gathered him into the safe harbor of her arms, and held him while waves of grief washed through him, leaving him spent, his head resting on the quiet shore of her lap. Placing her hands on the front and back of his heart, she opened to the Flow. Instantly, golden kailitha flooded through her hands to fill his dark and wounded heart. There was a deep silence as Kyr drifted, absorbing the healing Flow, releasing his rage and bitterness.

Chapter Twenty-One

Fearful Paradoxes

When Kyr woke early the next morning, a quiet melancholy and pensive confusion were all that was left of his storm of fury and grief. Hoping that fresh air would clear his mind, he donned his cloak, but for silence's sake, he carried his boots as he crept down the stairs, crossed the main room, and left the infirmary. Once outside, he shoved his feet into his boots and headed north along the path, away from Ravenhall.

In the pre-dawn stillness, the lake was a silver mirror. Tiny waves shushed and sighed, deepening the silence that filled Ravenvale. Kyr breathed deeply of the cool, crystalline air, letting it fill the clean hollowness inside him. The soft gray light brightened, revealing the forest dark against the shadowy guardian walls, scraps of mist drifting over lake and field, and a sudden scamper of rabbits dashing into the bushes.

He walked along, following the path as it curved along the edge of the lake. Rounding a bend, he looked up and stopped with an indrawn breath. Ravenhall rose up across the lake, sprawling over its hill. At this distance, it did not look like a place of ominous secrets. It seemed peaceful, its many levels, balconies, and windows a random yet harmonious medley crowned by the golden glory of the Ravens' Rookery. The massive old oak still held onto its leaves despite a few paltry storms. Unwilling to lose this rare morning peace, Kyr turned away and simply watched the rising sun paint the lake a soft pink, enjoying its warmth on his face.

But then, he gasped, as sudden light broke through his old prison of despair. *Maybe the Kailithana can free me from this web of evil and pain I've been trapped in. Oh Goddess, please!* But then, afraid to allow himself to believe in this new light, he shook his head. *Never mind, Zhovanya. No one can reverse the starcurse, not even the Kailithana.* Nevertheless, that strange, irrepressible lunacy called hope sent him hurrying back toward the infirmary.

Halfway back along the path, he saw a familiar figure and stopped in surprise. "Naran-ji!"

"Good morning, Kyr. Saw you leave the infirmary. Thought I'd see if I could catch you."

"Where have you been?" Kyr asked in a hurt tone. "I haven't seen you for days."

"Trying to help Rajani."

Scowling, Kyr demanded, "Why?"

"Zhovanya naralo." Naran looked at him with clear eyes, and Kyr looked away, discomfited by this reminder that even the worst offenders, such as himself and Naran, could be forgiven. He shook his head. "I can't forgive him. Not yet. Maybe never."

"That's up to you."

Kyr shrugged, his face burning. "I know."

"The important thing is that you're continuing with the Kailithara, eh?"

"Yes. It's tough...but good."

"Glad to hear it." Naran smiled. "Now, I have something for you." He felt in his pocket, and handed Kyr something small — a soaring bird carved of a reddish-brown wood. "I know how hard the Kailithara is. Hope this reminds you of who you are."

Kyr stared at the graceful figure resting on the palm of his hand, blinking away tears. "A Tawny Eagle," he said softly. "Thank you, Naran-ji." Their eyes met, and they exchanged a look of deep friendship and understanding. "When did you make this?"

"At the Sanctuary, after you turned yourself over to Gauday. I...missed you."

"Ah, Naran-ji." They clasped forearms as old friends and comrades on the hard path. Then they departed, each to his own challenge.

Kyr came to a halt just inside the front door of the infirmary. His heart sped up and his throat tightened. Jolanya sat at the table by the window, the pale sunlight gleaming in her silken black hair, her grey eyes shining warmly. *Merciless gods, how can I endure this? Opening to the Kailithara is hard enough. But letting the Kailithana go again....*

"Out of the way, son," announced Medari as he entered the room carrying a large tray.

"Oh! Sorry." Kyr stepped aside. "Good morning, heart-father. Let me help."

"Thanks. You take this." Medari gave him the heavy tray, and Kyr carried it over to the table. He glanced at Jolanya, and she gave him a welcoming smile. Tangled up in hope and doubt, he murmured, "Good morning, Kailithana," and busied himself setting out the mugs and pouring the tea, while Medari set out plates, forks, knives, a small crock of butter, and a pitcher of purpleberry syrup. When all was ready, the two men sat down at the table with Jolanya.

"Cook sent something you'll like, Kyr," Medari smiled. And with a small flourish, he removed the napkin covering the serving dish.

"Frycakes!" Kyr's eyes lit up, and he helped himself to an ample stack. Medari and Jolanya nearly forgot to eat, they so enjoyed watching him plow through his pile of butter-and-syrup-drenched frycakes. In moments, he was wiping up syrup with his last bite of frycake, and eyeing those on Medari's plate.

Medari laughed and forked one over. "I'll have to ask Cook for these every day. That'll put some flesh on your bones." The three of them lingered, drinking tea and watching the ravens swoop and dive above the lake in the chilly air.

Jolanya drank the last of her tea and set her mug down. "Are you ready to continue, brave one? I can begin the deeper healing work now."

Kyr's stomach clenched, and his mouth went dry. "But what about the star-curse? There's no point in going on if..." He took a swig of tea, and whispered, "Do you think you can...free me from it?"

"That's why I am here." Jolanya smiled serenely, still in touch with Jeyal's silver blessing.

"Alright." Kyr clasped his hands together under the table to still their trembling.

Taking their leave of Medari, Jolanya and Kyr climbed the stairs and entered his room. He carefully set the small sculpted eagle on the windowsill, shaking his head at the twists and turns of fate. *Ah, gods, these friends of mine: they have such faith in me. I hope I can live up to it.* He smiled. *Hope?* It was strange to have that short, vast word back in his vocabulary after so many months of despair.

After hanging up her cloak by the door, the Kailithana came over to join him at the window. "Ah, what's this?"

"A gift from Naran. I met him out by the lake this morning."

"It's so beautiful! Eagle is your soulkin, is it not? That's quite rare."

Not meeting her eyes, he turned away from the window and paced restlessly to the door and back, his mind roiling with dire questions.

"Alright, let's sit down, Kyr."

He stalked toward his bed, but abruptly sat down on the floor beside it, instead.

Jolanya took a seat on the floor facing him. "Now, what's bothering you?"

He glanced at her and looked down. "Yesterday, you insisted that I am Zhovanya's child. But...if I *am* Her child, then why all this pain and suffering? Merciless gods, I've been through *three* hells already!"

209

The Kailithana took a moment to touch into Jeyal's silver strength and connect with her own truth. Then she said, "This is what I believe: Zhovanya needed someone to rid us of our tormenters, and She chose you because you are the strongest of us all."

"Strongest?" Kyr shook his head in disbelief. "Ah, Kailithana, you have no idea how I have begged for death. And I lost all faith, that night Gauday left me out in the rain — and again when I learned of my star-cursed origin." And then, though the truth was ashes in his mouth, he had to speak it: "Besides, I'd never have survived the Soul-Drinker's Training, and all that came after, if it hadn't been for...Lanir." With this admission came a sudden grief for the loss of his inner teacher. "Gods and demons, I don't know whether to hate him or love him!"

Jolanya nodded. "It's not so simple as hating *or* loving, is it?"

"No, not with Lanir...nor with Zhovanya. I have felt Her Love, been taken into Her Heart, danced in sweet surrender to Her. Yet Her request to protect the Sanctuary sent me into Gauday's hands." He shifted restlessly, struggling to reconcile the fearful paradoxes of his life. "Are you *sure* She doesn't hate me? The Circle's ritual *was* black sorcery — and I *am* star-cursed."

Jolanya gazed at him with all the love and compassion in her heart. "She does not hate you, though you have every reason to think so. It's a way to explain our misery. But it is not the truth. You know that."

Looking into the Kailithana's lucent, gray eyes, Kyr took that perilous step into the void, moving beyond the certainties he had clung to since he'd taken in Rajani's memories of the star-curse ritual. "It seemed so clear. Thinking that She *wanted* me to suffer made some sense out of my whole life. But now..." He gave a lopsided shrug. "I don't understand anything."

Watching his zhan with her inner sight, the Kailithana saw that the most recent layer, the one that held the gray web together, was beginning to unravel. But there was a major knot that remained intact, and she sensed that it was the key to untangling the whole web. "What, exactly, made you think that Zhovanya wants you to suffer?"

"Well, let me see. At the Tower, I asked myself why She let me find my way to the Sanctuary. Right after the Soul- Drinker died, She could have kept the Sanctuary safe just by letting Gauday find me before Rajani did. Then Gauday would have had no reason to attack the Sanctuary. And I would have suffered quite enough at Gauday's hands. Then, it struck me: She sent me to Her Sanctuary so that I'd learn how good life can be, and let the ice melt. That made Gauday's torments seem even worse by contrast; and without the ice, I had no buffer against the pain. So I thought She must have wanted me to suffer."

Eyes dark, he brought his knees up and wrapped his arms around his shins. "Even after Gauday was dead and we'd left that cursed fort of his, the scars he cut and burned into me kept tormenting me. When I found out about the Circle's star-curse ritual, it seemed clear that Zhovanya had condemned me to suffer because I was an unnatural creature made from evil and murder."

"Oh, Kyr! You must hurt so much to think that She would be so cruel." Despite all her training as the Kailithana, tears trickled from her eyes, and she looked down, trying not to weep.

Kyr longed to touch her wet cheek. All he wanted in the world was to hold her and kiss away her tears. But in the next instant, his natural desire for her aroused a flood of old, unwanted feelings — obscene urges stemming from Gauday's sexual tortures. Sickened, he sat hunched up, head on his knees, unable to look at her. *Gods curse him! I* am *still tainted, even if Zhovanya does not hate me. I mustn't let Gauday's corruption touch the Kailithana.*

Fighting to subdue the vile desires surging through him, he imagined the frigid water of the lake washing through him, dousing the repulsive fires that burned in his mind and body. He was surprised when this worked. With a sigh of relief, he raised his head and straightened up.

Jolanya wiped her eyes and gave Kyr a wobbly smile. "I'm sorry. I shouldn't let my feelings interfere with our work."

"It's all right," he murmured. Unwilling to discuss what he'd just experienced, he quickly added, "Let's continue."

The Kailithana met his eyes straight on. "If that's what you want." She paused but he said nothing. "Alright. One thing I know, Kyr, is that it is *not* Zhovanya Who wanted you to suffer. But others have, haven't they?"

"Gods help me, yes! Certainly, the Soul-Drinker did — but then, he wanted *everyone* to suffer. Gauday, however, was fascinated with making *me* suffer. Of course, he had the excuse of carrying out our Master's last command."

The Kailithana's gaze sharpened. "What last command?"

"Just as he died, the Soul-Drinker screamed — in that horrible, mental voice of his — '*Capture Kyr and make him suffer forever. Never grant him the mercy of death.*' His command burned into the brains of all the mind-bonded Slaves. That's why Gauday didn't kill me when he finally got hold of me."

"Oh, Kyr! Don't you see? That command was burned into your mind, too. It was the *Soul-Drinker* who cursed you to suffer endlessly, not Zhovanya."

"What?" He stared at her, stunned. "Gods, I…" He shook his head, frowning. Then he said slowly, "That's true. The *Soul-Drinker* is the one who cursed me. Back then, he was the *Master,* and I saw him as an all-powerful god. He nearly was, with his sorcerous powers. Oh!" Kyr sat up straight, eyes wide.

"By all the hells! I've been mixing Zhovanya up with him!" His face went hot and he bowed his head. "Ah, Goddess, forgive me! I knew Your Love at the Sanctuary. You were with me whenever I truly cried out to You, even at that cursed fort. How could I forget?"

"*Of course* you forgot," the Kailithana said gently. "You only knew Zhovanya's Love for a short time at the Sanctuary. Most of your life, you have been at the mercy of those who wanted you to suffer. It's no surprise that you came to see the Goddess that way, too."

Kyr nodded. "He was a god to me, so I've been assuming that Zhovanya is like him."

"And, for this, you must forgive yourself," Jolanya continued. "You know Zhovanya does, don't you?"

"I guess so. I'm still reeling...I was so convinced that She hates me."

"Why do you think that you wanted to believe that?"

"*Wanted* to? Gods, I don't know! It's all so *confusing*!" Kyr jumped to his feet and started pacing back and forth. And then a wail burst out of him, a young, bewildered voice crying, "I killed my *Master*! I'm bad!" He fell to his knees in front of the fire in the hearth, breathing in short sobbing gasps.

The Kailithana crossed the room, knelt beside him, and placed her hand on his back. A Flow of kailitha surged through her hand into his heart, a soothing blue-green. In a few moments, he calmed down and murmured, "Ah, hells, I guess the Slave part of me still believed I deserve the punishment the Soul-Drinker commanded, and couldn't believe in Zhovanya's Love, despite all the blessings She has given me."

"Yes, brave one. It's so very hard for us to believe that the ones who raised us are not the source of the loving care we need and deserve, no matter how much suffering they inflict."

"Merciless gods," Kyr sighed, scrubbing the drying tears off his face. "How many times do I have to learn this?"

The Kailithana said gently, "The hard path is a spiral, not a straight line. We keep coming around to the same wounds, healing a little more each time."

"Hmph. Hard path, and *long*," Kyr muttered, with a rueful twist of his lips.

"Indeed." Jolanya smiled. "Shall we take a few moments to meditate?" Kyr nodded, and added a log to the fire. They settled down facing the hearth, sitting cross-legged, backs straight.

"Alright, brave one, let's remember Her blessings, and open our hearts to Her Love, as much as we can."

Kyr sat still, watching the friendly orange flames and reminding himself of Zhovanya's Love and Forgiveness, recalling all the times Her chant had saved his soul, all the times She had wrapped him in her great wings, or blessed him with gifts of counsel. But then he also recalled his recent rage and bitterness toward Her, and an anguish of shame and grief struck through him. Bowing his head, he whispered, "Zhovanya, narali. Goddess, forgive me." For a time, he silently chanted, *Zhovanya narali, Zhovanya narali.*

And then a soft breath of Her Love blew gently through his heart, melting the cold shell that he had built out of anger, grief, and horror. He shivered, feeling soft and vulnerable like Beran, the newborn baby, and dizzy with the feeling that the world had been upside-down, and now had come right-side up. With his hands pressed together before his heart, he whispered, "Ah, Goddess, forgiven once again. Thank You."

Then the Kailithana said, "Zhovanya naralo."

With renewed faith, he affirmed, "Zhovanya naralo." They smiled at each other in quiet joy at this homecoming.

Then he slumped a little, and shook his head. "I'm afraid it may take me a while to forgive myself. Or Lanir and Rajani."

"We can take all the time you need, brave one. This was a big step. Take the rest of the day to rest and be with Zhovanya. If you're ready, we'll continue tomorrow."

They got to their feet, and he bowed to her. "Thank you, Kailithana. I'm deeply grateful to you for helping me return to Zhovanya's Grace."

That evening, Kyr slipped into the penitents' small chapel just as they began to chant. Shy and weary, he sat in the back of the room and quietly chanted with them. During the meditation, he found himself near tears, so glad to come home after such a long, bitter time away from his brothers, from Her. Afterwards, he exchanged warm greetings with all four of the men. Sensing his quietness and reserve, they did not pressure him to stay.

"Sleep well?" Medari asked the next morning, as Kyr came down the stairs into the main room.

He rubbed his eyes and yawned. "Now I know why people say they slept like a log."

"I've eaten, but breakfast is keeping warm by the fire." Medari leaned down from his chair by the hearth and picked up the teapot. "Here."

"Thanks." Kyr took the teapot over to the table. "Have you seen the Kailithana?"

"She's out for a walk."

Kyr glanced out the window. "In this rain? It's pouring! What is she doing? Is she all right?"

"Yes, she's fine. Don't worry. She wrapped up well."

"Winter." Kyr shivered, then asked hopefully, "Does it snow here?"

"Sorry, no. Just rains a lot, gets pretty chilly."

Kyr grimaced, and filled his mug with tea.

At that moment, Jolanya opened the door, admitting a swirl of wind that made the hearthfire flare. Her face glowing, she laughed. "It's wild out there!" She shoved the door shut, hung up her dripping cloak, and hurried over to the fire to warm her hands. "Good morning, Kyr."

He smiled at her, entranced. She seemed so young, so full of life and delight. "You love the rain?" Rain, for him, was only a cold reminder of his torment at the hands of Gauday.

Jolanya grinned. "I love the change of seasons. Winter brings the power and excitement of storms, wind, and, yes, I even like the rain. We need it for the crops to grow — the trees, the animals — we all need the rain." She loosed her dark hair from its wind-frazzled braid, combed it with her fingers, and began rebraiding it.

Watching her, Kyr bit back what he longed to say: *For you, I would learn to love the rain.*

After fetching breakfast off the hearth and enjoying their raisin oatmeal muffins, bacon, and tea, the Kailithana and Kyr went up to his room. Jolanya took her seat in the padded chair and arranged her indigo robes and a white woolen shawl, while Kyr stirred up the fire in his small hearth. Then he sat cross-legged on his bed facing her, and nodded. "I'm ready."

The Kailithana bowed her head. "Zhovanya, ganaralai. Jeyal, ganaralai." After a few moments of meditative silence, she looked up. "It was a powerful day for you yesterday. How are you this morning, Kyr?"

"Not sure. Feels like I can't find the ground with my feet. I was so angry at Zhovanya, felt so lost. Now I'm glad to be with Her again, but nothing makes sense. I guess She loves me, even though I am star-cursed." He shook his head and shoulders as if he could rattle some sense into his difficult life.

"Think about it, Kyr. It all happened so fast: Lanir's death; the cleansing ritual; taking in Rajani's memories — one thing right after another. It must have been devastating for you."

"It was...overwhelming. When Lanir — Dekani — died, I felt abandoned — alone for the first time. Empty. Scared. Like my soul had been torn in half. Then all the rest of it happened." He sighed. "No wonder I got so confused."

His soul torn in half, the Kailithana mused. *Ah! Losing Dekani is what caused the black hole in his zhan.* Aloud, she said, "Ah, brave one, it must have been a terrible blow to lose your teacher. He was your steadfast support for most of your life. Then you found out how he deceived and used you. No wonder you lost trust in him, in everyone — even the Goddess."

"I do miss my teacher," he said forlornly.

"You haven't had any time to grieve for him, have you?"

"No. I've been too angry at him. And so much happened, as you said."

"Kailithos, think about this for a moment: Would *you* have done what he and Rajani did in order to end the Soul-Drinker's horror?"

"Hells, I don't know." He frowned thoughtfully. "I guess that if it was the only choice, I would, yes. The Soul-Drinker had to be stopped. According to Rajani's memories, the Circle tried many times to kill him, but no one could get through his sorcerous defenses. They were convinced that creating me through that evil ritual *was* their only option. "

"Can you forgive your father for using you so terribly?"

"I know he sacrificed himself — and me — to save all of Khailaz." He gave a startled laugh. "By all the little gods! I sacrificed myself to protect the Sanctuary. Like father, like son? Gods, I wish he had been able to *tell* me he was my father." Tears filled his eyes. He wept quietly, grieving for them both, trapped into such horrific sacrifices by the madness of the Soul-Drinker.

The Kailithana took his hands in her own, and sent blue-green kailitha flowing gently into his heart. After a time, he whispered, "Yes. I forgive him."

The Kailithana began to softly chant, "Zhovanya naralo." Kyr wiped his eyes and joined in: "Zhovanya naralo, Zhovanya naralo." As they chanted, quiet joy filled his heart, his soul.

After a time, they returned to silence. "Ready?" asked the Kailithana, feeling the kailitha surging up. He nodded, and stretched out before her on his bed. She placed one hand on his forehead, the other over his heart, and opened to the Flow.

The kailitha streamed through her hands, a warm red-gold, and she began the delicate work of restoring his zhan pathways. There was still much distortion and damage, and though the gray web was no longer blocking the kailitha, tangled remnants were strewn all along his zhan pathways. She had to tease each one loose as she encountered it, and then allow the kailitha to dissolve it.

Kyr only felt a delicious warmth creeping through his veins and nerves, his body relaxing bit by bit, until he was half-asleep, drifting on a gentle tide.

At last, many of the remnants of the web were cleared away, though the black hole at the core of his zhan had not changed. The Flow began to dwindle. Jolanya finished clearing the tangle she was working on and sat back, taking a few moments to return to herself, then opened her eyes. "That's all we can do today, brave one."

Kyr sat up and faced her. "Kailithana, how can Zhovanya love me and still send me into one hell after another? I don't understand."

"She needed you, remember?"

"But why would She need me to do anything? Why does She even allow such vicious tyrants as the Soul-Drinker and Gauday to exist?"

Jolanya smiled ruefully, remembering the painful years she had spent wrestling with this same kind of question. "Zhovanya is the Force of Life, of Love, of Creation. She works through us: we are Her hands, Her eyes, Her feet. Out of Her great Love and Wisdom, She gives us the wit and the freedom to make our own choices. We can always say 'No' to Her requests. We can always say 'No' to Love. But you have not, brave one. In the end, you have always said 'Yes.'"

A sweet pang brought tears to Kyr's eyes. *It's true. I almost always have tried to choose love, whenever I was allowed a choice; even when I barely knew what love was; even when it meant enduring degradation and torture.* Uneasy with this new view of himself, he protested, "But I have hurt so many people. Even here, I hurt Craith, and was cruel to Luciya." He took a breath, embarrassed and perplexed. "How can all of this be true — being star-cursed, born from evil — yet being one who chooses love?" He sighed. "Gods, I'm more confused than ever."

Jolanya smiled into his eyes, letting her love shine forth. And he — beginning to feel he might be worthy of love — shyly smiled back. Their eyes shone golden and silver, locked in a moment of sweet communion.

But then, Kyr dropped his eyes. Being seen with such radiant love by the one he longed for with his whole soul — but could not have — was unbearable. *Goddess, why does this love hurt so? Why does my heart yearn for this one who is forbidden to me?* He ached to take Jolanya in his arms, to kiss and caress her to ecstasy, as she herself had taught him. Struggling to keep control, he slid down to lie flat on his bed. *I've got to send her away.* "I'm sorry, Kailithana. I can't...I'm exhausted."

"I'm sure you need some time to take this all in. It's very important that you be kind to yourself, let yourself feel Zhovanya's love again. Don't try to figure it all out. Remember that Her ways are often unfathomable."

"Yes, Kailithana."

As she left the room, he realized that he truly was exhausted. *All these changes are overwhelming. And, Goddess forgive me, I want Jolanya so much! She was looking at me so lovingly. Maybe she... No! She is the Kailithana. I must respect that.* Heavy with fatigue, he shed his boots, crawled under his blankets, and closed his eyes; but his mind still nibbled on the puzzle of his life. *How can Zhovanya forgive me when I was* created *out of evil sorcery and brother-murder?*

Isn't that depravity woven into my bones and blood? Ah, hells, The Kailithana is right. I shouldn't be trying to figure it all out. He focused on the rise and fall of his chest with his breath, and started drifting toward sleep.

Then he remembered the first time he had seen the Goddess, and Her Dance that showed Her embracing all the best and worst of Life.

The Goddess danced, and as She danced, She changed. She aged and withered into a silver-haired crone, eyes deep with awareness and wisdom. She died and rotted away. Her white bones danced in the black void. She was reborn as a chubby infant, grew into golden young girl dancing in happy innocence, then a maiden dancing in sensuous abandon with Her lover. The Goddess died young, torn apart by childbirth. She was raped and killed. She was a mad-eyed killer, dripping with blood. She was holy and hideous. She was terrible and beautiful.

And now Her Dance deepened and She changed yet again. A stag with golden eyes ran panting from the hunters, bloody foam flying from his gaping mouth. A wolf howled to her pack-mates to come feast on the kill, her golden eyes glowing in the dark night. A golden-eyed hawk soared high, seeing small prey far below. A pair of golden eyes glanced upward in fright–and blinked out as a rabbit scurried into its warren.

Creature after creature danced through the darkness of the Temple–mating, birthing, feeding, killing, dying, and She was All–yet never did Her gaze lose its fierce serenity, nor did She stop dancing. For eternity, She danced through endless permutations of life and death, holiness and defilement.

Kyr sighed. *Well, maybe She can forgive me. She is the Goddess, after all.* Repeating the forgiveness chant in his mind, he fell asleep with a slight smile on his lips.

Chapter Twenty-Two

Healing Storm

The next morning, Kyr joined Medari and Jolanya at breakfast. They greeted him with glad smiles, which he returned with a brief nod, and silently took his seat, busying himself with filling his mug with tea and stirring honey into it. Their warm welcome clashed with his uncertainty of who and what he was, now that he had let go of the dark beliefs he'd adopted since learning of his star-cursed birth. He nibbled at his muffin but it seemed dry and tasteless. Shifting in his chair and exhaling raggedly, he stared out the window at the wind-ruffled lake, which danced in sparkles and whitecaps under a clear sunny sky.

Jolanya set her empty mug aside. "I can see that you are restless, Kyr. Shall we continue the Kailithara now?" At this, his agitation surged up with renewed force. But he knew that stopping the Kailithara now would be like trying to prevent Winter from arriving.

"Alright, Kailithana. But…it's so beautiful today. Let's go outdoors. The rains might come back any day." He shivered a little with the chill that still lingered deep in his bones.

"Fine idea!"

And the two of them each grabbed their cloaks from the hooks by the door. Kyr stepped outside, but Medari called them back: "Wait a moment. Take some water and food. You might be gone a while."

Jolanya nodded and went back inside, while Kyr fidgeted outside, pacing back and forth, hardly seeing the ravens who were soaring and cawing in the clear blue sky. Inside, Medari dug up a water sack and filled it, and Jolanya wrapped a couple of muffins in a napkin.

"Finally!" Kyr groused as Jolanya emerged, carrying their provisions in a small satchel.

"Yes, we can go now, impatient one," Jolanya laughed.

They headed up the path by the lake until they reached a swath of forest that went down to the lake's edge. Then they left the path, and explored the woods until they found a sheltered, sunny clearing carpeted with thick pine duff. The clearing was surrounded by dark green pines; peppered with white-barked aspen, now barren of leaves; and fiery red bushes. Looking around, Jolanya asked, "This will do, don't you think?"

"Let's get started!" Kyr snapped. Then, realizing how he sounded, he added, "Oh, curse it. I'm sorry. I don't understand why I'm feeling so unsettled."

"It's not surprising," the Kailithana said. "You made a major shift yesterday, which often causes fears and doubts to arise. But for you, there may be something else coming up. Shall we find out, kailithos? I'm ready if you are."

"Alright," Kyr grumped. "I should know by now: the only way out of this is by going through it."

"True," Jolanya said with a sympathetic smile.

They sat on the earth facing each other, their cloaks wrapped around them. Jolanya began to chant, praying for guidance for both of them: "Zhovanya, ganaralai. Jeyal, ganaralai." Kyr started to chant with her, but immediately he choked up, his throat tight with grief.

Jolanya brought the chant to a close, and asked gently, "What is it, kailithos?"

Seeing him rub his aching throat, she handed him the water sack, and he swigged down some water. "I wasted all that time feeling like Zhovanya hates me. It was...so lonely and...difficult."

"I know," she said softly. "It was that way for me, once, as well."

"You too?"

"Yes, for a while," she acknowledged, her eyes briefly lowered. "Mercifully, we now both know Her Love again."

Somehow it helped to know that someone else had gone through a similar experience of lostness. He gave her a brief flicker of a smile. "Thanks."

"You're welcome. Ready now?"

He nodded and stretched out on his back. The musty-sweet scent of pine duff filled his nose. Sitting cross-legged beside him, the Kailithana placed her hands below his heart over the core of his body, and opened to the Flow. Gently, she sent the kailitha — a steady stream of white, this time — to explore and heal his zhan pathways. Now that she had cleared out most of the gray web, she moved deeper into his inner swamp.

Goddess help us! The pathways here have almost disappeared! Ghostly lights flickered and flared over the swamp, revealing faint and broken pathways. Cautiously, she began to send the kailitha, now a golden flow, along the pathways, moving from one broken piece to the next, often stopping to search for the next piece. Weaving the pathways together was delicate, vital work, requiring all her skill and attention.

Sensing nothing of the Kailithana's subtle work, Kyr still felt tense and restless, but with Jolanya deep in her healing trance, he didn't dare move or speak. *Why can't I just relax?* But his unease increased. *What is bothering me? This isn't difficult or painful, just boring. All I'm doing is keeping still, keeping quiet. Reminds me of something.* He tried to turn it away, but the memory arose anyway.

> *"You must learn, boy, learn to endure the Master's favors, if you ever want to be a Slave." The mean Trainer was hurting him, pinching his leg with metal tongs.*
>
> *"OW, OW! STOP! Please STOP!" Kyr begged, writhing against the straps that bound him to the cold stone table.*
>
> *The Trainer only pinched harder. "Want the pain to stop? It's simple, stupid whelp. Stop wiggling. Stop squealing."*

Gods and demons! I was so young then, as young and innocent as that little boy, Jonir. He clenched his fists, roiling with rage at all the ways he had been used and hurt. *How many times have I had to force myself to be still and silent while someone hurt me? The Trainer; the Soul-Drinker; the Watcher; and last but not least, Gauday. And — if torture and degradation weren't enough — the Circle's ritual, and manipulation and lies by those who supposedly cared about me. Gods damn them, Gods damn them all! By all the hells, my whole life has been nothing but one rape after another — my body, my mind, my heart, my soul — all RAPED and RAPED and RAPED!* Smoldering with wrath, he nevertheless remained still under the Kailithana's hands, only because of the relentless self-control tortured into him by the Soul-Drinker's Trainer.

As the Kailithana wove a new pattern of zhan pathways in Kyr's core, she smiled, sensing his rage building. *About time!* she thought. Then, reconnecting one last pathway, she moved her hands down to his feet and sent the kailitha down deep into the bedrock of the earth beneath them, to link him to the solidity of stone. Then she rose and stepped back.

"Up now, Kyr," she urged him. "Move! Let your anger move you!"

Kyr needed no further encouragement. He leapt to his feet and surrendered into a stomping, whirling dance of outrage and fury. Burning hot, he stripped off his cloak and threw it aside. He whirled and leapt, striking and kicking the air, carried by the intense energy liberated by the Kailithana's work.

"Breathe, Kyr. Breathe, move, yell. *Now!*"

"Aaaaggghh!!" Fury — long-buried under his rigid self-control — poured out of him in wordless roars as he continued to leap, kick, and punch the air.

221

Then the Kailithana demanded, "*Tell* me, Kyr! Tell me!"

Kyr jumped around to face her, and stood with his eyes bulging, shoulders hunched up like a maddened bull, hands tensed into eagle claws.

"They *raped* me! *Used* me! I was *nothing* to any of them! Just a tool, a weapon! Gods damn them *all*!" Blazing with rage and potent with strength and power, he felt huge as a mountain, and began a stomping dance, each step seeming to shake the world.

The Kailithana grabbed two stones and began tapping them in time with his thudding feet, supporting his dance. Sweat poured from Kyr's skin, making his body shine in the afternoon sunshine, and darkening his hair and beard. He was as perilously beautiful as a raging inferno, and she was in awe of the power and grace of his dance of rage and self-reclaiming.

Every stomp of his foot crushed an adversary, every kick and fist strike affirmed his right to exist *for* himself, *as* himself. "They had no right! I *exist*! I am ME! Not a weapon, not a tool, not a toy!" A murderous fury claimed him and he roared out, "I'll kill them all! I'll kill *everyone*! I'll destroy the whole cursed *world*!"

His own words shocked him to a standstill, and he shook his head. "*NO!* I won't be like Dauthaz, like any of them. I *WON'T*!" From the greatness of his heart, in the center of his fiery storm, he made a profound, deliberate choice: to refuse to let himself be anything like those who had so grievously hurt him, and to turn once again away from the easy path of blame, hatred, and revenge.

Taking this stand in his true essence, he surrendered into a state of pure, translucent fire, flaming and raging into a transcendent dance. "*I AM!*" he yelled with each stomp and leap, each punch and kick. "*I AM!*" Furious outrage became fiercely joyous self-affirmation, and his body poured rapidly through the Martial Flowing Poses that Naran had taught him at the Sanctuary. His wild dance became a grace-filled paean of pride and passion, bringing Jolanya to tears.

After a time out of time, the fires of transformation began to sink down to glowing embers; and as Kyr slowed to a stop, he assumed the proud Spiritual Warrior Pose, feeling his strength and selfhood in a totally new way: deep, clear, and full. The Kailithana stood as witness to his new sovereignty, honoring him in her heart and soul. With hands at her heart, she bowed deeply to him.

Kyr accepted her respect and homage without reservation. For a while, he simply stood, breathing deeply, absorbing this new awareness of himself and his right to exist, and to live his life for himself. With the fire now burning as a warm golden-red light deep inside him, he knew himself to be worthy and strong, kind and valorous. And he knew that he would never allow anyone to use or abuse him again, or to take away his right to choose for himself.

After a few moments, his legs began trembling with tiredness. In wordless communion, he and the Kailithana sat down, facing each other. Wrapping themselves in their cloaks, they sank into meditation. Kyr went deeper than ever before, as a rock-solid quietness allowed him a deeper surrender.

Zhovanya's Presence lightly touched his heart, and he smiled, glad and grateful to return to Her Grace and Love. Yet something was different. A thrill, perilous and exciting, ran through him. No longer was he approaching the Goddess as a wounded supplicant seeking aid and comfort. Now he met Her as a man offering due reverence — perhaps even as a co-celebrant with Her. And now he heard Zhovanya laughing with delight, Her merriment filling his soul. Kyr began laughing out loud in pure joy and exultation. Jolanya glanced at him in surprise, but then, embracing his emergence into the fullness of himself, she happily joined in.

After a few moments, their joint laughter subsided into a deep, healing peace. As Jolanya sat quietly, she was surprised when the kailitha surged up, a deep-blue color she'd never seen, and she said gently, "Lie down, kailithos."

"Gladly. I'm exhausted." Kyr wrapped himself up in his cloak and stretched out on the soft pine duff. The Kailithana placed her hands on his forehead and chest. Kyr felt the kailitha flowing strongly yet gently, filling the now open spaces in his zhan, solidifying his new sense of integrity and wholeness. Overwhelmed by this huge transformation, he yielded to his tiredness and slept.

Jolanya sat beside him, allowing the deep-blue kailitha to do its work. Gladness filled her heart that he had reclaimed his soul; and she smiled, knowing that soon her work as Kailithana would end — and she could let herself love him fully.

But then a shadow crossed her mind. *Gods, what if he doesn't want me?* She shook her head. *I see you, fear. Of course, you arise now, when I am getting so close to my heart's desire.* And she allowed a trickle of that new blue kailitha to soothe her firesnake of fear back to sleep.

As the kailitha did its subtle healing work, Kyr slept deeply, resting on the Earth surrounded by graceful aspen and stalwart pine, and watched over by a raven perched nearby. Waking slowly, he savored his new sense of substantiality and inner spaciousness. Then he opened his eyes, and found Jolanya's gray eyes shining down at him with loving affection. He reached up to gently caress her cheek.

She smiled but pulled back from his touch. "Ah, kailithos," she said, with a slight emphasis on the second word. "You're awake. Good. We're finished for today, and it's getting cold. Shall we head back to the infirmary?"

He merely nodded, unwilling to break the inner quietness of his rejuvenated soul. They got to their feet and followed the path back through the wind-tossed woods, clutching their cloaks tightly against the chilly, pine-scented air. As they emerged onto the path by the lake, the late-afternoon sun sent golden rays to gild the snowy tops of the eastern cliffs and the frothy waves of the lake.

Kyr found it strange and wonderful to feel confident and relaxed in his own being; to feel that he had just as much right to exist and enjoy life as did Jolanya, or anyone else. His quiet smile of self-acceptance touched Jolanya's heart.

The Kailithana had declared a vacation for them both, after their day in the forest. And, as Kyr had predicted, the rains did indeed return: drizzling, pouring or storming every day. For the first two days after his healing transformation, he enjoyed resting and meditating, taking the time to become comfortable with his new sense of himself and the new vitality in his core. But then the rain's cold and damp crept into his bones, bringing back memories of being left out in the rain, yearning for death but giving in to Medari's pleading to stay alive, and enduring Gauday's torments. Now, after three days cooped-up indoors, breathing the warm air of the infirmary with its odors of smoke from the hearthfire, and of the pungent potions and salves Medari kept cooking up, Kyr began to feel glum and jittery.

On this third morning, the pale winter sun sparked honey-hued gleams in the oaken floor of Kyr's room. He glanced at this rare phenomenon, and jumped up off his bed to look out the window. "It isn't raining!" he exulted, and dashed downstairs, grabbed his cloak, and bolted outside. At once, he broke into a run, enjoying the freedom and spaciousness of being alone outdoors, happy for this chance to move and breathe winter's fresh, cold air. As he ran — heart pumping, blood surging through his veins — his gloom and edginess waned. Grinning, he sped up, running so lightly that he felt as if he could join the ravens soaring and cawing above the white-capped waves dancing across the lake.

Reaching a rise in the path, he stopped, taking in the expansive view of Ravenvale with its fields and forests, its scattered cottages and the sprawling mansion of Ravenhall. Far down the valley loomed the guardian cliffs through whose dark tunnel he and Rajani had entered this peaceful haven many months before. *I was so burdened then,* he thought, *so lost.* For a few moments, he reflected on all he had been through since he'd awakened in that strange new world of care and kindness at the safe house in the City, after the death of the Soul-Drinker; his journey through remorse, healing and forgiveness at the Great Tree and the Sanctuary; his fight to keep hold of his soul during his ordeal with Gauday; his long, dark night at the Tower. His heart softened with rare compassion for himself, and he smiled. *Difficult as this path has been, at this moment I'm not sure I would change it. Perhaps everything that happened has been a stepping stone to bring me here today.*

Grateful for his new-found sense of confidence and self-acceptance, he raised his arms, and shouted, "Thank You, Zhovanya!" A familiar-looking raven swooped overhead and circled twice, croaking gleefully. Kyr laughed and yelled, "Thanks to you also, friend raven!" With a waggle of its wings, the raven flew off to join its mob.

Later that day, as Kyr waited for the Kailithana, he stood by the window of his room, watching dark clouds swelling up over the western guardian wall. When Jolanya entered, he turned to her with a smile. She joined him at the window, and, with a smile of her own, reached up to pick a brown leaf out of his wind-tousled hair. "Ah, you've been outside."

"I went for a run by the lake." Smiling, he took the leaf from her and set it on the windowsill next to Naran's gift, the small wooden eagle. "It was refreshing."

"You look happier than you have the past few days. Do you need another day or are you ready to continue our work?"

For answer, Kyr stretched out on his bed and closed his eyes. The Kailithana settled onto her chair and closed her eyes as well, praying for guidance: *Zhovanya ganarali. Jeyal ganarali.* When she felt the kailitha arising, she placed her hands on Kyr's chest. The Flow began strongly; but as she sent it toward his core, the kailitha moved slower and slower, until it was oozing like thick mud.

The Kailithana took her hands away from his body, resting them in her lap. "Something is blocking the Flow, Kyr. Are you keeping something back?"

He sat up, hugging his knees to his chest, his eyes dark. "Yes," he acknowledged. "But I hate to speak of it." *Especially to you,* he added silently.

"It's that last month with Gauday, isn't it?" He shook as if struck by her words, but remained silent. "We're so close to completing the healing, Kyr. Don't let him win now. What makes this so difficult?"

"Gods, I'm not sure." His voice was harsh with pain and disgust. "I guess because it was so…obscenely intimate. And he was so lewdly delighted with my helplessness and suffering. Gods *curse* him!" His sudden outburst of anger startled them both. Kyr gave a shaky laugh. "I'm sorry, Kailithana."

"Keep going, kailithos."

He rubbed his face and took a couple of deep breaths. "Ah, gods and demons! What he did was so vile, I hate to go back into it." He got up and began moving about his room, picking things up and putting them down without looking at them.

Holding the small eagle that Naran had given him, he stared blindly out the window. "Gauday was trying to drag me back into the Soul-Drinker's hell. It wasn't just torture. He blended pain with sexual pleasure." Kyr shuddered. Sweat stood out on his brow, and he began pacing the room again, still holding the wooden bird. His breath came faster. "Must I go on? It's all coming back."

"Yes, brave one. Keep going."

With great concentration, he set the little wooden eagle on the window sill and gripped the edge of the sill with both hands, his shoulders hunched up, his knuckles turning white.

The Kailithana came to stand beside him, and placed one hand on his back and the other on his chest over his heart, sending a calming flow of white kailitha. His shaking slowly subsided, and his shoulders relaxed a little. Still leaning on the sill, he went on.

"The hardest thing was not to yield to Gauday. He wanted to be my new Master, tried to make me to see him as the source of all pain and all pleasure, like the Soul-Drinker was to us Slaves. Gauday used spellchants, trying to mind-bond me like Dauthaz did to his Watchers. If he'd succeeded, I would have been Gauday's obedient slave, doing any cruel, evil thing he wanted." He glanced at the Kailithana with haunted eyes. "It was terrifying. I'd rather have died than become his mind-slave!"

"Take a deep breath. Relax." The Kailithana reinforced her suggestions with an increase in the Flow. The kailitha turned red, bringing Kyr more into his centered strength.

"Gods," he complained, "I hate going over all this. But...let's get it over with." He straightened up and continued.

"I would get desperate for any way to end it, even if it meant yielding to Gauday. But Dekani — Lanir — wouldn't let me: kept singing that chant over and over. 'Zhovanya naralo, Zhovanya naralo.' Sometimes I hated him for that." Kyr sighed. "But when I was on the edge of giving in, he shielded me, took me down so deep that nothing Gauday did had any effect." He gave a little, painful laugh. "Frustrated the hell out of Gauday."

He picked up the little eagle and started pacing again. Jolanya dropped her hands and let the Flow ebb. "When Gauday realized I was resisting his spellchants, he started using noxious potions that clouded my mind. I got so confused! Couldn't tell what was real, where I was, who I was." He shook his head as if trying to clear out that confusion.

"And he kept on burning and cutting these damn scars into my body." His voice dropped to a murmur. "Worst of all, he used this sweet-smelling oil on me when he wanted sex, which made it so that I couldn't tell *his* pleasure from *mine*. That doubled pleasure was...overwhelming."

Kyr stopped dead, furious that he was getting aroused by speaking of Gauday's torments. "Gods curse his soul! He branded my body, my mind, my soul with his vile madness. And his mark is still deep in me: it's affecting me right now!" His hands tightened, and there was a sharp snap.

He looked down in dismay. Naran's gift lay in pieces in his hands.

"Merciless gods," he growled. "I *am* cursed. I can't keep anything good, no matter how small."

Jolanya wanted to protest: *You are not cursed!* But she merely said, "I'm sorry the little bird got broken, but you have every right to be angry, Kyr."

At this acknowledgement, all his tension and fury drained away, leaving only grief and exhaustion. He stood by the window, sadly tracing a broken wing with one finger. Then he set the pieces of the eagle on the window sill, trudged over to his bed, and sat on its edge.

The Kailithana came and sat in her chair, facing him. "You are no longer angry?"

"No, just sad that I broke Naran's gift." He sighed. "It's odd. I can indulge in anger now, but at the fort, it was my direst temptation, my worst enemy. To keep my soul, I had to soften. That was Zhovanya's word of counsel. 'Soften,' she said to me as I left the Sanctuary. I'm not sure yet whether that was a gift or a curse." He snorted softly. "No, it was a gift. If I'd hardened, if I'd fought, I would have broken, like that little eagle. I came close several times. Nearly went mad in that black pit Gauday kept me in."

"By all the gods, it is...difficult, this hard path." He shoulders sagged. "I almost let myself start hating Gauday," he murmured. "That would have been it, you know. If I'd let myself give in to hate, I'd have been lost in the Soul-Drinker's madness again. What Gauday did was so familiar. It's all we Slaves ever knew." He looked up with a slight smile. "But Lanir helped, and Zhovanya. They reminded me that my one advantage over Gauday was compassion. I had to forgive whatever he did. It was the only way to keep my soul safe from becoming mired in his foul swamp."

"Ah, brave one!" Jolanya's heart ached with pity for his terrible ordeal, and admiration for his greatness of soul.

He gave her little smile. "Not so brave. I'd never have been able to soften and forgive without Lanir's help and Zhovanya's gifts. When I was close to giving in — ah gods, *so* close! — She gave me another gift: to see Gauday through Her eyes." He looked down, silent for a moment, remembering how desperate he had been for a different blessing, how he had begged Her to end his suffering, to take him Home.

Sensing his pain, the Kailithana waited for him to look up. Then she asked gently, "And what did you see with Her second gift?"

Chapter Twenty-Three

Oblivion

Kyr sighed. It had taken him such a long time to understand what lay behind his tormentor's bizarre blend of cruelty and passion. He wasn't sure anyone could understand what he had discovered, except perhaps, the Kailithana. He searched her face. Seeing only openness and compassion, he decided to risk telling her.

"Behind all that arrogance and cruelty, Gauday's soul was so tired, so lost. His soul was suffering as much as mine was." He shook his head. "I wish I'd been able to help him. I tried, but he couldn't listen." It all came rushing back to him: the times he had tried to share Zhovanya's Love and Forgiveness with Gauday; and Gauday's furious rejection, scornful hatred, and gloating threats. "Merciless gods," Kyr whispered, hunching over, elbows on knees, resting his head in his hands. "So much pain, so much."

"Yes," said the Kailithana sadly. "Gauday's — and yours."

He looked up at her, his eyes glistening darkly with sorrow. *"Why?* Why is there so much pain in life?"

With a deep sigh, she said, "As far as I can tell, suffering is interwoven with the fabric of life in this world. And," she added softly, "so is joy...and love."

"Ah." His eyes met hers and flared amber for a moment as perilous hope arose in his heart. But then he clenched his jaw and looked away. *No, I mustn't let myself imagine that she could love me.* And with that thought, all that he had endured, and the cruel impossibility of loving her weighed heavily on him. Unable to bear any of it any longer, he lay down on his bed with his back to her.

Concerned and a little hurt by his posture, Jolanya bit her lip, unsure what to say to him. But then the kailitha surged up, powerful and insistent. "The Flow is strong, Kyr. May I work now?"

He remained silent, his back rigid, longing so intensely for the Kailithana that he could scarcely bear the thought of her touch. *Goddess,* he thought wildly,

You demand everything from me. But, he groaned silently, *I am your servant.* And he turned over to lie flat on his back.

"Thank you, Kyr." The Kailithana placed her hands on his chest and belly. The kailitha flooded through her hands, a warm golden-red: sweet, soft, and strong.

At first, Kyr welcomed the warmth of the kailitha; but, as it wove its way deeper into his zhan, old memories arose and he began to burn with shame. "Oh, gods! I hurt so many people!" he cried, remembering all the sacrifices whom he had tortured and killed as the Soul-Drinker's obedient Slave. All the torment and degradation and harm he had inflicted and endured began to pile up like a huge wave growing taller and taller as each moment passed. He clutched his quilt with tight fists, moaning, "Ohgods, Ohgods! No no no!"

"*Be* with this, Kyr," the Kailithana urged him. "Don't hold back."

"I…can't…it's too much!"

The Kailithana slowed the Flow to a trickle, and asked gently, "What is going on, Kyr?"

"The pain…the terror…all the memories. Dekani was always there, shielding me. Now he's gone, the ice is gone, and it's all piling up on me!" His breath came in short, shallow gasps. He had to get away from the mean man, all the mean men hurting and hurting him. But he couldn't — he was strapped down, chained, locked up. He shook with terror. They were coming: the Trainer, the Watcher, the Soul-Drinker, Gauday…

"KYR! Look at me," the Kailithana commanded sharply. "Tell me what you are experiencing." It was a command — and he obeyed.

"It's dark…I'm scared! I'm so little…I'm helpless…a tiny candle floating on the lake at night. There's a big storm brewing…a huge, black wave… it's towering higher and higher. I can't get away!" His heart sped up again, and he fought to stay still. "Oh gods, oh gods!"

"I'm here with you, Kyr. I'll help you stay afloat in the storm." She let the kailitha loose, and it surged through her hands, shining silver. "Keep breathing, Kyr. Stay with it."

The Kailithana's steady presence and the silver flood of the kailitha gave him courage; yet he shuddered all over with each deep breath, terrified of that looming wave of darkness.

"Let go, Kyr. It's the only way forward. Let go now."

It took all the courage he had, but he stopped trying to hold back that black wave. Memory upon memory crashed down upon him, until he felt as if he were being crushed under a huge, dark, blood-streaked mountain made of torment, degradation, betrayal, horror, agony, guilt, fury, grief. Kyr's eyes were wild with pain and fear. "Jolanya!" he panted. "I can't bear it! It's crushing me!"

She heard Kyr's agony and panic, but kept the kailitha flowing, praying more fiercely than she ever had before: *Zhovanya! Jeyal! By Your Light and Love, help me heal this wounded soul or take us both Home now!*

"Let go, Kyr! Let go *now!*"

After an eon of agony, his heart cracked under the weight and he wailed, "Help me! Goddess, help me!"

Deep within, Kyr heard a strangely joyful answer. *"AT LAST, YOU HAVE ASKED."*

Zhovanya's ethereal Presence filled the room with shimmering, translucent rainbow glory, and the Kailithana felt Zhovanya's Hands encompass her own. Then she knew the words that were needed. "Be with the pain. Accept it and let go."

"No, no!" Kyr's heart was thundering, and he was rigid with terror. *If I let go, I'll be crushed into nothing, into oblivion.*

In that instant, he realized *that* was all he wanted. *I'll let go and there will be no more suffering, no one to suffer.* Now he longed for oblivion as intensely as a lost child longs for its mother. And he surrendered, allowing the black wave to crash down on him, the bloody mountain to crush him. That small candle went out.

There was only the infinite emptiness of the still, black ocean.

For an eon, there was nothingness, emptiness, openness, peace.

There was only the Oneness, forever shimmering with causeless joy.

"Kyr?"

A wave shivered through the infinite depths.

"Kyr?"

Dissolving into laughter, awareness returned, awareness of the heat of someone's hands touching skin; of someone laughing, and proclaiming, "I'm not that! I'm not that!"

He's laughing! Jolanya stared at Kyr in astonishment. *What is he saying? He's not what?* As he kept laughing and repeating his amazing discovery, Jolanya found herself unavoidably laughing with him. He was glowing with the invisible fire of enlightenment, and she drew close, warming her soul by that ineffable flame.

The joy was so great that Kyr felt he would laugh forever, and never say anything but "I'm not that!" Yet after a few blessed moments, his laughter subsided to occasional chuckles. The black wave... the terrible, crushing mountain... were gone, dissolved into his being, leaving only substantiality and serenity.

Kyr opened his eyes to the limited world. Seeing Jolanya's smiling, bewildered face, he started laughing again.

In glad confusion, Jolanya asked, "You're not 'that'? Then, what are you? Who are you?"

Kyr was stunned and entranced by the last question. *Yes, who am I, if I am not that, if I am not my past, my suffering? Zhovanya,* he prayed, *show me who I am.*

An image appeared in his mind, accompanied by a feeling of great tenderness and gentle amusement. He saw a shining being of light, radiant with innate goodness and love. Yet this being was crouched over, clutching about itself a ragged cloak of patches and tatters, stained with blood and tears and darkness. Kyr found himself laughing and crying at once.

"What happened, Kyr? It must be wonderful. You are radiant!"

Kyr's laughter and tears were transmuted into a luminous smile. "Oh, Jolanya, I see it now. I am not what happened to me, not any of it. All that is just an old story. I am only this...this...." He groped for a way to express what went far beyond such small entrapments as words. "I am just this moment of awareness...and now *this* one...and now *this* one. Do you see? None of that old story happened to *this* 'me.' I don't have to carry any of it! I'm free!"

Now Jolanya laughed with joy to see the openness and awe on Kyr's face. But the Kailithana sensed that her work wasn't done. The wound in Kyr's core was still there, and the kailitha was not yet reaching it. "There's something more that needs to happen, Kyr. Can you stay still a while longer?"

He laughed again — gently, kindly, this time. "Yes, Kailithana, thank you."

"Zhovanya, ganarali, Jeyal ganarali," she whispered. Feeling Their Presence within her, she began sending the kailitha to clear and strengthen his zhan pathways. The Flow was gentle and full, a deep blue streaked with gold. To her surprise, the black gap in Kyr's zhan caused by Lanir's death began to shrink and change, at last. She watched in amazement as it became a smooth channel, similar to the one inside her through which the kailitha flowed. Now she knew what she must do: and carefully, she laced the zhan pathways together, making the needed connections to that new channel, weaving a fresh pattern of wholeness so beautiful that tears trickled down her cheeks.

As she worked, Kyr closed his eyes, feeling the changes wrought by the Kailithara sink deeper and deeper into his soul. Compassion filled his heart for the crouching being clinging to its cloak of memory and pain, ignorant of its own clear radiance; and for all those who had not been graced to see this truth about themselves.

Feeling a wholeness, a rightness in his core that he had never known before, Kyr saw again the being of light clutching its ragged cloak. Now, it dropped the tattered cloak of tears and darkness, and rose to standing, letting its light shine unfettered into the world.

Kyr suddenly felt vulnerable, and a little frightened. Witnessing these feelings with compassion, he realized that his mind was making up a story about what might happen if he let go of that old tattered cloak. *Ah, Goddess, help me,* he prayed. *Help me stay out of the story-trap. Help me let go.* And then he remembered all the times Dekani had reminded him to simply watch his breath. As he did this, the kailitha surged more strongly, and he relaxed into the moment, simply noticing the subtle changes taking place within him as the Kailithana worked, without hope or fear, without judgment or story.

When the Flow abated, Jolanya lifted her hands off his body. For a time, they were silent together, awed by the great blessing that Zhovanya had bestowed. Then Kyr rose up to sit cross-legged on his bed; and, putting his hands together at his heart, he bowed in reverence. "Ah, Zhovanya, how could I forget that You are also merciful?" He straightened up and laughed, a little ruefully. "I had but to ask!" He bowed again to the Kailithana in deep, wordless gratitude. She smiled back, awe and love shining from her eyes.

In a rich, glad voice, he began to sing, "Zhovanya naralo." Jolanya added her voice to his and they chanted together joyously. When they came to silence some time later, Kyr reached out his hands to Jolanya, and she left her chair and came up onto his bed. They sat cross-legged, facing each other in a peaceful silence, hands clasped, gently smiling into each other's eyes. No words were necessary to express his gratitude or her joy.

Kyr's golden eyes glowed with unshadowed serenity, and his face was soft, open, and radiant. Jolanya could feel a vast and delicate love emanating from him, filling the room, the building, the whole of Ravenvale. She basked in this Love that was flowing through him.

After a time, she became aware of her exhaustion, and her shoulders drooped. She knew she should leave but could not bear to be parted from him. The very thought made her heart sad.

"Kailithana, are you all right?" Kyr asked gently.

It took her a moment to realize that the vast Love in him was being focused on her, and another moment more to find her voice. "I'm very tired. I should go."

Struck by hope and anguish, Kyr stopped breathing and closed his eyes. He ached to hold her close; and dreaded losing her again, now that the Kailithara was nearly complete. He frowned in puzzlement. *I am free, yet there is pain.*

How can this be? After a moment, he saw what was causing his suffering: *Ah. I'm getting caught in a story about what blessings or pain the future may hold.*

With a sigh, he let go of those stories, and yielded to Love. He smiled and said "Don't go." With that simple plea, the Kailithana's discipline melted in the heat of her longing for him. Without another word, they lay down together, and he enfolded her in his arms, her head on his shoulder. Nothing had ever seemed sweeter to him. Banishing the past and the future, he kept his attention on the rise and fall of her breath, savoring each precious moment that she lay nestled in his arms.

As they rested together, an ancient memory stole softly into his awareness: his mother holding him close, cuddling him on her lap, before the Trainers came to tear him away from all love and kindness. A long-held barrier of isolation crumbled under an assault of tenderness for that bewildered little boy, and for his brave, sad mother. As he slid into a deep sleep, he felt worthy and beloved, held by the strong, welcoming arms of the Goddess.

After a time, they woke together and turned to gaze at each other. "Your eyes!" Jolanya said. "They're so clear now!" Laughing for pure joy, she looked at him with great affection.

Kyr blushed with shy pleasure, which made them both laugh again. He stretched and sat up. "Gods, I'm famished! I hope Medari has brought supper over."

Knowing that Kyr was in a new and tender state, Jolanya smiled and accepted his sudden shift of focus. She ached to speak aloud her passionate love and adoration of him, but something held her back. *The healing isn't complete yet. I can feel it, though I don't know what is needed. I must wait to share how I feel about him.* She stood up and rearranged her robes, patted at her hair, and began to redo her braid. "Shall I bring our supper up here?" she asked, resuming her role as Kailithana.

He tore his eyes away from the dark silken flood of her hair, her deft, graceful hands quickly returning it to its single severe braid. Feeling as new and open as Nyvali's infant son, Kyr realized that he wasn't ready to see anyone else yet. "Yes, please."

Downstairs, Jolanya found Medari just sitting down to supper. "We're eating upstairs tonight," she informed him. "Kyr's made an amazing breakthrough but isn't quite up to seeing anyone right now."

"Good news!" said Medari, his usually dour face lighting up with relief and joy. "He'll be all right now, I take it?"

"More than all right," Jolanya laughed. "But I should let *him* tell you what he will, in his own time."

"Fine, fine. Whenever he's ready." Medari handed her the kitchen tray he had left sitting on the chair next to him. "Here, you can use this to take your dinner up."

Jolanya filled two plates with roast chicken, green beans, and fresh-baked bread, added forks, knives, and a pot of tea and two mugs, and returned to Kyr's room. They ate in a warm and intimate silence, gray and amber eyes meeting and glancing away, exchanging brief glad smiles. A few chuckles escaped from Kyr as he savored his new freedom. After they had finished, Jolanya stacked the dishes onto the tray and set the tray by the door.

When she turned back, she found Kyr sitting cross-legged on his bed, a somber yet kindhearted expression on his face. She crossed over to sit in her chair facing him. "What is it, brave one?"

"I am seeing everyone differently now. My parents, Lanir and Alytha — they used evil sorcery, yes — but to achieve a noble purpose, sacrificing themselves for all of Khailaz. All from love. Rajani and Luciya, the whole Circle — also a mix of evil and love. Even Naran. And I don't know *your* story, but some kind of evil drove you to seek Atonement, to do great acts of love and service."

"Yes," Jolanya acknowledged, seeing her own life in a new way. Not wanting to interrupt his reflections, she said nothing more, and Kyr went on.

"Then there's Medari. Out of love for his family, he kept me alive to undergo Gauday's cruelties. But even Gauday's evil was a sort of love, crippled though he was."

"*Gauday's?*" Jolanya asked in disbelief.

"I know this is rather startling. But what I sensed was that Gauday thought he *loved* Dauthaz, and that the reason he hated me was because I killed his beloved Master."

"How could he — or anyone — love the Soul-Drinker?"

"Because the Soul-Drinker's viciousness was the only form of intimacy, of 'love,' that Gauday knew or could tolerate. He was actually trying to regain that kind of 'love' with me — with himself as the new Master."

And Kyr sighed, now seeing Gauday as a frightened being of hidden light, desperately clutching his familiar robe of darkness around him. Kyr bowed his head and said softly, "May his soul be restored by Zhovanya's Love."

Jolanya thought of her own tormenters, and tried to see them in the same way. She bowed her head and silently sent out her own prayers. After a time, the two looked up at each other and smiled, feeling their souls cleansed of the last traces of hate. They remained quiet, marveling at the intricate intertwining of love and evil in all their lives, and how each of them had been shaped by both.

Then the Kailithana asked him, "Do you forgive *yourself*, now?"

The question sent Kyr deep within. And he saw again those he sacrificed to the Soul-Drinker's greed; and the ones he had hurt since then: Craith, Luciya, Rajani. Closing his eyes, he prayed, *Goddess, help me understand. I am not my past, not the one who did those hurtful things — yet I am responsible for my actions, am I not?*

Her Presence came softly into his heart, and he felt held gently and sweetly. What came to him then was a procession of images: himself as an innocent babe like Beran; then as a child and youth in the grip of the Trainer and the Soul-Drinker, having no awareness of the possibility of choice. As the procession continued, he saw himself choosing the hard path; accepting responsibility for what he had done; seeking to atone for his offenses; finding his way to forgiveness and love; and sacrificing himself to protect the Sanctuary.

But, he objected, *here in Ravenvale, I hurt Craith, Rajani, and Luciya.*

In answer, he witnessed his own profound hurt when he discovered Lanir and Rajani's terrible betrayal of him. He saw himself as that being of light, spinning in a maelstrom of rage and pain, blinded by its cloak of bitterness. But he also saw the vast wings of the Goddess hovering over that pitiful being, and he smiled. *"You were with me all along, though I couldn't see You."*

As the vision faded away, he heard Zhovanya whispering, *"OPEN YOUR HEART, BELOVED."*

Calling on all his courage, Kyr opened his heart to the wounded, crazed man he had been when he had lost hold and attacked Craith. And with that came a deep realization of true innocence. *Given who I was and what I knew at each step of the way, I could have done no different than I did. And this is true for everyone. Ah, Zhovanya, I see it now. This is why You forgive us all.*

He opened his eyes and met Jolanya's gentle, compassionate gaze. "Yes, I forgive myself — and Zhovanya." With these words, a heaviness lifted from his soul, and his heart echoed with the forgiveness chant.

Zhovanya naralo, Zhovanya naralo, Zhovanya naralo.

Part Seven ~ Returning Home

"I surrender myself to everything. I love, I feel pain, I struggle.
The world seems to me wider than the mind,
my heart a dark and almighty mystery."

— Nikos Kazantzakis

Chapter Twenty-Four

A Grace of Service

The next morning, Kyr woke up laughing, all his body and being full of gratitude and lightness. Though dawn was barely showing her face, he rose, eager to meet this new day, this new life. He splashed his face with chilly water from his wash-basin, combed his hair with his fingers, dressed, and went downstairs. There, he stirred up the fire and gave it a new log, then, placing his hands together before his heart, bowed to the fire. "Thank you for your gift of warmth and light."

He turned and glanced out the window. Scudding clouds raced above wind-whipped whitecaps on the lake, and dead leaves tumbled across the ground. Not even the ravens were up yet. Instead of going for a run, he began moving in the basic Flowing Poses that he had learned from Naran at the Sanctuary, breathing with each movement. As he noticed each stretch and pull of his muscles, quiet joy flowed within his heart and soul.

The front door opened and Naran entered, along with a gust of wintery air. "Naran-ji!" Kyr turned toward his friend, eyes sparkling, arms wide. "I'm glad to see you!" Startled, the gray-robe took a step back. Kyr laughed. "It's all right, Naran-ji. I won't bite."

Naran's look of confusion dissolved, and a smile spread across his face. "Sorry! You usually don't reach out like this." Closing the door, he set his pack down and gladly accepted Kyr's embrace. Stepping back, he examined Kyr with delighted curiosity. "Gods, Kyr! You are so different! Your body feels so relaxed right now, so solid. That brittle wariness I sensed in you since you first came to Ravenvale has vanished. What in all the heavens happened?"

"All I can say is…I'm free, Naran-ji. And I owe it all to you, the Kailithana, and Zhovanya's grace. I'll say more when Medari gets here."

"Well, whatever it was, I'm glad to see you so…happy." Naran shrugged in amused frustration. "Pah! That's such a paltry word for what I sense in you, now."

Kyr gave his Aithané a warm smile. "And what brings you here today?"

"Rajani is getting along better, so I came to see how you are faring. Quite well, I see!" They both laughed.

Kyr was about to ask after Rajani, but the front door opened again, admitting another gust of cool, damp air — and Medari, carrying the breakfast tray.

"Good morning, heart-father," Kyr said, with a loving, open smile.

"You're looking, ah, quite well, son." Medari smiled briefly, went over to the table, and busied himself with setting out the dishes, mugs, teapot, a basket of sweet biscuits, and a bowl of boiled eggs. "Where's Jolanya? Is she coming for breakfast?"

Sensing his heart-father's reserve, Kyr merely said, "Last night, she said she might sleep late. It was…intense, yesterday, and she was tired." He gave the healer a warm look, but Medari wouldn't meet his eyes. *Well,* thought Kyr, *it is a big change. He needs time to adjust.* He smiled to himself. *So do I.*

They sat down at the table by the window and served themselves breakfast. Kyr silently savored each bite of sweet biscuit or salted egg, each sip of minty tea. Nothing had ever tasted so good to him. Overawed by his profound silence, Naran and Medari too kept quiet as they ate.

Then Naran swiped up the last bit of egg with his final bite of biscuit and washed it down with a swig of tea. "Well, Kyr, it's clear something has changed for you. Will you tell us what happened now?"

Kyr was quiet for a moment, reluctant to turn this most precious experience into just another story. But he wanted his friends to understand the transformation he was going through. At last, he said, "It was so obvious, once I understood. But getting there was rough." His laugh was easy and unshadowed. "Ah, how do I explain?" As Kyr searched for a way to share his awakening from the terrible drama of his life story, Naran waited patiently, but Medari fidgeted with his mug, twisting it back and forth on the table.

After a few moments, Kyr said, "Well, my friends, all I can find to say is that I realized that I am not the past, not what happened to me. That is just an old story. I let it go. I am…there is only…" He gestured with one arm, making a lazy circle. "This…here…now."

"Wonderful!" Naran exclaimed. "I'm so glad for you!"

But Medari said nothing.

"Heart-father," Kyr turned towards the healer, noticing his discomfort and wanting to reassure him. "I am forever grateful to you for all you have done for me at the fort and since then — especially for keeping me alive so I could reach this day."

"Despite it all?" Medari inquired in a challenging tone.

"Yes, in spite of it all." Though Medari nodded, Kyr felt as if he had run into a closed door. A shadow of hurt touched his heart, but he breathed it out and turned to Naran.

"Naran-ji, thank you for all you did for me at the Sanctuary: for hearing that terrible story; for bearing it with me; and for helping me begin to let it go. I'm deeply grateful to you for coming here to help me again, and for bringing the Kailithana here."

Naran smiled, but Kyr saw that his eyes were shadowed. "Ah, Naran-ji," Kyr persisted, "all this must have been so hard on you. I don't know how you managed to stay with me and remain so steady, so kind."

Naran blinked back tears. "I have to admit, it's been difficult, at times. But it's the best thing I've ever done in my life."

"Thank you, Naran-ji." Kyr's luminous gaze was both serious and joyful. "Bad and good, it's all just an old story. You can let yours go now, too."

"Ah! By the Goddess, you're right!" Naran's voice trembled with the truth of Kyr's words and tears filled his eyes. Overcome with relief, release, and gladness, he buried his face in his hands, sobbing quietly.

Across the table, Medari watched them, frowning. "What is this nonsense about stories?" He jumped up, banged the breakfast dishes onto the tray, and hurried out the door. Kyr glanced after him, but kept his attention with Naran.

In a few moments, Naran looked up. "Thank you, Kyr. By allowing me to be of service to you — the man who freed us all from the Soul-Drinker's evil — you have helped me complete my Atonement. And now, thanks to your example, I can drop my old story. I'm free, too!"

"I'm so glad, Naran-ji!" And they both grinned.

Despite his joy in Naran's freedom, Kyr found that in being with his friends, he was starting to lose contact with the truth he had learned the day before — starting to slip back into the old shell, the old story that he had thought defined who he was. Realizing that he needed time alone to savor and embrace his new freedom, he rose. "Naran-ji, I'm going for a walk before the next storm gets here. Will you tell the others for me?"

"Will you be all right alone?"

Kyr laughed. "I've never been more all right! But thanks for your concern, my friend. I promise to be careful, and to be back for supper." Then they looked into each other's eyes, and clasped each other's forearms, honoring each other as warriors on the hard path. Then Naran headed back to Ravenhall.

Kyr hurried up to his room, dressed warmly, put on his boots, grabbed his rain cloak, and left the infirmary for the world outside. Wanting to go somewhere he had never been before, he headed toward the foothills of the eastern guardian wall. The wind had calmed, and the pallid Winter Sun gave a whisper of warmth. Full of newly liberated energy, he strode along the path in the early morning light, enjoying simply being alive in the world, noticing drops of dew bejeweling a spider's web and sparkling from the tips of pine needles. He took deep breaths of the fresh, crisp air, and for a moment thought of all the many mornings when he had feared and regretted awakening. But with a shake of his head, he left that old story behind and went on.

Letting go of all thought, he immersed himself in the beauties of the world and his new-found joy. As he climbed the hills, the trees thinned and the wide sky arched overhead, pale and pure. Reaching an open area at the top of a hill, Kyr stopped and raised his arms in delight. Turning slowly in a circle, he gave thanks in his heart for this great blessing of freedom granted him through the Kailithara, and drank in the beauty surrounding him in every direction: the strength and grandeur of the dark guardian cliffs; the delicate tracery of leafless white aspens contrasting with the tall magnificence of dark-green pine and blue-green spruce; and, far below, the lake, a chalice of silvery mist glowing in the slanting light of early morning.

He paused as Ravenhall came into view, and thought of Rajani and Luciya, still lost in their terrible old story. "Ah, Goddess," he breathed. "Yes, I must go there soon." Realizing that he had just gone into a future story, he shook himself, let it go, and continued onward into the hills, resting as he needed to but always moving higher and higher, until he reached the base of the guardian wall itself. A narrow trail to the left beckoned, and he followed it for a time, skirting fallen boulders and piles of scree.

A cleft in the cliff echoed with the sound of trickling water. Thirst drove him to explore the shadowy opening. A small waterfall splashed down the right face of a large, fern-lined grotto into a dark pool. Graceful aspen trees encircled the small pool, and tiny lavender cupflowers dotted the pool's mossy green banks, giving off a delicate scent. Kyr bowed with his hands together before his heart, paying homage to the sweet beauty of the place, then knelt by the pool's edge to cup water with his hands and drink. The crystalline water made him shiver — or perhaps it was some apprehension of holiness.

The noon sun shone down, pooling golden on a flat-topped boulder nearby, Kyr took a seat on the sun-warmed stone, and sat soaking in the sun's warmth, pleasantly tired from his long walk. The steady trickling of the tiny waterfall enhanced the peacefulness of the fern-lined grotto. A solitary bird, hidden in the pines at the back of the grotto, sang a sweet, echoing refrain, deepening the sacredness of this natural chapel.

In the stillness, Kyr sensed the vast abiding Presence of the world as it is — in every grain of sand on the shore of the pond; in the great cliffs of stone surrounding Ravenvale; in every tiny flower and in every tall tree; in the heart of the hidden bird; and in his own blossoming soul. Some last tension in his heart relaxed, and he smiled. *This, too, is Home.*

Lulled by the warmth of the sun, he closed his eyes, and his mind drifted.

He was in the studio at the Sanctuary. There was something in his hand. He looked down. He held a chisel.

His head nodded forward and with a start, he woke — and stopped breathing.

The Goddess was standing on the far side of the pool, where the grotto narrowed. He knelt by the edge of the pool across from Her, and began to sing in reverence and gratitude for Her Presence: "Zhovanya naralo, Zhovanya naralo, Zhovanya naralo." Singing deep and strong from his healed heart, his voice echoed off the stone walls of this wild temple, deepening the sense of sacredness.

A gust of wind made the trees bend and sway. The sun's rays now reached across the pool, illuminating a large stone — a tall chunk of the cliff that had fallen long ago — standing where he had seen Zhovanya a moment before. Now he knew what had drawn him here. He walked around the pool, and slowly circled the stone, tracing with a sculptor's eye the lineaments of the Goddess Whom he would reveal. In awe and humility, he gave thanks to Zhovanya for this mercy of guidance, this new grace of service.

Tired, cold, and hungry, but serenely joyful, Kyr hurried home as charcoal clouds piled up above the eastern guardian wall. The sliver of the New Moon hung above the cloudbank, white against the darkening sky. From the west, the setting sun sparked roseate fire from the tops of white-caps surging across the lake. As he reached for the latch to the door of the infirmary, the wind tried to steal his cloak. Laughing, he dashed inside just as fat drops of rain splattered on the stone of the courtyard.

No one was in the main room, but Kyr heard the grinding of pestle and mortar coming from Medari's herbarium. He stepped closer, and poked his head in the door. "Good evening, Medari." The older man kept grinding herbs with his pestle, not even looking up. Kyr approached Medari's work bench.

"What is it, heart-father? What's wrong?" The healer continued his work for a moment, then set the pestle down with a thump.

He stood up, closed the door, and stood glaring at Kyr. "How can you *do* this? How *can* you just start acting as if none of it ever happened?" Medari's voice was low and furious.

The healer's anger struck Kyr in the heart, and he couldn't speak for a moment. The peace and joy of his day in the hills wavered. *Did I do something wrong?* And quickly, he realized: *No. This is Medari's difficult story, causing him grief and anguish.* Opening his heart, he tried to fathom his heart-father's pain and anger. "Do you feel as if I have betrayed you by letting go of the old story, the past?"

"It's *not* just an old story!" Medari snapped. "It's what *happened*! I can never forgive Gauday and his rabble for what they did to my family, to me — to *you*! How *can* you pretend it never occurred?"

Kyr's heart ached for his heart-father's pain, but in fierce compassion, he spoke his truth, knowing now that the only balm for Medari's soul was to shift his attention from the past into the present moment. "I am not pretending anything, and I have forgotten nothing." He leaned forward, trying to reach Medari with his eyes, praying that his heart-father would understand the necessity of his surrender. "I just couldn't live with all that pain any longer. It was crushing me. You of all people can understand that, can't you?"

The healer nodded grudgingly, and Kyr continued. "It's hard to explain what happened. I gave in to the pain, though I was terrified that I would go mad or die. But instead, Zhovanya showed me that what happened to me in the past is not who I am *now*. I don't have to clutch my dark cloak of memories and pain around me. I can let it go and simply be here now. I did — and, now I am *free*, Medari. You can be, too, if you let go into your pain."

"NO!" Medari roared. "Gauday fooled me into keeping you alive through all that torment. He tricked and used us both unmercifully, brutally! It's *unforgivable* what he did!" Medari raised clenched fists and shouted at Kyr. "He killed my *wife*! My *children*! For nothing, *nothing*!" His voice broke.

"I know," Kyr said softly. He put an arm around Medari's shoulders, led his heart-father over to a stool, and got him to sit down. Hunched over, elbows on knees, Medari buried his face in his hands. Jagged, angry sobs ripped up from his gut, a terrible sound to hear. Kyr stood close, his arm across Medari's shoulders, as witness and companion through the storm.

A long while later, Medari quieted and raised his head, looking exhausted. He sighed and glanced at Kyr. "I'm sorry...."

Kyr interrupted gently. "Nothing to be sorry for. We're family, and this is what you needed."

"I guess it was." The healer rubbed his face tiredly. "I feel...lighter. Maybe that is a little of the freedom you mentioned. But I doubt I can let go...." He shook his head sadly.

"Your journey is your own, and won't be like mine. But I will be here with you."

"Thanks, son. If it weren't for you, I couldn't go on." He rose and turned to face Kyr, and they hugged in silent solace and comfort. Then Medari stepped back. "Gods, I'm tired. But I feel calmer than I have in months."

"I'm glad." Kyr thought for a moment, and then offered, "Perhaps it might help to join the penitents tonight for meditation and singing the forgiveness chant."

"But what if I don't *feel* forgiving?"

"You don't have to feel or believe anything. Just come with me and see what happens."

Medari gave him a tired, bewildered look, and sighed. "Alright. For you, my wise heart-son, I will try it."

Kyr gave his arm a gentle squeeze. "I'm starving. That was a long walk I took today. Let's go get some supper." As they went together into the main room, Kyr became aware of how tired he was, and how shaken by his heart-father's anger and grief.

They found Naran kneeling by the fire, giving a log to the flames. Jolanya stood nearby, warming her hands. Their glad and welcoming smiles eased Kyr's fatigue and lifted his heart. He strode forward and took both of Jolanya's hands in his own. Looking into her clear, gray eyes, he felt again the wonderful blessing she had brought to him through the Kailithara. They shared a moment of unspoken joy.

"Have a good walk, Kyr?" Naran asked, as he dusted ash off his hands and climbed to his feet.

Kyr and Jolanya laughed, and he turned to Naran. "Wonderful!" Kyr exclaimed. "The world is so beautiful!"

"Indeed it is, when we have eyes to see." Naran rubbed his arms. "Cold storm tonight. It's drafty by the window. Let's move the table and chairs over near the hearth." Kyr helped with this, and with setting out their supper: venison and vegetable stew; warm rolls, and apple cobbler with honey-cream.

Though Medari was quiet and somber, there was a communion of love and friendship among them as they ate their supper together by the crackling fire. Kyr smiled, his eyes glowing amber with happiness. "For so long, I believed I'd never enjoy this quiet blessing of sharing food with friends again. Thanks to you all, I was wrong."

After the others headed off for their beds, Kyr sat by the dying fire, looking out the window into the dark, windy night, his joy tinged with a subtle grief. Allowing love had now awakened the pain of all the cruel and loveless years of his life. His grief swelled into a soul-deep pain, and he cried out silently, *"Goddess, help me! How can I truly forgive all that?"* He listened for Her Voice, but Her only answer was a gentle stillness of Presence.

He sighed, knowing that there was only one thing to do with his grief and pain: allow it and breathe with it. And so he did, reminding himself that it was all an old story and had nothing to do with who he was now. And after a time, the ache in his heart became a softness of compassion for the boy and man who had suffered so terribly.

L ater, as he lay in bed, Kyr thought, *I may be free of the past. But others, like Medari, are not. Life goes on, and it's still complicated. How do I help Medari? What am I going to do about Rajani and Luciya?* A ghost of his old anger at the Circle's heartless use of him lingered. He shook his head. Not me. The old angry ghost faded away, but his mind kept on raising concerns. *I've forgotten all about Friend. I hope she'll forgive me. Maybe I can bring her back here after the Kailithara is over. Gods, it nearly is, isn't it?* A newer grief arose at this thought. *How will I survive losing Jolanya again?*

Alarmed at his waning serenity, he prayed, *"Goddess, help me remember who I really am."* The radiant being of light She had shown him came into his mind, clutching its dark, ragged cloak of grief and fear again. "Ah," he breathed, and gently said to himself, "Let's not." Envisioning the being of light dropping that old cloak, he relaxed into the present moment, and his quiet joy returned. Keeping his mind on that vision of truth, he drifted into gentle sleep.

Chapter Twenty-Five

Pardoning the Unforgivable

After breakfast the next day, Naran ducked into the infirmary, quickly closed the door against a blustery shower, and hung up his damp cloak on the hooks behind the door. Turning, he found Kyr and Jolanya sitting on the couch by the hearth — Kyr with his legs stretched out toward the fire, ankles crossed, and hands behind his head, and Jolanya facing him, sitting cross-legged. Naran smiled at the peace radiating from them both. "Good morning. You two seem quite...relaxed."

Jolanya smiled. "We're taking the day off to let Kyr be with what he experienced yesterday."

"Good idea." Naran perched on the edge of one of the armchairs. "I hope you don't mind, Kyr, but I want to talk with the Kailithana about Rajani."

"Ah. I'd like to hear how he's doing."

Naran hesitated briefly. "It won't...bother you?"

Kyr regarded Naran with calm, sober eyes. "Not any more, Naran-ji."

"Good." Naran smiled. Then he turned his attention to Jolanya. "Rajani is taking better care of himself than before, but just barely. He seems almost immobilized by despair."

"Oh, how sad for such a vital man!" the Kailithana exclaimed. "What's going on with him?"

"I think he's brooding over the memories he absorbed from Kyr during the cleansing ritual. Neither I nor Luciya or Devanyi know what to do for him. Will you come to Ravenhall with me and see if you can help him?"

"I'm sorry," Jolanya said gently. "I can't work with him until after the Kailithara with Kyr is complete. Working with the kailitha is delicate and complex. It is too confusing to work with one pattern of damage to a man's zhan and then shift to another. That's why Kailithanas always work with one kailithos at a time."

"I see." Naran's shoulders slumped a little in disappointment.

"Why is Rajani dwelling on my memories?" Kyr asked softly, almost to himself. "That would be nothing but torture." Then he winced, remembering how sharply remorse and self-loathing cut the soul. "It's his guilt that's driving him, isn't it, Naran-ji?"

"Yes. He's punishing himself for his part in what you had to go through. Luciya and Devanyi have had to stop him from hurting himself several times."

"I think this is between Rajani and me," Kyr said. "I'll go visit him today. Perhaps I can help him get free from his story."

Jolanya frowned in concern. "Are you sure you're ready for that, Kyr?"

"No," Kyr said with a little laugh, "but I need to clear things up with him in order to be fully free of that story, myself."

As Kyr walked over to Ravenhall, he enjoyed the breezy day, with its woolly gray-and-white cloud-sheep grazing in the rain-washed blue sky, and the warmth of the strengthening Sun. Old memories arose, but he chose to focus instead on the wet pavement of the courtyard, admiring the colors in the flagstones that the rain had revealed, and the light sparkling on random puddles.

In Ravenhall, he found Luciya alone in the parlor, sitting in an armchair by the fire and staring out the windows at the wind-tossed lake. She seemed thinner, worn down by worry and sadness. Hearing his footsteps, she looked up and greeted him with a startled smile.

"Kyr! What...? Ah...welcome! Sit here by the fire. It's cool today, but I think Winter is on the wane."

Kyr smiled and took a seat on the couch facing the fire.

Luciya examined him warily. "It's good to see you, Kyr, and you look remarkably well, but...you were so...angry when you left. Why are you here, now?"

"I'm concerned about Rajani. Is he doing any better?"

"Concerned? How...kind of you." She smiled uncertainly. "Well, he takes care of himself now, but he eats very little." Sadness shadowed her face. "He sits in his room and stares out his window. Most of the time, he's oblivious to us. I think he's still dwelling on those memories he got from you. Maybe it's a way of punishing himself."

"Yes, that's what Naran thinks, too." Kyr met Luciya's doubtful gaze. "May I see Rajani?"

She stiffened. "I don't think that's a good idea," she snapped. "He's suffered quite enough. He doesn't need your accusations or anger."

"That's not why I'm here. Actually, I'd like to try to help him."

Luciya stared at him in disbelief. "Help him? But you have every reason to hate Rajani...me...the entire Circle!"

"I used to," Kyr confessed calmly. "But I've let all that go now, thanks to the Kailithana and Zhovanya. Maybe I can encourage Rajani to do the same."

"Let it go? I don't understand." But with a shake of her head, she waved that aside. "The truth is, we are at our wits' end with him. Do you honestly want to help him?"

"Yes. I promise not do anything to hurt him. All I want is to help him face and release his guilt and pain, and allow Zhovanya's Grace to reach him."

Luciya sighed, hope softening her pinched and careworn features. "I don't know why you would do this, but we'll try anything at this point." And, getting to her feet, she said, "Please come with me."

Kyr followed her upstairs to Rajani's room. Just before they reached his door, she stopped and said quietly, "I'll go in and talk with Rajani first. I'll call you when he's ready to see you." And she reached for the doorknob.

Kyr touched her arm to stop her. "Please: I want to see him even if he is resistant. I might be able to get through to him."

"Alright, but don't push him too hard. He might go into a rage." Kyr nodded, and she squared her shoulders, entered Rajani's room, and closed the door behind her.

Gaunt and unkempt, the Warrior Mage slumped on his shabby couch, which now was turned to face the window, staring out at the clouds. In shocking contrast to his former clean-shaven, neat appearance, he now had a scruffy black beard, and wore a rumpled gray tunic, wrinkled leggings, and worn felt slippers. He gave no sign of noticing Luciya's entrance.

"Rajani?" She crossed over to the couch and knelt in front of him. "You have a visitor. He's here to help you."

Rajani blinked a few times, and finally focused on her. "Help me?" he muttered in a faint and rusty voice. "Who would want to do that?"

She took his hands in hers and shook them a little, as if to anchor him in reality. "It's Kyr. He wants to help you."

"Kyr?" He pulled away from her, and hid his face in his hands, whispering, "Oh, gods, how he must hate me! What I've done to him..."

"I know, 'Jani."

"No, you don't!" He sat up and glared at her with reddened eyes. "You have no idea how much he has suffered, thanks to the cursed Prophecy — and me." He groaned aloud. "Gods and demons! What he went through as a little boy, being tortured into becoming the Soul-Drinker's Slave...unspeakable!"

Luciya frowned. "Did you forget that I was there then, spying on the Soul-Drinker, and helping Kyr when I could?"

"I remember, 'Ciya, but you haven't *felt* his terror and agony. I *have*. It was horrendous — and that was only the *beginning*! For most of his life, he lived in the Soul-Drinker's hell of pain and forced ecstasy, and learned to be a cold-blooded torturer and murderer." His voice grew louder and more agitated. "And that wasn't enough! After he recovered his soul from that hell, I let him walk into Gauday's hands, to suffer kinds of despicable abuse and sorcerous torture that you can't even imagine." With vicious self-loathing, he slammed his fists into his thighs. "Merciless! I am merciless!"

"Stop it!" cried Luciya, grabbing his hands. "We had no choice, 'Jani! We tried everything else. It was the only way. And you were compelled by the oath-bind."

"Doesn't matter. *I* am the one who made it all happen. I should never have let Granmere force me to take that damned…" His throat closed as the oath-bind took effect, and he slumped back in his chair, closing his eyes.

Luciya could see him sliding back into his dark pit of silent misery. Desperate, she grabbed him by the shoulders and shook him. "Don't you dare shut me out! Come back this instant!"

He groaned and blindly tried to shove her away.

"No, 'Jani! Enough! You can't wallow in this swamp of guilt and self-hatred any longer. The Prophecy is not yet completed." She shook him again harder.

"Gods damn you, woman!" he growled. "Leave me alone!"

"No." Luciya was adamant. "I won't let you alone until you speak with Kyr."

"Oh, cursed gods! If that's what it takes…" He opened his eyes and straightened up. "Let's get this over with. It's what I deserve, anyway."

Luciya let go of him, got to her feet, opened the door, and summoned Kyr. Turning back to the Warrior Mage, she begged, "Please let Kyr help you, 'Jani." Holding back sobs, she stumbled out of the room and closed the door.

Kyr stood still for a moment, taking in Rajani's disarray and gloom. *He's gotten stuck in his terrible story*, he sighed to himself. Then he crossed the room to stand by the window, facing Rajani.

The Warrior Mage sat on the couch with his arms crossed on his chest, stubbornly refusing to look up at Kyr.

Realizing that he had to break Rajani out of his locked position, Kyr said, "Come, let's sit by the fire. It's chilly here by the window." Kyr's gentle but resolute tone penetrated Rajani's armor of self-loathing.

"If you insist," he snapped petulantly. They moved to the wooden chairs by the hearth, and sat facing each other.

"What are you doing here?" Rajani demanded. "Did you come to berate me? Beat me senseless? Let's get to it. Whatever it is, I deserve it."

"I'm not here to help you punish yourself, Rajani."

"But you have every reason imaginable to hate me!" Unable to bear Kyr's luminous, compassionate gaze, Rajani hunched over and buried his face in his hands.

"I *did* hate you for a time," Kyr said, "after I found out about the Star-Curse. But I don't hate you now."

"How could you not?" Rajani muttered from behind his hands. "What you suffered because of what we, what *I* did..."

"Look at me. You will see the truth of what I am about to tell you." Kyr leaned over and gently pried Rajani's hands off his face.

The Warrior Mage looked at him, his eyes dark with despair, shame and guilt engraved on his haggard face.

"Please listen to me, Rajani." Kyr focused on keeping his heart open, and his eyes on Rajani's. "Through the grace of the Goddess and the blessing of the Kailithara, I have learned that it doesn't matter. None of what happened in the past is important. It is not who I am *now* — and I have let it go."

"But...what we did...the Circle...that hellish ritual...all the pain..." Rajani shook his head in an anguish of guilt. "No, Kyr, how can you just let it go? By all the gods, it's unforgivable!"

"It's only an old story now, Rajani. It's not who *you* are now, either. Let it go. Forgive yourself. Zhovanya naralo. She forgives us all."

Kyr's serenity began to penetrate Rajani's anguish. He looked at Kyr silently for a while, seeing no hatred, no accusation, no blame. Then, though it took more courage than going into any battle, the Warrior Mage knelt down facing Kyr, and dared to ask, "Do...do *you* forgive me?"

Kyr saw how Rajani held his breath, his eyes full of desperate apprehension — as if his sanity and his very soul were in the balance. He could hear Rajani's heart beating heavily in his chest and see sweat appearing on his skin. Knowing that he had to give a true and honest answer to this crucial question, no matter what, Kyr bowed his head and looked within to make sure that he actually *had* forgiven the Warrior Mage and the Circle.

When Kyr looked up, his eyes were clear and golden. "You and the Circle called me forth into a painful, difficult life."

Rajani cringed at Kyr's understated words. He knew all too well how very painful Kyr's life had been.

"Yet it was necessary," Kyr continued. "The Soul-Drinker was devastating the web of life, the soulkin, the hearts of the people — the very land itself. You and the Circle were right. He had to be destroyed."

251

"'Necessary,'" Rajani whispered, stunned and disbelieving. Kyr gave him a small nod and went on.

"Since then, you have devoted yourself to helping me. You rescued me from the Soul-Drinker's Watcher, and got me to Svahar to free me from the craving. You guided me to the Sanctuary to restore my soul, and you rescued me from Gauday. Now you have brought me here to Ravenvale, and freed me from the last remnants of the Soul-Drinker's and Gauday's sorcery." Kyr paused, again checking his heart for any vindictiveness. "Yours is a story of evil and harm intertwined with devotion and noble purpose."

The Warrior Mage looked down, his face flaming. Kyr had no idea that it was *he* who had sent him into the three hells of the Prophecy. "But you don't know…. The Prophecy…" He struggled to confess his guilt to Kyr, but his throat closed tightly as the oath-bind clamped down on him.

"No, Rajani, I *don't* know what this Prophecy says. But it is clear that you have sacrificed much for Khailaz. You gave up most of your life. You sacrificed your own brother." He paused, breathing through his heart. Finding no trace of rancor or bitterness, he was able to say with complete sincerity, "And yes, I forgive you."

"Oh, gods!" Rajani's eyes filled with tears, and he bowed his head to the floor at Kyr's feet, burying his face in his hands, his body clenched tight.

"Zhovanya naralo," Kyr said gently in response. And he began to sing the chant in a steady, quiet voice.

The Warrior Mage remained bowed down, his shoulders heaving with silent sobs. After a time, he returned to his chair, and tentatively, hoarsely, joined in the chant.

Luciya and Devanyi had been hovering nervously in the corridor outside Rajani's room, uncertain whether Kyr would be able to help Rajani and doubtful whether he truly wanted to. They were ready to rush to Rajani's aid if they heard one harsh word.

When they heard Kyr begin the chant, they sighed with relief; and when they heard Rajani begin to sing too, their eyes filled with glad tears. After a few moments, they looked at each other and Devanyi said, "If Kyr has forgiven Rajani, he has forgiven us as well, don't you think?" Luciya nodded, and they timidly entered the room. Seeing Kyr's welcoming smile, they sat with the two men and joined the chant. The room filled with Zhovanya's Presence, bringing them deep into a state of reverence.

Tears trickled steadily down Luciya's cheeks — tears of awe, admiration, and humility in the face of Kyr's unwavering devotion to the hardest path of all. *Ah, Zhovanya, Your ways are mysterious. That our evil ritual could call forth such a noble soul is incomprehensible to me. But I give great thanks that it is so. May the Prophecy now be fulfilled.*

When Her Presence faded from their awareness, they sat quietly for a while, then stretched and rose. Kyr noticed that Luciya was looking at him intently. *It's as if I were a mountain panther that might spring at her any moment, the way she looks at me.* "Luciya, I want to thank you for helping me when you were a spy in the Soul-Drinker's lair. It was you who showed me my safe cubbyhole, wasn't it?"

She nodded. "Yes, but I couldn't do much. I had to watch…." She choked up, tears in her eyes.

"Yes, it was a terrible time," Kyr said gently. "But it is only an old story now. I also want to apologize for my cruelty toward you after the cleansing. I hope you can forgive me?"

"Gods and demons, Kyr! It is *I* who should beg *your* forgiveness!" She shook her head, astonished at his generous spirit. "*Of course* I forgive you for your few cruel words," she said. "Do you forgive me for all *I* have done?" His ready, compassionate smile was all the answer she needed. She sighed deeply, and her own smile grew full and radiant.

Kyr saw that Devanyi was looking at him with tentative hope. "Devanyi," he said, taking her hands, "I want to thank you for your care at the safe house. You and Tenaiya were my first teachers of kindness." He laughed. "I was so baffled, at first. It was like discovering something bizarre and incomprehensible — something that I had been desperate for all my life without having any idea what it was."

"Oh, Kyr, you are amazing!" Her expression was such a mix of admiration and goggle-eyed wonder that Kyr burst out laughing; and everyone else joined him. The air in the room shimmered with the brilliance of the transformative power of forgiveness and laughter, warming their souls with subtle joy.

After a few moments, they quieted, and stood smiling at each other with bemused affection. But then Rajani burst out in a puzzled tone, "I'm starving."

"At last!" Devanyi exclaimed. "Do you know how many meals I've brought in that you've refused?" She caught herself and blushed. "I'm sorry. I shouldn't snap at you like that."

"I know I've been a difficult patient," Rajani said sheepishly. "Forgive me?"

She frowned, her hands on her hips. "As long as you eat properly from now on." Then she laughed and kissed him on the cheek.

"I promise." He smiled, but then looked down. "Goddess," he whispered. "How can I deserve all this forgiveness?"

After a moment, he looked up and hesitantly asked, "Kyr, will you join us?"

The man he had subjected to the Star-Curse nodded, and the four of them went down to the parlor.

The buffet held plates of sliced ham, cheese, and bread; pickled vegetables; and small bowls of warm cobbler made with dried berries and apples. Kyr found that he was as ravenous as the others, and smiled to himself. *Forgiveness is hungry work!*

They filled their plates and took seats on the stools at the round table by the hearth, where a fire burned steadily. At first, they ate in shy silence, unused to being together in amity. Rajani looked pale and worn-out. Luciya and Devanyi also looked tired, but relieved, and they smiled to see Rajani eating like a winter wolf. All three of them cast covert, uncertain glances at Kyr, unsure what to make of this calm, radiant man — so unlike the ravaged, raging creature they had seen after the cleansing ritual.

Luciya still felt on edge, as if that wild, furious man would take Kyr over at any moment. Finally, she had to break her mounting tension. "So, Kyr, may I ask how…I mean, you are so…different. What happened since we last saw you?"

Setting down his spoon, Kyr looked out toward the lake. Rajani, Devanyi, and Luciya sat unmoving, holding their breaths. Kyr's gaze went far away, into some unknowable realm. Then he looked back at them with a kind smile. "That's a story for another day. For now, I'll just say that I've gone through the third hell of your Prophesy…and I'm glad."

"Glad?" Rajani said in wonderment.

"Oh, Kyr!" Devanyi said reverently. "You seem to have found your way into the realm of angels."

"No, no," Kyr laughed. "I'm just…here, now."

Mystified but reassured, Luciya smiled. "Well, whatever happened, I'm very glad to see you so…serene. And I can't thank you enough for helping Rajani."

"I'm happy to be of service." And, indeed, Kyr's heart felt buoyant and contented to have helped Rajani and Luciya begin to move on from their painful stories.

The Warrior Mage had both elbows on the table, his head in his hands. At Kyr's words, he raised his head as if it were heavy as stone. "I can find no words sufficient…."

Kyr held up his hand. "No thanks needed, Rajani. I did this as much for myself as for you. Forgiving frees us as much as being forgiven, if not more." He smiled, feeling the truth of his own words in his enlightened heart. "I'll visit again, when you are ready."

"Alright. I'll let you know." Rajani slumped back in his chair, looking greatly relieved but wan and weary.

"Good." Kyr yawned. "I suspect we all need to rest now."

They all got to their feet. Luciya collected their dishes and set them on a tray on the sideboard. Devanyi came up to Kyr and whispered, "Thank you so much for helping Rajani!" Daring greatly, she stood on her tiptoes and placed a soft kiss on his cheek.

He smiled and kissed her forehead. Watching this, Luciya sighed ruefully, aware that Kyr had not flinched away from Devanyi's kiss, as he had from hers when he first arrived at Ravenvale. But then she smiled, glad to see Kyr restored to wholeness once again.

Chapter Twenty-Six

Forgiver and Forgiven

Two days later, Kyr and Rajani met in the Ravenhall parlor. Kyr was amazed how different the Warrior Mage looked now. Clean-shaven again, with his hair trimmed and tied back at the nape of his neck, he wore a dark green tunic, brown leggings, and short brown boots.

"You're looking more like your old self," Kyr greeted him.

Rajani shook his head. "I'll never be the same."

And indeed, Kyr saw that the Warrior Mage no longer carried his old stiff armor of barely concealed anger and despair. Smiling, Kyr said, "I'm glad."

"Me too...I think." Rajani gave a rusty laugh. "I hardly know who I am, now." He gestured toward the armchairs by the hearth. "Come, let's sit by the fire. Cook has set out tea and warm biscuits for us."

Feeling almost like strangers to each other after the transformative experiences they had each undergone since the devastating end of the cleansing ritual, they sat quietly for a few moments, sipping their tea and enjoying the sweet, buttery biscuits.

Then Rajani asked, "You have changed a lot yourself. How...?"

Kyr looked at him, clear-eyed and serious. "Are you ready to hear what I've been through, without turning it on yourself and returning to your morass of guilt and self-punishment?"

"I...don't know."

"What will you do if you find yourself sliding back into that swamp of despair?"

"Ah. Good question." Rajani searched within for a moment. "I will go to the chapel and pray for Her forgiveness."

"I suggest that you also join me and the penitents in their chapel for our evening meditation and chanting."

"You would allow *me* to join you?"

"All who wish to open their hearts to Zhovanya's love and forgiveness are welcome."

"Open my heart to Her?" Rajani whispered, and tears sprang to his eyes.

"It can be...difficult." Kyr sighed, remembering his furious defiance of Her at the Tower, and his painful road back to Her Grace.

"I don't know..." Rajani murmured. "I've been so angry for so long...kept my heart closed because I felt so...cursed."

"As have I," said Kyr quietly. "Zhovanya asks much from both of us." Their eyes met, topaz and azure, in a communion of mutual understanding and compassion. Then Kyr said, "Zhovanya naralo," and bowed his head. "Let's meditate for a little while."

"Zhovanya naralo," Rajani whispered. He closed his eyes, but doubted that he would be able to find any inner peace.

Kyr focused on the rise and fall of his belly as he breathed, reminding himself not to get lost in Rajani's terrible story, in which he had been ensnared before he was even conceived. Slowly, the tension in his body melted, and he relaxed into his new inner freedom — the clarity of simply being present to what is in this moment.

Drawn by the power of Kyr's presence, Rajani found himself deepening into a quietness that he had rarely experienced and had longed for without realizing it.

Then he heard Kyr say, "Alright, I'm ready to answer your question now."

With a sigh, Rajani returned to outer reality and opened his eyes. "Thank you."

"As I said before," Kyr began, "this is an old story to me now, and I have let it go. I am telling you only because you asked. I will keep it brief. Please just let me tell it without questions."

Rajani nodded, and Kyr continued.

"When I found out about the Star-Curse ritual from your memories, I was...devastated. I felt I was an evil creation *of* evil. I tried to kill myself, but Medari saved me. I fled to the penitents' house, where I lost control and attacked Craith. This only confirmed my evilness." Kyr sighed, remembering his total desolation; but with a silent blessing to his old self, he returned to the present moment. "I had to get away, where I could do no more harm. A raven guided me to the island in the lake, and to the Tower there."

Rajani's eyes widened at the idea that Raven had helped Kyr. But then he realized that Kyr was a scion of Ravenvale, just like Rajani himself and Lanir.

"At the Tower," Kyr continued, "I went through a very dark time, feeling betrayed by you, my father, the Circle, and Zhovanya."

Rajani held up a hand for silence, breathing through an upwelling of guilt and remorse. He yearned to apologize, to beg forgiveness; but in honor of Kyr's request for no interruptions, he kept silent. After a moment, he nodded, and Kyr went on.

"Then Eagle came to me in a dream, to teach me that I am who I choose to be." Kyr smiled serenely. "I examined all my choices, and concluded that I have chosen to be Zhovanya's servant and Medari's heart-son. So I came back."

"But how did you become so...?"

"I'm getting to that. My heart-father and my soul-healers, Naran and Jolanya, convinced me to undergo the Kailithara with Jolanya again. I dreaded it more than anything in my life. Ultimately, I had to face the mountain of pain that I've suffered and inflicted — and give in to it."

Rajani choked back a protest. But Kyr smiled, radiating joy.

"That mountain obliterated me — as I had so long desired. And I awakened cleansed, renewed, free." Kyr leaned forward and took Rajani's cold, clenched fists in his warm hands, and looked deeply into Rajani's blue eyes. "I now know deep in my soul that whatever happened to me in the past is not who I am now, in this moment. I don't have to believe in it, carry it with me, paw over it like a dog with an old bone. I am just here, now. As you are; as we all are." Releasing Rajani's hands, Kyr sat back. "And Zhovanya understands all of our struggles, and forgives us all — even you, Rajani. As do I."

Awed beyond words, Rajani could only kneel and bow down to Kyr.

"Oh, stop that." Kyr chuckled. "I'm just a man who lost his story. And I'm hungry. May I have the last biscuit?"

Rajani burst into startled laughter, resumed his seat, and handed him the biscuit.

A few days later, Kyr and Rajani met to go for a walk by the lake. The air was soft with the hint of Spring, and sunlight sparkled on the water. Rajani had resumed the black leathers of the Warrior Mage for his first time out in public; but he still looked pale, and his face bore new creases from his ordeal following the cleansing ritual. For the first time, Kyr felt years younger than Rajani — who was in fact his Fabro, his father's brother, as Naran had recently pointed out. In fact, Kyr felt younger than he had felt for years — light-hearted and free. He laughed out loud. "Isn't it a beautiful day? Do you think Winter is leaving us?"

"It's on the wane, for sure." Rajani sighed. "I'll have to check with Bru to see how the livestock fared."

"I'm sure he has it all well in hand." Kyr sauntered along, enjoying the fresh air and watching a flock of redfinches soaring together, turning as one. He pointed them out to Rajani. "They look like they are celebrating the return of the Sun."

"So they do." Rajani murmured. But he seemed preoccupied.

"What are you brooding about, Fabro?"

Startled, the Warrior Mage halted in his tracks. "What did you call me?"

"You are my father's brother, are you not?"

"Yes. I just didn't…I'm not used to hearing you call me that."

"It helps explain why you have gone to so much trouble to rescue me. I have wondered why you bothered. After all, I'd already destroyed the Soul-Drinker. You could have abandoned me after that. But you didn't."

"No, I couldn't do that," Rajani said warily.

Kyr turned to face him. "When are you going to tell me what is *really* going on?"

"Ah, what do you mean?"

"Don't you think you owe it to me to tell me what the Circle's plan for me *is*? I know you kept rescuing me and brought me here to Ravenvale for a reason. What else does this Prophecy of yours demand of me?" He regarded the Warrior Mage steadily, his topaz eyes calm and clear.

The Warrior Mage flushed in embarrassment and shook his head. "I'm very sorry, Kyr. I can't answer you. Things have to unfold without your foreknowledge. All I can tell you is that there will be no more suffering, and that what will unfold is of the utmost importance. Someday soon, you will understand."

In Rajani's voice Kyr heard pain and humility, mixed oddly with steely determination. He met Rajani's gaze and held it. After a moment, he said, "Alright. I will trust you."

The Warrior Mage was pierced through to his marrow by the keenness of Kyr's appraisal, and nearly crushed by the weight of his choice to trust him despite all that he had subjected Kyr to. Hands to his heart, he honored Kyr's valorous choice with a bow.

The next afternoon, they met again in Ravenhall's parlor for tea and biscuits. After a few pleasantries, Kyr set his cup down and quietly said, "I have something important to ask you. What was my mother like? I barely remember her."

Rajani choked on his tea, surprised by this unexpected question, and by the painful memories it evoked. "Sorry. Ah, well, let's see. Alytha was young, only about seventeen, but devoted to the Circle's purpose. The Soul-Drinker's Gatherers stole her mother when she was six. She hated Dauthaz with a fierce passion; but otherwise, she was kind and loving."

"Yes," Kyr said softly. "I recently remembered that she loved me."

"She was adept at mind-masking. The best of all of us."

"Ah. *That's* why she was chosen to be my mother. She could hide her secrets from Dauthaz." Kyr bowed his head, asking blessings for her soul. After a moment, he asked, "What did she like? What made her happy?"

"She grew up here in Ravenvale. She loved animals, loved her horse, always had a dog or two." Rajani smiled, remembering. "She got so excited when puppies came along, or even when chicks or ducklings hatched. Said they gave her hope."

"I guess I am a little like my mother, in this way." Kyr smiled. "Friend and Lady are important to me." He shook his head in dismay. "So much has been happening; it's been ages since I have seen either of them."

"Shall we go find them?" asked Rajani, hiding his relief at leaving behind Kyr's questions about the past and the Prophecy.

In the stable, they found Grena in the tackroom, polishing Lady's saddle, Friend asleep at his feet. At the sound of their entrance, Friend lifted her head, then joyfully leapt to her feet and rushed over to jump up on Kyr. Touched by her ungrudging welcome, he knelt and petted her, letting her lick his face for a few moments.

"Alright, girl, alright! That's enough." He wiped his face with his sleeve and rested his forehead on hers. "You know all about forgiveness, don't you?" he murmured, fondling her ears.

"Will you be taking her to stay with you, sir?" Grena asked, a certain regret in his voice.

Kyr looked up. "Well, how would that be for you? She's been with you for quite a while, now."

"She's a great dog," Grena acknowledged, "but she has missed you a lot, sir." And, twisting his polishing rag in his hands, he sighed regretfully. "She belongs with you. I'll bring her blanket and dish over to the infirmary."

"Thanks. Put them in my room upstairs, if you would. And thank you for taking care of her for me," Kyr smiled, adding, "I'll still need you to watch after her now and then. Would that be all right?"

Grena's face brightened. "Of course, any time."

Kyr got to his feet. "Alright, girl, let's go." Friend gave a happy bark, and followed Kyr and Rajani out the door of the tackroom. A short distance down the barn's corridor, she stopped and looked back over her shoulder at Grena.

"Go on, girl," Grena said, "I'll see you later. Go on, now." He made shooing motions with his hands, and closed the tackroom door. Friend stood there for a moment, gave a small whine, but then she trotted after Kyr.

As Kyr, Rajani, and Friend continued down the barn's breezeway, two large, curious faces — one black, one copper-red — poked out over the half-doors of their stalls. "Ah, Lady! There you are." While Kyr paused to greet her, Rajani went down the corridor to visit with his sorrel stallion, Akbara.

Kyr scratched the itchy spots behind Lady's velvety black ears. She shoved her nose against his chest, making him stumble back a couple of steps. He laughed. "I know. I've ignored you for much too long. I'm sorry." She snorted, and snuffled at his pocket. "Yes, I did remember." He took out a red apple and held it out to her. "I'll go for a ride with you soon, my Lady." Crunching the apple with her white teeth, she flicked her ears at him.

Once back outdoors, Kyr told Rajani, "I'd like to take Friend for a walk alone. Get reacquainted with her." This was true; but he was also feeling the impact of how Rajani's presence drew him back into the old familiar stories.

"Alright, Kyr," Rajani said. "And thank you. I am in your debt. If there's anything I can ever do for you…"

"Thanks," Kyr broke in. "I will ask." He called to Friend, and they started toward the gates. Instead of heading north along the lake, this time Kyr turned south, following the road around Ravenhall, and out across the fields and pastures toward the entrance to Ravenvale. Gray clouds wandered through blue vastness above, sending shadows trailing over the hayfields of wet stubble. Woolly sheep in green pastures imitated the clouds. In the distance, orchards of leafless fruit trees stood stolidly, awaiting Spring. Kyr took deep breaths, enjoying the openness and space of the wide fields, and started jogging. "Come, on, Friend!" Then, seeing how easily Friend kept up, he broke into a run. With a yip of joy, she galloped along with him, frisking happily.

Too soon, he was out of breath, and slowed to a walk. "I've been loafing around too much," he told Friend, and laughed. Then he sighed, thinking of all he'd been through since the cleansing ritual with Rajani. With a shake of his head, he dismissed the past again. Looking around for a place to rest, he spotted a lean-to not far off.

Inside it, the floor was covered with relatively dry straw. He sat with Friend, and hugged her to him. "I'm sorry I pushed you away, girl. I got…lost for a while." She looked up at him with serene brown eyes and licked his cheek. He smiled. "Forgiven, again."

Chapter Twenty~Seven

Diamond Light

leasepleasepleaseplease! Agony and aching need drove him to plead and beg mindlessly. His tormenter laughed in malicious triumph, teasing and taunting, but finally bringing the dreaded, desired culmination. Kyr woke to shuddering, humiliating pleasure. For a moment, he lay spent and panting. Then he curled into a ball of misery. *Oh, gods, no! I thought I was free of the past.*

A certain, sick desire to sink back into the old, familiar nightmare filled his gut, and an insidious inner voice whispered, *Maybe Medari was right. What makes me think I can just leave the past behind?*

NO! A stronger voice arose in him, and with it a refusal to dishonor the Kailithana and the deep healing and transformation that he had earned with her guidance. Taking some deep breaths, he calmed himself and brought to mind the being of light dropping its tattered cloak. *That is my true nature,* he affirmed, again sensing the vision's validity and clarity. Eagerly, he got up, threw on his robe, grabbed his towel, and headed for the bathhouse, with Friend at his heels. She happily nosed around outside while he took a quick bath. On his way back, Kyr noticed that another storm was looming over the western wall. When the first drops splattered down on his head, he laughed. No longer did he allow rain to drive him back to that dark night of storm, mud, illness, and lost faith at the fort.

After sharing breakfast with his friends in the infirmary's main room, Kyr asked Jolanya to come with him to his room. She nodded, and together they headed for the stairs. When Friend started to follow them, Kyr stopped to pet her. "Sorry, girl. You stay down here with Medari." Her ears drooped, but she went back and curled up on her raggedy blanket by the hearth.

In his room, Kyr sat cross-legged on his bed, and the Kailithana took her chair facing him. "What is it, Kyr?"

With clear eyes but a small, puzzled frown, Kyr told her of his nightmare. "I don't understand why this is still happening. I know it is just an old story and has nothing to do with me now."

"Yes, that's right," said the Kailithana. "Your true essence *is* that beautiful being of light that you saw, untouched by any hurt or degradation. But your body still carries the traces of what you have been through." She moved forward. "Let me see what the kailitha can do."

He stretched out on his back, and she placed one hand on his belly and the other on his chest over his heart. A gentle flow of kailitha trickled through her hands into Kyr's zhan.

Kyr focused on his breath, relaxing into the present moment and enjoying the soothing warmth of the kailitha.

"That's good, Kyr." A few moments later, the Kailithana felt the Flow increase and sharpen, and she said, "Now, it's time to open your heart, brave one. Remember who you really are, and face what you have endured."

Breathing through his heart, he closed his eyes, allowing the precious light of his true self to fill him. From this place, he was able to look clear-eyed at his tortured past. "So much suffering," he whispered.

"Keep breathing," the Kailithana commanded quietly. "Keep opening your heart. No judgment, no resistance. Breathe through it. What do you see?" The kailitha flowed diamond-clear and pristine, and she moved her hands so that one rested lightly on his forehead, and the other on the crown of his head.

"So much suffering," he repeated softly. "And...ah, I see. So much...willingness, so much...strength."

"Yes. What else?"

"So much viciousness and cruelty...and... so much help and love. My mother and father had so much love that they sacrificed themselves to free us all from the Soul-Drinker. Then there's Rajani and Luciya, always rescuing me," he smiled briefly. "And Tenaiya and Devanyi, caring for me, teaching me kindness; Svahar sacrificing himself to free me of the craving; and then, such gifts of compassion and healing at the Sanctuary...from Naran...Gaela... you." He opened his eyes and looked at her with gratitude and love.

But she was the Kailithana. She stopped herself from flinging herself into his arms, and kept the diamond kailitha flowing. "Look again, Kyr. What else?"

With a quiet sigh, he closed his eyes. And in a moment, he saw again the brilliance of the Goddess, felt again Her Love and Compassion for all his suffering, the suffering of all Her children. "Zhovanya," he whispered.

"Zhovanya." And they were quiet for a time as Her Presence gently enfolded them, subtly guiding the Flow in ways even Jolanya could not comprehend.

After a time, the kailitha ebbed, and their awareness of Zhovanya's Presence waned. Kyr shifted restlessly. Jolanya dropped her hands to her lap, and he sat up, cross-legged and facing her.

"What's happening, Kyr?"

"I'm feeling...tender and sad. Not sure why." He breathed through his heart, opening to this new feeling. "I have felt sad for Medari, for Rajani, even for Gauday. But this is different." Sensing deeper within, he said, "I'm feeling how...vulnerable I was, how much pain my body had to endure. I guess I am sad for it, for myself." He shook his head. "Well, that's no good, feeling sorry for myself over old stories."

"Oh, Kyr. It's all right to feel some tenderness and sorrow for yourself, for your body. It's about time that you allow yourself some compassion for all you have been through. You are strong enough, now." Her own compassion for him — for his strong, vulnerable human body — flooded through her. And she moved onto his bed to sit behind him, wrapped her arms around him, and rested her head on his back, offering his body the warm animal comfort of her own.

At first, he stiffened, battling his forbidden longing for her. But then he remembered to breathe through his heart, and his warm breath melted a last layer of hidden ice. Jolanya felt the tension drain from him as he began to weep. And they wept together, quiet tears of compassion and sorrow for his valiant and tender body, for themselves and their suffering, for all those who suffer in the dark innocence of the world.

The next afternoon, Naran and Kyr went walking by the lake, enjoying the early Spring sunshine. Though the stolid pines remained dark green as ever, the changeable aspens shyly displayed a haze of tender new green. The ravens were silently soaring and wheeling over the calm waters of the lake, while Friend splashed noisily and blissfully along at the water's edge, sniffing at the piles of broken branches and other debris left by the last winter storm.

A sudden cold breeze snatched Kyr's cloak to play with. He grabbed it back and wrapped it tighter. "Naran-ji," he began, then hesitated.

Naran glanced at him as they continued walking side-by-side. "What's bothering you, Kyr? You look sad."

"Ah, I... Well, the Kailithara is almost complete. And I am having trouble with stories I am making up...about the future."

"Ah," said Naran. "You fear Jolanya's departure?"

"Yes." Kyr sighed.

"Are you a prophet?"

"What?" Kyr stopped dead. Then he laughed. "No, Naran-ji. I'm not."

"Alright, then." Naran quirked an eyebrow at him.

Kyr smiled, releasing his fantasy of future pain once again. "Thanks, my friend. I will remember that." They walked on, and he turned his attention to the skirling wind; the green-hazed aspen trees swaying in the wind's embrace; the ravens quarreling over a silvery fish that one had found dead on the shore. Friend came up from the lake-shore, muddy-footed and panting happily, and they all continued their walk in companionable silence.

The setting sun thrust fiery lances between the clouds lurking above the guardian wall to the West. The sound of many voices chanting echoed over the lake. "Shall we join them?" Naran asked.

"The penitents? I've been ashamed to face them, after what I did to Craith." He shrugged, and laughed at himself. "But that's an old story. Alright, let's go."

Reaching the penitent's house, they left Friend in the kitchen with the guard, Nyx, and entered the chapel. Kyr looked around in surprise. *So many people here!* Rajani, Luciya, and Devanyi sat with Craith, Zurano, Kinar, and Jorem in a semi-circle in front of the altar. Kyr smiled, glad to see Medari sitting in the back. Beyond him were the widow Nyvali, and Chavri, the other guard.

Though the small room was already crowded, Kyr and Naran found seats next to Medari, filling the last spaces in the chapel. Kyr looked around. *We need a bigger space — but the only place larger is the chapel in Ravenhall.* He sighed, remembering the cleansing ritual that had taken place there, and its calamitous aftermath. *Ah, well, that was another stepping stone on the hard path. And it got me here.* He smiled, releasing the past and the future, and listened to his friends chanting together.

Two fat white candles burned on the low altar, gleaming off the polished stones and satiny driftwood that he had placed there eons ago, or so it seemed to him now. Someone had added a large, beautiful feather, the golden-brown of a tawny eagle. A thin column of smoke rose from a chipped pottery bowl, filling the chapel with the dusty-sweet smell of burning cedar.

Kyr joined the chant, glad to be reunited with his brothers and friends. As the chant continued, their voices blended together in rich, strong harmony; and for Kyr, joy rose up so strongly that he feared he might dissolve. Yet he opened his heart and soul to this perilous bliss, singing "Zhovanya naralo" with sure knowledge of its truth. A soft golden-yellow light filled the chapel, and Her Presence became palpable. They all fell silent, and were drawn deep into meditation.

Reverently, Kyr offered Her silent gratitude and honor. *"Ah, Zhovanya, forgive me for my doubts and fears. This life of mine has been…severe, yet it has brought me many treasures. I don't understand…."* And then it seemed to him that — until the moment that he had surrendered to the pain of it all — he had been absorbed in a strange and preposterous play. Yet behind the scenes, She always danced in Her power and grace, ready to welcome and dance with him, with everyone. And now he joined Her in spirit, swaying and turning together across the stars for a timeless while. His heart expanded with the gladness of being Home again at last.

But then people began to stir, and Kyr blinked, looking around the humble chapel. *Oh! I was* always *Home, if I had just known it.* The silent laughter of the Goddess filled the chapel for a moment, then slowly faded away. While the others filed into the kitchen, Kyr remained behind, absorbed in this wondrous blessing, this new realization. *Home is always here, always now.*

"Kyr? Won't you join us?"

Naran's words, uttered from across the threshold, sent a ripple through the deep quiet in Kyr's being. *Ah, I am called.* He stretched his arms and rolled his shoulders, bringing himself more awake in his body, and rose. "Yes, Naran-ji."

In the kitchen, the penitents offered everyone tea. Rajani and Luciya declined, saying they were tired, and headed back to Ravenhall. Everyone else stayed. Kyr accepted a mug from Kinar, and sipped the brew for a few moments, standing next to his heart-father.

"Thank you, son. This," Medari nodded toward the chapel, "is good." They exchanged fond smiles. Kyr sensed that his heart-father was now on the hard path toward healing and forgiveness, and he gave Medari a glad hug with his free arm.

But then, Craith, Zurano, Kinar, and Jorem gathered around him. Medari gave Kyr a nod, and went off to talk with Nyvali. She gave the healer a warm smile.

Craith greeted Kyr amiably: "Good to see you, Kyr."

"Yes, we missed you," said Kinar. Jorem and Zurano nodded.

"Sorry I disappeared on you. I had a lot to deal with. And — I'm here now." Shy of his clear and radiant gaze, they murmured, "Welcome back."

"Craith, are you well, now? I'm so sorry that I hurt you."

"No lasting harm done. You seemed…quite distraught."

"I was crazed by…" Kyr shrugged. "Never mind. That's an old story."

"But," Jorem protested, "how can we help you if we don't know what's going on?"

"I'm grateful for your concern." Kyr smiled. "But everything is all right, now. Best thing is to keep to your own journey on the hard path."

"Will you help us?" asked Zurano.

"Ah, let me see." He felt drawn into their stories, and then into his own old story, and winced inside. Then he remembered — the new sculpture of the Goddess was waiting for him. "I will help you as I can, but I have other work to do now."

Craith frowned. "We came here because of you, Kyr."

"That's right!" said Jorem, and the two pale Northerners nodded. "Didn't you come because you want to be free of the Soul-Drinker's poison?"

"Yes." Craith looked abashed, as did the other three men.

"Alright. Let me think for a moment." He closed his eyes. *How can I help them? They are like I was after a month or so at the Sanctuary. Ah.*

Opening his eyes, Kyr said, "I have a suggestion for you. Naran helped me tremendously at the Sanctuary. None of us would be here if not for him. Perhaps he can work with you, as he did with me. You couldn't do any better." Kyr nodded toward Naran, who was laughing with Devanyi by the doorway to the chapel. "Why don't you ask him?" He set his mug on the table and clasped forearms with each man, in the warrior's embrace. "Have faith, my friends, and keep to the hard path. Remember, Zhovanya forgives us all. Good night." Kyr slipped outside, needing time alone with the silent stars where his Goddess danced.

Inside, the four penitents approached Naran, and Craith took the lead. "Naran, sir, could we speak with you a moment?" Kinar, Zurano and Jorem hovered a few paces behind him.

Naran frowned briefly. "Sorry, Devanyi. I'd like to continue our talk. See you at breakfast?"

"Yes." She gave Naran a sweet smile, and nodded to the penitents. "Blessed night to you all," she said, then left for Ravenhall.

Naran studied the four men. "How may I help you?"

"Kyr has told us how much you helped him at the Sanctuary." Craith hesitated, but Jorem nudged him, and he forged on. "But we aren't free to go there. Since you are here now, we were wondering… Could you help us?"

"Help you, as I did Kyr?" Naran asked slowly, startled by this unexpected request. "Do you seek to atone for your crimes?"

"Yes," Craith said. "We want to find a way to face what we did; make amends if I can; and perhaps earn Zhovanya's forgiveness."

"It's not an easy undertaking, you understand?"

"We know," said Kinar, and the others nodded soberly. "Kyr told us some of what he went through."

"It's important that you accept responsibility for your actions and emotions, past and present, rather than blame others. Are you willing to do that?"

"Yes," said Craith somberly, and the other three nodded.

"If I were to work with each of you individually, it would take a long time." Naran pondered this for a moment. "But since you all have followed similar paths, perhaps I can work with you as a group. Would that suit you?"

Jorem nodded. "We four have shared much of our own stories with each other already."

"That's a good start." Naran paused, and looked each man in the eye. "Before we begin, there's something you must agree to: no lies, no secrets, no violence, no matter what. I can't work with you unless you can whole-heartedly agree to keep to these conditions."

They looked at each other, then nodded. Solemnly, each man in turn, said, "I so swear: no lies, no secrets, no violence."

"Alright, then." Naran smiled. "We have a deal."

"Thank you, sir," said Craith fervently. All four of the penitents bowed to Naran with deep respect and gratitude.

"And *I* thank *you*." Naran smiled. "I was wondering what to do with myself."

Part Eight ~ Consecration

*"Love exalts our earthly bodies to heaven,
and makes the very hills to dance with joy!"*

— Rumi

Chapter Twenty-Eight

The Star-Seer's Garden

For a quarter moon, Kyr spent much of his time meditating, or walking the hills with Friend in the soft days of early Spring, absorbing the great blessings he had received through the Kailithara and Zhovanya's Grace.

On the day of the first Full Moon of Spring, Naran and the Kailithana sat across from Kyr at the table after breakfast. Jolanya could not help but notice how the sunshine streaming in the window gleamed in his hair, which curled loosely around his face and almost down to his shoulders, now. *He looks like a mountain panther, all shades of amber.* She sighed to herself, longing to run her fingers through his red-gold curls.

Then, shaking herself slightly, she recalled herself to her duty as the Kailithana and checked his zhan with her inner senses. Her eyes widened as the kailitha sprang to life within her.

"Kyr, the kailitha is strong today. We need to continue the Kailithara." She paused, sensing the 'thirsty' quality of the kailitha. "And we need to be outdoors. It's lovely and warm, and I will need to draw on the zhan of Earth and Sky."

Kyr reached down to stroke Friend, who was curled up at his feet, and a slight frown creased his forehead. The idea of being out in the open made him feel uneasy, though he didn't know why. "Alright...but where can we go for some privacy? I'd rather not be out in the forest today."

"Good idea. Let's ask Rajani." Kyr turned to Naran, and said, "Looks like we'll be gone most of the day. What will *you* be doing?"

"I've worked it out with Rajani to interview each of the penitents today, prior to beginning our work together."

"Still helping others face their demons? You are the bravest man I know." Kyr smiled warmly at the man who had saved his soul.

Naran blushed and shook his head. "No, *you* are the most courageous one — ever."

"Men! Always competing over something," Jolanya remarked, and they all laughed. Then she stood up. "Let's go find Rajani." Friend too jumped up, eager for a walk.

They found Rajani in his office on the first floor, besieged by lists and plans and looking harassed.

"Here you are!" exclaimed Kyr. "Back in the saddle so soon?"

"Yes. Luciya is exhausted, after taking on all my duties *and* trying to care for me all this time. I'm helping out so she can recuperate." Jolanya started to protest, and he held up a hand. "Don't worry. I'm only working half-days for now, building up my strength."

He stood up and came around the desk to greet them. "I'm glad to see you. Any distraction is welcome." He laughed, and gave Friend a few pats. She licked his hand, and then started nosing around this new place.

"Sorry, Rajani, I'm afraid we won't be much of a diversion," said Jolanya. "We just have a quick question for you. Is there a place we can go outdoors that is secluded and private?"

Rajani's heart leapt in his chest at these words. *Oh, Goddess! This is just when Granmere said the Prophecy would be fulfilled — the first Full Moon of this Spring — and here they both are, looking radiant. This has to be it! Now I must send them to Granmere's sacred garden.* Looking out the window for a moment, he silently prayed, *Goddess forgive us, and bless these two. Guide them! Protect them!*

He took a breath, trying to calm himself down. Turning to the map of Ravenvale on the wall beside his desk, he ran his finger along a trail. "See here? Up this trail, there's a walled garden. It's quite private — but, I warn you, we haven't cleaned it up yet." He opened a desk drawer and pulled out a large ring of keys. Sorting through them, he found the one he wanted, and murmured, "Kaa'atay." The ring opened and he slid a large, antique key off it.

"This is the key to the gate," Rajani said as he held it out to Kyr. "It should be a good spot. I think my grandmother grew her healing herbs there and used it as a place to meditate. But it might take some work to clear a space."

"Sounds perfect," Kyr said, pocketing the key. "I could use a little exercise."

"You can get tools from Grif. And ask for some hinge oil. That gate hasn't been opened in years."

"Who is Grif?" asked Jolanya. "And how do we find him or her?"

"He's our head gardener. Not very tall, dark-skinned, curly black hair, bright green eyes. Can't miss him, for all he's so quiet. He'll be in the garden shed about now."

"Thanks, Rajani," Jolanya said. "We'll let you get back to work, now." Laughing at Rajani's disappointed look, she and Kyr headed downstairs, with Friend following eagerly at their heels.

When they reached the courtyard, Kyr leaned down to scratch Friend's ears. "Sorry, girl, you can't come with us today. Want to go see Grena?" Her tail drooped, and she wrinkled her brow. "It's just for the day," Kyr assured her. "I'll come get you this evening, alright?" She wagged her tail slowly.

The three made their way to the stables, where — after a briefing from Kyr — Grena promised Friend a good romp in the woods once his duties were done. Kyr knelt and hugged his faithful dog. "Good girl, good girl. Have fun with Grena. I'll see you later."

From the windows in his office, Rajani could see Kyr and Jolanya heading toward the Star-Seer's garden, and his heart pounded with joy. "Ah, Zhovanya," he breathed. "Soon You will be restored to your people, your land! Soon the web of life of Khailaz will be in Your hands again! We will all be free of the Soul-Drinker's long nightmare. And I will be free of this cursed oathbind!" He could barely contain his excitement.

Leaving the lists and plans scattered all over his desk, he hurried off to find Luciya and Devanyi. He quickly discovered them both in the parlor, sipping tea and chatting by the fire. "This is it!" he cried. "The Prophecy is finally going to be fulfilled!"

The two women turned to stare at him, wide-eyed. "How do you know?" Luciya demanded.

"It's the prophesied time, and I just sent Kyr and the Kailithana to Granmere's garden. As soon as I did that, the oathbind loosened its grip on my mind, the way it does when I'm on the right path."

"What does this mean?" asked Devanyi.

Luciya looked at her in surprise. "Oh, that's right. You haven't been a part of the Circle for very long, have you? It means that if all goes well, Zhovanya will be restored to Her rightful place as our Goddess, and the Sacred Balance will be renewed."

Devanyi's eyes widened. "Really? How...?"

"Come," Rajani broke in. "There's no time for discussion. All will soon become clear. Right now, we must gather everyone to pray for Kyr and Jolanya. Though these two brave souls don't know it, what they are about to do is perilous. If they aren't strong enough..." He shook his head. "No, no! They *must* succeed! And we must do all we can to help them." Taking command, the Warrior Mage said, "Devanyi, please find Ylana and ask her to come to the chapel. Luciya, go open the chapel and set out the candles and incense. I'll go ring the summoning bell. Then let's meet in the chapel to plan what to do."

The two women nodded, and left on their missions. Rajani hurried out of the parlor, ran up several flights of stairs, and stood panting before a small, arched door. "Curse it, I'm still out of shape!" He shoved the door open and clambered up the steep spiral staircase inside the bell tower. Reaching the belfry, he rang the large brass bell twice, then twice again, then three times. This pattern told everyone who was available to come to the chapel immediately.

The chapel filled quickly with the Ravenhall servers: Cook, Bru, and Grif. Companions, in their dark-green tunics, stood alertly by the doors. Long-time residents and new arrivals trickled in, wearing their everyday work clothes. A few sleepy-eyed ones showed up in their robes and slippers, hair awry. Murmuring questions to one another, the crowd shifted about, finding friends or family.

"What's this all about?" asked a farmer in his mud-splattered boots. "Are we being invaded?"

"You're new here, aren't you?" answered a silver-haired grandmother. "The bells said to *gather* here, not to arm ourselves. Don't worry."

Rajani stood before them, a dark figure against the golden altar, with the sunlight flooding in through the circular window behind him. Dancing light reflected off the lake, gleamed on the pale golden walls, and sparkled on the silver stars embedded in the dark-blue floor. The Presence Lamp above the altar remained the dead black that had replaced the Soul-Drinker's red glare when he died.

The Warrior Mage raised his hands. Everyone quickly fell silent and turned to face him expectantly.

"Thank you all for coming. There is something very important for all of Khailaz that may happen today. I cannot reveal what it is yet, but if our Liberator — Kyr — and the Kailithana succeed, there will be a clear sign. I will explain everything later. For now, we must all do what we can to help them."

Ylana, the Ritual Mage, came forth, wearing her green robes. The Warrior Mage bowed and yielded his place to her before the golden altar. Holding a burning taper, Ylana turned to the altar, lit two tall candles — one white, one black — and set sweet incense burning in its iridescent shell. Then she turned to face the crowd.

"We can help bring about this great blessing by praying for protection and guidance for Kyr and the Kailithana. Please join me in this chant." In her strong, mellow voice, she sang, "Zhovanya, dagantalo, Zhovanya, ganaralo."

Soon the chapel echoed with the deep and multi-layered resonance of many voices singing together.

The power and beauty of the chant gave Luciya chills. As the chanting continued, she, Rajani, Devanyi, and other members of the Circle prayed more fervently than ever they had before. The others in the chapel also prayed strongly, sensing the sacredness and significance of this mysterious event.

Meanwhile, Kyr and Jolanya stopped by the kitchen to ask for a basket of food for their noon meal, bringing along the gardening tools they had collected from Grif. Cook put together an ample basket, and handed to it Kyr.

"Thank you," he said.

"No," Cook answered gravely, "Thank *you*, sir."

"For what?" Kyr asked with a puzzled smile.

"For freeing us from the Soul-Drinker," Cook answered.

"Oh." Kyr blinked in surprise. "You're welcome." He smiled at her, then turned away, mildly disturbed. *How can I tell these people — that old story has nothing to do with me? In the first place, it was* Lanir *who killed the Soul-Drinker; and in the second, the man who made all those sacrifices isn't here now.* He smiled and shook his head. *Gods, I don't think I can ever make them understand. I guess it will just have to be my secret.*

"Here, I'll take the basket," Jolanya said. "You already have the tools to carry." She took the wicker basket from Kyr, and they set off, crossing the courtyard, and out the eastern gate. Following Rajani's directions, they took a narrow, grassy path that led them toward the back of the valley and up into some low hills hunched at the feet of the eastern cliffs.

Kyr took deep breaths of the lively Spring air, enjoying stretching his legs as they climbed. The sky was stitched with birds of many sizes and colors darting busily back and forth, courting or building nests. Their trills and songs made a sound tapestry in the air. He glanced at his companion, enjoying the sight of Jolanya striding beside him, her graceful form only hinted at beneath her indigo robes. "Gods, Jolanya," he exulted, "I am so happy to be alive! Thank you for this wonderful gift!" Right there on the trail, he dropped the satchel and spread his arms wide, embracing earth and sky.

Delighted by the miracle of his ebullience after his long ordeal, Jolanya set the basket down and danced around him. Then she gave him a playful little push, and raced up the trail. "Hey!" Kyr chased after her. Like two frisky colts, they capered up the steep trail, laughing and playing tag.

After a while, Jolanya had to stop to catch her breath. He took her by the arms, laughing. "I've got you now!" She looked into his eyes, entranced by the joy radiating from him, her heart melting. Seeing her love shining forth, a rush of flame and sweetness filled him. He yearned toward her, longing to kiss her soft, full lips.

But the Kailithana stepped aside, brushing her robes and straightening her braid. Softly she said, "You know Whom to thank. I am only Her servant." *And Yours, Jeyal,* she added silently.

Kyr sighed and let go of her arms, releasing her from his heart once again. "I think the garden is just around the next bend," he said, hiding his sadness behind a smile. "I'll go get our things." And he trotted back to fetch the tools and food.

Alone for the moment, Jolanya bit her lip, sad to see the disappointment in his eyes. *Soon, my love, soon. Perhaps this very day, the Kailithara will be complete.*

When Kyr returned, they headed on up the trail. A short way past the next bend, a surprisingly tall stone wall told them that they had found the right place. Kyr dug in his pocket for the key Rajani had given him. "I wonder why they made the wall so high."

Jolanya shook her head. "I'm not sure. Clearly, whoever built it wanted privacy. Fortunately, the garden faces South, so it gets a fair amount of sunlight up on this hill." Kyr tried to turn the key in the lock but it wouldn't budge.

"Here, let me try." Jolanya hunted in the tool bag for the narrow vial of hinge oil that Grif had given them. With a little oil and considerable wiggling, she got the key to turn. As they pushed the door open, the hinges screeched in protest, so she oiled them also. Then Kyr set the tools against the wall by the gate, and they both looked around the garden.

"Look at those roses," Jolanya exclaimed. "They have gone completely wild!" A tangle of long canes climbed all over the walls and into the lower branches of trees, boasting a profusion of scarlet, peach, and yellow flowers.

Kyr shivered as an odd tingling spread all over his body. "Hmmm. It's almost like I — or we — have been here before, or..."

"Yes, like we belong here... or are supposed to be here." Jolanya shook her head. "I don't know why."

They gazed at each other, mystified, waiting for they knew not what.

When nothing happened immediately, the Kailithana shrugged. "Well, whatever the reason is, I suppose we will find out. But for now, we need to clear out some space for our work." They spent the rest of the morning trimming back the brush and vines.

Kyr lopped off a dead branch from an oil-nut tree, and then stood staring through the opening he had created.

"Jolanya, look over there." He pointed at a small white roof showing through the opening at the back wall of the garden. "What's that?"

She came and peered over his shoulder. "I don't know. Let's go see." They took their sickles along so that they could cut a path to the small white stone building through the overgrown grasses and weeds. As they approached, they saw a narrow porch, its roof upheld by two slender columns — one black, one white — leading to a closed stone door that was bare of knob or handle.

"I think it's a temple," said Jolanya. "I wonder Whose?" And she pushed at the door, to no avail.

Kyr added his strength to hers, but the door wouldn't budge. He examined the door more closely. "I see no keyhole. We'll have to come back with some better tools to get this open."

"Perhaps we can ask Rajani how to get this open tomorrow." Jolanya sighed in mild frustration, and turned away from the enigmatic structure. "Well, we still have our work to do. Let's clear a space in that grassy area." They returned to the center of the garden, and began scything the tall grass in the open area. Jolanya started singing a simple song, perfectly suited to the rhythmic work. Kyr listened a while, then joined in.

"Wai ho, wai ho,
we clear the ground
for seeds we'll sow."

Soon, Kyr was hot and sweaty, and he stopped to strip off his tunic and stretch his tired muscles. Watching Jolanya swinging her scythe with easy grace, his throat ached with unshed tears. No matter how often he let go of the future and stopped himself from trying to be a "prophet," his heart stung painfully every time he thought of her departure — which would be soon. Perhaps even this very day, the Kailithara would be complete.

A clashing sound interrupted Jolanya's song. "Blasted rock! Now I'll have to sharpen the blade. Would you check to see if there are more rocks?" She searched out the whetstone from their bag of tools and started working on the dulled blade, the swishing of the stone against the blade making a counterpoint to the chirping of the redfinches hopping about in the rosebushes.

Kyr knelt and began to feel through the grass, which was now considerably shorter, though still about ankle-high. "Yes, there are quite a few rocks. They seem to be in a circle."

Jolanya looked up from her task. "A circle? Hmmm." Kyr started to pry at a rock. "Wait!" she said. "Leave it be. This might be a healing ring." Setting the scythe aside, she knelt at the other side of the small clearing and felt around with her hands. "Yes, look at this, there *is* a circle. This is wonderful! It will help our work a great deal." She continued feeling through the grass, following the curve of the rocks. "No, wait, it's a spiral. Even better!" Eagerly, Jolanya fetched a small sickle and began cutting the shortened grass from around the stones. "Come on, help me. We have to clear the grass from the spiral." Puzzled but willing, Kyr got the other sickle and started working.

As they cut the grass down, the stone spiral became more evident. At the center of the spiral was an open area. "Yes, look," Jolanya exclaimed happily. "It *is* a healing ring. See the five larger stones, one bigger than the rest? The person being healed lies with his head near the largest stone, hands and feet touching the other four. You'll lie there. And yes, there's the healer's seat." Eyes shining with excitement, Jolanya pointed to a flat gray-blue stone near the center. "Oh, Kyr, we couldn't ask for a better place!" *In fact, it couldn't be more perfect,* she thought, with a shiver of awe. *It's almost as if this place has been waiting for us.* She shook her head at this fanciful thought, and went back to cutting the grass.

At noon, they stopped to eat their lunch under the dappled shade of an ancient oak whose roots underlay the whole central area of the garden. Kyr removed an old ivory linen cloth from the top of their food basket, and spread it over the newly cut grass. Then he set out the bread, boiled eggs, apples, and an earthenware jug of mint tea. They ate in companionable silence, neither feeling free to speak the truth of their hearts, and unwilling to break the quiet peace of the garden with irrelevant chatter.

When they had eaten their fill, Jolanya packed the remains into the basket. Kyr watched her for a few moments; but then, fearing the growing strength of his attraction to her, he turned his gaze away and stretched out on the grass. Pillowing his head on a mossy hummock made by the old tree's roots, he closed his eyes and began to watch his breath. *Zhovanya,* he prayed, *help me be present to each moment. Help me let go of the stories spoken by desire and fear and hope.*

The warmth of the sunshine combined with their pleasant tiredness from the morning's activities to make them both drowsy. "I guess we won't get much done without a nap," Jolanya said, lying down nearby. Half-asleep already, Kyr gladly gave himself up to slumber. They both slept, bathed in the vibrant harmony of the ancient oak, the cascades of twining roses, the silent spiral of stones.

Sunlight crept onto Jolanya's face. She brushed at it, waking herself. Rolling up on an elbow, she watched Kyr sleep, studying his zhan. Suddenly she was wide-awake and tense with anticipation. *Yes, he's ready. I'm not sure what will happen, but it's something big.* She reached over and nudged him gently. "Wake up, brave one."

He woke with a lazy smile. "Gods, I haven't slept that well in ages, maybe ever." He arched his body, stretching full-length, then sagged pliantly back to earth. "What a restful place this is. I could sleep the rest of the day." Seeing her small frown of impatience, he sighed and sat up. "What do you want me to do?"

"It would be good for us to be fully in contact with the healing power of Earth, Air, and Sun. Do you mind if we shed our clothes?"

He swallowed hard. *Gods, does she think I am made of stone?* But he hid his qualms and began to undress.

Jolanya hung her robes from a low branch and turned around. Her handsome, supple body gleamed in the golden light of the afternoon sun. He looked down, fighting a rush of desire, and held his tunic in front of his groin.

Seeing the full extent of the small scars on Kyr's body, Jolanya bit her lip to keep from crying out in anger and horror. *Gods above and below, how did he endure that?* The lines of faded red scars twined around his arms and legs, curved around his belly and hips, and up onto his chest to end at his heart. If she could force herself to ignore their malign origin and purpose, the pattern the scars created was beautiful. *It's so extensive! No wonder I haven't been able to undo it completely.*

She took a deep breath and let it out, calming herself. "Alright, Kyr, lie down on your back, with your head and hands as I told you earlier."

"But…" Kyr hesitated, then shrugged. *What modesty do I have left, after what Gauday put me through?* But the thought of Gauday's sorcerous abuse instantly quelled his arousal. He breathed a sigh of relief, spread his cloak on the new-cut grass, made a pillow of his clothing, and stretched out in the center of the spiral, with his head next to the larger stone, hands and feet touching the four smaller stones. The stones sent ethereal ripples through his body. Despite the warmth of the sunshine flooding the garden, Kyr shivered with apprehension, wondering what more the Kailithara would demand of him.

The very air seemed full of expectancy as the Kailithana took her seat on the healer's stone. "I need you to keep still until the Flow of the kailitha stops. Are you ready?" At Kyr's nod, she placed one hand on his chest over his heart and the other on his belly, bowed her head, and prayed. *Zhovanya, Jeyal, ganarali. Guide me today. Let there be deep healing for this man who has sacrificed so much for us, for Khailaz, for You.* As she sank into her working trance, the zhan of the garden and its roses, of the ancient oak, of Earth and Sky augmented the Flow, enhancing her strength, clarity, and trust. Twin streams of kailitha poured through her: Jeyal's silver twining with Zhovanya's gold. She gasped at their power and intensity, and watched as her hands began to move of Their, not her, accord, following the pattern of Kyr's twining scars.

As the Kailithana lightly traced the pattern on his body, Kyr shuddered with remembered pain. *Ah, Goddess, why all this pain? Why did you send me into Gauday's hands?* The very questions evoked bitterness and confusion. But he knew such questions would destroy the precious peace he had found. Once again, he let go of the old story. *Forgive me, Zhovanya,* he prayed, returning to humbleness. *I am Yours. Help me remember who I am.*

The Kailithana watched as the kailitha, now a deep blue-green with ripples of gold and silver, filled in Kyr's scars and connected them together, completing the pattern that Gauday had tried to inflict on Kyr's zhan — but this time, in a healthy, beautiful way. When the pattern was complete, her hands settled on Kyr's midriff. The kailitha sank down to deeper levels of Kyr's zhan, where even she could not follow. But then she received a new song, and began to chant: "Surrender to the Earth, the Sky, the Flow. The Earth, the Sky, the Flow. The Earth, the Sky, the Flow."

As Jolanya chanted in her strong, clear voice, Kyr felt the resonance of her song opening him to the Flow, to the Earth and Oak cradling him, to the Sun and Wind caressing him. Taking slow, full breaths, he surrendered more with each exhalation. From the stones, the oak, the roses, the sky, a tingling clarity poured into him through Jolanya's hands, pulsing ever deeper until every part of his body was sparkling with it.

Soon, he could no longer tell where his body ended and the Earth and Air began. And then the tingling intensified almost to the threshold of pain, becoming intensely sensual, arousing his manhood to the fullest. Fearing he would lose hold, he clutched the stones near his hands, pressed down on the ones by his feet, and prayed, *Goddess help me!* He was panting with desire, aching for release, yet he found that he could not move. His body was pinned to the earth by the heavy Flow of kailitha.

Deeply linked with him through her working trance, Jolanya could feel his fear and desire, but she was helpless. In the grip of the strongest Flow she had ever experienced, she could only allow the flood of the kailitha to continue surging into him.

"The Earth. The Sky. The Flow." Her voice was husky with the desire that flooded her through their link, but she kept her hands in place, letting the kailitha work. In a small, frightened part of her mind, she thought, *Gods! How can I...we...contain this flood without flying apart?* She sensed her doubt starting to lessen the Flow. *Trust and breathe, Jolanya,* she reminded herself. *Breathe and open wider.* As she breathed more deeply and released her fear, the kailitha poured through her more strongly than ever, its intent beyond her ken.

The force of the kailitha within Kyr became more potent with each breath, until he was sure he was about to burst into a fountain of light. *Are you going to take me Home* now, *after all this? Ah, Goddess, why? Why now?* But then he smiled. *Why* not *now?* As the kailitha magnified even further, making him tremble and sweat, he took a deep breath and let it go. *I am ready, Zhovanya. I am Yours.*

In answer, the Flow reached a peak of such intensity that Jolanya sang out a wordless tone and Kyr's body arched like a drawn bow. Just when Jolanya thought they would both dissolve into ethereal flame, the kailitha imploded within Kyr. His long, wild cry of fear and exultation blended with her intonation, sending a thrilling resonance through both their bodies, vibrating through the stones, the oak, the roses, the sky.

They fell silent, and a vibrant hush filled the garden. The Flow gently receded, leaving Kyr lying supine on the earth. His awareness flowed down and down to an infinite point deep inside his soul. Then, from this imperceptible seed, a new pattern bloomed, flowering throughout his being — a crystalline, opalescent web, delicate and subtle, yet as strong as the ancient oak.

Deep in trance, Jolanya watched in awe and joy as all Kyr's scars and wounds were woven together with the new channel in his core to create a miraculous new symmetry and wholeness.

At last, the Flow dwindled to a trickle. Kyr lay, panting and stunned, unable to comprehend what had just happened. But he laughed to find that once again, it was not his time to go Home to Zhovanya's Heart. Instead, he felt reborn, and was glad.

Jolanya tenderly caressed his damp hair off his sweating brow, and he smiled up at her as sweetly as an infant. Profoundly relaxed, his eyes closed and he fell like a stone into a deep well of sleep, while the changes the Kailithara had brought about worked down through the deepest levels of his being. Pulling her cloak over them both, she lay down by his side, exhausted and awed by the transformation that the Goddess and the God had wrought through her.

Kyr woke to the sound of a dusklark's song thrilling though his body as the scent of lavender, and rose in an ecstasy of sensation. The subtle rasp of the soft cloak on his skin as he breathed, the slow hush of his breath, the silky-cool breeze on his face were exquisite luxuries. Even the touch of his tongue as he wet his dry lips was delicately sensuous.

The deep strength of oak and earth thrummed in his bones and muscles. His mind felt as clear and empty as sky after storm. For many moments, he lay still, reveling in the beauty of the world and his new sensitivity to it. High above in the clear air, he saw a pair of tawny eagles spiraling about each other. For the first time, he felt as free and clear as they, and his heart soared to join them in their exultant flight.

When at last he brought his attention back to earth, he looked over at Jolanya, sleeping peacefully by his side. *Goddess! She is so magnificent!* With his eyes, he traced her graceful curves, the flow of her darkly shining hair confined in its braid, the tender bow of her mouth, her long dark lashes against her smooth, dusky skin. A quiet flame of desire began to burn in him, yet he was content merely to take her in with his eyes.

As he looked more deeply, he began to see a shimmering around her. Startled, he blinked a few times and looked around. The trees, the grasses, the stones, even the air — all were imbued with a subtle dancing luminescence, denser and brighter in living things. The ancient oak took his breath away with its pulsing, golden glow. In this universe of light, there were no boundaries. The whole world was a web of light, living beings bright stars in the net. Awe and joy filled him, and great gratitude to Zhovanya.

Fascinated, he watched the play of light within and around the Kailithana. Some places pulsed more brightly than others in the web that was Jolanya. Without thought, he reached out a hand and touched one of the dimmer spots, sending his intention into the web of light that was all around them, then bringing the kailitha to that dim place in Jolanya's zhan where it was needed for her healing. He felt the Flow move through him and watched as that dim area brightened.

From the wholeness she had brought to him, he could now see the true pattern of her zhan. Noticing where there were areas of rigidity, old places of dark hurt, he directed the kailitha to these wounds, and watched in delight as they brightened and wove into the web of her zhan in a new and beautiful pattern.

The Flow diminished, and he knew that they were both ready — strong, hollow, and flexible as river reeds. *But what are we ready for?* He smiled at his own foolishness. *Of course. For whatever You ordain, Zhovanya, Jeyal.*

Jolanya came slowly to wakefulness with a feeling of utter contentment and joy. *God and Goddess, Your healing was so amazing! Kyr will be all right now, much more than all right. And I feel wonderful! My zhan feels so different…complete and whole in a way I never imagined. Thank You, thank You!*

Jolanya stretched and opened her eyes. Sitting up, she found Kyr sitting in front of her, gazing at her with awe and delight. And she saw that Kyr's body was now clear of the marks of torment, except for a pale tracery of twining scars, and that his zhan too was whole and complete. Joyfully, she realized, *The Kailthara is finished!*

Then she was drawn into the quiet golden flame of his eyes. Through the Earth, the Oak and the Air, the two of them were deeply linked. She felt his desire and the answer of her body. Knowing that her work was complete, she smiled an exultant and alluring smile. *At last,* she thought, *at last I can reveal my secret!* Slowly, she reached up and began to loosen the dark river of her hair from its severe braid.

Kyr trembled with deep joy, knowing without need of words that this meant she was letting go of her role as the Kailithana. He could hardly believe that she would now be his after all. Yet her eyes, her smile, her body told him it was so.

Chapter Twenty-Nine

In Sacred Time

B reathing deeply, feeling his connection with the oak and the earth, he opens his heart completely to his beloved, containing his jubilance and desire in stillness. For long moments, they look into each other's eyes, letting their passion build. A hush surrounds them: the world holding its breath.

A scream breaks the silence. Looking up into the limpid azure sky, they behold two great birds circling above them: the Firebird shining red-gold in the sunlight; the Night Eagle flashing silver, then dark as it circles in and out of the light. They clasp claws and whirl downwards together, diving straight at Kyr and Jolanya. Knowing that their ultimate fate is upon them at last, they stretch out on the earth, sighing in deepest surrender.

The great birds break apart, the Night Eagle alighting on Jolanya's chest. Crying *"BELOVED!"* the Firebird settles onto Kyr's chest; its claws of gold pierce deeply, ripping open his heart.

The silver silence of the Moon floods into her, swelling and receding like the tides of a relentless ocean, building higher and higher, reaching further and further into her until she fears she will drown in this perilous bliss, will be swept away and lost forever. Yet she yearns to surrender herself into the ocean of Mystery, into the deep peace of its dark and infinite depths.

The burning sound of the Sun pours into him, filling him with blinding ecstasy, scorching agony. Blazing hot, his body arches and his pounding heart shakes him until he is terrified that he will explode in violence, or shatter in utter exaltation. And he begs, *Take me Home to Your Heart, Zhovanya. Take me Home!*

"HOLD ME, BELOVED," whispers Jeyal, *"CONTAIN THE TIDES, THE DEEP, THE DARK."* And she fights the pull of the tides, knowing that losing herself in the ocean of Mystery would dissolve her ability to be

Jeyal's Vessel, leaving the Sun Goddess alone, scorching the world. But she is the Kailithana, adept at navigating the deep realms of the soul, and she keeps hold. Opening to the silver light of the God, she weaves strands of darkness and moonlight to cool and balance the blazing glory of her beloved.

"*BE MY VESSEL, BELOVED*," sings the Goddess. "*SURRENDER TO THE FIRE, THE LIGHT, THE GLORY, BUT DO NOT YIELD.*" And with the strength born of great discipline and his infinite devotion to Zhovanya, he fights his longing for annihilation in Her Flaming Heart, and welcomes the ferocious passion and fearsome light of the Goddess. The fires of three hells have served well to temper Zhovanya's Vessel.

And the Vessel of the Sun rises, his eyes burning with golden light; golden-red hair a flaming aureole; skin shining copper-gold. The Vessel of the Moon stands before him, silver eyes shining; face and body glowing with lunar radiance; stars shining in the night-dark flood of her hair.

Standing in the heart of the Universe,
Reunited at last,
The Divine Ones meet in an explosion of Light,
and They Dance
whirling together among the Stars,
Dancing across the Earth
as golden stag and silver doe,
leaping joyously through woods and leas;
soaring and screaming through the Air
as eagles mating in the sky,
tawny and black, talons locked, twirling in ecstasy;
as huge sea serpents, alabaster and obsidian,
twining together in the silken waters of an infinite Ocean;
as Man and Woman loving, gentle and deep.
An explosion of bliss, a cascade of joy,
Laughter swirling, spiraling, coalescing;
brilliancy bursting forth,
A resplendent Star burning
in the gentle embrace of the dark Void,
the Two burning in ecstasy as One
forever.
A deep, reverberating sound
a cosmic gong vibrating the Universe;

luminous darkness,
harmonious silence,
the profound stillness
and silence
of the
One.

The Two awaken in the Garden, smiling into each other's incandescent eyes burning gold and shining silver. He smooths her ebony hair. She caresses his glowing face.

Proud in their naked beauty, they arise. Hand in hand, they wander the glorious garden, where buds, blossoms, and fruit burgeon on every tree.

Reaching up, he plucks a golden peach and gives it to her. Gladly she bites into the luscious fruit, still warm from the sun, letting the sweet juices baptize her breasts and loins.

Laughing, she runs ahead, disappearing around a curve in the path. He speeds after her, already longing to be with her again.

Around the curve, he finds her standing, holding out a ruby-red apple.

With a bow, he joyously accepts her offering, and brings it to his lips, biting into the crisp globe, savoring its sweet-tart taste. He swallows, and closes his eyes as awareness blooms and blesses him.

Opening his eyes, he smiles, and says, "Beloved."

Golden and silver, Their eyes meet, glowing with love and desire. Breath deepens inward, flows outward, and is received by the Beloved in an endless circle. Delight inspires a sinuous dance with the Beloved. Light caresses bring shivers of delight, groans of desire. Kisses linger, lengthen, deepen, as hands trace contours of the Beloved's body.

The Beloved's moans inflame passion. The Beloved embraces and is embraced, penetrates and is penetrated, receives and is received. They are dancing in the heart of the Universe, starfire burning in Their blood, shining from Their eyes. Their cries of bliss meld with the eternal rapturous resonance of the Universe, and the Two are One.

At the peak of Their ecstasy, an ethereal golden-white Flame ignites and surges outward from Them through Air, Water, and Earth, reaching in a moment the furthest corners of Their land.

New leaves sprout from the gnarled twigs of the ancient oak, and a riot of color breaks forth across Their garden. Crimson rose and blue-star bush, lavender ilys and purple lovers' friend, scarlet firebrands and orange treasure cups spring into bloom, perfuming the air with their sweet scents. Dawnlark and dusklark, redfinch and greenjay, golden warbler and silver thrush burst into a chorus of celebration, embellishing the air with their songs.

Tears of devastating joy flow together into the grass and tiny blue flowers spring into bloom, forever after called Love's Tears. Embraced and embracing, the Beloved bodies sink limply into stillness.

Chapter Thirty

Revelations and Rejoicing

I n the chapel at Ravenhall, the Warrior Mage rose from kneeling and stood staring upwards. At the sudden kindling of the light above his head, joy burst through him. *Granmere, it worked!* he exulted.

Ylana smiled and raised her hands to end the chant. Then she sang out, "Zhovanya, volara donorulai! Jeyal, volara donorulai! We offer You our hearts!" One by one, everyone silently rose to their feet, staring in wonder at the newly kindled Presence Lamp. The dancing, opalescent Light shone gold and silver, blue and green, rose and orange — a benediction on all who beheld it.

Rajani knew that at this very moment, every Presence Lamp in all the chapels and temples throughout Khailaz were shining forth with the same new Light, heralding the Renewal of the Sacred Balance. His heart overflowed with gladness and awe at this tremendous blessing: that the Goddess and God held all of Khailaz in Their Hands once again. As he soaked in this new Light, the heavy yoke of his oath-bound duty lifted off his shoulders, at last.

Luciya turned toward him, brown eyes shining. "We did it, Jani! We fulfilled the Prophecy, at last!"

Stunned with joy, he shook his head. "I can't believe it's over."

She grabbed his hands. "We did it! We did it!" Feeling lighter than a feather, Rajani whirled her around, laughing.

"Ah," murmured Naran, coming over, "excuse the interruption. But what in all the hells — or heavens — is going on?"

Laughing, Luciya and Rajani whirled to a stop and dropped their hands. "Sorry!" Luciya said. "This means so much to us, after all the years we have worked for this day. I'm so excited! I forgot that most folks don't know how wonderful this is." Luciya took Rajani by the hand and they turned to face the silent, wondering crowd.

"Alright, Naran…everyone," Rajani said. "The new Light of the Presence Lamp tells us that Kyr and Jolanya succeeded. Now we can explain what's happened, but we must be brief. We need to reach Kyr and Jolanya, make sure they are all right."

He nodded to Luciya and she gestured toward the glowing Presence Lamp. "I know you are wondering what this new Light means, and why Rajani and I are celebrating. Oh, my friends, it is the most wonderful blessing! For ages before the Soul-Drinker subjugated our land, the fertility and well-being of Khailaz were renewed every Spring by the reunion of the Goddess and the God. When this Renewal was achieved, the Presence Lamp reignited, assuring us that Zhovanya and Her Consort, Jeyal, held us within Their Love. Now, the rekindling of the Presence Lamp tells us that the Renewal has been completed for the first time in six generations. Zhovanya and Jeyal are fully Present with us again!"

Catching fire from her enthusiasm, many in the crowd shouted, "Zhovanya is with us!" Those more in the know — members of the Circle, and the Companions in their dark- green tunics — cheered mightily. Others, having heard very little of the long-suppressed history of Khailaz, still looked bewildered:

"What Goddess?" demanded a newly arrived, velvet-clad merchant.

"There's a God, too?" a young man asked in awe.

A white-haired, hunchbacked woman, a former drudge rescued from the Soul-Drinker's labyrinth, trembled in fear. "What will They do to us?"

"Don't worry." Luciya raised her voice so all could hear. "The Goddess and God are nothing like the cursed Soul-Drinker. They are merciful and just. They care for the land, our soulkin, and the web of life. With Them, our land will recover from the blight caused by the Soul-Drinker, and flourish again."

At this, most people looked relieved, and many began to murmur excitedly to each other.

Only Naran seemed not to take in the astounding news. Instead, ever-concerned with the well-being of his friends, he loudly demanded, "What does this Renewal have to do with Kyr and the Kailithana? Where are they?"

The Warrior Mage held up a hand. "Patience! Let me explain." He paused until the crowd simmered down. "Usually, the Renewal was carried out by a man and woman chosen by a Ritual Mage, like Ylana. But at this time of greatest need, Zhovanya and Jeyal chose and shaped their avatars for this Great Renewal. These avatars are Kyr and Jolanya. As far as we know, this hasn't happened since the first time the Presence Lamps began to shine, ages ago."

Naran frowned impatiently. "Rajani, what did you mean you 'need to make sure Kyr and Jolanya are all right'? Are they hurt?"

"I don't know, Naran. They were chosen to become the Vessels of the Goddess and God. That's why each of them had to go through such intense suffering and atonement — and transformation. But no one knows what happens to those Vessels once they have fulfilled their destinies." Rajani glanced around. "I see that some of you still look confused, upset, or angry. Please let me finish, then we'll go find them."

Naran nodded, and the Warrior Mage sat down. Everyone else joined him, sitting around him in a circle to hear what he had to say.

"My grandmother, Lyriana, was the last Star-Seer," he began. "*Her* grandmother, Kyrana, was a Star-Seer and a great Prophet who lived during the time the Soul-Drinker enslaved our land. From her study of the star cycles, she learned that in our own lifetimes, there would be a unique opportunity to destroy the Soul-Drinker and restore the Goddess Zhovanya and Her Consort, the God Jeyal, to us. And so she formed a secret Circle dedicated to fulfilling her Prophecy, and trained my grandmother Lyriana as a Star-Seer.

"Kyrana foresaw that if a twin-souled boy-child was conceived when the Seven Wanderers formed the Dire Cross under the Firebird star-pattern, then that boy — as a young man — would be able to slay Dauthaz and bring about the Great Renewal, although at a terrible cost to him. After Kyrana's death, Lyriana continued the search for the sequence of star-charts that would lead to this star-cursed man — whom we know now as Kyr, our Liberator."

"Twin-souled?" Naran murmured. Then, comprehending: "Ah, Lanir and Kyr."

"Terrible cost, indeed!" Medari snapped at Rajani. "What cursed Prophecy gave you the right…?"

Rajani glared at him. "Would you rather have the Soul-Drinker ruling Khailaz forever?"

Medari shrugged irritably, but fell silent.

"No, I didn't think so."

Luciya quickly took up the story. "The stars also told the Star-Seer that a woman would be shaped to be a Vessel for Zhovanya's Consort, Jeyal. If this woman could be united with Kyr, they would make possible the Reunion of Goddess and God, thus bringing about the Great Renewal that has happened today." Luciya looked around with a sad yet proud smile. "For six generations, we of the Circle dedicated ourselves to the salvation of Khailaz. Many of us gave our lives for this cause. Today, all the sacrifices are vindicated."

Naran sighed. "Well, one thing is sure. When Kyr sacrificed himself to save the Sanctuary, he proved that, if he'd had the choice, he would have been the first to volunteer for the chance to destroy the Soul-Drinker."

"As his father did," said Luciya, her voice soft with old grief for Lanir.

293

"Yes, and his mother, too," added Rajani, remembering Alytha's courage and grace.

In her quiet, yet earth-strong voice, Devanyi said, "I pray you, let's be gentle with each other, and allow ourselves some joy over this wonderful change that the Circle — and Kyr and the Kailithana — have brought about. I suggest we go make sure they are all right."

In the garden, the bliss of Oneness slowly ebbed away, leaving the two stranded on separate shores. Like an infinite ocean pouring into a narrowing well, the vast cosmic awareness slowly shrank to human form: limited, exquisite, touchingly vulnerable. Eyes looked out and beheld the same awareness looking back. There were names attached to these eyes: Kyr; Jolanya. There was laughter at this quaintness. Separateness that would have been intolerable was made delightful by the shared knowing of Oneness. Smiles glowed, fingers lovingly traced the delicate, beautiful chrysalis-bodies of these precious, named forms.

But then these bodies shivered with the evening chill, bringing a poignancy of limitation, an awareness of abandonment. "Oh, Kyr, They left us!" Jolanya wrapped her arms around him and buried her face on his chest, sobbing. When the wave of sorrow ebbed, she pushed back a bit and looked into his eyes. "Why, Kyr? Why didn't They keep us with Them? It's so terribly lonely without Them." She saw a serene acceptance in his unclouded eyes.

"They didn't, not really." Kyr spread his arms wide, and his gesture included the garden, Khailaz, the entire world. "This is *all* part of Their Dance, my love. They are always with us."

A deep sigh shuddered through Jolanya's body. She reached up to caress his face. "I am so glad *you* are with me. I couldn't bear this alone."

Kyr clasped her closer. "Nor I, nor I," he whispered, smiling a little at the return of that peculiar little pronoun.

For a time they clung together, like children abandoned in a foreign land. Yet soon, a knowing of Oneness superseded sadness, bringing a peaceful assent to the continuation of this illusion of separateness. For a while longer, they held each other with tender fondness for these deep, sweet bodies, this vulnerable human flesh shaped for surrender to love and union. Then the evening chill reminded them of human needs and they rose and helped each other find their scattered clothing.

Jolanya pulled on her robes and then looked down to find her sandals and slip her feet into them. Looking up, she did not see Kyr immediately, and a small frisson of loss shivered through her. She turned around, searching for him. He was standing not far away, tenderly tracing the petals of the lush red blooms of a tree rose. She moved to his side. Glancing at his face, she saw tears tracing a path down his face. "I'm here, beloved," she said.

Kyr gave her a quick, luminous smile and wrapped an arm around her waist. "I see now why it all had to happen as it did."

"Yes," she said. "We were needed." She reached forth a gentle finger and touched the tears trickling from his eyes. "Something is making you sad?"

He turned to face her, clasping her waist with both hands. "I'm thinking of Gauday. I wouldn't have been ready, if not for what he did."

She nodded, knowing that all they had suffered had prepared them to endure the excruciating ecstasy of Divine Presence.

Kyr sighed sadly. "He sacrificed so much: his sanity, his whole life. In his soul, he must love Zhovanya very deeply to play such a role."

Jolanya looked at him, tears shimmering in her gray eyes, thinking of those who had shaped her, as Gauday had shaped Kyr. "Zhovanya naralo," she whispered. Kyr rested his forehead on Jolanya's, and his tears mingled with hers. Silently, they grieved for their tormenters, who had sacrificed their minds and hearts to play their roles in this story.

Unheeded, their mingled tears fell upon the dark red rose. When they looked up, all the roses of this one tree shone a gold-tinged white in the evening gloom. Awed, they stood before the miracle rose, feeling the world, the stars, the whole universe wheeling around them, all in perfect harmony; darkness and light, defilement and holiness, together creating a majestic dance of unfathomable beauty.

Turning in a circle with raised arms, they paid homage to the Goddess and the God, the Two Who Are One, and to all those who had sacrificed their minds, hearts, and lives to bring about this Great Renewal. Filled with humble joy, they turned and turned, softly singing a wordless song of devotion and praise.

As they slowly came to stillness, Kyr caught a glimpse of something shining at the back of the garden. He caught Jolanya's hand and led her toward the small temple. In amazed silence, they saw that the door now stood open, and a soft, opalescent light spilled forth into the evening-darkened garden. Together, they stepped inside.

They found themselves in a small, bare antechamber. The light radiated from a passageway at the back that led into the cliff. Hand-in-hand, they walked down the passageway and came into a huge marble-floored chamber carved by Nature and by human hands out of the goldstone of the cliff. A shimmering, iridescent light emanated from the far side of the chamber. In awe and trepidation, they approached.

Looking up, they saw that the slowly shifting light came from a large round alabaster Presence Lamp, finely carved with a tracery of thorny woodrose vines in bloom. Its light fell upon a huge statue of the same alabaster, glowing dimly, and they beheld the Goddess and the God clasped in each other's arms, dancing together in eternal bliss.

Longing for that vast ecstasy of which they were no longer the vessels, they knelt in silent worship, still holding hands. After a time, a knowing came upon them and they each put their free hand on the base of the statue, allowing the kailitha to flow through them. Slowly, the statue began to brighten until it was filled with the same rippling opalescent light as the Presence Lamp.

In Kyr's mind, Zhovanya spoke — as did Jeyal in Jolanya's — saying, *"THROUGH THY SUFFERING AND FAITH, THE SACRED DANCE IS RENEWED ONCE AGAIN. BLESSED THOU ART AND SHALL BE."* For a timeless while, they dwelt in the Divine Presence, giving and receiving love and gratitude.

At last they were released, and returned to their ordinary senses. Looking around, they were amazed to find the hidden temple filled with many people, kneeling in deep reverence, staring in awe at the glowing God and Goddess. In the forefront were Rajani and Luciya, Nyvali and Medari, Devanyi and Naran. Behind them knelt Craith and Jorem, Kinar and Zurano, Bru, Alenya, and Grif, and many more, every face alight with joy and wonder.

Avatars of the Two Who Are One, Kyr and Jolanya rose and, with Their eternal rhythm pulsing through their mortal bodies, began to sway and dance. Jolanya called out, "Surrender to Their Sacred Dance. Let Them move you. It is time to celebrate!" She began to clap out Their rhythm, and everyone began to dance, filling the Temple with swirling color and joyful laughter.

Standing by the central column of the chamber, Craith noticed stone wands hanging from braided leather cords tied around the column. Taking up a wand, he began tapping the column in time with Jolanya's clapping. Jorem approached and the two smiled at each other, touching hands as lovers do. Jorem took up another wand and added a counterpoint rhythm to Craith's steady beat. A deep pulsing resonance rang out from the stone pillar, filling the temple, and soon all were moving in a stately dance, like the stars circling the heavens.

While most continued dancing, a few people hurried out to spread the wondrous tidings. Rajani went with them, striding out of the Temple as if he had something important to do. But once outside in the garden, he tore off his black leather tunic and threw it on the ground. Clutching his chest, he stumbled over to the old oak tree, sagged to the ground, and leaned against the trunk. The pain in his chest grew worse, and he groaned, "Goddess, help me!" And then he felt Divine Hands encompass his heart. He groaned again as the pain peaked — and then the obsidian shell around his heart shattered. The Warrior Mage dissolved into tears, his long battle finally over.

Luciya looked around for Rajani. "Where is he? He should be here!" she murmured to herself. Not finding him anywhere, she slipped outside and searched the garden. A dark figure sat hunched, head in hands, at the base of the faintly glowing oak, and she hurried over. "'Jani, what's wrong?"

"Nothing, I just...needed time," he mumbled, wiping his eyes. He glanced up at her, fearing to see her habitual anger at him for slaying her beloved Lanir in the terrible ritual that had made this wondrous day possible. "I'm so sorry for..."

"I know, 'Jani. You did what was necessary, and what Lanir wanted. Without your steadfastness and selfless courage, this glorious day would not have been possible." She reached out her hands and helped him to his feet. With a radiant smile, she said, "And...I forgive you."

Startled and doubtful, Rajani asked, "After all this time? Why now?"

"When I saw that beautiful Light fill the Presence Lamp, my heart softened and opened. The Light came in and washed away my old grief for Lanir, and my resentment toward you." She sobered, and said softly, "I'm so sorry, 'Jani. I know how long I kept you at bay out of loyalty to Lanir. He sacrificed himself for Khailaz: so noble, such a martyred hero! How could I not remain his loyal grieving widow?" She shook her head at her own folly.

"I understand, 'Ciya. You had a right to hate me for killing him."

"No, no. You had to do it, and now it has all paid off! Khailaz is free and in the hands of the Goddess again." She looked at him with loving eyes. "I know you have loved me all this time. And now that my heart is clear, I know that I love you, too. I hope you can forgive me?"

"Oh, 'Ciya...," he whispered, and opened his arms to her. "Of course I do. Zhovanya naralo."

"Zhovanya naralo," she whispered, and stepped into his embrace. Released from the terrible burden they had shared for so long, they wept from joy, their long-hindered love now blossoming.

A few moments later, they drew apart, and stood smiling into each other's eyes. Then Luciya laughed. "It's time to celebrate!" Hand in hand, Rajani and Luciya slipped back into the Temple to join the dance.

New arrivals poured into the Temple Cave and stood staring in awe at the glowing statue of the Two Who are One and the huge Presence Lamp, and bathing their hungry souls in Divine Light. Some had brought baskets of tall candles, or vases full of flowers. After a few moments, they set the candles on rocky ledges and lit them, while others set the flowers around the base of the glowing statue, filling the cavern with beauty and light.

Others arrived carrying a variety of stringed instruments and flutes. Inspired by the God and Goddess, the musicians sat down to begin attuning themselves and their instruments. Then they wove a joyous melody into the rhythm that Craith and Jorem had set, the tones of strings and flutes awakening subtle and exquisite overtones from the goldstone walls of the cavern. The sacred Temple, which had been hidden for so long, empty and dark, was now filled with laughter and music and dancing; with joy and gratitude and reverence.

The iridescent Light of the God and Goddess pulsed within Their statue in time with the music. Craith and Jorem glanced at each other, smiled, and increased the rhythm. The Divine Light beat swifter and brighter, and everyone matched the new tempo, leaping and twirling gladly and gracefully in the rippling light of the Two Who Are One.

Laughing exultantly, Kyr clasped Jolanya's hands in his own and swung her into a swirling dance that was wild and graceful and reverent. She was all he had ever wanted, and now she was his and he was hers in a deeper way than he could ever have imagined. Jolanya's eyes sparkled with delight, grateful beyond measure to be free at last to love Kyr as her heart bade. Through their divine ordeal, they were bonded soul-to-soul, and never again would they be parted. Even the loss of the Oneness they had known in the sacred passion of the Goddess and God could not dim their joy.

Epilogue ~ Walking the Spiral

With his dusty tunic thrown over one shoulder, Kyr came in the door, his hair damp from washing up at the pond in the grotto, where he worked every day on his new sculpture. From his deep surrender to the agony and beauty of life, he was carving his love and reverence into the dark stone, bringing forth the terrible magnificence of the Goddess in her many guises.

Jolanya smiled, admiring his bronzed strength, which was subtly enhanced by the twining of his faded scars. His final healing in the Star-Seer's Garden, and two months of hard work on his sculpture of the Goddess, had transformed him into a robust, vibrant man, tanned and muscular. With his hard work and the summer heat, he'd shaved his beard and cut his hair close to his scalp. He looked like the young man he truly was — except for the depths of wisdom in his topaz eyes.

He chuckled as Friend plodded in and flopped down on the hearth rug, panting. "She's worn out from chasing her raven pal all over the hills." Dropping his tunic in the basket by the door, he enfolded Jolanya in his arms, resting his cheek on top of her head. They were silent, breathing in each other's scent, allowing their hearts to come into rhythm together. "Welcome home," she whispered, and he smiled into her hair, thinking gratefully, *Ah, Zhovanya, home indeed. I finally know the true meaning of the word.*

At last, Kyr and Jolanya let go of each other. No longer did she wear the dark robes of the Kailithana, but a loose dress of blue and silver. Her hair, freed of the Kailithana's severe braid, flowed in a shining flood down her back. He could never get enough of looking at her, his beloved, whom he had believed would never be his. Yet now they lived together quietly in a cottage that a grateful and reverent community of Ravenvale had built for them in the foothills of the eastern guardian wall, near the sacred grotto where his new sculpture was taking form.

He knelt and embraced Jolanya again, gently pressing his face against her belly. Awe filled him as it always did at the wonder of their coming child. "Hello, little one," he murmured.

Jolanya stroked his damp hair. "Aren't you hungry?"

"Starved!" He released her and took a seat on a stool by the polished plank table.

Jolanya set a pot of chicken stew and a basket of flat bread on the table, enjoying the eager look on Kyr's face as he sniffed the aroma of the rosemary and thyme she'd used in the stew. She was still surprised at how much she enjoyed caring for her beloved and their home. After all the trials and glories of her previous life, each day of quiet domesticity was a restful treasure.

She took her seat beside him. "How did the work go today?"

"I ran into a roadblock. Couldn't see what to do next, until I sat down to meditate with the stone. Now I have even more of a challenge." He shook his head. "Zhovanya and Jeyal showed me that They are equals now. The sculpture must include Him, not as Her Consort, but as Her Beloved Partner." Kyr gazed at *his* Beloved Partner and smiled so lovingly that Jolanya stopped breathing for a moment. Then she turned toward him, wrapped her arms around his neck, and kissed him long and thoroughly.

When she let him go, he gasped for air, laughing. "We can continue this 'discussion' later. Let's eat before that heavenly-smelling stew gets cold."

She smiled, and they bowed their heads, silently giving thanks for their many blessings, then served themselves and began to eat.

"And how many people came for your counsel today?" he asked.

"A young couple came. They are newlywed and needed some help with their love-making. Such sweet innocents!" She smiled, then sobered. "And Naran sent Craith to talk about the after-effects of Gauday's torments." Her face darkened. "That man..."

"Gauday was also Zhovanya's tool," Kyr reminded her gently.

"I know." Looking at her hands, she murmured, "But there's so little I can do now, without the kailitha."

"I'm sorry, beloved. I know it's difficult losing your abilities as the Kailithana."

"It is, but I don't regret it." She gave him a loving smile. "And it's someone else's role now. I wonder who the Sisters of the Moon selected. Ah, never mind. I'm sorry to run off to the past and abandon you in the here-and-now."

They laughed together, and turned their attention to the delicious food. When they finished their meal, she reached across the narrow table and clasped one of his hands in hers. "Shall we go back to the Star-Seer's garden tonight? The Moon is Full. We have to face this sometime."

"Are we ready?" He smiled uncertainly. "You know it can never be what we experienced that night with Zhovanya and Jeyal. That was so…"

"Overwhelming, beyond words, I know. But now we have this life together, and I love you so much! I want to share love with you in all ways. What is making you hesitate?"

"I know it can't be like it was with the Goddess and God, but…" He glanced at her and blushed. "What if you don't like it when it's…just me?"

"Don't be silly." Jolanya smiled at him affectionately.

He laughed. "Ah, there I go again, making up a story about possible future pain."

"I have to confess, I'm nervous too."

He leaned forward and kissed her hand. Meeting her eyes, he nodded. Jolanya scraped the good bits off their plates into a bowl with other scraps and set it on the floor for Friend, and they left her safe in their cottage, still sleeping by the hearth.

Summer's first Full Moon lit the path, as they returned for the first time to face the scene of their transcendent ordeal. Crickets and frogs filled the air with their symphony, and a gentle breeze carried the musty-sweet scent of warm pine trees. They held hands, as they often did now, happiest when in physical contact with each other. People had begun gently teasing them for their nearly constant closeness, but they didn't expect their friends to understand their wistful longing for Divine Union, and their deep love forged in fires of suffering and surrender.

Kyr walked along in silence. At last, Jolanya asked, "What are you brooding about, dear one?"

"Sorry, off in the past, remembering…it was so…intense, being the Vessel for Zhovanya. It went far beyond what the Trainer did; beyond the agonizing pleasure of the Soul-Drinker's Rod; beyond the torture of the craving; beyond anything Gauday did; beyond those dark days at the Tower — beyond all of those put together."

Jolanya met his darkened eyes with her clear, gray gaze. "Ah, love, that perilous bliss is lost to us. We will never know it again."

"I know." Kyr sighed. "I see now that all the suffering, all the torture, allowed me to endure Zhovanya's terrible ecstasy."

"Yes. All I have gone through was necessary also. I had to learn to keep hold of myself in the deep ocean of Mystery, or I would have drowned in the sweeping tides of Jeyal's Presence."

At the gate to the Star-Seer's garden, Kyr paused. With a shaky laugh, he said, "I'm terrified." Jolanya reached out to him, and they embraced, two castaways clinging to each other. Then they stepped apart, and entered the garden.

For a little while, they wandered about in silence, remembering. At the entrance to the healing spiral in the heart of the garden, they paused and gazed into each other's eyes. Then Kyr nodded and they entered the spiral.

Each step awakened a faint echo of the Divine passion that had consumed them. When they reached the heart of the spiral, desire flamed up and they made love, tenderly and slowly. They had both feared that their sublime travail as Vessels of the Divine would make ordinary, mortal loving seem insignificant. But their awareness of their shared loss of Union only made their vulnerable human love more poignant, more precious.

Afterwards, they lay together, hearts pulsing in rhythm, smiles and tears becoming quiet laughter of knowing, of acceptance that all their suffering and struggles were recompensed by this hearthfire love of theirs. Never again would they know the starfire passion of the God and Goddess, but this — this was enough.

Hand-in-hand, they walked the spiral back into the world.

—∿—

"What is one man's and one woman's love and desire,
against the great revolutions of our lifetimes,
the hope, the unending cruelty of our species?
A little thing.
But a key is a little thing,
next to the door it opens."

— Ursula LeGuin

Glossary

PRONOUNS

Lo – us all, me, you, us, them – exact meaning depends on intention of speaker
Li – I, me
Lai – we

CHANTS

"Zhovanya naralo" – The Goddess forgives us all/ Goddess, forgive us/me/them.
"Zhovanya dagantalo" – Goddess protect us.
Zhovanya ganaralo" – Goddess guide us.
"Ganarali ya zhanto abaharo" – Guide me to this lost spirit.
"Zhovanya, ganarali vida!" – Goddess, guide me home!
"Zhovanya dagantalo. Valanera moruba le zhanto." – Zhovanya, protect us. Dissolve the evil that binds this soul.'
"Jeyal, volara donorulai." – Jeyal (Moon God), we offer You our hearts.
"Jeyal sumaralai." – Jeyal, we call You.

MAGICAL COMMANDS

"Shai!" – "[Let there be) Light!"
"Shai la vi." – "[Let there be] a dim light."
"Shai'ya!" – "Burn!"
"Kaa'a-tay!" – "Open!"
"Kaa'a ta lak!" – "Break!"
"Vaa'a lan ti! – "Be whole!"
"Vaa'a lan!" – "Unite!"
"Waa-Rah!" – Command to raise the wind
"Waa-Rah Tavor!" – Command to raise a whirlwind
"Kiiiyaaa, KA!" – Command to direct an arrow to its target
"Ta'a Kor!" – "Sword"
"Ji Tal!" – "Stop!"

WORDS USED AT THE SANCTUARY

Kailitha (Kai-LI-tha) – Divine healing energy
Kailithana (Kai-li-THAHN-a) – The high priestess who channels the kailitha to heal those most damaged — for example, by torture and rape.
Kailithara (Kai-li-THAR-a) – The healing journey led by the Kailithana
Kailithos (Kai-LI-thos) – One who is going through the Kailthara
Kailithama (Kai-li-THAM-a) – Sacred chamber in which the Kailithara takes place
Aithané (AI-thahn-ay) – Listener, Confessor
Phanaíthos (Fa-NAI-thos) – Speaker, Divulger
Phanaithara (Fa-nai-THAR-a) – Divulgence, Confession, Journey to Forgiveness and Self-Forgiveness

OTHER

Final Grace – Death, granted by healers to those in intolerable pain who cannot be cured or helped in any way
Oil of Tramantha – A very rare sorcerous oil that unites and enhances the pleasures of sexual partners until it is impossible to distinguish self from other
Shanawa Elixir – A magical restorative elixir
Soulkin – Nature spirit with which one's soul is most akin (aligned)
Zhan – The life force of a being, and of the web of life

(Note: *Zhovanạya* is the adjectival form of *Zhovanya*)

Thank you for reading *Perilous Bliss!*

The Star-Seer's Prophecy trilogy, as well as my own inner work and my career as a psychotherapist, are dedicated to ending the personal and societal culture of hatred, revenge, and punishment, and evoking an inner and outer culture of compassion, forgiveness, and healing.

I hope that reading Kyr's story has inspired you to treat yourself with greater compassion and forgiveness, and to be more forgiving and compassionate toward others. If Kyr's story has illuminated your own healing journey, may your vicarious journey with our "star-cursed" hero help bring *you* into a life of love, connection, and wholeness.

———∾∿∾———

If you have been touched or inspired by my books,
please spread the word.

Charles De Lint, one of my favorite and very successful fantasy authors, writes:

> *"Word of mouth is crucial for any author to succeed. If you*
> *enjoyed this book, please leave a review on Amazon. Even*
> *if it's just a sentence or two, it would make all the difference*
> *and would be very much appreciated."*

———∾∿∾———

This is even more true for me.
Thanks so much in advance!

———∾∿∾———

Dark Innocence: https://www.amazon.com/dp/0981627838

Fierce Blessings: https://www.amazon.com/
Fierce-Blessings-Star-Seers-Prophecy-Book-ebook/dp/B0137NGF9Q

Perilous Bliss: Please visit either of the above links, and scroll down a bit to find this book's page on Amazon. Thanks! (Link not available prior to publication.)

I love to hear from my readers. Let's stay in touch!

For a FREE gift, updates about special sales, events, or giveaways, and articles devoted to supporting you on your healing journey, **subscribe to my newsletter:**

www.starseersprophecy.com/subscribe/

You will receive a gift from me:

The Star-Seer's Story

A short Prequel to *The Star-Seer's Prophecy* trilogy.
Discover how Lyriana came to be the Star-Seer and foretell Kyr's fate as the Liberator of Khailaz.
A fascinating read even for those who have read any, or all, of the Trilogy!

Other ways to stay in touch:

Like my Facebook Author Page: https://www.facebook.com/StarSeersProphecy/

If you have questions or comments, please write me at: info@starseersprophecy.com

Afterword

The Three Purposes of *The Star-Seer's Prophecy*

In my Author's Note for *Dark Innocence* (Book One of this trilogy), I wrote: "The main focus of Kyr's story is the amazing capacity we humans have to recover our true essence from the darkest of ordeals, and to retrieve the light of our souls from the depths of despair." My hope is that you have been inspired by this story to continue or begin your own journey on the hard path: to search for your own healing, and to recover the light of your soul.

In my Author's Note for *Fierce Blessings* (Book Two), I wrote that the underlying purpose of this trilogy was "to end the inner and outer culture of hatred, revenge, and punishment, and to evoke an inner and outer culture of compassion, forgiveness, and healing." In this same Note, I also wrote: "*The Star-Seer's Prophecy* confronts the evil and cruelty that we humans suffer and inflict in our dark innocence, and holds forth a vision of the healing, compassion, and forgiveness so needed in our world."

In this third and final volume, *Perilous Bliss*, the focus is on *how* we move beyond this old culture of revenge and punishment, and live from our true essence. For Kyr, it begins with realizing (with his soulkin Eagle's help) that he can be who he chooses to be. Then, with the Kailithana's help, he confronts his own inborn innocence; faces and feels his pain and rage at how he has been betrayed and abused; and reclaims his "right to exist *for* himself, *as* himself." Next, he allows himself to stop holding off the "black wave" of all that he has suffered, and surrenders to oblivion.

Eventually, he awakens to his true essence as "a shining being of light, radiant with innate goodness and love," and drops his "tattered cloak of tears and darkness." In other words, he drops his identification with his suffering and with all that has happened to him in the past, and steps into the present moment. In a sense, he is reborn each moment. From this place of freedom, he can forgive those who have betrayed and hurt him so terribly, because he is no longer that victim.

So in the end, our "star-cursed" hero emerges triumphant from his long, redemptive journey on the hard path. With help and guidance, and his own willingness and courage, he:

- Transcends his prior life of incredible hardship;

- Accomplishes (with his true love, Jolanya) the long-hoped-for union of God and Goddess;
- Brings about the Great Renewal that heals the entire land of Khailaz; and
- Gets to live an "ordinary life" of love, connection, and wholeness (deeply informed, of course, by who he has become by choosing the hard path).

I hope that reading Kyr's story, as it evolved through all three volumes of this trilogy, has inspired you to treat yourself with greater compassion and forgiveness, and to be more forgiving and compassionate toward others. I hope you may also see the freedom that can be ours when we drop our identification with our past, and begin to live in the present moment, neither brooding over the past nor worrying about the future. Perhaps you may even find yourself seeing with the eyes of the Goddess: able to see our true essence as beings of light and love, and to see beyond the cruelty of our enemies or abusers to the suffering and torment of *their* souls.

To whatever extent Kyr's story has illuminated your own story, may going through this vicarious journey with our "thrice-cursed" hero help to also bring *you* into a life of love, connection, and wholeness.

If you would like to let me know what you think about the trilogy, or how Kyr's story has affected you, please visit: **www.starseersprophecy.com/contact**. I'd love to hear from you!

Many blessings for your journey,
Rahima Warren

—◦◦◦—

"As freely as the firmament embraces the world,
or the sun pours forth impartially his beams,
so mercy must encircle both friend and foe."

— Johann Christoph Friedrich von Schiller,
poet and dramatist (1759-1805)

"A Story that Heals:
An Interview with a Survivor"

The first book of this trilogy, *Dark Innocence*, has been helpful to some readers, inspiring them to return to or continue on the "hard path" of healing, recovery, and transformation.

Here is an excerpt from an interview with Tetja Ann Barbee, who graciously allowed me to interview her about her experience of reading the book.

"...By living vicariously through the characters...I could safely start to heal old wounds, and question things about my own beliefs. And it all happened through the story's presentation of terrible suffering, acceptance, and growth....

I cried and laughed a lot, and consciously decided that if these characters can face such horrendous pain and evil, and come out to a place of lightness and beauty and love, so can I. As a result, I have been able to forgive someone with whom I was very angry for a long time.... I have committed myself to deepen my recovery process. And I'm enjoying the effects of personal realizations about my own path in life....

Rahima, I want to thank you for having such a keen sense of a person's suffering, and the hurdles one can face while dealing with it... and for helping me jump the first hurdle!"

For full interview, go to: **www.starseersprophecy.com/tetja**

Resources

If this story has stirred up strong feelings or difficult memories for you, please seek the support of a counselor or group. For referrals, contact the local chapter of professional organizations such as:

→ AAMFT – American Association of Marriage & Family Therapists: **www.aamft.org**

→ AHP – Association for Humanistic Psychology: **www.ahpweb.org**

→ APA – American Psychological Association: Referral Service: **http://locator.apa.org**

Acknowledgments

I am very grateful to Book Developer extraordinaire **Naomi Rose**, my editor and publisher (Rose Press), for her unfailing faith in and support for this story and author. Her great sweetness, patience, and wisdom, combined with her editorial skills and ear for nuance and connection, are rare and invaluable.

I want to acknowledge the importance of several of my teachers and their approaches to inner work: **Strephon Kaplan Williams**, Jungian-Senoi Dream-work; **Gisela Schubach De Dominico**, Sandtray Worldplay; **Natalie Rogers**, Person-Centered Expressive Arts Therapy; and **Chris Zydel**, Painting from the Wild Heart. From them, I learned to listen to, trust and safely express whatever is arising from within, dark or bright, ugly or beautiful, horrifying or inspiring. From my experience with these approaches, I learned to listen to the messages of the darkness as well as of the light. This trilogy is a direct result.

Much appreciation to **Christine Angell** for her friendship and support, and for her thoughtful comments about my books.

Most of all, I am forever grateful to my beloved husband for his infinite support for my unfolding; for his patience and delight with his mad-artist wife; for reading various drafts, catching typos, and pointing out incongruities in the manuscript with his logical engineer/physicist mind; and for his devoted technical support.

And always, I bow to that mysterious Source from which this story flowed into my awareness, through my heart, and onto the page.

About the Author

Rahima Warren is the author of *The Star-Seer's Prophecy* trilogy, a deep, compelling fantasy of the healing journey. A retired psychotherapist with over 30 years' professional training and experience, she draws her vivid storytelling from her own healing journey and spiritual practice, as well as from her work guiding others toward wholeness. Through this work, she gained an intuitive understanding of the universal human experiences of wounding, healing, and transformation — the source and theme of her trilogy.

"In my work with clients recovering from abuse," she says, "I was awed by the human capacity to heal, and to reach new levels of forgiveness, wholeness, and happiness. Delving into the deep mysteries within, I've retrieved many gems of wisdom and healing. Through an unexpected alchemy, these inner gems coalesced with my love of fantasy fiction into the writing of this mystical and redemptive trilogy adventure — and in the process, transformed me into an author."

The author hopes that this archetypal story will support and inspire you for your own journey on the "hard path" toward healing, forgiveness, and freedom. Her website is **www.starseersprophecy.com**.

About Rose Press

Books & Other Fragrant Offerings
to Bring You Home to Yourself
www.rosepress.com

In our time of reading for information, Rose Press seeks to offer you books and other fragrant offerings that will live in your heart like an eternal time-capsule, releasing their healing medicine as you need it.

"Fragrance" is not usually associated with books. Books, we tend to thin, in our speeded-up age, are about ideas, entertainment, steps for helping us to be more new and improved.

And yet there have been books that are mirrors to the soul — or marvels of excavation, revealing the vast treasures hidden within. There have been books, the journey of whose reading swept readers up into their remarkable world, leaving them at the end with the passage of that journey in their bones, and the fragrance of that atmosphere still hovering impossibly near. There have been books so deeply entered into by their authors that turning the pages of these books transmitted to their readers more than a whiff of the understandings and evocations embodied in the book: they helped to form the readers' very being.

This is the vision of Rose Press books: that in taking them into yourself, you discover what is truly in you, and it opens your heart like petals opening to the light. That said, getting to the more subtle fragrance — the distillation of more earthbound, sometimes sludgy experience — is often what book writers dream of and work in the trenches to do. Behind the most exquisite fragrance left with a reader by a book is the author's composted experience (all the years and memories and ideas and possibilities dreamed of and lived through, written and refined) that produced such perfume. So what is left on the page is the offering: the "fragrance," one might say. All the dregs have been churned up and left to sink to the bottom, leaving only the gift of the book.

This, then, is what the reader gets to experience: a hint of the churning process, but ultimately, the fragrance.

When 10,000 rose petals are gathered in the dark of early morning, placed into retorts filled with solvent, and heated over time until their oil rises as a liquid distillation, then you have just 16 ounces of that most prized (and expensive) of aromatics, rose essence (rose absolute). In the same way, Rose Press Books are the distillation of their authors' essence, distilled over time and many revisions to bring you into contact with the gift of something fragrant and indescribably beautiful within yourself.

Writing these books entails a journey, and reading these books is also a journey. And you, afterwards, will be the carrier of that journey in the world: burnished, more yourself than before, and smelling — even after everything — like a rose.

Questions for Contemplation and Discussion

Continuing the Conversation and the Healing

If you have been affected by this book — indeed, by the entire trilogy — then you may sense the value of having a way to talk about it with other people, both for your own healing and to connect with others on this deeper level. Here are some suggestions and starter-questions. You need not feel limited to these; perhaps something unique will occur to you that you can interest others in exploring along with you.

For Book-Club Discussion Groups

If you are in a book club, or want to start one based on *The Star-Seer's Prophecy*, you may find the following questions a good conversation-starter:

1. How did you experience the book(s)? Were you immediately drawn into the story, or did it take a while? Did you find Kyr's story intriguing, sad, gripping, disturbing, inspiring, touching, or…?

2. Were the characters believable, fully developed as complex human beings, or one-dimensional? What are their motivations? Do any of them learn, grow, or change? If so, how?

3. Did any character(s) or event(s) remind you of your own life? Why?

4. What are the major themes of the trilogy? Are they relevant in your life? Did the author effectively develop these themes?

5. Was there redemption for any of the characters? If so, who? Is this important to you in reading a book?

6. Is the plot engaging? Is it a fast page-turner, or does the plot unfold slowly with a focus on character? Were you surprised by how the story evolved through complications, twists, and turns?

7. Did certain parts of the book make you uncomfortable? If so, why? Did this lead to a new understanding or awareness of some aspect of your life?

8. Which passages strike you as insightful, inspiring, or profound?

9. Is the ending of the trilogy satisfying? Why or why not?

10. Has Kyr's story helped you heal, or learn something new about yourself or your life? How?

NOTE: You can also use the questions listed below under "For Individuals Doing Inner Healing Work."

For Individuals Doing Inner Healing Work

If we choose to explore our lives beyond the conditions with which we were raised, there comes a time when those beliefs and artifices are stripped away. Then we face the void as Kyr does, feeling abandoned, betrayed, and lost: not knowing who we are, what to believe, or where we belong. At that point, we have the option of retreating to the seemingly safe shell of the confining personality that others told us, or assumed that, we are — or of choosing for ourselves who we will be. Like Kyr, we may find this an arduous and painful process, but ultimately a freeing and fulfilling one.

Part of this process is to stop denying or suppressing our own feelings of rage and betrayal, depression and self-hatred. Once we have faced and felt these intense emotions (preferably with the support of trained and experienced therapists), we can begin to stop identifying with being the victim of abuse or betrayal. This in itself brings us into a new level of freedom and awareness, of self-acceptance and empowerment.

As Kyr shows, there is a further step we can take: to let go of the past entirely and live in the present moment, responding appropriately in each situation, no longer from reactivity to past trauma. We can forgive those who have harmed us and, undefined by the past, we can be the kind of person we choose to be. We can discover our true essence as beings of light and love, and live with joy, enthusiasm, and creativity.

Here are some questions that may catalyze your own healing:

1. Have you ever realized that the person you were taught to be is not who you really are? How did that affect you? Did you feel abandoned, lost, betrayed, or something else? What did you do to get beyond that?

2. Have you been able to let go of identifying with being a victim? Whether you have or not, how does that affect your life?

3. Have you found a way to let go of the past, forgive your abusers for the sake of your own freedom, and live more in the present? If so, how has that changed your life? If not, what might enable you to do so?

For Therapists Who Wish to Use *The Star-Seer's Prophecy* as Bibliotherapy

Using *The Star-Seer's Prophecy* trilogy as bibliotherapy provides your clients a safe distance and an engaging imaginative context for recognizing and addressing their own traumas.

Sometimes, reading a book is a safer, more accessible way for someone who has experienced psychologically scarring abuse to vicariously enter into a different version of their own experience and come out the other side. Literature is particularly powerful when it takes universal themes and particularizes them into a specific, detailed world that, is different from the reader's but that, on a deeper level, speaks to the universality of human experience. This allows the reader to relate to the characters' traumas without defensiveness.

Healing for *her* readers was certainly a prime motivation of retired psychotherapist Rahima Warren when she wrote the story of Kyr — a "dark innocent" raised to know only abuse, cruelty, and depravity — who unwittingly embarks on a healing journey to discover his true nature. Throughout the trilogy, he learns to love and trust, forgive his tormentors — and, just as importantly, himself — and ultimately emerges whole, empowered, fulfilled, and a leader towards a better way of living and being.

Discussing this trilogy with your clients can offer them the following profound supports:

1. Common ground with the hero of this book, who undergoes unendurable suffering but chooses the "hard path" that frees him;
2. A tangible roadmap of the healing journey and its internal stages; and
3. The opportunity for transformative openings in the client. "Remember when Kyr couldn't believe anyone really wanted to help him?" you might ask, in a moment when your client was fighting off kindness, support, or love. Your clients' identification with Kyr's journey can bring them to the realization that even people who have been subjected to the most horrendous experiences can find a good life on the other side.

To explore doing bibliotherapy centered on *The Star-Seer's Prophecy*, as well as to inquire about bulk-discounts purchases, please go to: **https://starseersprophecy.com/healing-through-books/for-therapists/**.

For Societal-Healing Groups and Individuals Seeking a Deeper Understanding of The Psychology Underlying Social/Political Forces

The tendency to look at difficult societal situations as having only external and socio-political influences has been strong in our society. And yet there are always inner forces and conflicts within human beings that underlie socio-economic and political events. A deep study of the inner life of those in power, and/or of our own inner lives, may help us see political events and public figures with greater understanding of the hidden psychological forces at play. Certainly, bringing the "outside" "inside," as *The Star-Seer's Prophecy* does in all three volumes, may enhance the perspective from which you view life events — and perhaps enable you to be a participant, even a leader, in opening up healing possibilities from this new perspective.

Whether you are an individual or part of a group seeking to understand what really brings about positive change in a culture, reading and discussing *The Star-Seer's Prophecy* in this light will, at the very least, open your heart and mind to deeper levels of understanding and connection, and allow forgiveness and compassion in your own heart the chance to open doors for you and the world in which you live.

Many of the characters in this book played out onto others abuse that they themselves had been subjected to: Kyr; Gauday, and his minions Larag and Viro; Naran; and Craith, for example. Yet not all of them took the identical path towards continuing this abuse. What, for you, are the differences in character and direction taken among these characters in the trilogy? What made them some of them continue in the direction they had been subjected to? And what made some of them change direction? And for those who chose to change direction, what was their effect on their community?

Recommended Reading

- Byron Katie, *Loving What Is*. Byron Katie provides a challenging way to look beyond our assumptions, and free ourselves from our past.
- Eckhart Tolle, *The Power of Now*, and *Stillness Speaks*. Eckhart Tolle offers experiences and guidance to living in the present — in the stillness and peace that is our essence.

Recommended Websites

- http://gratefulness.org. Founded by Brother David Steindl-Rast. Grateful living is a way of life which asks us to notice all that is already present and abundant – from the tiniest things of beauty to the grandest of our blessings – and in so doing, to take nothing for granted. We can learn to focus our attention on, and acknowledge, that life is a gift. Even in the most challenging times, living gratefully makes us aware of, and available to, the opportunities that are always available; opportunities to learn and grow, and to extend ourselves with care and compassion to others. Small, grateful acts every day can uplift us, make a difference for others, and help change the world.

- http://learningtoforgive.com. Based on the work of the Stanford University Forgiveness Project. This ground-breaking approach offers insights into the healing powers and medical benefits of forgiveness. Dr. Fred Luskin offers a powerful method in which the emphasis is of letting go of hurt, helplessness and anger while increasing confidence, hope and happiness. Through these powerful techniques individuals can learn how to release unwanted hurts and grudges and open themselves to happiness, peace and love.
- http://self-compassion.org. Based on the pioneering work of Dr. Kristin Neff, who says: "Instead of mercilessly judging and criticizing yourself for various inadequacies or shortcomings, self-compassion means you are kind and understanding when confronted with personal failings – after all, who ever said you were supposed to be perfect?"

To Hear More From the Author

To ask the author to speak to your book club, at your conference, for interviews, and so on, please contact the publisher: Naomi Rose, Rose Press, at rosepressbooks@yahoo.com.

www.ingramcontent.com/pod-product-compliance
Lightning Source LLC
Chambersburg PA
CBHW030657120726
47905CB00001B/254